S0-AGX-226

SUDDENLY, A FAINT NOISE SOUNDED
BEHIND ME.

Instantly I flattened against the wall. Some detective! Would that ruse make me invisible, candle and all? Muffled voices breathed out from the sitting room door a few yards away. What an opportunity! I might find out what the inhabitants of Cloisters thought of me! Heroically snuffing out my candle with my fingers I tiptoed forward. I pressed close and peered into the room. Primrose and Hyacinth sat at a gate-legged table in the corner diagonally across from me. They were playing cards. Beat Your Neighbour or Happy Families? I smiled. Rather sweet their staying up past the hour when nice old ladies should be in bed.

"Ace takes king," Hyacinth reproved, tapping her cards on the table.

"A priceless combination of rare wit, satire, and riveting action, along with some of the most amusing—and confusing—characters I've run into in a long time."
　　　　　—Susan Kenney,
　　　　　　author of *Garden of Malice* and *In Another Country*

"The story is written with a sprightly pace. The mystery is unveiled a bit at a time, and even the craftiest readers will be left guessing until almost the very end. . . . Ms. Cannell does indeed lead unsuspecting readers down a garden path. It's a pleasant walk."
　　　　　　　　　　—*Indianapolis Star*

Bantam Books by Dorothy Cannell

THE WIDOWS CLUB
DOWN THE GARDEN PATH
MUM'S THE WORD

Coming Soon:
THE THIN WOMAN
FEMMES FATAL

DOWN
THE
GARDEN
PATH

A Pastoral Mystery

Dorothy Cannell

BANTAM BOOKS
NEW YORK • TORONTO • LONDON • SYDNEY • AUCKLAND

*This edition contains the complete text
of the original hardcover edition.*
NOT ONE WORD HAS BEEN OMITTED.

DOWN THE GARDEN PATH
*A Bantam Crime Line Book / published by arrangement with
St. Martin's Press*

PRINTING HISTORY
*St. Martin's Press edition published 1985
Bantam edition / September 1989*

CRIME LINE *and the portrayal of a boxed "cl" are trademarks of
Bantam Books, a division of Bantam Doubleday Dell Publishing
Group, Inc.*

*All rights reserved.
Copyright © 1985 by Dorothy Cannell.
Cover art copyright © 1989 by Tom Hallman.
Library of Congress Catalog Card Number: 85-12520.
No part of this book may be reproduced or transmitted
in any form or by any means, electronic or mechanical,
including photocopying, recording, or by any information
storage and retrieval system, without permission in writing from
the publisher.
For information address: St. Martin's Press, 175 Fifth Avenue,
New York, NY 10010.*

*If you purchased this book without a cover you should be aware
that this book is stolen property. It was reported as "unsold and
destroyed" to the publisher and neither the author nor the
publisher has received any payment for this "stripped book."*

ISBN 0-553-26895-3

Published simultaneously in the United States and Canada

*Bantam Books are published by Bantam Books, a division of Bantam
Doubleday Dell Publishing Group, Inc. Its trademark, consisting of
the words "Bantam Books" and the portrayal of a rooster, is Registered
in U.S. Patent and Trademark Office and in other countries. Marca
Registrada. Bantam Books, 666 Fifth Avenue, New York, New
York 10103.*

PRINTED IN THE UNITED STATES OF AMERICA

OPM   14   13   12   11   10   9   8   7   6   5   4

*To Lena and Leslie Cannell
with love and appreciation
from your daughter-in-law*

DOWN
THE
GARDEN
PATH

Prologue

The Vicar's Daughter

To the residents of Flaxby Meade in the Cotswolds, the avenue was known as Abbots Walk, a remembrance of a gentler time, of centuries gone by, when the famous monastery, Chantwell, stood near this place welcoming beggars to its alms-gate and tending the infirm and ailing. Those were Popish times, and the village was now staunchly Church of England, but the residents could be tolerant—when they chose. On both sides of the walk's earth-trodden pathway, ancient elms arched upwards in graceful latticework to meet at last in gentle supplication: a cathedral ceiling of green, fragile as filigree. This was September and radiant afternoon sunlight filtered through the leaves, turning the ground to a mosaic of gold and brown. Somewhere high in the pure blue sky a bird chanted its eternal song. Surely a monk, or even the abbot himself, might still pass this way; his tonsured head bent low, fingers tolling the beads with the patient ease of daily ritual.

Some of the superstitious old folk claimed the walk was indeed haunted, and sometimes children hid amidst its trees, whiling away the hours, playing jacks or cat's cradle, waiting to glimpse a spectral brother dressed up for the outing in his best hair shirt. There were also the cowards—namby-pambies afraid to pass along that shadowed pathway—but Abbots Walk was a sacred place, not a place of treachery and evil. Serenity, a gift from the earth and its history, had laid a hand upon it in benediction. Stillness and peace were the offerings bestowed here, woven in quiet shadows across the ground. Many the passerby who gazed upwards, awed by the rich carving

1

of bark and jade, and bowed his head to pray a mumbled verse or two.

Tessa Fields was certainly praying as she precariously pedalled a rusty old bicycle into Abbots Walk. She was belligerently demanding that the Man upstairs drop any paperwork with which he was presently occupied and take care of that arch-demon of them all—Harry Harkness—pronto. Harry was the one who had insisted on the bicycle. He was the one who deserved to meet his Maker fifty years before his time—not her. At twenty-one, Tessa wasn't ready for the Pearly Gates . . . but she would make her grand entrance if she flew over those handlebars and was impaled on an outstretched branch. Damn! she thought. Those trees were snickering at her. And she really couldn't blame them. To meet one's end taking a toss from a bolting black stallion held a certain poignancy; a fatal fall from a piebald metal nag was a sick joke.

The bike erupted over a moss-covered rock, bucked wildly, and shied to the left. No wild screeching of brakes; the brute didn't have any. A tree stump loomed in their path, and Bronco reared wildly before plunging to a whimpering halt. The whimper was from Tessa. When she opened her eyes and adjusted to the sunlight filtering dappled gold and green through the trees, she found she was in the middle of the walk. And walk was what she should have done, she mused bitterly. Her friend Harry had insisted on the bicycle, claiming it was essential to everything the afternoon entailed. Had it mattered that she had never even mastered a tricycle? Not a bit! Harry had informed her it was all in the mind—like parachute jumping. Yesterday, when giving her that ten-minute lesson, he had assured her that her only problem seemed to be confusing fore with aft. She did, however, recall his admitting that pedalling might have been a tad easier if Bronco had possessed pedals instead of steel rods.

Tessa shook back her thickly curling mop of wild, honey-colored hair without prying her hands off the handlebars, and gave the bike a vicious kick. Decidedly un-Christian of her. This palsied metal beast was not the one to blame. Harry was the only villain, and he was compounding his sins by being late. "Men!" she seethed. Not one of the Creator's finer achievements. But, as Fergy would say, practice makes perfect—look what He achieved with one spare rib only minutes after His trial run with Adam. Straddling the bicycle, Tessa peered towards the opaque green light at the end of the walk. "Come on, Harry!" she muttered under her breath. "The least you could do is show up on time." She didn't exactly like all this hushed beauty. Made one feel like a turkey smelling Christmas on the wind.

Speaking of birds. There were plenty of those, twittering and tweeting away. Tessa could sense their eyes, hundreds of little black stabs of darkness, pinning her onto a piece of paper like a dead butterfly. She wished Harry would get here. Harry with his laughing eyes. . . . Ages ago, when she had been madly (and childishly) in love with him, she had written a poem to his eyes, likening them to bluebells on the first May morning. Now she winced at such sentimental gush and damned Harry's eyes. He was going to ruin all their fantastic plans for this afternoon. Already he was two and a half minutes late. Even the trees tensed and the light at the end of the tunnel clouded. Something waited there. Something human? Tessa was surprised at her unease. What she and Harry planned for this afternoon would never have met with her father's approval, but until minutes ago she had been convinced that it was what she wanted, that it was right. The ruffled collar of her cream silk blouse brushed her neck like cool quick fingers. If only Harry had not informed her that this place was haunted.

"Hello! Anyone there?" Tessa called. Banish Harry's quip about earthly abstinence making for very lusty ghosts. She was wearing her brown corduroy knee-length britches with the dozen minuscule buttons down the front. Let Vapour Fingers try having a go at those! Instantly she was sorry. Vulgarity was not acceptable here. Even the birds had stopped tweeting, as though their beaks had fallen open. Quickly she crossed herself. Her father was very ecumenical in spirit. A slight breeze stirred, surprisingly chill.

A dim form stepped forward, and something else gleaming silver was hunched by its side.

"Harry, is that you?" The whispered words were drowned out by a gust of shrill twitterings. She saw now that the silver monster was a motorbike which the creature had leaned up against a tree.

"Hey there, my lovely!" The voice was male and not the

least bit vapourish. His only resemblance to a monk was that he wore brown—a dark brown leather jacket and form-fitting taupe trousers. He walked leisurely, almost indolently, towards her, eyes glinting in his sun-darkened face, thick chestnut hair lifting a little in the breeze. Those eyes—alert, yet somehow amused—made her think of fire and ice, and idiotically she was a little afraid. Perhaps it was the too-sleek clothes. She disliked leather jackets on men, and despised silk cravats knotted at the neck.

The man was carrying a small branch, flicking off leaves in a little trail as he came. He was tall, but tilting her neck to look at him was not what caused the cold tickle down Tessa's spine.

"So I can find my way home." He flicked off another leaf, watching her eyes watching him. "Remember Hansel and Gretel?"

"That was bread."

"I got hungry and ate the lunch my mummy packed in my little kerchief." He smiled slowly, displaying exceptionally fine white teeth. Thumbing back at the silver monster, now several yards behind him, he continued, "You think it safe for me to leave Petrol Breath by that tree? I haven't seen any 'No Parking' signs posted, have you?"

She shrugged. "I'm just here minding my own business."

"Guess I'll chance it." He smiled again. "You're not trying to scare me, are you, standing there eating me up with your big bad eyes? What about you, Little Red Riding Hood?"

Tessa's knuckles ached from gripping the handlebars, "I'm not unescorted. I'm meeting a friend. He will be here any minute."

The man had stopped a pace or two away from her, still yanking leaves off the branch. Tessa half expected to hear a series of "ouches" as they fluttered to the ground. "That's a good one," he said. "Almost as good as my favorite line—the cheque is in the post." Reaching out long brown fingers he unclenched her hands from the bike and gave the handlebars a playful jerk. Looming over her, his breath fanned her face. Then, lips tightening, he directed the tree branch at her like a pistol. "Stand and deliver, my lovely. Ah, how this place fires up the imagination!" He covered the lower half of his face, masklike, with his free hand, then dropped it. "Don't you love those old yarns of highwaymen appearing out of no-where on deserted stretches of road? Such high old times those jolly dogs had despoiling innocent damsels." His voice surged to a rasp and Tessa jerked back, scraping her shin on the mudguard.

"A high old time and a swinging one, too, at the end of a gibbet," she tossed back. Fear sharpened her voice to an unnatural pitch.

"My, what big beautiful eyes," he said in a soft, almost musing voice. "You know, I consider myself a connoisseur and I don't believe I have ever seen anything quite like them. Topaz. No—sherry, warmed lovingly in a crystal glass. Eyes to drink a toast to and then smash." He extended the word—toying with it with his tongue. "The glass, of course." The timbre of his voice had deepened again and his breath-ing became decidedly ragged. Tessa tried to yank the bike backwards, but he held on. "And the way your mouth tilts down at the corners—charming. The only part I am not sure about is the hair." Reaching out he flicked at it with the stick. "Gorgeous colour and masses of it, but I don't care for the style. Too unkempt. What it needs is brushing—lots of brush-ing; long, smooth, languorous strokes." Eyes baiting her, he tossed the stick away. Catching up a handful of hair he forced her head backwards. "Red Riding Hood, you really are something."

"Not something, someone," she snapped back, the tangled cloud of hair flaring out as she pulled free. The bike stood between them like a chastity belt.

"Oh, cripes! Don't come over all bloody high-minded." He closed his eyes and sucked in a pained breath. "Life's too short not to pounce on each chance encounter and wring every last drop of pleasure from it. Come on! You look like a girl who's great at thinking up highly inventive fun and games. Know what else I think?" His voice was gentle now, almost beguiling.

"No." Tessa tilted her head sideways as she rammed the front wheel of the bicycle into his legs. His eyes darkened.

"I don't think that friend of yours is coming," he said slowly, as if savouring every word. "But the way I see it, his loss is my gain." In one lithe movement, he reached out an arm and lifted her from the bike. Holding her for a moment before releasing her, he picked up the bicycle as if it were a child's kite and flung it across the walk, where it shuddered into a tree stump.

"Calm down, precious." The man had both arms around her now. "Don't fight the inevitable. I could break every bone in your body just by blowing on you. But be a good little mousey and this nice tomcat will play with you first."

"You've been going to the pictures too often." A separate part of Tessa was listening, not to this creature with the steel arms, but to the quivering silence. She had the feeling of being watched by secret eyes. "Look." She was shouting now. "You're not scaring me—you are not going to murder me. No one in his right mind would pull something like that in daylight, in a place that isn't"—her gaze shifted around the walk—"all *that* isolated."

"Oh, but it is . . . and you see, my pretty, I make no claim to being in my right mind. Not when I look upon those eyes. By the way—if you give me your address before we're through, you have my word that I will write something really touching on the card attached to my floral offering."

She was choking as his lips sidled, warm and hungry, up her neck.

"Relax," he breathed, teeth nipping at her ear. "This is what you want, isn't it?" His voice was a creeping-crawling thing holding her mesmerized, the muscle and steel of his body and hands moulding her against him like melted plastic. "This is what all you women want, isn't it? None of that sissy drivel that made your mothers froth with delight. You want a man who will do his stuff and not ask you how you enjoyed it, right?" The words stopped when his mouth clamped down on hers.

"No," she gasped, twisting her mouth away, heart knocking wildly in her chest. She had to make him stop. She should never have come to this place. Beneath the beauty and serenity lay something evil. The ghosts weren't nice people. "Harry!" she gasped.

"Harry isn't here." The man smiled. "There's only me, Mr. Evil Incarnate."

"Don't be so stupid." Tessa tried to blink away the tears of rage and fright but they were trapped in her lashes. She could smell the sun on the man's leather jacket. She could smell the dark moistness of the earth following that morning's shower; the woody fragrance of the bark; the green pungency of the leaves. Such a lovely day. The lump in her throat threatened to choke her. And then she heard it—the crunch of twigs underfoot. Someone was coming. Someone perhaps to disturb those sly twittering birds, and whatever else lurked amidst the trees.

"Scoundrel!" shouted a high, quavering female voice. "Rapist! Murderer!"

Tessa wrenched sideways, peering over the man's shoulder. A flurried elderly lady in a grey-and-white striped dress was thrusting her way through the trees, hampered somewhat by a wide straw sunhat. A bulging string bag swung from the crook of her arm, and her lavender crocheted shawl kept getting snagged on twigs.

"Unhand that girl at once if you know what is good for you."

The man snickered. "Ah! What I like best! An audience!"

"Sneer if you must, sir." The elderly lady unpinned her shawl carefully and checked for damage. "But beware! My nephew Marmaduke, otherwise known as Muscles, is right behind me."

The man tossed Tessa away, sending her sprawling on the ground. "The old hen's lying. What say you, little temptress? Shall we adjourn our merry romp for another time?" He lowered his voice. "If I hang around too long she may recall where she saw my wanted poster. But despair not, I am the faithful kind. I will see you again—some dark and stormy night."

Before Tessa could struggle to her feet the man had sprinted down the walk and they heard the surging roar of the motorbike. She was shaking violently all over.

"My poor child, are you all right?" The elderly lady nipped spryly over and placed a tentative hand on Tessa's arm. "There, there! Such an appalling thing. In my young day, a girl would never recover from such an outrage. Indeed, it would have been considered a shade unladylike if she had. Now, my dear, that rogue was rude but truthful in calling me a lying old hen

7

in reference to my nephew Marmaduke. The boy lives in America, so we cannot place any dependence upon his assisting us. We will have to manage on our own. Should one call in Scotland Yard, one wonders? An exciting prospect! But I have the notion that they really do prefer murder. And can we risk offending Constable Watt by going over his head? With strikes rampant, one *does* have to pander to the sensibilities of the working class, doesn't one? But as my dear father always said, one doesn't chase down a solution with a wooden club. First things first. When we get back to the house we will both have a nice hot cup of tea to settle our nerves, so we can think straight, then say a little prayer of thanksgiving that I reached you before all was lost."

Tessa looked into the crumpled tissue-paper face with its gentle pansy-blue eyes. "You're very kind," she breathed, slowly raising a limp hand to her brow. "Excuse me, I feel rather faint." Groping with her other hand, she met unresisting air, dropped forward and—before the elderly lady could catch her—slipped into a heap upon the dark, sun-warmed ground.

Were the ghosts enjoying themselves? Behind her closed lids Tessa could see them, squirming shadows thick among the leaves. She could almost hear the murmur of their watching . . .

Ten-year-old Bertie Krumpet had just experienced the most gruesome time of his life, even worse than the time he accidentally got locked in the henhouse one night when Aunt Maude was gone on a case. Worse even than his memories of the orphanage in the East End before his adoption. Worse than being sent to the butcher's and seeing all those stiff carcasses hanging from the ceiling, the dried bloodstains on the sawdust floor.

Most times he enjoyed coming to Abbots Walk. Him and Fred often went there. They wasn't afraid of spooks. People was what frightened them—people like the Squire with his weird toddler's voice and sissy clothes, and that gypsy lady with the big black eyes that took X-rays of your innards. Weird, they was. But they wasn't wicked like the man in the leather jacket. No one was that wicked except on the telly. Funny about that. . . . For a while, as he and Fred peered down from their perch midway up one of the elms, Bertie felt like they was watching a play. Sort of comforting in a way. You wasn't expected to rescue people on the telly, however awful they got knocked around. Must have been the young lady's being so pretty what gave that make-believe feeling. Bertie had only grown frightened when he realized that her fear was real. And it weren't as though the man had done something awful like sticking a knitting needle in one of her ears and out the other. It were his voice—all thick and slimy—what told you he was wicked and spooked you half to death.

What a stroke of luck, the old girl bopping along in the nick of time like that! And now the young lady had come over queer and fainted! Awful, but exciting! What next? Miss Primrose Tramwell was gentry, a breed for which Bertie felt immense pity. Imagine never prowling round Woolworth's or munching fish and chips out of newspaper while walking home from the flicks on a dark wet night. But Miss Tramwell weren't just gentry, she were batty; she and her sister both. A very weird pair—Miss Hyacinth and Primrose Tramwell. The whole village said so.

From the tree branch, screened by leaves, Bertie and Fred had continued to watch, fascinated, as the frail elderly lady reached into her string bag. Drawing out a jar of pickled onions, she unscrewed the lid, and waved them under the girl's nose.

"That pong'll bring 'er round," said Fred comfortingly, and some of Bertie's guilt at not having scrambled to the rescue began to fade. He was almost beginning to enjoy himself. The girl's eyelids quivered open and she was staring about her in a frightened way.

"Where am I?" she whispered.

Bertie's question was, Who was she? Flaxby Meade being no longer than a clothesline in any direction, stood to reason there was no one living there he didn't know. Same went for Leather Jacket. He weren't Flaxby.

Miss Tramwell carefully replaced the lid on the pickled onions and set them down. She was now wafting her lavender shawl before the girl's face. "Shock is what you are suffering from, my dear. Men! And people continue to feel sorry for the old maid! I expect we will find your assailant has a bicycle fetish and cannot control himself."

Bertie swore enthusiastically under his breath. "Cor bli-

9

mey! Fiddle-assing around! Why can't the old girl 'op on that there bike and chase the man down?"

"Come off it," said Fred, always Bertie's voice of reason. " 'ow's she going to nail a motorbike? Ain't as though she could 'ave nicked a look at the license plate. Know what, Bertie? We should 'ave crept down and tried to get a quick dekko. But then . . . Aunt Maude would 'ave worried if we'd bin late 'ome for supper." Fred was great that way. Bertie felt a lot more cheerful knowing that their failure to act the heroes was based in some measure on consideration for Aunt Maude and her mutton pie.

The girl inched slowly upwards into a sitting position. She was now rubbing her forehead. "Oh, please, please! Where am I?" She gazed wistfully up at Miss Tramwell through thick dark-gold lashes. "And who are you?"

Miss Tramwell breathed a tremulous sigh of relief and bent to wrap her shawl about the girl's shoulders. "My dear, words cannot express . . . I really was not sure the onions would work. No one faints these days. It's quite out of fashion . . . but all's well that ends well. Dear me, I must not go rambling on. My sister Hyacinth is always remonstrating with me. We may be a fidgety pair of spinsters, she says, but there is no need to keep giving the game away. I know you will like Hyacinth. She is older than me, but really she does a remarkable job of keeping herself up. I am sure very few people notice that she dyes her hair. Now, my dear, if you will let me help you to your feet. There we are. Now we may be on our way."

"Our way?" breathed the girl.

"To Cloisters, naturally. The home of the Tramwells for four hundred and twenty-four years. Now, as you will see"— she patted the string bag on her arm—"I was on my way to pay a sick call on Dr. Mallard. He has his thirty-second cold this year. The man's a hypochondriac, so I will just catch him when he is laid up again, in a fortnight or so."

"Oh, Gawd!" muttered Bertie. "She's a bloody record." But just when he began to wonder if old Celery Legs was intentionally prolonging the agony, she ran out of wind. The girl stood up, wide expressionless eyes fixed on Miss Tramwell's face.

"I don't know who I am," she murmured dreamily. "So

sorry . . . I seem to have gone all funny from that faint. You I fainted, didn't you? Why am I here in this wood? I don't know *anything!*"

"Weird!" sighed Bertie ecstatically, shifting as noiselessly as possible in his tree.

The girl was sinking into a kneeling position on the ground, arms cradling her body as if to protect it from the outside world. "Who am I?" she demanded angrily, as though the information had been stolen from her.

"Dear me," sighed Primrose. "We seem to find ourselves in even more of a pickle than first supposed. Whatever is one to do?" she fluttered. "Even if old Quack-Quack—Dr. Mallard, that is—weren't indisposed, he knows nothing about the inner workings of the mind. Most people hereabouts think he's been out of his for years. Hyacinth and I put more stock in the old folk remedies than in modern medicine. Come to think of it, only last week we were reading an article about amnesia in one of those do-it-yourself health magazines, and I remember particularly the author suggesting that a judicious thwack with a blunt instrument on the back of the head is worth months of arduous psychotherapy."

The girl gave a violent start.

"Remember anything? Oh dear; paltry of me . . . but I really don't believe I have the fortitude to pick up a tree branch and slug you. Best to go and talk matters over with Hyacinth, I dare say."

"I—I don't want to impose." The drooping girl straightened. Eyes wild, she twisted around as though searching for a means of escape. (Bertie did not think the bicycle would be much help. It, too, looked as though it had been attacked.) "And I am sure I don't need medical attention. In a few minutes . . ."

"I understand completely. The last thing you need to see right now is a man. And doctors do have a nasty tendency to be male. . . . Good gracious, how very foolish not to have thought of her before . . . our visiting nurse, Maude Krumpet."

"Aunt Maude," said Bertie and Fred as one.

"Yes, your Aunt Maude!" Miss Tramwell stopped brushing leaves and twigs from the skirt of her dress and looked up into the boughs. "Come down from that tree, Bertie Krumpet, and run home as fast as your sneaky legs will carry you. If

11

Nurse is in, tell her she is needed at Cloisters. Otherwise, look until you find her."

Old Celery Legs was a witch. How had she known they was up that tree? Old women like her was supposed to be deaf as doorposts and blind as teddy bears. Bertie sidled down the trunk, scraping his knees and angry that Fred would not come with him. He glowered up at Miss Tramwell through his fringe of spiky ginger hair. The beautiful forgetful miss must be thinking him a real sop. He wished he was thin and tall, like Fred, instead of short and pudgy with a face all over freckles. Miserable old Celery Legs. Fred might not come back for days.

"Be off with you, Bertie!" Miss Tramwell flapped her hands at him. "And no skipping stones in the brook, mind."

Bertie went. He was so miffed that he did not give Miss Tramwell even grudging admiration for not only having caught him out but remembering his name. It was the other one who had caught him in the garden at Cloisters and warned him that she had counted all the apples on the big tree so she'd know if one was missing.

"How did you know he was there?" the girl asked as Bertie vanished.

"My dear child." Primrose Tramwell patted her prim silver curls and adjusted a couple of invisible hairpins. "When you are as old as I, and have spent as many nights quaking in your bed, listening for a burglar's footsteps on the stairs, you will discover your hearing is remarkably acute—when necessary. At other times it is quite as useful to be a little hard of hearing. Dear me, there I go rambling again; this is nothing to you, is it, poor child! How white you look. Are you ready to go? I know you will feel so much better when we reach Cloisters and have a nice hot cup of tea—with lots of brandy."

Yes, indeed, thought Tessa. A stiff dose of medicinal brandy is exactly what I need. This may not be quite as easy as you and I planned, Harry, wherever you are. Perhaps even *more* of a challenge, especially if Hyacinth turns out to be anything like her saccharine-sweet sister. Still, if things get sticky, I can always feign a swift return to my faculties and make a getaway. But, oh, Harry, I hope it doesn't come to that! This is so important to me. We plotted everything so well—the parts we were to play. Except that rehearsals are never quite the real thing, are they? Coming at me like that —you scared me, Harry, you really did. . . .

1

Our housekeeper, Mrs. Ferguson, always blamed my wicked ways on my origins. Don't get me wrong: Fergy wasn't referring to Dad's being your typical gentle, absent-minded clergyman or to the fact that Mum—dear cosy redheaded Mum, with her wonderfully appalling taste in clothes and equally wonderful taste in what little girls like to eat, play with, and have read to them on rainy afternoons—had died when I was ten. Neither was Fergy referring to my being an only child, our living at Kings Ransome, a small nondescript village near Warwick, or that I had always had pets, had gone to boarding school at the age of eleven, and had never learned to ride a bicycle.

When she spoke of my origins, which she did often with immense relish, Fergy spoke from a literal interpretation of the dictionary. How I was Begot. Tradesmen and lost souls seeking guidance to the local pub became her captive audiences, but her greatest source of pleasure was any newcomer to the village who joined her group, the Joyful Sounds or, in plainer terms, the Ladies' Choir. These ladies, mostly charwomen or housewives escaping from punitive children, held their meetings every Tuesday afternoon in the vicarage kitchen. This may not sound very grandiose, but you have to realize that they all wore hats like the Queen Mum and did not remove their gloves while partaking of sherry cake and China tea. The sherry was always Harvey's Bristol Cream and the tea was always poured by Fergy from the silver teapot. And why not? Dad preferred his from the earthenware one. He had no objections to Fergy keeping the silver "primed," as she called it. After Mum died, the only ladies entertained at the vicarage were the Joyful Sounds. Dad was too shy to be social, except in the pulpit where somehow he became impassioned and magnificent like Laurence Olivier. Fergy had stressed upon him that a widowed clergyman brought out the animal in most women. "Just won't leave poor Vicar alone." And I had to agree that Fergy might be right. Phone calls in the middle of the night. Distraught females taken suddenly bad with terrible attacks of conscience that could only be assuaged by immediate confession. Fergy's answer was to tell the twerps to turn R.C. and hang up on them. But one of Dad's special talents was for listening. And it must be admitted there were some advantages to his clerical allure. Our larder was always "proper bursting" at the seams with gifts of appreciation. Pork pies, crabapple and quince jellies, green tomato chutney, gingerbread, and brandied peaches were handed through the kitchen door into a very uppish Fergy's often floury and always ungrateful hands. What did some people think she was doing draped over the cooker all morning, drying her hair? Her lack of appreciation may have been the reason some of the offerings were left in wicker baskets, covered with tea towels, small notes attached, on the back doorstep. Which brings us, very clearly I must say, right back to how I was Begot—for it was in a wicker basket that I was discovered on the vicarage doorstep. Only in my case the note was pinned to a white hand-knitted blanket.

Such were my origins. Heaven only knew where or what I had come from! Of course Mum had told me the story from the time I was very small and I had never tired of her relating how she had come out for the milk and found me, and how she had rocked me all that day, scared that someone would come and take me away. I loved to tell the story myself until one of the girls at school screwed up her face and stuck out her tongue, jeering, "Why, that's even more stupider than the stork in Wellington boots fib. You need to buy your mummy a book on where babies really do come from."

That incident occurred shortly before Mum died. She was ill at the time but I remember lying on her bed, feeling her thin arms around me, and her telling me that not only did she and my father love me, but that the woman who had given birth to me had also loved me. "She had her reasons

for bringing you to us," Mum said. "Sometimes when I am
half asleep I almost remember: I see this face—we're sitting
side by side talking like friends. Nice, nice face, but then it's
gone, I'm looking out a window and it's raining—all dark and
blurry." I stayed with Mum for a long time after she fell
asleep. The wind was gusting outside, battering against the
grey stone walls of the house, but I was always safe and warm
wherever she was.

About a month after Mum's funeral the Tuesday meetings
of the Joyful Sounds resumed. With one week of the summer
holidays still remaining, I was at home, not only unhappy but
bored. My dog, Slobber, was at the vet's being treated for
some minor ailment and I could not bring myself to play with
my other old companion—my doll, Agatha Slouch. Mum had
made Agatha for me, and it hurt every time I looked at those
crooked embroidered eyebrows and the button nose with four
nostrils instead of two. So there I was sitting cross-legged in
the wash house, peering through a crack in the kitchen doorway
listening with all my might. Fergy's conversations were always
stimulating, running the gamut from who had to get married
that month to who had been caught shoplifting at Boots. The
ladies were all seated royally around the cloth-covered kitchen
table, and I spotted a newcomer in their midst. A thin woman
with a chin like a shoehorn and eyebrows like poor Agatha.

"A right treat this is an' all, your joining us, Mrs. Stark."
Fergy was pouring tea in a thin golden stream into fluted china
cups from the sitting room cabinet. "Hope you an' yours will
have nothing but happiness in Kings Ransome. Not but you
won't find it a proper dead-in-alive-hole if ever there was one.
Nothing happens here. Never has. Excepting for the business
of our Tessa. You'll have heard about that, I'm sure."

Mrs. Stark opened her mouth but Fergy rode right on.
"Talk about give a woman a fit! There she was right next to
the milk bottles, not more'n four or five days old, doctor reckoned. The prettiest baby I've ever laid me eyes on. Dressed
up like for a christening, she was." Fergy poured a cup for
herself, stirred in three lumps of sugar, and blew on it. "Bless
me, if I didn't die of shock! Not what the doctor orders for a
woman with my weak heart, let me tell you! I couldn't as much
as lift a feather duster all day. As for the Missus, she was

carrying on like it was the virgin birth. Doctor had told her, you see, after she had her 'overalls' took away, that she was finished as far as all that was concerned."

Mrs. Stark was trying to arrange her spoon in her saucer so it wouldn't fall off with an uncouth clatter. "Turned out all right, has she? Never stops being grateful like, I suppose, for being tooken in and given a good 'ome."

"Not on your life!" Fergy gave a royal snort. "Proper little madam she is; as a rule, that is, a bit off form at the moment what with the Missus being taken. But if she don't grow up to rob Buckingham Palace, I don't know knickers from a fur coat. Like to see a photo of her, would you, Mrs. Stark? Can't fetch her down to meet you—the rules is against children at the meetings, but won't take me a sec to tootle up and fetch one of the snapshots off me dressing table."

At the closing of the kitchen door a heavy silence settled on the room for exactly three seconds. "What I says"—this from Mrs. Baker, the bank manager's char, wearing the red satin toque—"and I don't care who 'ears me—it's all right, she'll be 'alfway up the stairs by now—if I'd bin Vicar nor 'is Missus I'd 'ave been a mite more cautious about taking something off the street like that! Why, you all know me, I won't buy floor polish door to door. And as for a mongrel pup off market—you couldn't pay me! When I got my Corgi I forked out four quid, would 'ave bin ten but for 'im only 'aving one ear, but I got papers. That way I knew what I was bloody well getting."

"'Course you did." Mrs. Salmon, a woman with four chins and a face as red and scaley as her name, nodded. "Stands to reason, don't it?"

"Correct me if I should haippan to be wrong," wheezed posh Mrs. Smythe. (Her husband's name was Smith.) "But from what I haive overheard by way of the grapevine, so to speak, the little girl is worse than plain naughty. There's something not quite right there, if you asks me. Mentally, I mean! Let Jimmy Edwards's butterfly out of the jar he was carrying to school, she did. Said she would report him to the RSPCA."

Mrs. Stark gave an unassuming little cough as she gripped her spoon in both hands. "I know as 'ow I shouldn't say nothing, being a new member and Mrs. Ferguson so gracious in 'er 'ospitality, but did any of you ladies see that film years ago, called *The Bad Seed*? Ever so frightenin' it was. The nicest couple you'd ever wish to meet adopted this pretty little girl and . . ."

"Sad, really." The bank manager's char had a cautious eye on the door as she spoke. "Her own mother not wanting her and now this one gone. Still, I suppose it ain't the same really. Couldn't be. As I always says, if you don't suffer to 'ave the little blighters you can't love 'em."

"Oh, how true." Mrs. Smythe nodded as the kitchen door creaked open and Fergy came in with her snapshot. Hands clasping her ample middle, Fergy watched complacently as the photo made its round of the table to "Oohs" and "In't she lovely—should be on telly or in one of them Pears' adverts."

"Well, I never," said Mrs. Stark. "What my Bill wouldn't give for some of that 'air. Sort of like an 'alo, in't it?"

"A halo? On our Tessa? That'll be the day!" Fergy took the frame back and wiped the glass with her apron. "Worse than a gnat bite she is—enough to drive you right up the wall. Still, between you, me, and my dead Uncle Harry, I always says the goody-goodies either need their tonsils out or a good dose of salts."

My conviction that Fergy would be a lot better pleased if I grew up to be a striptease dancer than a doctor or Member of Parliament could not take the sting out of the other women's comments. At several points I had been tempted to get up off the cold stone floor of the wash house and rush into the kitchen to beat them up. But wouldn't that only prove to them how wicked I was? A bad seed. I stayed put and thought about my mother. Not Mum, but the woman who had brought me into this horrible, critical world. Why had she given me away? It could not be because she had not liked me, surely—because Fergy had said I was a pretty baby. And if my wicked tendencies came from my biological mother, she could not be expected to object to them. Any thoughts I gave to my birth father at that time were fleeting. The male role in reproduction was still what Fergy termed "mercifully vague," so to me this man—whoever he might be—was very much a bit player in the drama of my existence. Later I dabbled with him a bit— tacked on a black moustache and a French accent, or rendered him a hopeless invalid—to suit whatever story I was weaving about my mother. But he was never real to me because, I think, Dad was real. I could touch Dad. I could hold on to him. He would climb a ladder, even though he was afraid of heights, when my budgie flew out the window and the other birds pecked at it from the top branches of the copper beech.

Dad was working on his sermon when I crept out of the wash house that afternoon. The study was my favourite room in the house; untidy, rather dark on account of the narrow latticed windows, but friendly. Right for talks. And we had a special talk that afternoon. I sat on the footstool in front of the fire and he told me how much he and Mum had wanted a child. "Tessa, when you send a present, does the mode of transportation matter? Does it matter if the postman drives up in a van, comes pedalling along on a bicycle, or walks?"

"No."

He reached out and touched my hair. "So, should it matter what mode of transportation God uses to deliver his children, as long as he gets the names and addresses right? Those women in the kitchen—you should feel sorry for them, Tessa."

"Sorry?"

"Think how small the world is to people who pass through life sticking labels on others. Think how many special, interesting people they miss knowing. As blind as me without my specs—they never see all the miracles big and small that happen every day. Miracles!" He gave a wistful chuckle. "You were your mother's miracle, and mine—although, coming as you did on the twenty-seventh of December, Mum liked to call you a Christmas box from my employer." He took off his glasses and polished them, his grey cardigan buttoned wrong as always. "What a day that was—soft and hazy. No frost in the air. We'd had an unusually mild winter and there were still a couple of roses blooming on that bush near the back door."

"Tell me again about Mum . . . asking you to have the church bells rung."

He kept polishing the glasses. "You remember old Greenwood, Tess. He came on a bit uppish at doing overtime—all bluster, mind, he would have slept with his bells if he could. Mum wanted them rung for two reasons—to express our joy and to let whoever had left you know you were safe. We were certain she was somewhere close by, waiting. That little hot water bottle in the blanket was still quite warm, so we knew you could only have been left minutes before Mum went out for the milk."

"But Greenwood did ring the bells, didn't he?"

"Indeed he did. Kept them ringing until half the county started telephoning to ask if a war was beginning or ending." Dad put his glasses back on. "What a day! Your mother glowing. Fergy 'coming over queer.' The doctor arriving and sending me off to boil water—for tea! No one who hasn't been through the disappointment of being turned down by one adoption agency after another can know how Mum and I felt. We'd married latish, as you know, and her health not being tiptop, we'd been told our prospect of becoming parents was practically nil. I had almost resigned myself, but not Mum. She told me that she found herself talking to strangers in shops, in queues, on buses about her longing for a child. She never gave up. She kept right on praying for that miracle."

Unable to speak, I moved off my stool and curled up against Dad's knees.

"The best thing that ever happened to us; that's you, Tessa." Dad stroked my hair. "Our only concern at first was that we might not be allowed to keep you. But that note pinned to your blanket won the day for us in court. Remember what it said, Tessa?"

"Tell me again."

" 'Dear Reverend and Mrs. Fields. This is your daughter, Tessa. I want none but you to have her.' You were a gift from a loving woman. Don't let anyone ever make you think otherwise."

I knew Dad was right. But questions remained. Questions that I did not ask him because he could not have the answers, and even to raise them would have seemed disloyal. He had enough to bear without me adding to his problems. I smiled and kissed him, telling him I was fine, but I went up the narrow, rather dark staircase dragging my feet. If my mother was such a loving, good woman, why had she parted with me? Poverty? Fergy said no one was poor anymore, but I supposed it was possible. Or could my mother have been weeks away from death—the victim of a rare disease? No. I didn't like that idea. Don't even think about death: I *had* to be able to find her. I wanted her healthy, and rich, and beautiful. *That* would

21

be something for the Joyful Sounds to choke on. What if . . . what if Russian spies had been after her and, terrified they would get her baby, too, she had done the only thing a noble, wonderful mother could do—sought sanctuary for me at the church? Our history class had read about people doing that. Of course, the vicarage doorstep wasn't the church proper. But I liked the idea. Mum would have liked it, too. She was always reading what she called cloak-and-dagger books.

The idea of becoming a sort of detective in my own interest took hold of me that late afternoon. I see now that my motives were mixed, that I had both the desire to discover where I came from, and a need to do something that would keep my mind off the emptiness in the house. I went over to the window seat in my bedroom and picked up the basket that had been my first cradle, and which was now occupied by Agatha Slouch. Sitting her down on the window seat I turned the basket upside down in the hope of finding some previously missed clue. A name cleverly woven into the wicker perhaps. Nothing. But I was not done yet. Down the hall I went to Mum's room (Dad now slept in the box room) and opened up the top drawer of her dressing table. Carefully lifting out a pile of blouses I held them against my face for a moment before putting them down and picking up the note which I knew was underneath. Dad had repeated its message accurately, and indeed I already knew it by heart. It was the lettering I studied now. Did it slope backwards because written left-handed by a normally right-handed person? The paper was a pale mauve and still faintly Devon violet-scented. Fergy considered "smelly paper" horribly common, something my mother could never be—so was this another ruse to mislead, or was there some hidden meaning? Dad would not have minded if I kept the letter but I wanted it to stay in Mum's drawer. When I was putting it back I remembered something else. Reaching under a pile of petticoats I pulled out the little hot water bottle which had kept me snug and warm in my basket. Sitting cross-legged on the floor, holding it in my hands, I felt comforted again; not only because of its associations but because there was something jolly about it. A small stone flask, not more than six inches long, shaped like a monk—a tubby, smiling-faced monk, one eye closed in a wink.

"You'd help me if you could," I said, patting his bald pate, and we huddled together on the floor until the shadows took over the room and Fergy called me down to tea.

Often, until I went away to boarding school, I would go up and talk to my friend the monk, and I never quite forgot him even after I found a more substantial friend—one who argued more, was given at times to daunting criticism of my behaviour, but who was almost as good a listener. Harry.

Harry Harkness lived with his widowed mother, Vera, at the other end of Vicarage Lane. And if that makes him sound like a knock-kneed bookkeeper and her a grey-haired old lady complete with rocking chair, nothing could be further from the truth. Vera was a chestnut-haired vamp, who had buried two husbands and divorced a third. Harry, son of number two, was a gorgeous chestnut-haired vampire. Ten years older than I, he had an evil reputation for sucking the breath and guts out of everything female within a twenty-mile radius.

We met when I was twelve, home for the holidays. My dog, Slobber, ran off one afternoon while taking me for a walk. Slobber was doing the drawing room scene that summer. On this occasion he entered the Harknesses' drawing room through their French windows with me in hot and muddy pursuit. Vera wasn't present, but Harry was entertaining a lady who, from the various items of her clothing scattered around the sofa, suffered from the heat.

A squeal and a flurry of cushions blotted out my horrified mumbled apology. The lady fled the room and, moments later, the house. I never saw her again. Harry told me afterwards that she'd moved to the Outer Hebrides. He may have been joking. That was part of his charm for me—I never quite knew when he was being serious or what he was thinking. He was also a superb host. Minutes later Vera came in and, while she chatted to me, Harry rustled up a splendid tea of sausages, bread and butter, and rock buns. Having sat in a tin and been forgotten those buns certainly lived up to their name, but dunked in mugs of steaming tea they were really quite good.

That afternoon stands out as one of the happiest days of my childhood after Mum's death. I found myself telling Vera and Harry about her and about my birth mother. (Increasingly, the latter was becoming a fantasy figure to me, endowed with beauty, brilliance, and charm of international proportions. In this I was spurred on by my schoolfellows who now thought my foundling history at once deliciously romantic and pathetic.)

My special friendship with the Harknesses, mother and son, had begun. Harry, of course, was more than a friend. He was my hero, the stuff of which schoolgirl dreams are made. And as time went on, hiding my monumental crush from him, under a mask of a tomboyish younger sister, took more and more doing. At last I decided that perhaps what was needed was to put some distance between Harry's concept of me as a pal and my emergence as a woman. So one year I didn't come home for the Christmas holidays. Instead I spent them with a friend at her family's home in Bournemouth. The Jeffersons were wonderful people and made a great fuss over my birthday (celebrated as four days prior to my arrival at the vicarage), but guilt at leaving Fergy to fill Dad's stocking and her own, and missing out on stirring the Christmas puddings for luck, almost made the sacrifice unbearable. The days until Easter seemed unending, and when I did at last get back to Kings Ransome it was to discover Harry was away on business for the agricultural firm he represented.

Hadn't Fergy always warned that not stirring the puddings would fetch forth seven years of bad luck? She was so often right in her ominous predictions. Indeed, the new month began with nine straight days of rain, a sure sign that evil forces were in ascendance. Still, I repeatedly told myself as the summer term dragged on that people made their own good or bad fortune. If I wanted to find my mother one day soon, I would have to go and look for her. If I wanted Harry now, I would have to go and get him. I took a good look in the mirror (something I was inclined to avoid because my reflection reminded me that, unlike most people I knew, I looked like no one but myself), and assessed my looks. Yes, I supposed I was pretty in an Old Masters kind of way. I would have preferred lush black hair and slumberous dark eyes, but my figure was coming along nicely, especially the upper portion, as a result of applying a herbal cream purchased at an exorbitant price via my friend Rosie Jefferson's brother. And Harry had not seen me for almost a year.

On a trip up to London to view the Houses of Parliament, I feigned illness and asked to be allowed to sit in the ladies' cloakroom until I recovered. Knowing Miss Whale's delicate sensibilities I was confident that visions of my being disgustingly sick would keep her at bay long enough for me to whip outside and down one of the side streets to the boutiques. Success. In one I found exactly what I wanted, a splashy black dress with a gravitating neckline and only inches of skirt. How smug I was as I sat on the train going back to school in my blue-and-gold-striped blazer and my demure straw hat, the dress concealed in my satchel. And how foolishly I forgot another of Fergy's warnings: "God doesn't sleep. He only pretends."

I was to be punished for my deviousness. My great plan to get Harry in a compromising situation from which the only decent outlet would be immediate marriage ended in catastrophe. I should have scented trouble ahead when things went too well—at first. Dad was glad I wanted to visit Vera and Harry. He liked them, and although he wouldn't have liked the black dress, it was concealed under my raincoat. As I had known she would be, Vera was out at bingo that night, but Harry's pleasure at seeing me eroded the instant the raincoat came off and he inhaled the first wave of the perfume I had sloshed over my body from the toes up. Could this be the man I had idolized for years, callously propelling me out the door, calling me a child—of all disgusting names? And, to add insult to injury, he said he was too fond—*fond*—of me to do anything that would hurt me.

I would never forgive him. I didn't plan to live long enough to forgive him! Back in our damp, chilly, black-and-white-tiled bathroom I tried to drown myself, but being the immature child I was, I couldn't even do that right. The pungent scent of my Floral Passion bubble bath kept bringing me back.

Something had to be made of the rest of my miserable existence, but for weeks I could not think of anything worthwhile, except making the lives of those around me as rotten as my own. The trouble with Dad was that he was so disgustingly understanding. After telling me that he was ready to listen and talk about whatever was troubling me, he left me alone. When I came to dinner one evening with my hair a brilliant purple and my cheeks streaked with black blush, he merely smiled at me through the spectacles drooping down his nose and asked if I had had a pleasant day. Curled up in bed that night with my grey flannel rabbit with the pink velvet ears, I had one of my "talks" with Mum. The next day I went out and worked in her rockery, and three hours later came in and asked Dad if, instead of going back to school in September, I could go to a secretarial college in London.

Life in the city would make me forget. Theatres, museums, the zoo, art galleries—I haunted them all on weekends. They were a great deal more cheerful than my bedsitter near Oxford Circus. Besides, if my despised former teachers were right and the most important part of a girl's anatomy was her head, I had better start using mine.

Early in my London sojourn, I did go along to an organization named FIND, which assisted adoptees in locating their birth mothers. But although they were eager to help me they were unable to discover any more than I already knew —that there appeared to be no record of my birth prior to my adoption, meaning it was unlikely I had been born in a hospital or nursing home. All right, so I had been born at home; but then how had my mother dealt with the doctor or, more likely, the midwife? That question continued to plague me, just as Harry's failure to write or telephone pleading for forgiveness plagued me. And then something happened. I began to enjoy myself. Mainly because of Angus Hunt.

Mr. Hunt wasn't a dashing young man about town, and he didn't fall madly in love with me. He was a middle-aged, large (tall *and* fat), shaggy lion of a man, and he offered me a job in his art gallery. Or what I at first believed to be his gallery. He didn't, I found, own The Heritage. But he *was* The Heritage. Strange, our paths crossing as they did; and stranger still that they should divide and recross later.

Still, I shall always wonder if the worst day of Mr. Hunt's life was the one when I went to view Umberto Bosky's showing. I remember it was my birthday and I stood in a crush of hundreds craning with gasps of wonderment at the sole exhibit, a ten-foot canvas with a six-inch spider-legged crescent, just sufficiently off centre to announce that Bosky spurned the ruler.

"The sheer power! Do you know from which of his periods it comes?" boomed a six-foot woman in a deerstalker hat, standing on my foot.

"His midlife-crisis period," I said as, scowling, I turned to press my way through the surge of damp overcoats. Out of the morass of heaving humanity a hand gripped my elbow. And that was it—my meeting with Mr. Hunt. His lack of outdoor wear told me that he was a member of The Heritage staff, and I told him what I thought of stuffing the place with Bosky bunk. Mr. Hunt disagreed. Repellent as he personally found such art, it brought people in at a trot and, at £2.50 a head, crowds like these helped buy the real treasures. He offered to show me one, a suspected Rubens he was hoping to authenticate. Half an hour later he offered me a job as his girl Friday.

Typical Angus Hunt. His warmth, his spontaneity, his enthusiasms were as vast as his size. "Ach, lassie, don't think about art. Feel it." On the rare occasions when one of his brilliant impulses turned sour, he would hunch his massive shoulders under the rumpled linen jacket, shake his untidy mane of grey hair, and say, "Worth the gamble. Always worth the gamble."

I had been working for Mr. Hunt for about eighteen months when I received an up-beat "how are you doing" letter from Harry. My immediate reaction, after my hands stopped shaking, was to use it to line my budgie's cage. That word "child" still rang hatefully in my ears, but was there some small hope that one day the man might be brought to realize what he had tossed away like a wilted cabbage leaf? In my chatty up-beat reply, I filled two pages on what fun it was to work for Angus Hunt, his passion for fruitcake, baked and sent to him every fortnight by two "maiden aunts" in his native Scotland, his intriguing collection of pocket watches, and his occasional jocular hints at a secret vice.

The right approach. It worked, didn't it? On a gimlet-grey evening as I sat on the window seat trying to cheer myself by painting my nails red with white polka dots, I spied a motorbike pulling up to the curb. Footsteps creaked up the stairs to my third-floor room. Frantically blowing on wet polish, and attempting to pick the newspaper up from the couch with my elbows, I vacillated between ecstasy and rage. It would be spineless to forgive him immediately, but then Dad prized charity—loving charity—above all other virtues. I wanted Dad to be proud of me, didn't I? But . . . I opened the door and

Harry stood there, hand lifted ready to knock. His eyes as brilliantly blue as ever. Gorgeous. He was still the most gorgeous man I had ever seen and when he said, "Hello, Tess," with that faint blend of amusement and appreciation in his voice—exactly as though we were meeting accidentally at the bus stop after not seeing each other since the day before yesterday—I hated him. The idiot *did* love me. I knew he did and yet he had stayed away! Perhaps now, with the wisdom of maturity, I could appreciate that Harry had displayed a certain gallantry in not succumbing to the lure of the black dress. But the man could add, couldn't he? I hadn't been sixteen for quite a few years.

He was handing me flowers, and I hid my face in them. The door was closing and we were standing like actors in a bad play on the hearth rug. Ah, now he was speaking his lines. Telling me that he had wanted to give me time to grow up, to be sure of my feelings. He was taking something out of his coat pocket, a small velvet box, handing it to me with what would have been a pretty fair display of reticence if I hadn't known him so well, if I hadn't been able to read confidence in the tilt of his chin and the way his hands moved.

Not so fast, Harry darling. I told him that, having aged considerably since we had last met, my eyesight was failing. Excusing myself, I went over to my bureau, picked up a magnifying glass, came slowly back to the rug, opened up the box, and through the lens examined what was inside. A pearl and cinnamon diamond ring. How had Harry known I had always loved that ring when I gazed at it through the window of the village antique shop?

"It's lovely," I whispered, looking up at him, but he was staring at the magnifying glass.

I tried to make words come out of my throat, to tell him that I had only been teasing. But he wouldn't have believed me.

"I'm sorry I disturbed your busy evening," he drawled. Looking pointedly at my smudged nails, he turned about and left.

For three hours I sat in a corner, a sodden lump, biting my wretched nails and alternately plotting how I could get even. Years of emotional reconstruction down the drain. London wiped out. And, come to think of it—this with a ferocious sniff—apart from Angus Hunt and The Heritage I loathed London. I was a country girl, and as Angus would say, "What I wouldna' gi' reet noo for green stillness and dreaming church spires." And Dad . . . and grumpy, bullying Fergy, and the new puppy . . .

The telephone buzzed exactly as it would have done in a bad play. A play where the heroine had forgotten not only her lines but the part she was supposed to play. Harry, ringing to . . . ? I fell over the sofa reaching for the phone. It was Dad on the line. And now my heart pounded from fear. Dad never used the phone by choice; he was afraid of the instrument. What was wrong? Nothing. Dad said he was ringing to impart some good news, and he was making a wonderful attempt at sounding chipper. The bishop had deemed that at sixty-plus Dad was ready for semiretirement, and had arranged for him to move to a village even smaller than Kings Ransome, in Devon. Yes, it was a bit of a wrench but Fergy, bless her, was going, too. She was already cleaning out cupboards and packing to beat Pickford's. I could hear her voice in the background. "What? Let Vicar go off into the back of beyond to face the good Lord only knows how many deprivated spinsters? I knows me duty when I sees it!"

And I knew mine: home. I could almost taste Fergy's treacle pudding. The next day I gave Mr. Hunt notice, and he was kind enough to say he would miss my deplorable typing and poisonous coffee. On parting, a week later, he handed me the lady's silver pocket watch he was wearing, and at my protestations that I couldn't take it, blew out his gigantic cheeks, shook back his mane of hair, and stumped away from me muttering, "Nothing, nothing but late nineteenth-century rubbish." That was the last I saw of him, for a while.

Those weeks at the vicarage, taking down and packing up, were both happy and sad. Memories came flocking back. On the day the Joyful Sounds were to come for their final meeting, I knew I couldn't stand to be in the house with them, so I went on an excursion trip to Stratford with a stopover at Flaxby Meade. This was another small village like a hundred others —softly green with its string of thatched cottages, a hint of past villainy in the glimpse of its stocks, and—a pottery. The Monk's Pottery by name.

It was all meant. I would not go down to Devon with Dad

and Fergy at the end of the week. I had another journey to make before I joined them. A journey back into the past. My past.

"Dig up an old grave, and you'll find maggots," Fergy had always warned. It started to rain as I got out of the coach back at Kings Ransome; it rained for several straight days, but I forgot to count them. I was too caught up with planning how I could make my truce with Harry.

2

The petulant part of me would have liked to think that in rejecting me Harry's life had been blighted. But in some ways he had done rather well for himself. As he had told me in his letter, Fortune had smiled on him the previous year in the timely death of his Uncle Victor, aged ninety-two and of miserly habits. Harry had been able to abandon agricultural sales and purchase some land where he could raise horses. This equine passion of his had been the one thing about Harry that had not quite thrilled me. I only like the kind of animals I can take to bed with me. Wickersley—Harry always did think he had a way with words—lay about six miles from Kings Ransome. And that distance was the reason we had not so far collided with each other. Vera had not moved with him to his new abode, but neither had she remained in her old one. She now chose to divide her time between a cottage in Wales, also courtesy of Uncle Victor, and her sister living in Devon, not far from where Dad would be.

The day I went to see Harry, I was alone in the vicarage. Dad and Fergy had left the day before and the new incumbent would not be arriving for a month. What to wear took some thought. I had already realized that in reestablishing a relationship with Harry I must appeal to his memory of the innocent golden days of our friendship before passion reared. And I wasn't sure I had a platonic-looking dress in my wardrobe. But there it was, right at the back. Black. The longer length had been in when I was thirteen and I had worn this when accompanying Dad to funerals. Wearing it, my unruly hair pinned on top of my head, I felt that I was the very epitome of the Victorian governess. Or would be if I sucked in my chest. I never wore makeup because it made my face blotchy,

31

so I didn't have to bother fussing. A tuck of stray curl here and there and I was off.

I took a bus to within a mile of Harry's place and walked the rest of the way down a lane made narrower than need be by the wild honeysuckle hedges burgeoning on each side. Something else burgeoned over my right shoulder with heart-stopping suddenness; the head of a very large horse shaking out yards of tongue.

Gulping down a scream I whispered, "Nice horsie." Blackie must be a clue that I was close to my destination. A sign cutely marked "Private—Trespassers will be Persecuted" appeared. And I beheld a vista of field inhabited by groupings of horses—russet, cream, and black—shading themselves from the midday sun under gently spreading oak trees.

Harry's house stood on a small knoll. It was a converted labourer's cottage with an ornate brass plate on the black-hinged white front door saying, "Tradesman's Entrance—Others Round Back." After a friendly rap or two fetched no response, I opened the door and stepped inside. Vera and Harry had never stood on ceremony in the old days and I had to psych myself into believing the old days could be resurrected. I called out to Harry but there was no answer. The house, being small, had no hall. I found myself in a pleasant sitting room, a good portion taken up with a corner staircase and long stone fireplace. The room did not appear cramped because the walls and woodwork were painted white and the furniture was of natural pine or upholstered in oatmeal and sage-green tweeds. For several minutes I wandered about the room, peering out the windows at the front and the back. Harry must be with his horses, feeding them probably. The thought of even a bag of hay made me feel ravenous.

I opened a door next to the sideboard, leading, I hoped, to the kitchen. I wondered if preparing lunch for Harry might not be an ideal way of breaking the ice between us and getting back on the old footing. I had received the worst marks in the history of my school in domestic science but I could certainly butter bread and open a can of corned beef.

I was right. That door did lead to the kitchen, but as I entered my plans received a check. On the kitchen counter, next to a bottle of sherry and a bowl of fruit, stood a golden-crusted meat pie covered in plastic wrap. My, my! How the landed gentry do live. Harry must have a woman come in mornings to do for him. I filled the kettle, went to get out some crockery from the cupboards, and then noticed that some had been left out on the pale orange Formica. I took a glimpse at Mr. Hunt's watch, strung true governess fashion from my belt and tucked into my skirt pocket. I wished Harry would come.

Some of my bravado was deserting me, but he was so necessary to my plans. I could not let the memory of that terrible last meeting completely intimidate me. My hands felt sticky and I had to fight the urge to bite my nails. I drew a deep breath, causing a slight rip in one of the side seams of my bodice, but otherwise I felt better. Hmm! Perhaps a quick poke around the house . . . Unwise. It was often unwise to ignore Fergy's golden rules. "Don't poke your nose through other people's keyholes. You may get it stuck."

Facing me as I reached the top of the staircase was a closed door. And, as my hand turned the knob and thrust it open an awareness came that I was making a mistake. A look at the rumpled bed confirmed the feeling. It sprang, not from the fact that tidy Harry had not made his bed, but that the mound of green candlewick bedspread was moving. Something below its surface squirmed like an underwater swimmer, wriggled, kicked, and came up gasping, laughing for air.

"Harry, I'm sorry I fell asleep. You did say you wouldn't be long . . ." it breathed huskily, and then stopped. All I could see was a stormy mass of black hair and a flash of large dark eyes. The sheet was covering up her mouth. But I could see enough. This . . . this creature personified my idea of female beauty.

Taking quick shallow breaths and with my eyes locked with those of the lady of the harem I told myself there was a bright side to this—Harry could have been in bed with her. Should I have found them locked together like Siamese twins, I would have died. As it was . . . I must remember I had come to urge Harry to be my accomplice . . . nothing more.

"Good morning," said the hussy. "Don't you think we should introduce ourselves?"

Twisting my hands behind my back I lifted my chin and tried to force my lips into a superior smirk, but it was hard when they kept quivering.

"Come on," came that marvellous breathy voice. "You must be someone very close to Harry to make free with his house. What are you, his sister? His mother?" She was laughing at me! And Fergy thought *I* was born to be a wicked brazen thing!

I unfroze. Leaning forward I gave the bedspread a jerk, which sent her backwards against the pillows. This creature rated meat pie, sherry, and fruit, did she? All I had ever got were burnt bangers and stale cakes! "His mother!" I hissed. "I'm his wife, you poor deluded fool. When I think of what I have suffered with all his women, I wonder I don't throw myself in the nearest river." I ground my teeth. "And I would in a minute, if it weren't for the little ones. Six of them I have downstairs, crying for their daddy." With that I walked with noble tread to the door. That should fix her! But the muffled sound of her throaty laughter followed me downstairs. Slamming the kitchen door I leaned up against it, blinking. Behind me I thought I heard another door open and close. Return of Lord Harry Heartthrob? No. At least not by way of the front door, because at that moment he came in through the one next to the pantry. Head down, he was pulling out a bottle of cream and a packet of cheese from a brown paper bag.

"What did I tell you? Mrs. O'Leary was only too pleased to oblige with . . ." He looked up. "Tessa!" The bag, cream, and cheese all slipped and he made an automatic clutch at them. "This is so—unexpected." What was unexpected was the look in his eyes.

He was pleased to see me. Nothing could disguise the delight in his dark blue gaze before it travelled furtively to the door which had edged open when I moved away from it. Through the gap he would have a good view of the staircase.

"Well, isn't this nice. I have a guest." His hearty tone was an attempt to reach the upper regions and warn the other guest to dress before descending. A waste. The bird had already flown. A calm settled over me, bred of a mixture of amusement and sadness.

I pointed at the pie. "You seem to have been expecting another guest. Harry, I'm sorry, my stopping by like this was a real cheek. I shouldn't have walked in without your being here."

His eyes changed, became enigmatic. "Contrary to rumour, bachelors don't all exist off diets of bread and dripping and marmalade sandwiches. I really do rather well for myself. You will stay for lunch, won't you? We'll celebrate with some wine. I can't believe you're here, Tess. That last time I saw you . . . I'm afraid I rather went off the deep end. . . ."

"Forget that. I want us to be friends, Harry."

"Friends." He paused, looked away from me, then back again. "Yes, I suppose. . . . You do look splendid, but then—look, I'm sorry, I drank an ocean of coffee this morning, and if I don't hit the loo . . ."

He fled through into the sitting room and leapt up the stairs four at a time. Seconds later he came bounding halfway down again, pausing, eyes narrowed. Suddenly he grinned. "I should have known," he said. Leaning back against the staircase wall, he folded his lean brown arms. Marvellous how in the faded blue jeans with the rip above the knee he still managed to look like a model from a *Horse and Hound* magazine. His lip curled. "What did you do with her? Bury her in the cellar?"

"Don't be silly." I looked up at him. Was he angry? Was it possible that he really cared about that woman? Was he realizing now that my nose was undignified and that the way my mouth tilted downwards at the corners was not wistful but bizarre? "What a fuss," I said, brazening the situation out. "Your friend was extremely inhospitable to me. I believe she left by the front door as you came in the back."

"You haven't lost your entrancing nerve." Harry leaned over the bannister rail and clasped his hands to his chest à la the Balcony Scene, panting down at me, "Tessa, Tessa! Have you perchance come here to beg me to make renewed application for your hand, now that your father the vicar is forcing you into a loveless union with some elderly widower?"

"I told you, I want us to be friends."

"Your wish is my command." Harry swung nimbly over the rail and landed almost noiselessly at my feet. "I will convey your apologies to my—friend, when next we meet. Now, let's eat."

I flounced after him into the kitchen, where with Spartan efficiency Harry readied lunch. The cheese, cream, a cut loaf, and a packet of butter got tossed on to the table and he stabbed a knife into the pie. "Don't need a plate, do you?" He hurtled some cutlery in front of where I sat at the table. "Here's your serviette." Seizing a piece of paper towel he made to tuck it down the neck of my dress, but I flipped it away and spread it demurely on my lap.

"Sorry," he leered. "The baser side of my nature momentarily ascended. Eat up, you wicked temptress, you."

That disarming way of his was most unfair. I could not stay angry with him but perhaps that wasn't all bad. Perhaps it meant I really had outgrown being in love with him. "Speaking of wickedness"—I toyed with my fork—"I have decided finally to do something meaningful with my existence. I'm taking up a life of crime. And my reason for being here is to ask you—delightful rogue that you are—to be my accomplice."

"I failed Greek at school." Harry moved back to the table with a pot of tea.

"Okay: translation. I am going to stage a crime with me as the victim and you, hopefully, as the perpetrator."

"Are you on something?" He leaned forward solicitously, raised one of my eyelids and appeared to study the pupil. "Apparently not, so the only other explanation is that you have been consorting with some very strange characters. I'm surprised at you. A vicar's daughter should be above all shady activity."

"That is the whole point." I leaned my elbows on the table and trusted my wistful look was in evidence. "I am not by rights a vicar's daughter. I am in reality a nameless nobody who doesn't even have a proper birthday."

Harry leaned back in his chair. "So tell me, what's the crime? Do you want me to kidnap half the population of the U.K. between the ages of thirty-five and sixty and hold them hostage until one of them confesses to being your long-lost mother? Let it go, Tessa. You've had wonderful parents. Do you plan to disown them when you find the real thing? And have you ever considered that perhaps you are being a little greedy? One father, one mother is the general rule. Hold on a minute . . . are you asking me to break into some welfare office or courthouse—wherever adoption papers are stored—and sneak your file out under my raincoat? No, that can't be it, because you said something about me villain, you victim. Right?"

"Right. And you wouldn't do any good trying to filch my records because I already know that officially I didn't exist before arriving at the vicarage. But you are kind of on the right track. This does concern my search for my origins." I pushed my cup towards him and he refilled it. "Thanks." I took a sip and hoped that I could get through my explanations without Harry thinking I had lost all touch with reality.

"Last week I went on a day coach trip to Stratford."

"A bit touristy but harmless."

"Stratford is only relevant because it explains why I happened to be in Flaxby Meade, which is . . ."

"Quaint. But minus the Bard to give its thatched cottages and sloping green meadows substance. Actually, it does happen to be the birthplace of . . ."

"Will you please stop interrupting! Such a jolly little group we were—I don't remember when I last saw a heartier throng of middle-aged women in grey berets and navy blue blazers. We broke our journey for morning coffee at a wizened little Tudor café just inside Flaxby Meade. Nothing exceptional about the place except the really terrific Chelsea buns, but it was while we were sitting at the tables with their blue-and-white-check cloths that something momentous happened. The coach driver was taken deathly ill."

"What fun for one and all," said Harry.

"I don't mean to sound heartless, but it wasn't as though the poor man died, and it was all so providential. You know what Fergy would have said. 'It was *meant*.' One minute he was fine—jolly and fat—swilling down his tea at a corner table, chatting to a sweet white-haired old lady, a local, not a member of our group, and the next thing he was crawling on his hands and knees to the Gents. Only the Ladies was closer. He almost fell through the door, nearly getting trampled by a stampede of frantic women."

"What's the punch line? Had the sweet old lady stirred a teaspoon of arsenic in his tea? Okay, I'm sorry—continue your tale."

"Thank you. I don't know the cause of the man's indisposition—maybe eating smelly kippers for breakfast—but it gave us, the passengers, an hour to kill before his replacement arrived. One of the women in the grey berets, an enormous creature exhaling command, suggested we take a look at . . ."

"Ah-ha, let me guess." Harry closed his eyes. "The monastery ruins?"

"Clever! We do know our guide to Warwickshire, don't we? You'd think with my vicarage background I'd be all het up about Gothic relics, wouldn't you? But, Harry, they sort of scare me. Much more so than graveyards where you can feel fairly secure the remains are safely underground. Then, when I got there, I remarked to one of the rubble buffs—just to be chatty—that had those pillars of stone been five instead of five hundred years old, the town council would have ordered them carted away. I nearly got murdered. Only in the very nick of time was I rescued by one of Dad's soul mates. Bump! Bump! Down the lane that ran in front of the Ruins came this bubble car . . . up it pulled, and the driver hopped out, introducing himself as the Reverend Egrinon Snapper."

"Odd name."

"He was an odd little man altogether. Not at all like any clergyman I ever met. Fergy declares you can tell one by his walk, and this one didn't walk anything like Dad. He kind of slithered. He also had frizzy orange hair and a nose that could pick locks, but he certainly was . . ."

"Charming?" Harry enquired.

"Let's say convivial. Spotting a mini-congregation he leapt right into the pulpit. He couldn't stop talking about those old Gilbertese monks."

"Gilbertine."

"Probably. He told us he was on holiday from Kent and spent part of every day sitting in what had been the refectory, soaking up atmosphere. Communing with the spirits, which according to him beat communing with the natives—a sullen, close-mouthed lot, he said."

"Even the local clergy?"

"I don't know." I took a sip of tea and munched down thoughtfully on a forkful of pie. "But I could imagine Egrinon rubbing my placid Dad the wrong way. Even for a Protestant there was something overly enthusiastic in his recounting the excesses of monastic life. Seven-course dinners off gold plates, lurid ambition, monks slothing on their bunks all day reading dirty Geoffrey Chaucer. Henry the Eighth should have had Reverend Snapper on the payroll at the Dissolution. You should have seen how his nose quivered when he said the brothers didn't get their sensual thrills only from books. His topper was a Scandal Most Sordid!"

"The monk who impregnated the village virgin and got her with unholy child?"

"You are swift." I took another sip of now cold tea. "But I suppose that is an old story in more ways than one. What makes this one grislier is that the monk hanged himself."

"Fascinating."

I glared at him. "Don't you dare sneer. It was all very sad. The wretched girl's family booted her out of the house. And don't tell me that was the done thing in those days. Even for the sixteenth century (and this happened shortly before the Dissolution) they must have been hateful people. Where could she go? Pretty ironic when you think that the usual source of succour would be the monastery."

"It may still have been. Going on the premise that all monks are brothers, that baby was not short of uncles. Wouldn't surprise me if the jolly old chaps set to and raised the little tyke while Mummy went gadding off to be a nun as penance for her sins."

"How can you snicker like that! You're exactly like the Reverend Snapper. He positively seethed with delight when relating how that poor girl barely survived the stocks and a dunking in the village pond, to say nothing of the death of her spineless lover. Standing in those Ruins I could feel her horror, feel how she must have felt when her baby—a little girl—was born. Who would dare help her even if they wished? Okay, I know I sound soppily sentimental, but there is a reason. That young mother wrapped her child in a blanket, put her in a basket, and left her on the doorstep of some local gentry, people who were childless and kind. She also left them a note which read 'This is your daughter Tessa.' Oh, Harry, can you imagine how I felt when I heard that! The monk's name was Tessail. Those people did raise her and she grew up to marry a cousin of the family."

"Very interesting, though long-winded. But . . ." I sensed rather than saw Harry stiffen in his chair.

"But nothing. The cousin inherited the property through an entail or something, and Tessa's descendants still live in the old ancestral, Cloisters—a house that, ironically, was built on the monastery land a few years after the monks were given the push."

"Jolly good. All's well that ends well." Harry stood, stretching languidly, muscles rippling under the wool shirt.

"Not entirely." I didn't have to fake the wistfulness in my voice. "Tessa never knew what became of her mother."

"So saith your gleeful little cleric. What an incurable dreamer you are, Tess." Moving towards me he twined a loose strand of my hair around one of his fingers. "The legend would lose much in the telling if the fallen woman had ended her days fat and happy, swilling down mead at the local tavern. Don't glare at me. I don't want you agonizing . . . seeing yourself as the reincarnation of this namesake."

"Harry, that isn't it at all."

He stepped away from me. "Give yourself a break, Tessa. You can't blithely assume, because your own history bears something of a resemblance to a dubious folk tale, that your mother ever lived anywhere near Flaxby Meade. All right. I'll grant you are dealing with an interesting coincidence. But thousands of day trippers will have heard some version of the story you were told. If this is to be fantasy time, I suggest that some woman found herself pregnant under difficult circumstances and decided her child would have a better chance in life if presented to the world with a romantic flourish."

I took a patient breath. "Please listen. We have the legend. We have F.M.'s easy proximity to Kings Ransome and now we discover the Monk's Pottery. Conveniently placed, I might add, right next door to the café. And guess what I found among the monk salt and pepper shakers? A monk flask. An absolute double of the one left in the basket with me."

Take that Harry. Start taking me seriously.

But he didn't. He was now leaning up against the kitchen counter quirking a compassionate smile at me. Every moment brought greater clarity that he was not, after all, the man for me.

"The following day," I said, "I paid a second visit to Flaxby Meade by car. What I hoped for I am not really sure. I know enough about small villages, even discarding the Reverend Snapper's dour commentary, to realize that I would accomplish nothing by tapping on cottage doors, making discreet enquiries into my origins. So there I was, back in the café eating Chelsea buns, when inspiration struck. The inspiration that is to start you and me upon a life of crime." I smiled—bewitchingly I hoped—up at him.

"Will it be something lip-smackingly vicious and obscene?" He inched a shade closer and panted into my neck.

"Hardly, considering whence came my inspiration," I said, eyes on my hands, primly folded over my governess frock. "I got my fabulous idea from two elderly but sprightly spinsters. They were sitting at a corner table when I noticed them. It would have been impossible not to notice them. All they needed were signs round their necks marked Endangered Species. Amazing. I had believed that women like that were extinct outside of books. And speaking of books! The legs of their table were hidden by stacks of books. Library books."

"Could I interest you in a glass of cider to wet your voice?" Harry had turned and was rummaging in a cupboard. "Sorry to interrupt, but before you get too far along, I think I had better admit that I have never felt that manly urge to knock little old ladies over the head. . . ." He paused, holding a glass in each hand. "However"—the word came out slowly as he poured the cider—"roll out the yarn—what did these funny old birds look like?"

I stood up and we tapped glasses. "The shorter one was wearing a pale lavender-blue twin set above a long striped wool skirt, cherry net gloves even while she ate just like the Joyful Sounds, and a preposterous hat. A goldfinch perched in a nest of feathers! But the other one . . ."

"Her friend?"

"Sister, as it turned out. She was wearing an inky-blue-and-red peasant dress, lime-green patent shoes, a muddy dishcloth shawl, and the most enormous dangly earrings. Enough to knock her silly every time she moved her head! A head of suspiciously black hair all swept up into a great big thundercloud. She looked like an aged beatnik. Strange. They were both strange!"

Harry downed the last of his cider. "I don't know. They sound the spitting image of two of my father's elderly relatives."

"Really?" I nearly got sidetracked. "I didn't know you had any relatives except that aunt in Devon. You positively must have her get in touch with Daddy. Anyway, seeing their piles of books made me think it wouldn't be a bad idea to spend the morning hunting up a definitive work on that weak-kneed Tessail and his victims. Then I heard the old girls talking. They were discussing Regency romances. You know—earl meets girl, et cetera. Let me tell you, they were passionate on the subject, squabbling over who should get first dibs on *The Highwayman and the Hangwoman.* It was rather sweet really. Whatever would they do if one cold and blustery night a highwayman did come leaping at them out of the bushes? I was sitting there hidden away behind a potted plant sprouting plastic oranges and lemons, toying with the notion, when the waitress went up to them—all of a bob and curtsey—and spoke to them by name. The Name. The name of the family who took in the first Tessa."

I walked slowly across the kitchen and then turned back to face him. "It was all *meant,* you see."

"Meant?"

"Yes. When I heard that name I knew what I had to do."

"Pass yourself off as a member of some historical society, enquiring if the old girls knew of any twentieth-century take-offs on the old family saga?" Harry was smiling as he pulled at a loose thread in his shirt. "You needn't have gone to all that trouble. If you really think those two old ladies can help you, I . . ."

"Would what? Recommend the direct approach? Harry, you don't listen. I have been describing two women past sixty, living in a fantasy realm where the most daring intimation of sex is a bare ankle. Let us suppose that twenty years ago a member of their family or household had a child, and all was hushed up. Would they glibly spill the beans at the first 'Hello—does the name Tessa Fields ring a bell?' No. Of course they wouldn't—but perhaps if they were to get to know me . . ."

"That shouldn't be too difficult," said Harry thoughtfully, and I felt a little spurt of hope. Despite himself, he was becoming interested.

"Well, it wouldn't be difficult to get to know them casually, I am sure. One can always manage something of that sort. But that wouldn't be enough. I would need time. Quite a bit of time in which to break down their defences. And the only way to achieve that would be to somehow wheedle a visit to their house."

"Afternoon tea?"

"Oh, no." Absently I stuck a pin back in my hair. "I am sure I would need to remain for at least a week. And that is where you come in, Harry. In the guise of a modern highwayman."

"What?" He picked up the cider bottle and studied the label. "Maybe this has a higher alcohol content than stated."

I waved him back to the table. "Come and sit down—this isn't as drastic a measure as it sounds. I'm not asking you to rob the old ladies. All I need is for you to stage a heinous attack upon my person—causing such palpitations and attacks of the vapours (very much the in thing in Regencies) that I will suffer a nasty bout of amnesia—to be witnessed by one or both of them. That part I haven't quite worked out . . . fixing them on the scene, I mean . . . but I'm sure between us we can solve that small problem. Now what else should I tell you?" I couldn't read the look in his intensely blue eyes and decided it was probably just as well. A strand of hair had fallen over my left eyebrow and I blew it away. "Let's see . . . the ladies' name is Tramwell. They live in this vast house called Cloisters. And, really, I don't anticipate any trouble at all in luring them into offering me hospitality until I simultaneously recover my memory and uncover my origins."

Harry did not sit down with me. He shook his head with disbelief. "Of all the outrageous, arrogant schemes. To assume that because these women are old they are also completely senile. I almost think it would serve you right if I let you go through with it—and spend a week in an atmosphere of mothballs and woodworm." He thrust his hands deep in his pockets, and looked at me. "In plotting this little drama, didn't you give any thought to the police being brought in to investigate? And do you seriously suppose you would escape a thorough medical before being carted off to the padded cell?"

I should have known! Hadn't he failed me before when I desperately needed him? Rising, I thrust my chair back with a wonderful grating sound, and made an ostentatious display of looking round for my bag.

"You didn't bring one."

"Huh! I should have remembered what a spoilsport you are, Harry Harkness." Stalking across to the kitchen door I flung it open, stood glaring at it for a moment, swung it back-wards and forwards biting down on my lip, and waited. Wasn't he going to say anything?

"Goodbye," I said with awful finality.

"Tessa, nobody wants you to be happy more than I. What-ever has happened between us, you are still the most important person in the world to me. But . . ." As a declaration of af-fection it was spoken in a strangely flat tone. And that was what touched me, what forced me to blink back the tears. He wasn't hiding behind flippancy anymore. Turning, I ran to him, twining my arms around his neck and burying my face against the comfort of his rough shirt. His fingers moved slowly, gently, through my hair shaking out a spray of pins, and I forgot our quarrels, the woman in his bed. We were a team. We had always been a team.

"I still say"—his voice was muffled—"that your plot is mad, outrageous, and in all likelihood pointless."

Disengaging my arms I moved slowly away from him. I had to be reasonable, coherent, and imperturbable, all difficult when I was breathing in the giddy scent of his aftershave, becoming lulled by the idea that nothing was really that im-portant outside this room.

"Why mad, outrageous, pointless?"

"Mad—because the chance of pulling the thing off is less than minimal, without a hidden ace—or two. Outrageous—because you know nothing about these women, and point-less—because you have no proof that your connection is to their family."

"Okay." I tucked a strand of hair behind my ear. "We do have an ace up our sleeves. The Tramwells' thirst for romance. Poor old pets, you only had to look at them to know the high points of their lives are shopping at Harrods twice a year and Princess Diana's having another baby. In a way I think it is rather splendid that we can let them live out one of their fantasies. And as for not being related to their family, maybe I do want to believe I am descended from that other Tessa because it would all fit so well, but if I am wrong about that I still may discover something about my origins through being in that house. If my mother . . ."

"Tessa, why aren't you more curious about your father?"

"What do I need him for? I have Dad."

"But you can't just ignore his role, even if you have no desire to know him."

I shook my head. "Fergy always said that she reckoned he was a sleeping partner in more ways than one, but I see him more as a hit-and-run motorist. If he had been around when my mother needed him, she wouldn't have had to do what she did. Harry, you are going to help me, aren't you? Please."

I reached out to him with both hands and he took them slowly.

"Yes," he said. "But for my reasons, not yours." And I was too happy to wonder then what he meant.

3

For all my bravado I did experience the occasional twinge of conscience at the prospect of tricking two innocent old ladies. And on the morning of the great event I could not get warm. Fergy's words kept knelling in my ears. "God pays debts without money." Although fortunately for her peace of mind she had no idea of what turn my wickedness had taken. She and Dad believed I was engaged in a farewell bed-and-breakfast tour of the Cotswolds. She wrote saying future correspondence would be directed to the Kings Ransome post office, that she was busily occupied in founding a new chapter of the Joyful Sounds, and in keeping the ladies away from Dad. What could be more captivating to predatory female instincts than a new clergyman with a spotlessly kept house? Yes, Fergy could see her work cut out for her, especially as Dad had displayed a certain uncharacteristic waywardness in inviting Vera's sister Ruth to tea and actually requesting the silver pot.

How innocent it all sounded. If Fergy had seen me that first night at Cloisters, lying in a narrow bed in what had been the nursery fifty years ago, she would have dragged me out by the hair. Lying back on my pillows, I looked about the room. Impossible not to feel the eeriness. A faint scent of dried lavender hung in the air, but it couldn't cover the deadness. All those relics of spent childhood; the ink-stained desk, the arthritically slouched rocking horse, frayed picture books, and dolls. Those dolls were the worst, with their blind-eyed stiff china smiles. In the centre of the room was a full-sized swing suspended on thick ropes from rings in the high-beamed ceiling. Creak, creak. I did not relish waking in the dark to the sound of a gibbet out on the windswept moor.

Well, what was I complaining about? My amateur theatrical production demanded atmosphere, didn't it? It also demanded that Hyacinth and Primrose play the parts assigned to them. And so far, in a sense, they had. The stage-managing of the production had been almost disconcertingly easy. I had experienced that unexpected feeling of alarm during the feigned attack, but I quickly realized that this was a primitive female reaction to the idea of assault; nothing really to do with Harry himself. And other than the appearance on the stage, when the scene shifted to Cloisters, of a couple of rather colourful bit players and a guard dog capable of flaking the flesh from one's bones, all had worked like a charm. No intrusive introduction of policemen or doctors. So why was it that the Tramwells' falling for the Old Regency Masquerade scam no longer seemed as easy and harmless as it had when talking it over with Harry?

Harry was the one who had suggested Abbots Walk as the setting for Act I. He had reported back to me a few days after my visit that he had done a bit of research, disguised as a binocular-slung American tourist in the public bar of the Golden Goose. He had uncovered information that each Monday Miss Primrose Tramwell passed along the walk at approximately three in the afternoon on visits to the needy. That's one of the characteristics of elderly people. I had nodded. They are so wonderfully predictable. It's leading those dull lives, I suppose. But Miss Primrose Tramwell will be meeting adventure very soon now.

So merrily complaisant; but this afternoon when we had come tottering out of the walk, I had wondered if the break in her routine might not be too much for one so frail. And yet, when she had suggested thwacking me over the head to cure the amnesia hadn't I sensed a hint of steel under the feather duster? Or had I been reacting to that breathless hush of evil in the atmosphere? Harry had said Abbots Walk was considered almost a sacred place by the locals, so was it my conscience that was stalking me . . . or what?

"Cloisters," Primrose had said as we finally got away from the trees, "is not a palace. Only seventeen bedrooms and five receptions, not counting the parlour. Some people find the idea of the house being built on monastery grounds a trifle unearthly, but the family joke is that having taken a vow of silence, our ghosts don't answer back. A very old joke because we have lived in the house since the first of April, 1561. Henry gave us the land, Bloody Mary took it back, and construction did not begin until Queen Bessie returned it. . . . Oh, well! Without royal bickering, we wouldn't have history books, would we? Earlier we—the family—lived on the site of what is now Cheynwind Hall."

"What a splendid memory you have," I said, my pensive sigh uttered to show that my infirmity had been brought home to me.

"Dearest child," trilled Primrose with a silvery laugh, "I did not say I was speaking from personal recollection. It is Flaxby Meade itself that has the long memory. The stories are handed down. There is the one about the duel between my great-great-grandfather and the squire of the day. They fought it out on a dining room table with fish knives instead of swords. And, bless me! There was the time Maude Krumpet's father was thrown in gaol by my own father for poaching. He had been shooting blackbirds out of our trees."

We veered slightly left on coming out of Abbots Walk, passed the Ruins on our right and the common with its stocks on the other side of the narrow cobbled road.

"Would you believe that this road once went all the way to Warwick?" Miss Tramwell chattered on. "Progress. But at least we have not been boxed in by rows of semis. The only house within a mile of us down the road belongs to our dear friend Mr. Deasley." I slackened our pace further as she coughed gently, a slight flush mounting her cheeks. "Cloisters—you will glimpse it now just ahead—will go to a cousin's son after Hyacinth's and my day, so we are the last of the direct line. Our only other surviving sister, Violet, lives in America and will never return. Once colonized they can never readjust to our plumbing."

A delicious quiver of excitement trickled down my spine. "What charming—perfumey—names you all have." (Violet. Devon violet paper!)

"How very dear of you! Yes, our mother adored flowers. And how fortunate we were all girls. There were four of us, you know. Lily was the one who died."

The trickle turned to ice. Which was stupid: Lily could have been six months or eighty when she passed away. I opened my mouth to say, "I'm sorry, was she . . ." but Primrose was twittering on. A rise of stone appeared beyond a clustering of elm.

"Not a word to Hyacinth, but I will tell you, primroses were always Mother's absolute favourite flower. Here we are —a few more yards, and do be careful of those two steps at the gate. Down the garden path we go. Cloisters, you notice, has only a modest front lawn these days. People just don't go in for the lodge keeper at the gates anymore."

She may have rambled on. I wasn't listening. The lawn did look as though it had been cut from too skimpy a piece of green cloth, but the house was positively splendid. It actually *belonged* in one of those Regency novels and I fell instantly, madly, passionately in love with it. Built of Cotswold stone, somewhere between Jersey cream and warm custard, its gabled roof had faded to a pigeon grey, blushed with the faintest hint of rose. Ivy traced the walls in a delicate mesh of twine and leaves. A stone trelliswork decorated the pinnacles, and an arched jade and lavender stained-glass window flamed above the triple-arched portico.

The door should have been opened by a superbly aloof butler, but Primrose let us in herself. We were in a vast hall, and my eyes lit on a topsy-turvy grouping of Wellington boots in one corner, a plate of dog biscuits tucked under a table, and a stack of hot water bottles sitting on a chair. The fantasy faded, but this was even better. Real people lived in this unreal house. No everyday clutter could disperse the antiquity wafting in the air. Ancestors in gloomy oils scowled down upon us from the wainscotted walls. Angus Hunt would have scowled back at them. But would the first Tessa be among them? The Reverend Snapper had said the family had moved into this house when she was a young woman.

We were standing at the foot of a magnificent dark-oak staircase, which owed its rich mellow sheen more to age than to Johnson's lavender wax. Fergy would have said that the place looked like it hadn't smelled a polishing cloth since World War I. She would also have taken exception to the way the faded Persian rug lay sprawled unevenly across the floor, but she would have termed the general air of shabbiness "proper classy." To Fergy, anyone reduced to buying furniture hadn't come from much.

"Home Sweet Home," chirped Primrose. On her last word

a nearly invisible door in the oak panelling sprang open, releasing the ugliest, most rabid-looking canine (of bulldog extraction) I have ever seen. With one fell, ear-splitting swoop it came yelping and slithering across the floor, juicy fat tongue lolling, yellow eyes bulging in what I desperately hoped was a near-sighted glare. No such luck. It was making directly for my legs. Would he—she—bury the bones under the sofa? Terror had me dodging behind Primrose's back, clutching her breathlessly and whispering "nice doggie" over her shoulder. Incredible! The creature fell back and lay spread-eagled, flattened, pretending to be dead. The peculiar angle of the Persian rug was now explained.

"Good girl! Sweetie baby," purred Miss Tramwell, beaming down fondly at the canine monstrosity. "Minerva dearest, sit up and offer our guest a paw. That's the way."

I timorously accepted Minerva's overture, trying to ignore the hungry look in those yellow eyes as she sniffed my hand.

"Now, Minnie, this is Miss . . ." murmured Primrose. "Oh dear, how very awkward. Or, dare I hope, child, that you have sensed some indication of incipient recovery?"

This was tricky. If I made my case too hopeless, the Tramwells might deem me beyond the powers of a Maude Krumpet. On the other hand, to underplay my part would defeat my object. Clasping my hand to my brow, I whispered regretfully, "Strange—as your dog came across the hall, a memory—frightening . . . someone trying to hurt me, but it is gone. Everything is a complete . . ."

"Fog," supplied Miss Tramwell with a bright little nod. Setting her string bag and shawl on top of the hot water bottles, she was about to lead the way across the hall when that door in the panelling opened again and the other Miss Tramwell materialized. Today she was wearing a knitted orange suit which sagged at the shoulders and dipped at the hemline. The violent colour emphasized her sallow skin and made her black hair not only suspicious but blatantly dishonest. Had I noticed in the café how dark and hooded were her eyes?

"Primrose, my dear, tea is growing cold. You know how I dislike . . ." She broke off when she saw me. "Good afternoon." The heavy lids descended even lower. "I believe you are the young person who called the other day, collecting for the Uninsured Motorist Fund. Surely our butler told you then that we do not give at the door. Primrose, really, you must not be so soft-hearted."

"Hyacinth, you are mistaken." Primrose gently ushered me forward. "Something frightful has occurred," she whispered. "I came upon this poor girl being attacked by some ruffian in Abbots Walk. The most contemptible fellow in a purple silk jacket with a cravat at the throat. And yes! I am positive he limped. So fortunate that my memory has not yet failed me. Oh dear, how frightfully insensitive. The terrible truth is, Hyacinth, that this abused girl has completely lost her memory. Knows not who she is, where she comes from, or who that villain was."

"So she hasn't come collecting?" Hyacinth sounded more relieved than anything. "Such an annoyance, strangers rapping on the door, particularly when"—a meeting of their eyes from which I was somehow excluded—"when You-Know-Who's little problem prevents our keeping petty cash around."

Both Minnie and I pricked up our ears, hoping to hear more of You-Know-Who and his problem. But we were out of luck. The sitting room into which Hyacinth led us was another room of ample proportions. Pictures hung thick upon its walls. A time-muted carpet covered the centre of the oak floor, flanked by two sagging rose-and-green chintz sofas. In front of the massive stone fireplace lay a lumpy patchwork blanket where Minerva immediately disported herself, giving us full benefit of her unique profile. On a walnut coffee table between the sofas, tea awaited. Graceful curves of a silver teapot spout and handle protruded from a bumble-bee-striped cosy. A Wedgwood biscuit stand, stacked with an assortment of broken digestives and custard creams, stood next to the blue-and-white-striped milk jug and sugar bowl and the mismatched assortment of plates, cups, and saucers for three.

Hyacinth gestured for me to sit down on the sofa facing the French windows overlooking the lovely back garden but I hesitated, eyes on the china. "Excuse me, I must be very much in the way—I see you are expecting company."

Primrose understood at once. She gave her pretty tinkling laugh. "Dear child, you will think us very silly, but Minnie always joins us for afternoon tea. Hers is the Queen Victoria

coronation cup. Makes our big girl feel important. But I am
sure she will be a kind, unselfish person and let you have it,
seeing that you are feeling poorly."

"Please, no!" I cried. No faking the faintness in my tone
this time. "Minerva is quite put out by the idea!"

"I fear so." Primrose wagged a reproving finger at the
inert lump. "The trouble with you, Miss Minerva, is that being
an only dog you have never learned to share. I will ring for
Butler and have him bring us another cup." She did so, but
repeated jangling of the bell rope failed to bring the sound of
hurrying footsteps. A shame, because a butler named Butler
was something I very much wanted to see. Primrose went to
fetch another cup.

Picking up a Royal Doulton cup and setting it in a Woolworth's saucer, Hyacinth poured a tepid trickle from the silver
spout. "You must take some refreshment," she insisted, "and
then we can talk about your situation. Do you take milk and
sugar?"

I opened my mouth, then closed it. Hyacinth's lips, orange
to match her dress, lifted into a half-smile. "Forgive me. How
about milk no sugar?"

I would rather drink poison than sugar in my tea. "Thank
you," I sighed as Primrose came back through the door.

"Odd," she said. "Butler is nowhere to be found, and this
is Chantal's day off." She turned to me. "Our maid—of gypsy
blood and a wonderful worker, when she's here. Takes two
days off every week; but they do hate to be cooped up, don't
they? And Nurse Krumpet did warn us that being too strict
with the girl might be a mistake; possibly even dangerous. By
the way, Hyacinth, Nurse's boy Bertie was in the walk, and I
sent him to fetch her."

"Splendid!" approved her sister. "Fortunate that boys are
such a ubiquitous breed. A pity the same cannot be said of
Butler; ah! I hear him." Hyacinth's dangling earrings bobbed
against her long neck like Egyptian mummies. I was looking
at the door until I noticed that she and her sister were gazing
at the fireplace.

The next moment I was half rising from my seat, spilling
tea in a sickening warm slither down my legs. A huge, right-
hand section of the fireplace was caving in on us. Hyacinth
handed me a serviette to wipe myself dry as Primrose stood up.

"Most irritating," she said. "Hyacinth, that catch has stuck again. We should have had someone in to fix it, but working on priest holes is another lost art. Excuse me, my dear." She moved in front of me and, reaching forward, pressed a stone in the lurching cliff. Slowly it creaked outward, displaying a murky cavity within. "All right, Butler, I have released the spring. You may come out."

A flicker of golden light and that classic figure of upper-crust British life emerged, candle held aloft. At the moment he bore a striking resemblance to another musical comedy breed, the chimney sweep, but his aplomb was magnificent. Blowing out the candle, he set it down on a pie-crust table.

"Pardon me, mesdames, it would seem I have rather lost track of time. Tut! And you having to serve your own tea! With a guest and all! May I be permitted to make up for my shocking lapse by fetching you fresh tea and a plate of your favourite fish-paste sandwiches?"

Hyacinth winced as his grimy hands shot forward to pick up the tray. "Do not touch a thing! What can have occupied you so long in the priest hole?"

"It had come to me, madame, in the pursuit of my domestic round, that your late govenor's—that is, your h'esteemed parent's—bottles of brandy might benefit from a dab with the duster."

Hyacinth sniffed, apparently unimpressed by her hireling's zest for work. "I trust you have not been polishing them off in more ways than one."

Butler's expression became, if possible, more imperious and inscrutable under reprimand. So far he had not accorded me more than a cursory glance, but I got the oddest feeling that if faced with a thirty-second quiz, he could have named my shoe size, the date I had my ears pierced, where I spent my last summer holiday, and the name of my perfume.

"Will the young person be remaining for the h'evening repast, mesdames?" he enquired. "Tonight, being Monday, it should be baked beans on toast, but for something a little more festive I could top that off with a poached h'egg. Chantal did inform me she will not be back until late. She is visiting an acquaintance confined to bed."

"Yes, yes, Butler," flustered Primrose. "A fresh pot of tea would be very nice, please."

Flicking out his hands like a penguin's wings Butler picked up the tea tray with his wrists and padded around the back of my sofa. (Butler wasn't wearing shoes.) As he passed behind me on his way out of the room he murmured, "Lovely scent, miss. Concubine h'if I don't mistake?"

A shiver passed down my spine. He was right, of course.

As the door closed behind him Primrose murmured vaguely, "I do wish we could persuade him to wear shoes, but then we've been so successful in rehabilitating him in other ways. Butler was a burglar, and a very successful one—only one visit inside—before coming to us."

"A burglar?" I put my hand over my teacup to stop it rattling on its saucer.

"Yes, indeed. His whole family was in the 'trade,' as he calls it. Most reprehensible, but in many ways marvellous training for a servant. Unobtrusive. So light and quick on his feet, and not the least fear of heights. I don't think the attic windows had been washed outside for thirty years before he came." Primrose was moving over to the priest hole door, which was still hanging open. I could see now that it was not solid brick, but a false front adhered to a wooden back. "I really don't know, Hy, what we are to do about that catch." She pushed the door shut. "If one of us were to go down while the house was empty . . ."

A terrible desire to giggle almost overcame me, and I had to take refuge in drinking my tea. My plight was rapidly taking a back seat to household difficulties.

At that very moment a loud knocking sounded in the distance, causing Minnie to lurch off her blanket and dash whining to the door. Sturdy footsteps approached and Butler impressively bowed the visiting nurse into our presence.

I had told myself I was getting off lightly by being checked over by a nurse rather than an august M.D. Now I was less sure. Nurse was a large woman with the look of an oversized Dutch doll about her. Her greying brown hair was bound in tight plaits across her head, and her face was large, round, and rosy, making her blue eyes appear small. Those eyes were merry, but shrewd.

"Well, this is a right to-do." With bustling warmth she came forward. Reaching out one of her large hands, she touched me gently. "Bertie has been telling me such things about a wicked man and a beautiful young lady. The boy does have a lively imagination but I see he had some of it right. What a pretty thing you are! Feeling any better, dear?"

Again I had to strike that fine balance between natural distress and creating the kind of alarm that would see me whipped off to hospital. Covering one hand with the other I crossed two fingers.

"Physically I feel better." I languished. "So peculiar—this sensation of not being able to remember and yet . . . I know it is all there, behind a sort of curtain . . . if I can only rest for a little while, I am sure I will be fine. My memory has to return soon. Surely this sort of thing doesn't last long?"

"When the cause of amnesia is peremptory—sudden shock rather than long-term distress—the recovery tends to be speedy. My guess is that in a few hours or after a night's sleep you should be yourself again." Bending over me, Maude lifted up each eyelid and raised my wrist to take my pulse. She nodded encouragingly at the sisters. "I'm pretty sure that when Dr. Mallard sees her he will say much the same thing."

Hyacinth compressed her orange lips. "Now, Maude, you know precisely how we feel about doctors—particularly that malingering old bird. Where have doctors ever been when we have needed them?" My ears pricked up at the bitterness of her tone. "Our family has always favoured the home-brewed medical remedy. If the young lady so desires, I suggest she stay here until the fog clears."

"Not such a bad idea, perhaps." Maude's shrewd eyes were fixed thoughtfully on Hyacinth's face. "A homey atmosphere may well bring her round faster than hospital wards. But what of her family? They'll be jumping off the walls when she doesn't turn up wherever and whenever she was expected."

I held my breath on that one.

"Terrible," piped up Primrose. "One feels their distress, but if she cannot tell us who she is, she will not be able to tell the doctors."

Excellent. Or was it a little too glib? No—these ladies might be a little odd but they were certainly kind and hospitable.

"Then what about the police?" Maude sat down with a weighty thud on a spindle-legged chair. "What did our friend Constable Watt say on the subject of this madman in the walk?"

"We haven't yet spoken to the police," said Hyacinth as my heart set up a racket I was afraid could be heard across the room.

"Not . . . ." The chair spun under Maude as she turned to stare at her. "Miss Tramwell, you can't mean to keep mum on this. There may be a next time, and some other poor girl may lose more than her memory. Believe me, I am not trying to frighten anyone, but people do get murdered in lonely spots like Abbots Walk."

Primrose had fluttered across the room to the bell rope; now she came back to sit beside her sister on the sofa across from me. "Nurse dear, you must have some tea before you leave us. Butler just promised to fetch some when you arrived. So kind of you to come so quickly; but as for murder, oh, I really don't think so! In Flaxby Meade! We have never, in recent years, been exposed to anything quite that sordid. And as for dragging Constable Watt out here when our friend is quite unable to tell him anything . . . dear me, I do rather feel that would be something of an imposition." She turned to her sister for corroboration.

"When it comes right down to it," said Hyacinth, "what crime did the man actually commit? Please"—she turned earnestly to me, the earrings penduluming back and forth—"I am not minimizing the moral aspect of your suffering, but I can't see the police being more than mildly interested in . . ."

"Some very degenerate language and ungentlemanly manoeuvring for a kiss and a cuddle," supplied Primrose. "I was never more shocked, but I think you are right, Hyacinth, the police would want bruises and her clothes torn and in disarray. Hard physical evidence I think is the term."

Maude looked thoroughly unconvinced, but Hyacinth nodded briskly, the Egyptian mummies lurching forward. "Good. Because really I do not think Butler would at all appreciate having the house cluttered with bobbies. And I have no idea when or how we could replace him if he decided to give notice. Nurse"—a flash of the black eyes in that lady's direction—"I know we can rely on your absolute discretion in this matter. So regrettable that our families have not always

56

dealt well together—your father and our father—but we have always had the highest personal regard for you. Your patients so devoted, and your taking in that homeless boy. By the way, how is he doing?"

The room was beginning to fall into shadow. One slid across Maude Krumpet's homely face. I saw her hands squeeze the white of her apron into a taut ridge, her eyes fixed almost blankly on my face.

"Bertie is adjusting splendidly, considering he was a much abused child before finally being abandoned. But I do worry about his being on his own so much. This week school is out, due to some problem with the plumbing." She shifted in her skimpy chair. "For his sake, his being a witness, I could certainly do without a police hue and cry." Her words came out slowly but her eyes were focussing now. "I won't talk about any of this, and I don't think Bertie will gab. I'll warn him, but it probably won't be necessary. Tell him a secret and he sees himself as the Count of Monte Cristo." Maude gave her thick body a shake and stood up. "What still worries me most, dear, is your family." She came over and felt my forehead. "You weren't carrying anything that could possibly identify you?"

"Oh!" I managed a creditable start. "I never looked on the ground to see if I had a handbag with me."

Primrose preened herself a little. "Ah, but I did. Not a sign of one."

My mouth drooped and I lifted a trembling hand to thread a loose curl behind my right ear. "That's that, then!"

"I wouldn't discount hope." Hyacinth reached across and patted my knee bracingly. "We will check your clothes for labels. See if we can discover where they were purchased. You know I really do begin to see the fascination of the detection business. Perhaps if you find, upon recovering your memory, that you do not urgently have to be elsewhere, you would remain with us for a little while. We could put our heads together and see if we might not uncover the identity of your attacker."

It was working! They were falling prey to the romantic lure of the highwayman. So why this funny feeling of something lodged unpleasantly in my throat? Certainly it wasn't a fear of wrinkled old labels disclosing who I was. My clothes had all been bought at Selfridge's. Was it an attack of conscience? Or that the Tramwells' quirky old-maidishness left me winded? Nurse Krumpet's solid ordinariness served to emphasize their oddity. She passed another hand over my brow. "No headache, dizziness, or nausea? Splendid! I really do believe you will do just fine." Her voice was a little absent-minded. Thinking of something else—a case perhaps. A baby she had to deliver?

At that moment I did experience a decided dizziness. Deliver a baby! I was very likely in the same room as the woman who had delivered me. My lack of birth certificate had always pointed to my being eased into the world by someone who could keep her mouth shut. Someone with personal loyalties. Wasn't Maude Krumpet proving that, despite old feuds, when the Tramwells called she came? When they asked for discretion she complied? She was buttoning her cape, still looking at me.

"His being in the walk, I can't help wondering . . ."

"Roaring around the countryside on his motorbike, nothing odd about that," said Hyacinth.

"Nasty, noisy things." Maude did up the last button. "But as I say, I do wonder if he might be an acquaintance of your Chantal. Lovely girl. Would think she'd bring men buzzing round your back door like flies, but keeps to herself, doesn't she? Only time I've seen her with a man was a week or so back. Yes—it was in the walk. I caught a glimpse of her standing just inside the trees as I pedalled past. Remember, because I thought him an odd sort of man and . . ."

"A tourist, I expect. Even though the season is ending we still get some gawking at the Ruins." Primrose reached down to pat Minerva, who had ambled to her side. "But, dear me, I suppose it could have been him. Was he tall and handsome in a brutish piratical way?"

"No, he was short, kind of skimpy, and . . ."

Nurse did not finish because Butler came through the door with a tray. With dust and grime removed he looked more than ever like his fictional namesake. Deferential, unobtrusive, of regal bearing—but other than that I would have been hard put to describe him. His hair was neither dark nor light. He was somewhere between tall and short and his eyes were a blend of green, grey, and brown. The perfect servant merging impeccably into the background of lives eased by servitude. As he left the room Nurse gulped down her tea, glanced at her watch, and said she must be off. If she was needed she would be at the Fletchers', and then up at the Hall. The Squire's mother had suffered another of her turns.

Brushing away my murmured thanks Nurse left the room accompanied by the Tramwells, and I was left watching a sudden rain, slipping tearily down the windowpanes. I moved to the window. Was Harry out there? Hovering to make sure all was well with me? Silly of him if he were. His part was played. I wasn't worried that the Tramwells would discover his identity and see him thrust into gaol, but I was worried that in the interest of chivalry he would get himself soaked to the skin. Rubbing a small clear space in the clouded pane I peered out into the gathering darkness. Like all unknown gardens, this one looked extremely oppressive at night. Nothing much moved. A sway of tree branch and a flap of deck chair canvas on the verandah immediately outside the window. Nothing else that I could see. But I believed that someone was out there watching. And that the someone wasn't Harry. I felt the way I had in Abbots Walk that afternoon; hemmed in by something furtive, threatening, and inexplicable. What utter idiocy! The curtain dropped from my hand.

The Tramwells were either saying a lengthy goodbye to Nurse Krumpet or consulting together. Somehow, I was going to have to arrange a consultation of my own with Maude. Settling back against the sofa cushions, I wished there had been a fire in the grate. It would have been cosy to have curled up and dozed a little in the warmth . . . yawn . . . this had been a long and stressful day. Perhaps forty tiddly-winks . . . I was dreaming of a low, husky voice singing a plaintive ballad of love and betrayal. . . . The room flooded with light so strong it pierced the back of my eyelids and I sat up with a jolt. Hyacinth and Primrose were back in the room, indisputably real but another voice was somewhere close by. The gypsy maid Chantal?

I wondered if she would be the one to serve dinner, but an hour later when we sat at the round oak table in a parlour across the hall it was Butler who did the honours. Austerely, he explained that Chantal had unexpectedly returned for an hour, prepared the meal, and left again. I was disappointed, but I would see her tomorrow. Excitement was still playing cat's cradle with my insides, but I thoroughly enjoyed her sausage and chips and the apple tart with the flaky golden crust. Very soon after dinner, the sisters suggested that I get an early night and escorted me up the satin-smooth steps of the great staircase.

"Hold on to the rail when coming down tomorrow," warned Hyacinth. "You don't need a wrenched ankle or worse on top of all your troubles."

At the turns the steps did narrow to wedges the size of the slice of apple tart I had just eaten. I would remember to be careful. We reached the second hallway, an enormous gallery lined with doors. About a foot above these ran a thick time-blackened ledge crammed with a miscellany of objects. A baby alligator, stuffed but once alive, caught my eye.

"I trust you won't mind sleeping in the old nursery." Turning into a small arched alcove, Hyacinth pushed open a door. "We always keep sheets on all four beds in here. Foolish, but Primrose and I tend to be sentimental. The memories that old swing brings back! Violet liked to scare us by flying out so far we were afraid she would take off the door. Now, are you quite sure you will be comfortable here? W.C. next door; bath down the hall. We could prepare one of the other rooms, but that would mean getting a fire lit and opening up the windows at the same time. Butler and Chantal each do a splendid job but they have as much as they can manage with the rooms we use."

Before I could reply, Primrose broke in. "You know, my dears, I have been thinking about Chantal and wondering if —should the amnesia not abate—she would agree to look into her crystal ball and see if she can arouse any images that might prove helpful."

I felt as if a trapdoor had sprung out from under me. Fergy had a fearful reverence for gypsies and their dark powers. The wash house at the vicarage had held enough pegs to keep a fire going all winter, purchased in desperate hope of keeping the evil eye away. After the sisters left I undressed and washed in the blue-and-white china basin on the rosewood stand. Then, shivering, I struggled into the great floating folds of white lawn nightdress which the Tramwells had left for me at the foot of the small bed nearest the door. The material was exquisite. Reams of drawn threadwork and minute tucks, but the smell of mothballs would cling to me for a year. Moodily I stared at the swing hanging from the ceiling. Better to sit than lie down. I wasn't Baby Bear. That sister who had died —Lily—perhaps she had been a tall child and died from cramp. In the dim and distant days of the Tramwells' youth people died of everything. Indigestion. Acne. Childbirth.

Childbirth! I told myself to take deep slow breaths, but ignored the advice. I had never ever considered the possibility that my mother might have been dead; that someone other than she had left me on the vicarage doorstep. And I didn't want to consider it now. But . . . if I had killed her in being born, wasn't it possible that those who had loved her had wanted me gone—removed immediately without any of the lengthy fuss of conventional adoption procedures? My eyes filled with tears and I bit hard on a nail. A murderess. That's how they would view me. No! Harry was right. No jumping to wild conclusions. Remember the Devon violet paper. Violet, the sister who had gone to America, was a much better prospect! And I could not discount other possibilities. Had the four girls had a governess—an impoverished gentlewoman, perhaps a distant family connection? A friend or cousin who had come for visits? Harry, of course, had kept insisting that there was every chance that even if my mother had lived in Flaxby Meade she might not have been a member of the Cloisters' household. But I felt in the very marrow of my bones that he was wrong. If only there were some physical resemblance between the two of us. The way Maude had looked at me . . . Was it possible she had recognized some resemblance to someone? Was that why she had not pushed harder to present my case to the authorities?

The portraits in the hall! Why had I not thought of them before? Reaching for Mr. Hunt's watch I clutched it against me, its ticking a small friendly heartbeat. After midnight! Creeping stealthily out of bed I crossed to the door, halting at every groan of floorboard. How close were the sisters' rooms? A blessing at least that old people favoured early nights. But I could not risk turning on the hall lights. I had noticed a candle with a box of matches lying beside it on the mantel. It would light my way down those dangerous stairs and illuminate the portraits.

All set! With small flickering flame held aloft, the hem of

the nightgown held cautiously off the ground, I set off. I was halfway down the stairs when I heard a muffled noise and the hideous prospect of Minerva leaping over the bannisters at my jugular made me pause, heart moving chokingly up into my throat. Silence. But I didn't feel much better. Why hadn't I thought that Butler or Chantal might still be up and about? The candle flame quivered and I cupped it with the hand that had been holding my nightgown. Keeping the hem tucked under my elbow would take some doing but I started moving again. If I did meet either of the servants I would explain loftily that I was going down in search of a glass of warm milk.

The first portraits were a disappointment. Bewigged and, in many cases, clearly befuddled, none of them looked like me. One coy, ringletted lass, flesh mounding like enormous meringues over the top of her low-cut emerald satin gown, did resemble someone I knew—the barmaid at the Royal Thistle and . . . just a hint of someone else in the expression of the roguish blue eyes. Or was I imagining it? Must be . . . unless Primrose . . . when she had talked about Minerva's coronation cup? The eyes were a similar blue, but . . . no. I moved on. The gentleman in the next frame was soberly dressed and portly. His wig was a modest little number and his mouth primly pursed, but, whether by trick of the candlelight, his protruberant eyes were decidedly and gloatingly fixed on the cleavage next door. His mistress? Couldn't be, or her portrait would have hung in the cellar. Nothing of interest for a few yards except that . . . surely I had seen the young gentleman with the tricorne hat, hand resting on the silver-topped cane, before . . . or had I seen a portrait very like it, perhaps by the same artist, at The Heritage Gallery? Lifting the candle flame closer I searched for the signature and then realized this wasn't an original. It wasn't even a particularly good copy.

A faint shushing sound which might have been the wind or a door opening somewhere far off in the house prodded me and my candle onward. At some time the Tramwells must have lost ownership of the original and . . . wouldn't it be marvellous if as a reward for all their hospitality I could arrange for Angus . . . ? I forgot Angus. I had found Violet. Her name was in the left-hand corner of a muddy green background. A heavy, ponderous work, but then it could be that Violet had been a heavy, ponderous child. Hyacinth's description of her rocketing back and forth on the nursery swing had not made her sound that way, but . . . I peered as closely as I could without setting the portrait alight but I couldn't detect any likeness to myself. Inching forward, I reached Lily. A better painting and a totally different subject. Here was a laughing, elfin-faced little girl of about seven, her short hair a mass of silvery bubbles. Not pretty exactly. What was so special was that although she was standing, black-booted feet together, she seemed to be moving. Lily would always be moving—whirling, running, laughing. Again, I had one of those strange feelings that had beset me since coming to this house. I knew that whatever had happened to Lily had been terrible. She hadn't died peacefully in her bed a few years ago, after a happy and fulfilled life. I was afraid. I didn't want her to look like me, and she didn't. (Another weird flash. I knew—absolutely knew—that this was the best-loved child. How had Hyacinth and Primrose and Violet felt about that?)

I glided on past the other portraits, none of them arranged in any particular sequence. Women with acid faces wearing stiff black dresses, men wearing gold watch chains stretched across their pompous fronts. An eighteenth-century rake in white wig and foaming lace at his throat. And beside him a girl of about my age in weighty blue velvet, an Elizabethan ruff under her round chin. Eyes wide and alive stared right into the candle flame. She was no beauty; heavy-set, plain features, round face. She looked jolly, and knowing, as though she understood my reasons for being here and did not condemn my masquerade romp. A small brass plate in the right-hand corner gave her name. Tessa Tramwellyan. I gritted my teeth to stop my breath rushing out and extinguishing the candle. This was my namesake. Had to be . . . because a quick glance farther down the row showed no other Tessas. I moved back to her. My hand shook and shadows moved in the hall. Ridiculous, but I could have sworn she winked at me. A pity her looks weren't more dramatic. With her romantic history Tessa should have been a great beauty, with a hint of sorrow in her eyes.

Suddenly, a faint noise sounded behind me. Instantly I flattened against the wall. Some detective! Would that ruse make me invisible, candle and all? Muffled voices breathed out from the sitting room door a few yards away. Amazingly, fear evaporated. What an opportunity! I might find out what the inhabitants of Cloisters thought of me! Heroically snuffing out my candle with my fingers I tiptoed forward. Fergy had always said luck was my patron saint. A faint crack of light showed that the sitting room door stood a finger-width ajar. I pressed close to that strip of light and peered into the room. Primrose and Hyacinth sat at a gate-legged table in the corner diagonally across from me. They were playing cards. Beat Your Neighbour or Happy Families? I smiled. Rather sweet their staying up way past the hour when nice little old ladies should be in bed.

"Ace takes king," Hyacinth reproved, tapping her cards on the table. "I knew when you threw the three of spades and ducked the jack of hearts that you were not concentrating. I realize this has been an unusual day, but excitement generally keeps you on your toes."

"So sorry, dear," Primrose sighed. "I was thinking about the girl."

"Wondering, no doubt, if she may not be a great deal of trouble." Hyacinth picked up the cards and shuffled them before fanning them swiftly into two stacks. "One thing I will say for her, she does not appear to eat horrendous quantities. Watches her figure. Humph! Can't say I blame her."

"I imagine a great many men do likewise." Primrose sounded thoughtful. "I have been fussing with the notion that she might be rather useful to us. Clearly well brought up as well as quite lovely. I imagine don't you, my dear, that she would be rather pleased to make some small return for our hospitality?"

Not quite what the heroine had in mind, I thought, but assisting Butler and Chantal with a little light housework would provide excellent cover for my investigations.

"That might be treading on sticky ground." Hyacinth was examining her cards. "Can't feel he would be pleased, and in all fairness one could not blame him."

Butler?

"One faces the question of propriety," she muttered. "Capitalizing on her youth and physical attributes isn't quite nice, is it?"

How quaint and old-fashioned they were. Jogging three or four laps around the rooms with the Hoover wouldn't kill me. Unless . . . if the house had to be swept from attic to cellar with a dustpan and brush I could see her point. Primrose did not.

"Fiddle. I think, my dear, you are exaggerating what would be asked of her. Not that I suggest we actually voice a request . . ."

Had I made a slight sound? Naturally I felt a little miffed at the prospect of being given orders like a parlour maid, but I didn't think I had gasped in outrage. Primrose had, however, turned her head towards the door. I must not be caught here like a thief in the night. I must make for the stairs. But, alas, hampered by having to hold up my skirts I was prevented from feeling my way. Speed was out. All I could do was mentally cross my fingers and trust the sisters would attribute any sound to the wind, whimpering dispiritedly around the house. But all was well. No cry of "Halt, who goes there?" My body brushed the bannister knob and I stole up the stairs. Slowly, steadily, one tiptoe at a time. I was in no state to fake a desire for warm milk. Almost at the top. Almost safe. What . . . what was that? The wind? But the wind had not sounded so fierce a moment ago.

Now it had broken through the house and with a huge gusting rush slammed into my back, pitching me painfully forward. Not the wind. The snarling menace that held me pinned down against the floor and was burrowing into my neck had a face covered with fur and a huge wet tongue.

4

Being used to dogs, I realized that Minerva's greeting was violently enthusiastic, not hostile, and she had the decency to exercise sufficient restraint not to bring the Tramwells running. No wild crescendo of barks! Crawling out from under, I told her she was my favourite animal in the world, but could we please get better acquainted in the morning? Reaching up for a fingerhold on the next step I continued my wary ascent, with man's best friend making playful snatches at my hem. Couldn't this prove a nightmare with me waking to find myself scrunched up in my pygmy bed? Scratch the nightmare idea. In the ways of their topsy-turvy horror, I would probably find Hyacinth and Primrose had flown up to wait for me, glassy-eyed, at the top of the stairs.

But it was Butler who was waiting there for me. Dared I hope that in my shroud nightgown he would take me for the house ghost, not the house guest?

The master of unflappability did even better.

"Pardon me, miss. It would seem that you have been sleep-walking. A very trying—indeed dangerous—habit, I'm sure." He reached out a deferential hand to assist me up from my grovelling position. "Brought on no doubt by a very 'arrowing day. May I fetch something to settle you, miss? Say a cup of hot chocolate?"

What a wonderful noble thing the Tramwells had done in reforming this man! What a credit to their benevolence!

"Hot chocolate would be lovely, Butler. Thank you." Minerva was lying on my feet but I managed a brilliant smile at the blurred figure of my rescuer.

"At once, miss," he responded with that marvellous blend of aloof respect. "Shall we say your room or mine, miss?"

I quailed. What was this, blackmail? Somehow I managed a whisper. "How silly of me! I have just remembered that I don't know whether I like hot chocolate or not. Better forget it. Goodnight. Coming, Minerva? Sweet of her—she seems to have taken a fancy to me. Wants to sleep on my bed."

In the safety of the nursery—key turned in the lock and a chair pushed against it for good measure—I told myself firmly that Butler had lapsed briefly into cockney humour. In the morning I would actually believe it. Surprisingly I slept well even with Minerva slumped across my middle, and I awoke to find sunlight gilding the furniture and to a feeling of boundless energy. Better make immediate use of it. However gracious the Tramwells' hospitality, my time here was limited. I would have been on my way downstairs in five minutes if I could have found Angus's watch. I was sure I had put it down on the table with my charm bracelet after checking the time, but perhaps I had dropped it down on the mantel when lighting the candle. My watch wasn't there and I couldn't think where else . . . unless Minnie had whiled away a wakeful period in the night playing hide and seek with it? Slipping on my charm bracelet I jingled it at her. But she missed the implication that it was mine—mustn't touch—and made a snapping leap at my arm.

We met no one as we reached the downstairs hall. But even if the sisters weren't yet up I was sure the servants would be, and that this would be an excellent opportunity to meet and speak with the enticingly mysterious Chantal. What psychic powers I possessed were strong enough to suggest I would find her in the kitchen, but not sufficiently developed to tell me how to get there. I opened three doors into wrong rooms, all gloomily bare save for a few humps of furniture draped in yellowing sheets, before I found the kitchen. It was at a right angle from the siting room, down a short flight of stone steps.

The kitchen was empty of people, but I loved it anyway. In size it was about half the dimensions of the front hall, and positively brimming with Gothic delights. A huge open fireplace, complete with a spit equal to roasting a mediaeval martyr, dominated one stone wall. Two black cauldrons hung in side alcoves. A foot or so farther down the wall stood a cast-iron cooker capable of baking enough loaves to feed all the village poor. Only these days those unfortunates would have shiny gas cookers of their own purchased on the never-never, and glossy no-wax lino on their floors. This floor was stone, each flag about the size of one of Harry's paddocks. Only the sink looked modern, circa 1906. On either side of it ran a stretch of marble very likely pinched from the Taj Mahal. A half-dozen Welsh dressers crammed with bone china, Woolworth's plastic, tarnished silver, brass, and empty jam jars, filled up some dead space. But there was still an island of room for the huge deal table in the centre. Fergy would have given both arms and a leg for one like it.

A seemingly dead black cat by the fireplace sat up and joined Minerva under the table in devouring an unpleasant blob of pressed pink meat out of a Chinese porcelain bowl. We had a smaller one in the same silkworm pattern in our front room cabinet, and The Heritage owned a magnificent version presently on loan to the Art Institute in Chicago. Minerva snarled at the cat and it skimmed across the room to leap up a step-ladder standing beside one of the dressers.

"Sure an' away 'tis a dog's life, Minnie," I sighed. She bared her teeth in a grunt, showing no memory of our night together. Turncoat. Amnesia must be contagious. That feeling grew when Butler, entering by a side door opening off a flight of narrow stairs, evinced no sign of embarrassment at having even jokingly made a pass at a guest of the family.

"Good morning, miss." Slight inclination of the head. "May I h'assume you are here to advise how you wish your h'eggs prepared?" (Butler had that tendency of the reformed "H" dropper to add them occasionally in inappropriate places.) "The ladies like theirs lightly boiled." He gave no indication of noticing that Minnie had taken hold of one of his trouser legs and was worrying it fiercely. "On h'egg days, we always send in extra toast so they can cut it into soldiers—for dipping."

I was about to exclaim "That's exactly how I like my eggs!" when I caught myself and said, "Sounds lovely, Butler."

He bowed again. "Very good, miss. If you care to h'adjourn to the breakfast parlour you should find the ladies already down."

He was easing me out of the kitchen, and resentment surged. Fergy was queen at our house so it wasn't his august manner that bothered me but the feeling that below it lay contempt. Why? What had the Tramwells told him about my reasons for being here? I watched Minerva amble off to sit, belching, by the fireplace. If only Chantal would come in. I stalled for a little extra time.

"I do hope I am not making a great deal of extra work for you, this is such a vast house to keep up, if I can be of help in any way—some dusting or . . ."

"You're a guest, miss."

"But I wouldn't mind, really. I like"—a slight stumble, I was about to say I liked old houses—"I like this house. It's almost like a person."

"Yes, miss." Butler's voice had mellowed a fraction.

"Really a very beautiful house."

"And a great many clocks, sixty-five until the ladies parted with one recently."

Now he had almost a glow about him and, puzzled, I could only say, "No excuse for anyone to ever be late, then."

"Certainly not, miss, so I won't keep you." Impassively he held open the kitchen door. "I'm very partial to clocks. They have always been rather a speciality of mine. My father 'ad—had—a similar enthusiasm for cigarette cases and my mother—she worked on the trains—took up lighters as a hobby."

"A lot more interesting than stamps" was all I could think to say before Butler bowed again and I found myself out in the hall. I still hadn't met Chantal, and I still hadn't asked Butler what he had been doing on the second-floor landing last night. Checking for burglars, perhaps?

5

One clock chimed and another one boomed and I headed hurriedly in the direction of the little old ladies.

The parlour was the room in which we had eaten dinner last night. It was considerably smaller than the sitting room but with similar French windows opening on to the same view, a wide terrace set out with clay pots of wallflowers and scattered with a few deck chairs. Beyond was a large garden reached by moss-grained steps. The lawn was shaved to a soft green plush and the flower beds were cut into a wide circle of crescents glowing with every shape and colour of rose from deepest pink to apricot, pale yellow, and champagne. Dad would love this place.

Dear Dad. For one whole second I thought I saw him, sitting at the small round table with Hyacinth and Primrose. But, other than not having much thatch on top of his head, the elderly gentleman leaning forward to pat Hyacinth's veiny hand with its ruby-red fingernails was nothing like Dad. Come to that, Hyacinth did not look like the Hyacinth I had previously seen. She was positively dimpling, and the flutter of her eyelashes was enough to cause a severe draught. Primrose, sitting with her lavender shawl hunched around her shoulders, looked chilled and curdled—if not actually sour. Could it be: sibling rivalry at over sixty? Gentlemen callers before breakfast! What was the older generation coming to! A giggle stirred but almost immediately subsided. How sad if Hyacinth and Primrose had never experienced romance when young. Why shouldn't Hyacinth have a little flirtation now before it was too late? Then she said something to the man and, despite myself, I was a little shocked by the decidedly come-hither look in those black eyes. Out of nowhere came an amazing thought.

Who would have better reason to conceal a pregnancy and ferret the child away than a fortyish spinster?

"Ah, there you are, dear." Primrose's pressed-flower face lost its discontented expression, and I realized how pretty she must have been twenty years ago. "I do trust you slept well."

Her small hands twittered upwards to pat silvery curls, and I breathed again. She couldn't be my mother. Neither could her sister. The very idea would be like a naughty French farce. And I hadn't waited all these years to discover I was some sort of joke.

"Clyde, you must meet our guest," said Hyacinth.

The gentleman had risen on perceiving my entrance. Sunlight winked off his rimless glasses, giving his eyes a decided sparkle. He was coming around the table towards me, very dapper—if a trifle stout—in his navy pin-striped suit. His surprisingly mod Italian shoes also winked at me.

"Good morning," he beamed. "And if it weren't, you would certainly make it one!" Turning back to include the Tramwells in the warmth of his approval he continued to pump both my hands in his squashy paws. "Allow me, dear young lady, to introduce myself—Clyde Deasley. And may I say the pleasure of this meeting is all mine!" A nod to the sisters and a quiver of pencil-thin silver moustache. "Lovely, quite lovely."

Hyacinth sniffed. "Clyde, sprightliness is not becoming in a man a sneeze away from his old-age pension. Let the child sit down. Here comes breakfast now and she certainly needs fattening up. Much too thin, whatever the modern obsession with trying to resemble an ironing board."

"How delighted I am that I gate-crashed your little breakfast party. Not doing things formally this morning, Butler?" Clyde, chortling up at Butler, spread his serviette over the dome of his waistcoat.

The family retainer was not amused; nose elevated, he proceeded around the room with the tray. My h'egg was passed to me looking rather sweet and inviting in its Bunnykins cup. But the atmosphere was not one of cosy sunshine, and I attributed this to an antipathy between the two men. However, when Butler left the room, Mr. Deasley had only the nicest things to say about him.

"Come along splendidly, hasn't he? Take back every word

I said about your being totally mad in not only failing to turn him over to the police but actually giving him a job when you came home to find him robbing the place." Beaming at the Tramwells, he knocked the top off his egg.

I stared at them all.

Primrose tapped her shell daintily. "We were raised on the principle of 'the one sinner who repents.' Besides, after sitting down with Butler"—she looked at me—"not his real name, of course, but he has had so many aliases I don't think he remembers what he was christened, we found much that was commendable in him."

"Certainly," agreed Hyacinth. "A man who listens to the Albert Hall on the wireless while he works and had displayed the delicacy not to go through our lingerie drawers could not be all bad."

"Clyde, your cup is empty," Primrose said. "May I pour you another?"

"Delighted, dear lady." Mr. Deasley's hand reached under the table to pick up his dropped serviette. Primrose, seated beside him, exhibited a pastel blush.

Returning his hand to full view he reached over and raised her quivering fingers to his lips. No one had ever kissed my hand, and I wondered if the moustache tickled. The clock on the mantel gave off a silvery chime. Mr. Deasley looked towards it.

"Another Butler blessing. He has got your clocks going. Not in perfect accord"—another ping-ping began behind us —"but it's good to know that there is life in the old tocks yet."

Hyacinth looked at me. "Mr. Deasley has more than a passing interest in old things. He owns an antique shop called the Silver Rose in the village, and timepieces are one of his special enthusiasms. Isn't that right, Clyde? Along with books and coins and . . ."

"Anything except brass crinoline-lady bells and World War I medals." Mr. Deasley beamed at me.

Rising from her chair, Hyacinth said, "Occasionally our friend gives us advice on . . . insuring some of our pieces. So if you will excuse us, my dear, we will leave you for a few moments while we go to the library for a little business chat."

"Of course," I replied as Primrose scuttled out of her chair, and Clyde raised a hand to smooth out the fuzz on top of his head. Why did I get the feeling that the gesture was a little studied? Almost embarrassed. If it were, he recovered instantly. Bowing over his tummy he did a disappearing act through the open French windows. Back he came holding a full-blown, almost lavender rose in one hand. His elevated nose and the way he held the flower rigidly out in front of him reminded me of Butler with the tray.

Breathless of voice, he stuttered, "Ro-oses a-re r-red, vi-violets bl-blue, su-sugrhh . . ." A sneeze, a veritable earthquake of a sneeze, enveloped him and Primrose stepped forward to pry the rose from his clenched fist.

"Such foolishness, Clyde—with your severe hay fever! And after my removing the flowers from the table when you came in! You could give yourself a heart attack. We knew a man who sneezed himself to death at a funeral, didn't we, Hy?"

Mopping at the tears rolling off the crests of his full cheeks, Mr. Deasley gasped apologies. "Should have express-sses-ed admiration more simply." With his glasses resting on top of his head his eyes appeared over the handkerchief rim. "Ah! But come to think of it, I have not as yet been presented with the pleasure of your name."

The earrings for once immobile, Hyacinth regarded him acidly. "Why should I enlighten the wicked purloiner of one of my roses on any subject?"

A wave of emotion, stronger than any I had felt since coming to Cloisters, flooded through me. Gratitude. The Tramwells had not regaled their gentleman caller with the truth about my presence in this house. And then she spoke words which, if I had been a sprig-muslin heroine, would have caused me to faint dead away. "Severe memory loss, Clyde. I am beginning to think you suffer from that effect of encroaching old age." Her back was as straight as the wall behind her. "Surely, Prim or I told you that our charming house guest's name is Tessa."

6

Horror settled like a custom-made shroud about my shoulders. I was discovered. Gratitude indeed! But how did the Tramwell pussy cats know?

"Tessa!" Clyde Deasley rolled the word around on his tongue. "A flower indeed among names and, need I say, it suits you to perfection!" Lifting my nerveless fingers he brushed a kiss across the tips. The moustache did tickle. My mind focussed glassily on that small revelation. He was moving to the door alongside Primrose when Butler glided in and started clearing the table. Hyacinth delayed following the others. She instructed Butler to leave the dishes for ten minutes as Miss Tessa would like to have another cup of coffee.

When we were alone, she said, "I saw no reason to supply Mr. Deasley with the details of your sorry plight. He is an old and dear friend, but even the best men do tend to gossip."

Behind my back my hands squeezed each other for courage. "Why then, why did you tell him my name was Tessa? Is it?" No need to fake the tremor in my voice this time.

"Dear, dear!" Hyacinth's unevenly painted ebony brows moved into squiggly but fairly level lines. "I never thought about raising false hopes. Tessa was simply the first name that came to me. It's a family name although traditionally used as the second Christian name. My sister Violet is Violet Tessa. Years ago—hundreds—a baby named Tessa was abandoned on the doorstep of a former ancestral home of the Tramwells. Her father was a young monk and her mother a village girl. Primrose and I are descended from her because she married into the family and indeed lived in this house after it was built. We were talking about her last night after you went to bed."

I had lowered my face to hide my immense giddy relief;

74

now I raised it. "What was she like? If I am to be named after her temporarily, and I do take that as a great compliment, I think I would enjoy learning something of her history. Was she a colourful character?"

Hyacinth's dark eyes looked more hooded than ever. "If by that you mean did she run off with a duke or smoke cigars—no. From all the family stories she was the ordinary motherly sort. But what's ordinary? Despite the intolerance of the times she persuaded her husband, so the family story goes, to let the gypsies camp in the woods behind Abbots Walk. Remarkable, since it was said a gypsy had cursed her father —the monk—and the spell took. He died by hanging, I am sorry to say."

"How awful." I glanced out the window to where the Ruins shone soft and grey in the sunlight. "In his cell?" The Reverend Snapper had not said where the deed was done.

"No. In the grounds," said Hyacinth, and I tried not to refrain too obviously from looking towards the window. "Chantal can probably tell you as much as I about the family curse. Her people have been in these parts as long as ours."

"The family curse? Was the hex upon the monk's descendants also?"

"All nonsense, of course, but Tessa died from a fall down the stairs . . . and through the years other"—she paused— "happenings have caused it to be said that the curse is still in force."

I drew my hands up to warm my arms. "Does Tessa have any other descendants in the village outside your family?"

"Not direct ones. The younger sons and daughters tended to move away, but her mother's family were village people. I suspect one-quarter of the present population is distantly connected with Tessa, if they would acknowledge it." Instructing me not to worry at showing no sign of returning memory, Hyacinth left to follow the others, with me staring after her.

What had she meant by that last remark? Restless, I went out the French windows into the garden. Was Tessa also considered a bad seed? The morning was fairly warm but the sky was combed with clouds in shades of pearl and charcoal. No need for some choleric old gardener to tell me it was going to rain soon. Did the Tramwells have a gardener? Yes, I was sure that was a man's jacketed sleeve protruding around the for-

sythia. I was about to walk over and speak to the old codger
when I realized that would mean more questions; awkward for
me and unfair to the Tramwells. Turning back to the house, I
suddenly felt immensely happy. By lending me Tessa's name
the Tramwells had provided me with a marvellous excuse for
asking questions about the family. I was at the windows when
my mood changed again just as swiftly. The gardener wasn't
clipping away at that bush. He was watching me. And it wasn't
a nice kind of watching.

Back in the parlour I conjured up Fergy's scolding voice
telling me the only one watching me was the Man upstairs and
felt better. I was being wicked and deceitful but I was sure
God would see it was all in a good cause. No one was likely
to get hurt by my masquerade and when "I came to myself"
I would tell the Tramwells that I believed Angus Hunt had
the original of the copy in the portrait gallery.

An urge to look at the gallery again in daylight took hold
of me. I might meet Chantal in the hall. But no—Butler was
in the hall, and he informed me that Chantal had taken the
family car down to the village on errands for the ladies. I was
seriously beginning to wonder if the girl existed in solid human
form.

I was about to turn with a mental flounce in the direction
of the portrait gallery when Butler emitted a confidential
cough. "Pardon me, miss. H'I am talking out of turn, but if I
was you, I'd be on the watch when it comes to a certain gentleman presently on the premises."

"That nice Mr. Deasley!" said I, sounding suitably
shocked.

"Kneesley Deasley, as he's known in these 'ere—here—
parts. On account of his having a keenness for touching ladies'
knees in church."

"No!" I gasped.

"A harmless divershong some might say, but I have my
two ladies to consider. I would wager my grandmother's pension he's not here to do them any good."

"But he might genuinely want to—court one of them," I
suggested.

"Precisely, miss." Butler elevated the tray on his fingertips
and went into the parlour.

I stood for a minute or two after the door closed and went

76

along to the gallery. This part of the hall was rather dark, so I switched on a light. In its whitish glare I searched again among the long-dead faces for some hint of resemblance to myself. Finding none, I fleetingly pondered which, if any, had suffered violent death. Cloisters must have had its share of religious heretics, beheaded Royalists, and oppressors of the poor. This man, Sinclair Tramwell, in a heavily embroidered waistcoat and wearing his own hair, in 1756, looked a wily old reprobate. The kind to drop dead at his daughter's coming-out ball—from a knife wound in the back. Smiling, I moved on but when I reached the copy my amusement ebbed, like blood seeping from a death thrust. Last night I had not noticed the name of the subject. I saw now that he was the Marquis De Salutare. A sliver of memory slid into place—Angus telling me that the reason the original was extremely valuable was that it was painted by a brilliant artist of the French court who had been guillotined during the Revolution. The majority of his work had been destroyed and the marquis himself had been killed after ferrying many of his fellow aristocrats across the channel to freedom.

Why was he here among the Tramwells? If he had been a family connection, it would have been friendly to put him over some fireplace, but . . . Butler came out of the parlour with a loaded tray and I moved away from the wall. The sight of him in the mundane occupation of carrying crockery to the kitchen forced me back to reality. This picture might mean nothing more interesting than a need to cover a damp spot on the wall. The Tramwells wouldn't want one of their own growing musty, would they? I meant to look again at the Tramwell sisters, but Butler was walking extremely slowly and I did not want him to think me well enough for prolonged art gazing. I would have to return to the parlour, or the sitting room, and stifle. I glared at the grandfather clock in its alcove to my right, its wheezy tock-tock bursting into splintered booms as I passed. Time was wasting. No Chantal. No Maude Krumpet—unless I sprained an ankle to fetch her here. I might have to resort to that ploy yet, or I would soon begin to think of myself as a prisoner, completely cut off from the outside world.

Hand on the sitting room door, I hesitated. Not completely cut off. The telephone! However quaintly old world they might be, the Tramwells must have a phone. I had not seen one in the sitting room or parlour, so it should be out here—and surely if I were quick and quiet I could call Harry. I lifted cardigans and hats off tables and chairs, looked behind vases, peered behind curtains, searched under tables and inside small chests. All to no avail. I was close to concluding that the Tramwells had not succumbed after all when I heard a strange burping sound. Cloisters *was* possessed of a phone, and it was ringing. From somewhere in this hall. Where hadn't I looked? Burp-burp. Hurry. And suddenly I knew. The cupboard under the stairs! Crouching down, I opened a small wooden door, reached into darkness and pulled out what might have been one of Minerva's buried bones. A long curly tail was attached and I knew all was well. Lifting the bone to my ear I spoke into the mouthpiece in a breathy rush, success making me giddy. "Tramwell Ancestral Home."

A responsive giggle. "Oh, you funny thing!" The voice sounded like a child, I could not tell which sex, but the next words were jarringly those of an adult. "But, please! Spare me any more gush, Chantilly, is it?" I opened my mouth but the voice gurgled on like a playful but chilly little brook. "I'm taking Mumsie out in a teensy bit to get her fitted for a new coat. Oh, that it might be a strait jacket! Will you be a pet and tell them tomorrow evening, that's important—Wednesday—not Thursday this week. But still at the usual time. Dinner naturally. I've bagged some plump juicy pigeons so we should have a simply mouth-watering time. And do tell them, will you, girl, not to wear black again. It does cast such a pall. Hold on a minute"—pause and then—"all right, Mumsie, I'm coming, yes, Mumsie, I am talking to a lady. I haven't asked her to marry me yet, but I will. Promise." Another pause while a lot of muttering went on. I was wondering whether to say something when the caller whispered down the line, "Remember—tomorrow, Wednesday," in that squishy baby voice.

With the receiver dangling from my hand, I forgot all about phoning Harry. The Tramwells had some strange friends. Pigeons for dinner! Everyday fare in the Regency era, but . . . I crept out from the cupboard. The phone message was not sufficiently urgent to warrant my interrupting the Tramwells in their private discourse with Mr. Deasley.

I would sit on one of the sofas in the sitting room and

think about Harry . . . no, maybe that wasn't such a good idea.
I might get too clear a picture of him and the woman with the
sultry eyes. Much better to search the bookshelves for something on the Tramwells of Warwickshire. Unfortunately, all I
discovered were novels I had already read and the same in-
spirational volumes sent to Dad at Christmas by people who
thought that kind of thing light reading for a vicar on rainy
afternoons. Anything documenting the history of the Tramwells must be in the library where the sisters were entertaining
Mr. Deasley. Plodding about the room, I inspected ornaments
and peered at pictures on the walls. Having grown up in a
shabby old house where little money was to be found for re-
furbishing I recognized many little dodges that made up thrift.
And I wasn't much surprised that people in the Tramwell
condition—all those Welsh dressers in the kitchen stuffed with
silver and crystal, Minerva dining out of an Oriental bowl—
should resort to them. Dad had an elderly and immensely rich
cousin who sent us an obviously reused Christmas card each
year.

I set down a brass bell and walked in a slow circle around
the edge of the carpet. Mum would have liked this room. She
had also been ingenious at putting cast-off items to unconven-
tional use. In one corner sat a rose-patterned chamber pot
blooming with trailing ivy. On one of the bookshelves an iron
boot jack did duty as a book end. On the open bureau shelf
lay a torch and a mother-of-pearl handled fish knife. Pretty
and perfect for slitting open envelopes.

Continuing my prowl I noticed something else. Many objects in the room came from the Far East. Those brasses . . .
that silk screen brilliant with jewel coloured peacocks, blocking
any draught between the fireplace and . . . I looked down at
the hearth and saw that the fire dogs were a mottled sickly-
green pair of dragons breathing open-jawed resentment at having their backs burdened with pokers and shovels. Stuffed
alligators upstairs, dragons down. What a fey, mischievous
house this was! Turning back to look at the wall hangings I
found several hand-inked maps with the signature Sinclair
Tramwell in their right-hand corners. Sinclair . . . ? Of course!
And I smiled smugly. The knife in the back at his daughter's
coming-out ball might have been a bit far-fetched, but I had
been right about the man being a colourful personality. Com-

mander of one of the King's vessels or, better still, a pirate? An exquisitely embroidered Indian shawl placed sensibly under glass hung over a black lacquered, gilt-inlaid chest. Were both souvenirs of Sinclair's travels? The idea that this man's blood flowed in my veins was decidedly intriguing.

In a sudden rush I remembered the priest hole. I moved over to the fireplace, running my hand down the brick on the far right-hand side of the mantel. Thoughts of the Tramwells' imminent return would not deter me; I was bored, and who knew what secret family documents I might find below? I pushed, pulled, and rubbed, felt a nub of cement, thought of Harry's bedfellow's nose and gave a vicious pull. Then a yank and a twist. An anguished vibrating groan and the stone door swung slowly outward.

I listened. No one was coming down the hall. If I took a very quick peek, bearing in mind that the chance might not come again . . . I was about to enter the black void and hunt for a light switch when I remembered Butler emerging with his candle. Mmm . . . nasty palpitating things, candles. I had had enough of them last night. What I needed was a torch. Fetching it from the bureau shelf I pressed it alight and with a half-glance over my shoulder stepped heroically into the black hole. Careful! Mustn't become over-confident. Cripes! I had almost closed the door behind me. That would have been fun, Tessa. With that faulty catch I might have been stuck in the nether regions for a long, long time. Okay—mustn't overdo the Gothic bit. If I did get stuck my voice would carry through the wall. Someone would come, wouldn't they?

I left the door agape, for my blood pressure. Hopefully, anyone glancing casually into the room would never notice. This was fun. I loved the heavy dank smell that settled about me, and the chill. A few firm strides forward brought me to a flight of stone steps leading down into nothingness. Built today, that staircase would never have met nit-picking safety code regulations. It lacked a rail. All I could do was hug the brick wall to my right as I felt my way down. The torch wasn't much help, throwing out only an inch or two of furtive shadow. Wise Butler. A candle would have been better. Wise and resourceful, for how he had whiled away an afternoon down here I could not imagine. Must be part mole. The smell—damp and earthy with a hint of underground habitation—intensified. I was, I sensed, about halfway down. Thank you, God. Murky shapes were beginning to take form below me. Another dozen steps and I recognized some of the shapes as two upturned wooden cartons and rows of bottles on shelves. I reached the bottom and the floor was flagstone like the kitchen, only dustier and many degrees colder. On one of the cartons was a cluster of candles stuck in bottles, a large box of matches lying beside them. Igniting a cheery little blaze I warmed my hands for about ten seconds before snapping to my senses. Mustn't linger. And really, when I looked around the small dim chamber, I wasn't greatly impressed; no heavy coil of chains lying snake-like in a corner. No rack. No thumb-screws. No stack of family papers marked *Top Secret* that I could see. Huge disappointment. My lurid imagination had confused dissident's refuge with dungeon.

I should have known when the sisters discussed the priest hole as though it were a vacuum cleaner with a faulty switch that its present function was sadly prosaic. At some time, after priestly heads stopped rolling down Tower Hill, someone had converted this place into a booze cellar. Most of the wine racks were now empty, but I did spy about thirty bottles in an odd assortment of sizes and shapes. Picking up one, I dusted it off (Butler must have missed it) fully expecting to find a French label. What I read was hand-inscribed—Parsnip: 1963. Another lifted at random—Rhubarb: 1971. I found only three bottles of venerable old port. Being an "after the ladies leave the gentlemen to their cigars" beverage, maybe the sisters had given Daddy's supply away to the heir so he could acquire a touch of the gout in preparation for his impending change in circumstances. Coming to the sisters' stock of brandy I was sure he would not be overwhelmed by that portion of his inheritance. Only a few had French labels.

What could have kept Butler down here so long or brought him back to the sitting room covered with grime? The bleary yellow beam of the torch pricked into the gloom of distant corners, settled on a group of small wooden kegs, then went wavering along the wall below the sitting room fireplace; nothing there but a towering expanse of brick and a gigantic tattered cobweb that hung wisply down from the ceiling. My arm brushed along the wall, snagging on something. I let out a yelp of pain, and the torch slipped out of my hand. Either I had pressed the switch or the wretched thing died in the fall, for I was immediately adrift in shadow Blast! But I was still curious. Reaching up, I felt a metal tip like a nail or picture hook. Nerves brought on a feeble giggle. Had someone once tried to liven up this place with artwork?

Sobriety returned with a rush. I couldn't find the torch and I was too far from the aura of candlelight for it to aid me in my search. Time was against me, too. Any moment the Tramwells might notice the gaping door and, disgusted with my snooping ways, decide to toss me out of the house. I had been very foolish, and nothing was gained. Stumbling, I made my way to the candles. I would use one of them for the return trip. A pair of absent-minded old ladies would not find anything ominous about a misplaced torch. I blew out all but one candle and, holding this aloft, made my way slowly up those steps. The return voyage wasn't fun. What was that noise above? What if one or both sisters had a wacky sense of humour and were to screech out "Boo" just as I neared the top? The very thought almost made me trip. My palms began sweating and the candle felt like a stick of melting butter. I squeezed it hard. What if I dropped it? Hurry, hurry! I could not cup the flame to keep it safe as my left hand was fully occupied in feeling the way up the wall; one small slip and . . . my breath whistled out in a gust and the candle promptly went out.

I wanted my mother. And I did not mean the fabulous, fascinating woman of my imagining, but the Mum who had sat with me through thunderstorms and come in with the broom to beat out the witches who had moved in behind my wardrobe. My hand was sliding wetly off the wall. Calm down. Think happy thoughts. Think how Harry would miss me if I died. Or would he marry that naked creature under the sheets? Oh no! I drew a deep steadying breath. Those two were not getting rid of me this easily. All I had to do was pretend I was climbing a rope at school. Claw my way up an inch at a time. Surely I must be getting close now. My foot felt for another step and I came close to fainting. I was back in the little alcove. Success could not have tasted sweeter to Sir Edmund Hillary. Only seconds more, and I would be pushing open the hidden door. Please God, let the sitting room still be empty and . . . *please let the door still be open!* Why couldn't I find the crack of light? My hands beat frantically against the walls like a bird trapped in a chimney. But it was no use. The door—and I knew I had found it by its wooden back—was shut as tight as the corner shop on early closing.

I pushed, shoved, and jostled while telling myself fiercely that the wind had done this. It had howled in through that gap in the French windows, whipped around the silk screen, and slammed the door shut. The members of this household knew about the faulty catch. They would not close the priest hole without first checking to see if someone were down there. Not unless one of them was secretly bonkers and incurably evil.

Being discovered in a ridiculously unflattering situation was now the least of my problems. When rescued I would tell the Tramwells that my twentieth-century highwayman had come leaping at me through the window and, remembering the priest hole, I had fled to safety, drawing the door shut before he could follow. My first scream wasn't much more than a squeak, so I could hardly believe my luck when I heard a faint grinding noise and slowly—painfully slowly—the door moved outward as if my rescuer were not quite sure he, or she, was doing the right thing in letting me out.

7

He looked like a ghost. And yet he—not your heroine—was the one who looked ready to pop out of his skin. I had also never heard of a short, freckle-faced ghost wearing knee-length check trousers, purple socks bunched around the ankles, and an orange jersey.

Those freckles stood out fiercely on his pudgy cheeks, his round brown eyes reminding me of one of Harry's horses about to bolt. Poor little nipper. A glance around the room showed me we were alone, and my gratitude towards him was boundless. He had saved me not only from imprisonment but from disgrace with the Tramwells. Pushing the priest hole door firmly shut behind me, I took a deep breath of relief and tried to think what I could bestow on him in reward.

"You're Bertie, aren't you?" I said.

Eyes widening, his lips crept into a joyful smile. Seems I had given him his reward.

"Cor, miss! Fancy you remembering. And you so sick an' all yesterday! Wait till I tell Fred!" The pudgy fists burrowed into the pockets of his trousers. Bertie grew two inches before my eyes.

"Fred?"

"Me mate. We was playing ball an'—an' it sort of rolled into the garden. Couldn't find it nowhere when . . ."

"Maybe the gardener got snotty and took it?"

"Gardener, miss? There ain't no gardener. Aunt Maude's always saying the old girls is wonderful, keeping the lawn an' flowers an' stuff up theirselves."

I wouldn't let myself conjure up any more horrors. That sleeve obtruding from the forsythia must have belonged to shy

Fred. And that silly feeling of being watched had come from two boys playing.

Bertie was fumbling for words, his ears edged with red. "You see, miss, we come to the winder to ask one of the ladies to—to let Aunt Maude know if they ever come across the ball, when we saw you go into that there wall. You left the door open a wedge, didn't you, miss?"

"Right. Did you see how it came to be closed? Did anyone come into the room?"

He stared at his feet. "I—I dunno, miss. We, Fred an' me, couldn't get no one to 'ear us at the winder, so we went back to scour the rosebushes. No luck, an' when we looked through the glass again the fireplace was all bricked back up. 'Cripes!' I says. 'Wonder if Miss is all right.' Aunt Maude told us about that dungeon place and how the door kept getting jammed. Dangerous, she called it."

"You didn't have any trouble finding the secret spring?"

"Not me, miss." The orange jersey swelled importantly. "Were easy. Read all the *Famous Five* books I 'ave. So's Fred, but he wouldn't come in."

"Bertie, you are my hero." Solemnly we shook hands, but all the time I was wondering why he had looked so scared when the door opened. My hair couldn't have turned white from terror or my nails grown into claws in so short a time. Moving towards the French windows I asked, "Where's Fred now? If he's a friend of yours I would like to meet him. Is he shy? Or afraid—of something in this house?" I turned back to face him. "It's a very old house and there must be a lot of stories, even scary ones, about it."

"Fred's afraid of people." Bertie spoke with fond superiority. "But he thinks you're a princess. Even better than Diana, honest. And we in't neither of us bothered"—the wind rattled against the windows and Bertie jumped—"about that monk what got 'anged nor any other ghosts, 'ere or in the walk."

"Have you heard a lot of stuff about that monk? It's a pretty good yarn, isn't it?" Could I edge Bertie towards more recent gossip?

"Only a trickle, miss. Funny thing is, people turn a mite funny when you ask about old Tassel or whatever 'is name was.

85

Aunt Maude said some television people come down once and wanted to make a play about it, an' they got told to buzz off or get a boot up the . . ."

"I get the general vicinity." I'd been right in thinking that honest enquiry into my origins would have been futile, but I was surprised that the villagers were still bent on hushing up a mild scandal several hundred years old. "About your Aunt Maude," I said. "Why do you call her that, not Mum or Mummy? You're adopted, aren't you?"

Bertie's round brown eyes showed surprise. "Never really thought about it, miss. Names don't mean nothing, do they? Ever since she come an' brought me 'ome she's been the tops to me, an' she knows 'ow I feel about her."

He was a really decent kid. And he could have no idea that he was making me feel vaguely uncomfortable. His kind of loving was so uncomplicated, so clear. Could the word I was looking for be "mature?"

Voices out in the hall. Voices at the sitting room door.

"I'd better 'op it." Bertie's ears turned a darker red. "I'd die for you, miss." Then he darted out the window. He might not be scared of ghosts but he wasn't keen on facing either of the old ladies. Hyacinth's crisp tones rose above Primrose's soft patter, but a man's voice was overriding them both. Bother. Mr. Deasley must be staying for lunch. Disposing myself on the sofa facing the windows I assumed my wistful, little-girl-lost expression as the door opened.

Primrose trotted in ahead of Hyacinth, her crumpled flower face puckered with consternation. "Dear child, the oddest thing has happened! We don't quite know what to think."

"No, but I insist that Maude Krumpet not be blamed." Hyacinth's tone indicated that some bickering had occurred regarding that lady. "The boy must have blabbed. Annoying, but no point in recriminations. Tessa, a doctor has just arrived—a tourist, it seems. He was in the tobacconist's shop and overheard a rumour about a girl suffering from amnesia."

"A tobacconist's!" huffed Primrose pettishly as I sank limply back against the sofa cushions. "An M.D. should not be frequenting such premises. And indeed, I do not at all like the look of him, or the sound of his name. Dr. Hotfoot. How unpleasantly . . . perspiry."

I was the one perspiring. Standing up, I felt the room shift unpleasantly and sat down. What was to be done? What chance had I of fooling this meddlesome medic? Hateful man to come trudging out of his way to tend the sick. "Please," I cried, clasping my clammy brow, "can't you get rid of him? I really don't feel well enough to see a doctor."

A coy, questing rap sounded at the door and Primrose began fussing with her curls. "No escape, I fear, but we will remain with you, Tessa dear." The next words came out in a bright gush. "Come in, doctor! Yes, here is the patient, most anxious to see you. So, good of you to . . ."

Primrose rambled on but the words jibber-jabbered into an incomprehensible whirl of sound. Dr. Hotfoot strode omnipotently forward as the sisters sank on to the opposite sofa, his eyes fixed on my ghastly pallor. In rising out of my seat again, I almost stumbled and had to catch the sofa arm for support.

"Well, well." He twitched his little black bag. "And how are you today, young lady?"

The menace. I would gladly have strangled him if I could have grabbed hold of his stethoscope. He was unravelling it an inch at a time from that evil bag, beaming encouragement at me from under bushy eyebrows. Gold-rimmed glasses slid halfway down his nose and a heavy moustache drooped over his upper lip.

"May one enquire, doctor, the location of your practice?" Hyacinth's long hands flexed on her lap, the nails glowing like small coals.

The doctor smiled gently upon her. "At a charming Gothic prison for the criminally insane. Studying the minds of society's deviates has been a life-long passion."

Primrose sniffed deprecatingly as I cringed farther back against the cushions.

Clasping the stethoscope around his neck, Dr. Hotfoot rummaged deep into the bag. Out came a small bottle of dark topaz liquid and he shook it vigorously, holding it up to the light. "In layman's vernacular—truth serum," he announced. "Now, if you please, I would like to speak with my patient alone. Nothing must be permitted to distract if I am to achieve results."

The sisters did not rise. "I really think, doctor," fluted Primrose, "that one of us, at least, should stay with Tessa. A temporary name, but one that suits her, don't you think?"

Somehow I managed to force words between my teeth. "Perhaps I should see the doctor alone." I garnered strength. "I think it might be best."

"You are quite sure?" Hyacinth nudged Primrose up and they moved with reluctance to the door. "Remember, we will be right outside in the hall. Call if you should need us."

The door shut softly and I sat watching Dr. Hotfoot, mesmerized with anger and fear.

"Relax," he breathed. Setting the little bottle down on the coffee table he drew a syringe from the bottomless bag. With one eye half closed, he studied its gleaming silver tip. The moustache twitched. "Now, young lady, if you will roll up your sleeve we will have you spilling your life history in no time."

"Oh no, you don't," I whispered, leaping up and darting to safety behind the sofa. "The patient wishes to hear a little more about your background, doctor. Do tell where you acquired your medical licence and how long you have had it."

"My dear Miss Anonymous, I completely understand your misgivings. To be examined by a stranger . . ." His voice was low enough not to carry to the hall. "But you need have no fear; I will not ask you to remove your clothes—immediately." That overweight moustache crept up slowly into a furry smile. "As for my licence, don't worry your pretty head about trivia. It would never have been revoked but for that one unfortunate fuss. A pity. She was a devoted wife and I do miss her."

"You're mad." Screeching in a whisper was hard on the vocal cords. "You are certifiably insane. Come one inch closer with that needle and I swear I will jab it where it will do permanent damage."

"Oh, damn it, Tessa! You are such a spoilsport," sighed Harry. "One teensy stick with this, practically painless I promise, and I would have you exactly where I want you—flat on the sofa."

"You—you toad." Yanking the syringe out of his hand I threw it into the black bag filled, I now saw, with horse paraphernalia and a couple of bottles of stout.

"Admit it, Tess." Harry lounged against the fireplace, the

heel of one shoe resting on a dragon's head. "You are pleased to see me."

"I am not." Slashing the zip across the bag I glared at him. "For starters, you overdid the ruffian stuff yesterday."

"You got exactly what you asked for, my sweet. Attempted rape isn't pretty. What did you expect me to do? Touch my forelock and shout abuse from a kneeling position? In my own humble opinion I was great. And just consider my range. Villain one day—noble physician the next." The glasses slid farther down his nose and he seesawed that monstrous moustache about on his lip.

"Will you get out of here?" Stamping one's foot silently takes rigid self-control.

"Then spill the beans. I'm not leaving until you tell me what progress you have made. Any regrets?"

I stole across the room, listened at the door, and tiptoed back. "None. When I go down to Devon I may set myself up as a private eye. Don't laugh. I really think I have the knack."

"Your nose always was one of your best features." Harry jiggled a poker with his foot.

"How glad I am that I didn't marry you. But, Harry, what do you think of this? I have discovered that the Tramwells had two younger sisters."

"Had?"

"One is dead. The other went to America. There's a gypsy curse on the house, half the village is related to the first Tessa but not pleased by the connection. So I can't see one of them naming a child after her. The visiting nurse has an adopted son, so she is bound to be sympathetic if I can gain her confidence. A portrait has been switched in the gallery, and . . ."

Harry moved away from the fireplace, took hold of my hands, and smiled down at them. "Well, as long as you are enjoying yourself."

Seething, I pulled away. "Don't patronize me. I am going to find my mother."

"Tessa, your mother is dead. You won't find her in some stranger. And will you be satisfied with a different kind of affection, friendship perhaps?" He lifted the black bag, swinging it gently. "I heard someone singing as I came in. Tunefully, so it couldn't have been you. Does either of the old ladies fancy herself as an opera star?"

89

"Don't patronize them either. They are really rather—special. The singer must be the maid, Chantal."

Harry adjusted his moustache. "Have you met her?"

"Not yet. Let me tell you, anyone looking for unobtrusive household help would find her a rare gem. She's a gypsy. The butler is a reformed—or semireformed—burglar; the Tramwells hinted that he suffers the occasional lapse. Such fun. And my bedroom has every luxury, including its own private swing. Oh, and Harry—" My irritation evaporated. "This morning positively flew." His raised finger warned me to keep my voice low. "I spent much of my time escaping from priest holes." A gesture towards the fireplace. "Over there. Someone accidentally locked me in."

His bushy eyebrows met. "Who?"

"I don't know. Harry, were you outside, in the garden earlier this morning?" Before he could reply, a knock came at the sitting room door. Hyacinth held it open as Primrose entered with a tray, chirping, "Are we decent? What is the verdict, doctor? Will the patient live?"

Something was different about both of them. They had dressed for lunch, Primrose by donning a rose-pink cardigan over her white silk blouse and Hyacinth by trailing plum lipstick across her mouth. Were they always this formal, or was the brightened plumage a response to the male presence?

The gallant doctor, true to his name, hotfooted it over to Primrose. Removing the tray, he lowered it gently as a newborn infant on the coffee table. As the ladies took their seats he planted his hands behind his back, focussed on their expectant faces, and took a professional grip on himself. "The straight facts, ladies. We are dealing here with a very sensitive, we might even say precarious, situation. But"—his chest expanded—"some small headway has been made, the veil is lifting."

The sisters exchanged dubious glances.

"Now." He raised bespectacled eyes ceilingward. "It must be left to flutter free of its own accord. If it were to be brutally wrenched away in the clinical atmosphere of some backward cottage hospital I fear this girl could be thrust over the brink into the final abyss."

Stuff it, Harry.

"Dear me," murmured Hyacinth and Primrose.

90

Dr. Hotfoot absently accepted the cup of weak tea handed him. "Gentle interrogation while the patient was in the semi-comatose state revealed that she was especially susceptible to the amnesia due to an already unsettled state of mind. A recent distressing love affair." Tea slopped over the sides of the cup. The Tramwells would think him professionally distraught, I knew he was laughing. "The man must have been an animal. Any gently reared young girl would have been . . . but I will not elaborate."

"Indeed we would not wish to hear," tutted Primrose.

"I don't know, perhaps we ought . . ." said Hyacinth.

Dr. Hotfoot pursed his lips and I was terrified the moustache would fly off. He stroked it back down and continued. "A sad case. One shock following another, coupled with her appearing to be quite alone in the world, may delay her complete recovery somewhat. But I do believe it could be accelerated if you good ladies will continue providing a quietly sustaining atmosphere. One in which she may learn to trust humanity again." He now calmed himself by a deep swallow of tea, leaving the moustache half drowned.

Would he never leave?

Hyacinth squared her already rigid shoulders. "Have no fear, doctor. My sister and I were raised to know our civic duty."

The doctor looked at the mantel clock. All urgings that he remain for lunch were hurriedly refused and, black bag in hand, he bowed over the sisters' extended hands. Turning to me, he suggested that if I would show him out he would describe a series of simple mental exercises which might prove efficacious.

"I'll be in the Ruins every morning at three A.M. should you need to talk. You might want to bring a letter for me to post to your father," he whispered at the front door and I nodded, almost pushing him out. I felt, rather than heard, Butler come up behind me.

"Luncheon is served, miss. In the parlour."

The sisters were seated at the table contemplating a chicken salad when I rejoined them.

"Not an offensive man, considering," said Hyacinth as I sat down and unfolded my serviette.

"Considering he is a doctor?"

"That, and the moustache. Violet once had a very handsome admirer, but Father insisted that any man who wore a moustache was hiding something, so it all came to nothing. Shall we say grace?"

The rest of the afternoon passed placidly. As we sat in the sitting room Hyacinth asked me to help her wind some wool, a rather pretty pink three-ply, for Violet's youngest. The children did enjoy getting presents from England. But when I was at the point of asking more about this sister—when and to whom she was married—a knot was discovered in the wool. Primrose hovered over us, blocking out the light as we tried to unpick it.

"Such a vast, brash country, America," she said. "I never can quite understand how Violet has adjusted to the way of life, spirited though she always was. They don't use bread and butter plates, I hear. No, we have never been. Violet has often urged us to visit, but her husband . . . a deadly man." A small titter hastily suppressed. "Yes, the least said about him the better, and Hyacinth and I have never been much for travel. Surprising if you believe in heredity. Our great-great-great-grandfather Sinclair Tramwell went all round the world."

"This Sinclair, he was an officer in the navy?"

"A tea taster," Hyacinth responded, the restored wool gliding once again through her fingers. "The first member of the family to go into trade. Considered highly deplorable at the time, but he did bring home some nice knick-knacks."

"People were so narrow-minded years ago." Primrose sat down and put her feet up on a small stool. "One of our ancestors married the innkeeper's daughter; you'll see her in the gallery—looks well-endowed. But Sinclair is the only one in our family to have had sea fever, along with the gambling spirit. Tea was gold in his day and he quite restored the shaky family fortunes."

"I saw his portrait in the gallery." The ball of wool rolled to the edge of my lap and I started winding again.

Hyacinth nodded. "Has the look of a pirate or a smuggler, doesn't he? Either term would undoubtedly fit. Today he would simply be called an astute businessman. From stories told he was extremely popular among the tenants—not home to bother them much and when he was, lenient and open-handed. But of course a man like that has his enemies. He and the Squire of that time were always at each other's throat. Here in this house, at dinner one night, old Grundy created an uproar, insisting the pilchards were off. He accused Sinclair of trying to do him mortal harm."

"One of my favourite anecdotes." Primrose beamed. "The way Father told it, Sinclair leapt four foot above his chair shouting, 'Churl! Such was not my intent in asking you to dine, you leprous fool, but I am more than ready to oblige!' With which he lunged across the table crunching china to fragments and pinked the Squire good and proper."

"Was he badly hurt?" I asked, delighted.

"Not bloodily so. Squire Grundy was mainly outraged that Sinclair had not bothered to wipe off his knife before taking a poke at him, and that he got pilchard juice all down his starched white shirt. However, one must bear in mind Father's own delight in the dramatic."

"Do you think your father may have resembled Sinclair in . . ."

"Flamboyance?" Hyacinth's wiggly black brows burrowed closer together. "Perhaps, but there was no resemblance in the financial sense. Father considered money the most vulgar word in the English language and forbade us even to think about it. He was a kind, loving, incredibly naïve old . . ."

"Scallywag," supplied Primrose. "When we were young most fathers did not participate much in child-rearing. He did. He even taught us to knit. He adored us all. The hours he spent playing tin soldiers, golden steps, and blind man's bluff . . . but he was never the same, after Lily." Primrose moved the stool back and stood up. "My word, how dark it is getting. I'd better draw the curtains."

Father and Lily. What was it about that combination? The cheerful reminiscing mood in the room was what had suddenly darkened. Not the day itself. Had the adoring playful parent turned harsh and violent on discovering that his beloved—favourite—daughter was with child, and thrust her, unprotected, out on her own? Wouldn't the mother have had something to say about that? I had such a strong feeling for Lily. Did that mean . . . ? But I would not be cheated again. America was only hours away by air. And I would travel a lot farther to see and touch the woman who had held me as a baby. Tessa, slow down! Explore other avenues.

"You say your father taught you to knit, didn't your governess . . . ?"

"We never had one," Primrose replied. "Father thought them frivolous."

So . . .

I snapped back to my surroundings to hear Hyacinth say, "On the subject of squires past and present I am rather surprised we haven't heard from Godfrey. He had mentioned a problem with Thursday, saying he might prefer having us for dinner tomorrow."

"Couldn't you have phrased that some other way, dear?" Primrose sat down again. "You make him sound like a cannibal and us the main course."

"Well, if the main course is to be . . ." Hyacinth stopped and stared as I gave a small gasp.

That phone message! I had forgotten to relay it to the sisters. Biting the edge of a fingernail, I murmured guiltily, "Would the Squire be a person with a rather high voice and a mother in need of a new coat? He rang this morning to say Wednesday does suit him better this week and pigeons are on the menu."

"Perfect," replied Hyacinth briskly. "I will go and phone Godfrey now to sort out the details. Take this wool, Prim, and Tessa's ball. We can finish later."

She was only gone for a few minutes and on re-entering flicked the electric light switch by the door. "Yes, I know it is early, Primrose, but I don't suppose Tessa finds sitting with only one lamp on as cosy as we do."

These rich people and their petty thrifts! But I forgot my amusement when Hyacinth casually informed us that Squire Grundy had been excessively enthused to learn they had a guest, and that he had invited me to join his little dinner party and the card game to follow. I could hardly contain my glee. What luck. What a splendid opportunity to meet other residents of Flaxby Meade. The Grundys were bound to include several other local people among their guests.

"Oh, but I couldn't," I murmured.

"Oh, but you must," insisted Primrose. "You will so enjoy

seeing Cheynwind. It is quite magnificent although much more modern than Cloisters. And, unfortunately, the Grundys are still considered something of outsiders, as their family has only been in residence for the past couple of hundred years. Besides which, several of the Grundy males have not married for rather obvious reasons. Not that I wish to imply that Godfrey is one of those pixie persons who are always coming out of the wardrobe these days . . ."

As fluttery as Primrose, I ran fingers through my tangled mop of curls, opened my eyes wide in wistful appeal and released a sighing breath. "How kind of Mr. Grundy to include me, but I don't have anything suitable to wear for evening, and I don't . . . remember if . . . I play cards." Under cover of one hand I crossed two fingers into a knot. A close call that.

"Indeed, child, I would not suggest your joining the play. The friendliest game of whist can be emotionally taxing. Not at all what Dr. Hotfoot ordered. And as for clothes—Primrose reached out a childlike eager hand for me—"the romantic fashions being so much back in vogue we are bound to find something suitably delightful for you in one of the trunks in the attics. Hyacinth, wouldn't she look delicious in white organza, an Empire waist, and those adorable puffed sleeves?"

Hyacinth declined to join our expedition to the upper regions, saying she wished to gather up all the overdue library books. By the time we reached the rickety stairs leading to the attic I began to feel that my whole day had been spent climbing up and down mildewed staircases, but stepping on to the wooden floor of the attic was not quite like entering the priest hole. The illumination from the porthole window showed that this space was as congested as the other was barren. Trunks, crates, disused furniture, stacks of pictures, and mounds of tattered lampshades created a maze of pathways, wavering in the gloomy half-light. The whole place reeked of the past. A shivery tingle iced down my back. But it wasn't unpleasant. The ghosts here would be the house-wifely sort, not the kind in Abbots Walk.

I was smiling to myself when I noticed that the attic was inhabited by a presence. A tall slim figure in a simple grey dress that clung like the Yorkshire mist about her body as she stood, back turned to us, gazing up at the window. Was it to her a mirror? Arms lifted in a graceful arc, a silver lace shawl over her floating dark hair.

"Why, Chantal," wheezed Primrose from beside me, "stargazing, I see. Do they tell you anything of interest?"

"Certainly, madam," came the softly throaty reply. The woman's hands slid down, and she bent to pick up a picture lying face down on the floor, placing it on a trunk. Without turning she moved closer to the window. "They tell me many things about the second Tessa. And I will be happy to reveal them all, if she will cross my palm with silver."

Now she turned, slowly, the heavy hair moving with her in a dark sea wave. With the soft starlight falling around her I recognized her at once. Chantal was the girl in Harry's bed.

8

Blackmail! As I wafted up and down on my bedroom swing that night, growing sicker and fainter by the minute (I had been unable to force down a bite of food at dinner), that one word kept clanging inside my head. All the while Primrose and I had been riffling through forgotten finery I kept telling myself that Harry would never have discussed me, and the amnesia stunt, with a casual bedmate. Met at some pub, doubtless, between here and Kings Ransome. But he wouldn't have needed to tell her anything. She was psychic, wasn't she? Fergy had the sight herself. She often knew what I would do before I had finished plotting. But Chantal's kind of vision was different. Evil. She had to be evil because she must have recognized me, as I had her. Blackmail. Blackmail. I floated down on a queasy wave. Why hadn't she piped up with, "Lawks, Miss Tramwell, ma'am, the young lady is the friend of a friend of mine. If she don't remember her name, he will"?

I closed my eyes to stop the room from shifting. I must be providing immense amusement for her. And a superb opportunity for revenge. The swing shimmied to a standstill. My hands were chafed and I rubbed them against my face. To be, reluctantly, fair, I could admit that Chantal might be justified in feeling some spite for me. Especially if Harry had told her that he was . . . interested in me. Harry! Was he her reason for keeping silent about my identity? Did she see herself having a better chance with him the longer I remained in never-never land? I got off the swing, steadying myself on a rope. Was it —was it possible that she was genuinely infatuated with him? I felt chilled through in my shroud nightgown. Harry was more than a highly desirable man, he was . . . I was looking at the window which I had left slightly open. No wonder I felt cold.

I clutched tighter at the rope. I'd given myself the creeps thinking about Chantal. It was stupid, but I hadn't felt this scared in the priest hole.

The priest hole. She had already enjoyed some revenge, had she? Good, because she wouldn't get many more chances. And she wouldn't get Harry . . . tonight at any rate. Until now I hadn't given another thought to his promise to be in the Ruins at three in the morning, but . . . an apple tree stood directly outside my window. A quick flit down that and a race across the lawn—nothing could be simpler or safer so long as everyone was in bed. What time was it now? Instinctively I made for the bedside table, quite forgetting that I had not yet found my watch. There it was, lying in a neat coil of silver chain. Butler or Chantal must have found it—fallen on the floor—and put it back. Holding it was a kind of magic. White magic. I felt safer, stronger, more lovable. I missed Angus Hunt. He would have told me to tackle the powers of evil with a flourish.

· At the moment, alas, I couldn't do much of anything; it was only a little after midnight. Rather than lying on the bed and risking sleep I drew a chair up to the window, and rested my chin on the ledge. I may have dozed. At any rate it did not seem much later when I lifted the watch chain away from my neck and saw that it was five minutes to three. Wide awake, I raised the latch, pushed the window outwards and heard the sound of enthusiastic barking, saw a rush of deeper shadow, and knew myself to be a prisoner. Even if Minerva went in within minutes I could not chance someone still being up when I descended. It was almost as if that *someone* had known. And might there not be more to her knowledge than the psychic gift? Chantal had been in the house during Dr. Hotfoot's visit. He had mentioned hearing a woman singing as he came in. Was it possible that she had recognized Harry under the false moustache and hidden eavesdropping in the hall when we arranged the meeting place?

As I crawled into bed I faced up to two choices. I could somehow find a way to deal with Chantal's knowing more about me than was healthy, or I could walk downstairs tomorrow morning with my memory intact and say a quick round of polite farewells. Rather like choosing between the hangman's rope and the headman's axe, Fergy would say. But I knew as my eyelids drooped that I wasn't going anywhere tomorrow, except of course to Cheynwind Hall. As I drifted towards sleep, the image of Chantal was still with me. Harry wouldn't have forgotten if she had told him she worked at Cloisters as a maid. So what persona had she created for herself? Model? Actress? Opera singer? Wretched Minerva! If only I could have met Harry tonight, seen his face when I told him whom I had met in the attic. Funny about that . . . vast yawn . . . other than stargazing, what was Chantal doing in the attics Primrose had said no one ever visited these days? *Borrowing* old finery for her days out? I ground my teeth.

Tomorrow, tomorrow. All would be made plain tomorrow. Untrue.

I woke late feeling fusty and cross. I had to rush to get down before the sisters finished breakfast, and found myself distinctly peeved that neither asked how my amnesia was doing. Primrose twerped on instead about Minerva's recent habit of wanting to be let out in the middle of the night.

"Pretends she wants to go to the bathroom, but we think she has a gentleman friend. Don't we, Hy? I do hope she didn't disturb you, Tessa. It's bad enough that Butler or Chantal has to get up. Naturally Butler is a nocturnal person, always up and about at the most inhuman hour, but even so . . ."

My vision blurred, but I was not allowed time to coax myself back to vigour with a second cup of tea. Primrose chivvied me upstairs to a little turret room, reminiscent of the one where Sleeping Beauty came to grief with a spindle. My appointment was with an ancient treadle sewing machine.

I had come to enjoy sewing after Fergy told me that men married women who could turn collars. The treadle hummed on, one seam flowing into another. Before starting on my evening finery I altered some day clothes Primrose and I had found in the attic. I only left the room once during the morning when I discovered I was thirsty and went down for a glass of water. From the discordant booming, chirping, and ding-dings of the clocks it must have been about eleven o'clock. Glancing over the bannister rail as I reached the last few stairs, I saw Primrose talking with Mr. Deasley in the hall. He was holding a book in one hand and was patting, or rather stroking, her arm with the other.

"Dreadfully childish of me." I barely caught her words. "But I feel such a sense of . . . amputation parting with any book, even ones from the public library, but you understand that, Clyde, and I know your friend will respect *Evelina*, volume I, and not use a cigar for a bookmark or . . ." The pudgy hand gravitated towards her shoulder. They looked up, saw me, and Mr. Deasley rushed to assist me to ground level. "Ah, the lovely industrious Tessa."

"Clyde has dropped by to borrow a book for a sick friend. Unfortunately he can't stay even a moment more." Primrose almost scuttled to the front door and held it open. "Have a pleasant walk home, my dear." She practically bundled him out of the door and then turned with a serene—almost absent-minded—expression on her face. "Tessa." She took my arm and led me down the hall. "I would be so appreciative if you wouldn't mention to Hyacinth that Mr. Deasley was here. She's been working in the garden all morning and might resent my socializing when I should have been giving Minerva a bath."

I agreed solemnly. If Primrose in the midst of her maidenly fluster wanted to delude herself that Hyacinth was unlikely to spot the elderly swain wending his way homewards, that was all right with me.

I did not see Chantal all that day. Primrose brought me up a sandwich for lunch, then a slice of Victoria sponge and tea late in the afternoon. Minerva, ambling up with her, remained nestled down on the mound of scrap material on the floor until the room began to darken. Grunting awake she nosed to the door as I snipped off the last thread and shook out the soft floating material. Time for my ablutions and the fun of dressing up. Through the high lozenge-shaped window I could spy a heavy surging of cloud, and by the time I reached the nursery a spasmodic spatter of rain could be heard. A quick bath would warm me up if I could ever find the bathroom. It would have to be especially quick if I wasted many more minutes opening wrong doors into rooms furnished only with a few stray cobwebs.

Back in the nursery later, I stared in mild panic at my watch, and laid it with my charm bracelet on the bedside table. Neither were suitable accessories for my ethereal attire. Sighing wistfully, Primrose had supplied me with silk underwear and stockings from her "bottom drawer." In the attic we had found a pair of ivory shoes that exactly matched the dress. (I had no idea of the age of that dress. Its style was timelessly simple, and long evening gowns did keep bouncing in and out of fashion.) As the cool rustle of the ivory material slid over my head I felt myself slipping back into a distant, more elegant past. For a brief moment I had another of those crazy feelings that the real world was the figment of my imagination; and then the symphony of clocks struck up. Dignifying the occasion by approaching the cherub mirror above the washstand for the second time in one day (my habit was a pause as I dodged past in the morning) I decided my hair was all wrong. Not having a brush I ran my fingers through its still damp mass and thrust it on top of my head, securing it at strategic points with some early Victorian hairpins I found in a Coalport bowl on the wooden ledge in front of me. Enough. Hyacinth and Primrose would be having kittens if I didn't get down to the sitting room immediately.

"Splendid. Right on time. You look lovely." Hyacinth settled an enormous tartan knitting bag over her arm as she circled around me. Primrose, striving to disentangle her shawl from her handbag clasp, joined enthusiastically in the verbal applause. So what could I do but tell the sisters they, too, looked splendid? An outrageous lie. Hyacinth's gown like mine was long, a slinky sleek number in salmon satin. Matching feathers gusting at the neck and sleeves. Tonight her elongated earlobes bore the weight of enormous blobs of rhinestone glitter and across her non-bosom lay tier upon tier of the same sparkling reddish-purple stones. I tried to tell myself that Primrose's navy blue schoolgirl gym slip wasn't that bad. It was frightful. It made her look a hundred years older, and the mini-length accentuated her sparrow legs. Why? Why was she wearing lavender fishnet stockings? Silly me! To coordinate with her shawl, of course!

"So glad you think we look nice, dear," she preened, forcing me to look into her face. Round patches, like pink cement, stood out on her cheeks, and her lashes had been dipped in tar. Her lipstick, raspberry red and sticky, made her look like she had been eating jam.

The door opened noiselessly and in came Butler, notifying us that he had brought the car around to the front door. Suddenly I didn't want to go. How could I concentrate on ferretting out information if the other guests were snickering behind their sherry glasses at the Tramwells? The elderly are so vulnerable.

And so, on occasion, are the young. The drive to Cheyn-wind Hall brought out insecurities concerning life and death which I had not known I possessed. Butler did not drive us. He did no more than open the doors of what looked like a vintage model hearse. It was Hyacinth who took the wheel as Primrose and I settled ourselves beside her.

"Everyone cosy? People grimaced twenty years ago when Wilkinson's went into cremation in a big way and we bought Old Reliable. But we knew we were on to a good thing. These have to be one hundred percent dependable. Wouldn't do to have the dear departed stalled in the middle of a traffic jam, would it? Should you feel tired on the way home, Tessa, you can lie down in the back on Minnie's eiderdown. She does enjoy the occasional jaunt." Hyacinth's foot hit the accelerator and I made a clutch at the door handle as we rocketed off into the dark. A dark unalleviated by the beam of headlights: she refused to turn them on because the glare bothered her eyes.

"Miss Tramwell, have you had your driver's licence for many years?" I asked through bitten lips.

"What's that? Licence?" Hyacinth reached out a finger and made a peephole the size of one eye on the steamy wind-screen. "Never had one of my own. Use my mother's—for sentimental reasons. Ah, here we are! Cheynwind Hall."

The hearse jolted and jarred its merry way down the long winding drive, pounced on an unsuspecting tree, did a brief detour over part of the lawn, and halted with a roar. Easing up from my ungainly sprawl across Primrose's lap I realized I still lived but might be left with a permanent tremor in my extremities. Ducking out into a fierce whistling wind and a burst of sudden rain, we made the short dash across a hard surface and up two steps in record time. Still, we got rather damp. Skirts winding around our legs, we clutched at each other to save ourselves from being blown away. To the impeccably austere butler who opened the door we must have resembled members of a chain gang.

Do butlers attend classes to perfect that look of disdain? This one accepted our wraps, with the veriest tips of his fingers—rather as though they were newspapers used for wrapping fish and chips—and dropped them into the arms of the hovering underservant.

"This way, if you please."

We followed his rigid back across a glassy expanse of parquet flooring and past a marble statue of a virile Greek god. Primrose averted her eyes. And I had to fight to suppress a nervous giggle. This place was more of a museum than The Heritage. All that was missing were red plush ropes to cordon back the masses and £1.50 admission. Barely had I regained my pose of debutante demureness when a pair of lofty double doors were slid open and the butler proclaimed, "The Tramwell party, sir."

I went in hopefully, almost happily. That drive over had been a deepening experience. Life was wonderful.

It can also hit one over the head with a sandbag. But I didn't feel or see the sandbag descending in those first seconds of looking around the drawing room. The people scattered about, seated or standing, were as yet faceless cardboard figures. If the hall was baronial, this was royal. A huge chandelier dripped a pool of silvered light onto a sea of rosewood, marble, glass, and velvet. From the ceiling-high windows velvet midnight blue curtains streamed to the floor. A semicircular ivory silk sofa faced the marble-and-gilt fireplace, and daffodil brocade chairs nestled against small inlaid tables. In one corner a triple-panelled glass screen reflected the jewelled light of the chandelier and the ruby sparkle of the fire. Every ornament, every lacquered cabinet must have been worth the Royal Mint. Frozen into a gawking trance I was impeding Hyacinth's and Primrose's progress into the room. A gentle nudge from one of them and I moved forward. It was then the sandbag hit me. Two of the cardboard figures immediately in front of us moved apart. One, a Little Lord Fauntleroy type with bulging yellow eyes and obviously permed locks, wearing a pink velvet jacket, came sashaying forward. The other metamorphosed under my beseeching, horrified gaze into Angus Hunt. The room rocked. Blindly I held out a hand and felt it lifted. Knew that it was being flapped up and down by my host, Squire Godfrey Grundy. Heard myself murmur "Delighted to be here" over Hyacinth's droning introduction. Angus, stalled in his tracks for a merciful minute or two by a stout, white-haired lady, was now ploughing towards me, floorboards creaking under his enormous bulk. Any minute it would all be over. He was beaming at me, his several chins quivering in welcome.

"My oh my, what a gorgeous thing you are!" Godfrey cooed. "I was only saying to Mumsie before the rabble came trooping in that I can't do a thing with this room. Horridly insipid. And now here you are, adding just the right touch of sparkle. That dress . . . exquisite! You must tell me where . . ." Angus was upon us. Nothing to be done. Nothing. I took my hand back from Godfrey and tried to hold it out to my former employer, but my arm wouldn't bend at the elbow.

"Ach, this is a rare pleasure, one I didn't expect for a wee moment when I came here tonight." His hands came out to envelop mine in vast warmth. He was looking from me to the Tramwells, including them in his pleasure.

My voice rang in my ears, cool, clear, and immensely prim. I would hate myself forever. "It's a pleasure to meet you, Mr.—umm—" He held on to my hand and instantly I felt the tensing of his fingers, followed by an enquiring squeeze. I squeezed back and forced myself to look into his eyes; they now held the blandest of expressions. My pulse steadied a fraction but the pain deep within my breastbone worsened. Godfrey was prancing around us making the introductions, explaining I was a guest of the Tramwells. Would Mr. Hunt be a dear and get the old ladies a drink while he showed me off to the other guests?

"Old ladies?" said Mr. Hunt in a tight voice, looking around. "I canna say I see any of those but I will be delighted to share a noggin with these two fair lassies." Tucking a hand under the elbows of each of the sisters, both dipping their eyelashes and uttering delighted disclaimers, he looked at me. "As I said, a rare pleasure to . . . make your acquaintance."

"And yours. Perhaps—perhaps we can talk later." I had to fight the urge to turn and look back as Godfrey drew me towards a burly red-faced man who looked far more the "rides to hounds" squire than ever my host did.

"Ah, Mr. Whitby-Brown, dearie, this is Tessa . . ." Vaguely I realized that Godfrey believed my surname was Tramwell. "A distant connection of those wacky old hoots over there."

"Delighted, I'm sure." My hand was being wrung dry

once more, and cigar breath wheezed in my face. Would Mr. Hunt with all his expansive generosity be able to excuse my web of deceit? I had once heard him described as a brilliant man with a clay foot—too damn honest for his own damn good, or anyone else's.

I could feel his mind working from across the room. Angus, I'm sorry. The stout old lady with beautifully waving white hair appeared at my elbow. "Did I hear Goddy say you are a relation of the Tramwells? What a pretty, pretty child you are."

I nodded numbly. Out of the corner of my eye I could see Hyacinth and Primrose with Angus. What were they saying? I strove to hear even as I smiled fixedly at the old lady.

"Tell me, are you one of Violet's girls? She does have something of the look of Vi, doesn't she, Goddy?" She twinkled across my head at him. "And you know you always did have your eye on her, didn't you, son?"

"Never, never did. She was the one who gave me the dead frog for my birthday present. I'm not a bit surprised that the gruesome thing would . . ."

I looked like Violet?

Angus would understand when I spoke to him. I would make him understand.

I inhaled deeply and Mr. Whitby-Brown, with a covert glance at my inflated bosom, excused himself and went off in a fog of cigar smoke to join two other gentlemen at the far end of the room.

"Now now, dear, you can't blame Violet's marrying beneath her on a dead frog," chided Mrs. Grundy. In her black silk dress with the cameo brooch pinned at the lace collar she exuded a kind of cosy familiarity, as if she were someone I had met or at least seen somewhere before. Here was a nice ordinary woman who would adore talking to someone young and lively. As Godfrey picked up an ashtray and dodged after Mr. Whitby-Brown, I told her I wasn't one of Violet's daughters and, unfortunately, didn't even know much about her.

"Then I don't feel quite so bad about what Godfrey just said." She patted my arm comfortably. "Being an only child, he's been overprotected. Dreadfully shocked he was when Violet turned Catholic after that marriage. I keep telling him the R.C.s are human beings just like the rest of us. But, between you and me, it's the mumbo-jumbo he doesn't like—all those idols and the smelly smoke signals. Now, dear, what is your connection to the Tramwell family?"

I told her it was "rather vague," and that this was my first visit to Cloisters.

"Not too vague a connection." Mrs. Grundy chuckled. "Or your name wouldn't be Tessa. That can't be a coincidence, can it? Tell me, have you encountered any cold shoulders? The villagers still consider that old business a blot on their copy book. Bless us, here at Cheynwind the Grundys have always been extremely proud of their old scandal, one of the most famous unsolved murders. Goddy told me that one gentleman here tonight, the clergyman—he's standing with his back to us—is writing a book about that sort of thing."

"How interesting." I smiled limpidly at her as the butler handed us each a sherry. Somehow I must find a means of speaking to Angus alone. Try to explain.

"I was only saying to Goddy earlier that something is always happening in Flaxby Meade. I cannot for the life of me understand why Nurse Krumpet took in that boy—from goodness knows where."

"Nothing known of his origins, I suppose?" The sherry was very dry, but even if it hadn't been I would have thought it bitter. Across the room I could see Hyacinth and Primrose still talking with Angus, and suddenly I liked their outfits—monstrous tartan knitting bag, fishnet stockings—a lot better than a black silk dress and cameo brooch.

"Sad to say, poor little thing—that type of child has only one place of origin—the gutter. Bertie! The very name is common, isn't it?"

"Oh, I couldn't agree more. I always thought as much when I heard George VI was called that by the immediate family." My simper was perfection.

"A place for everything, of course. But I did breathe a word of warning to Mrs. Gregory when I ran into her in the Spider Web Café last week that she was running a risk letting her boy Ricky—such a silly name—associate with a child who has definite mental problems. My late husband was a scientist, you know, and he felt most strongly that . . ."

"Bertie—mental problems?"

"You didn't know? Oh, how indiscreet of me, but as I was

saying to Goddy earlier, if he had ever talked to people who weren't there—and someone called Fred, at that—I would have rushed him straight to a psychiatrist."

Fred. Imaginary!

"It's all in the way they are brought up, isn't it? Goddy, apart from liking to dress up in my clothes every now and then, has never given me a moment's worry. Ah, here's my boy, coming to escort me in to dinner. A mother's privilege, dear, although I am sure he would like to do you the honour." Her large face billowed into a smile.

"Really, I don't need an escort." But I did. Arm in arm with Angus, I could whisper in his ear that all would be explained later.

Goddy, with a flabby-lipped pout, jabbed out an elbow for Mumsie to take his arm, and they went off to stand at the alcove leading into the dining room. Bother! Hyacinth was crossing the room on Angus Hunt's arm while Mr. Whitby-Brown and the other two gentlemen—one with a bullet-shaped head shaved to shadowy stubble, and the vicar interested in murder—shifted their feet and slowed down their hand gesturing. I took this as a sign they were about to make a move. Meanwhile, Primrose scuttled over and clutched my arm. "That courtly Mr. Hunt wanted to take me in to dinner, but Hyacinth turned pettish, and he suggested that I permit that bristle-haired man with the monocle to . . ."

Embarrassed, because her treble voice carried, I suggested we escort each other. The men were ambling in a leisurely way towards us and I got my first front view of two of them. My breath went down the wrong way to the wrong place. It couldn't be! Finding Angus Hunt here had done something to my brain. Now, I was seeing spectres from my past at every turn. . . .

The vicar was the Reverend Egrinon Snapper. Time to succumb to a fit of the vapours. My past was encircling me. It had me by the throat. Fergy says unpleasant coincidences are really the devil leaping out and crying "Gotcha." But twice in one night. Had I really been that wicked?

Herr Fritz Wortter, with a click of heel, offered me his arm. Like a condemned woman I took it, waiting for the axe to fall. No time for a last prayer . . . but, amazingly, I remained alive. Reverend Snapper gave nary the teensiest sign of recognizing me as part of the group who had visited the Ruins. What a pansy I was! It had been a good-sized group, he had been carried away like any genuine fanatic by his theme, and I had no distinguishing features—like *his* nose. Uncanny the way it twitched when he uttered the conventional pleasantries, but at that moment I wouldn't have minded if he picked up his socks with it. He was harmless.

"Two men all to myself. I shall have to take care not to let the occurrence go to my head." The pink cement of Primrose's cheeks cracked a little in excitement as Mr. Whitby-Brown and the Reverend Snapper soldiered up on either side of her, and we all marched in to dinner.

I would even eat pigeon now with equanimity. But when we passed through the velvet-hung archway and sat down at the table lavishly set with white linen and lace, crystal, and hothouse flowers, I discovered that fowl had been left off the menu entirely. The genetic makeup of the soup was a bit of a mystery but delicious, as was the lobster mousse, the roast lamb, and the queen pudding. But, alas, the dining experience was itself not without its unpleasant incidents. The first was Mrs. Grundy's false teeth. She removed them when the lamb arrived—and she did so discreetly, behind her serviette—but then she slipped them into her finger bowl, saying the lemon slice would keep them fresh. Seated beside her, there was no way I could avoid the sight of those floating choppers for the rest of the meal. Beautiful white head nodding, Mrs. Grundy squeezed my arm. "You will excuse me, won't you, my dear, but I really can't chew with the things and at my time of life my only pleasures are Goddy and food."

"But not in that order," squealed the beloved son.

"Always one for a joke." Mrs. Grundy sliced into her meat, the knife and fork almost lost in her large hands, and I may have imagined the edge of steel in her voice. "Even as a boy Goddy tended to be rather exuberant in company. My husband, like most scientists, was rather solitary, and now I'm pretty much past the social whirl. I have my turns, you know."

"Oh, I am sorry. Your heart?" The butler refilled my wineglass, and Herr Wortter on the other side of Mrs. Grundy claimed her attention, leaving me free to listen in on the other conversations around the table. Angus was discussing a picture, reputedly by van Gogh and recently acquired by The Heritage.

How hard it was for me not to display enthusiasm. I was relieved and saddened that he never looked directly at me.

"Hunt is a recognized genius at uncovering frauds,"
Godfrey burbled. "So beware"—he wagged a finger—"those
frauds amongst us." Everyone, except Herr Wortter, who was
fussing with his monocle, laughed mightily while my insides
shrivelled up.

Angus, chins jostling, responded to Godfrey's compliment, "Ach, I'm no genius. I've made more than my share of
mistakes. Art is a passionate, demanding, magnificent mistress.
Aye! And sometimes it's hard to keep a cool head in dealing
with her."

Conversation continued. Mrs. Grundy, signalling to a
hovering servant, had him fetch her the coffee pot. All Mother
Knows Best, she poured a cup for the Reverend Snapper,
chiding benignly that he really should have had wine like
everyone else—and then poured another for Godfrey. Reaching into a pocket in her dress, she pulled out a lace hanky
and a small packet. "Glucose," she said. "Vicar, you will join
me in a sprinkle. You should, too, Goddy. So much healthier
than sugar." Godfrey looked mutinous and Snapper silly,
while the rest of the group listened to Hyacinth talking about
drains.

"Bad plumbing has always been the scourge of this country. In my opinion, it is what prevents our keeping up with
the Americans and the Russians."

Who would snicker first? It wasn't Mr. Whitby-Brown.
Leaning forward he thumped a fist on the table. "Couldn't
agree with you more—especially in cases where a body is
stuffed down inside the main drain, eh, Grundy?" Now came
the laughter. A gleeful titter from Godfrey.

"So you've heard about our jolly little murder of 1803,
have you?"

"The padre here was mentioning earlier . . ." Mr. Whitby-
Brown waved two fingers as if holding a cigar.

"Yes, yes, I was indeed." The Reverend Snapper set down
his coffee cup, hitting the rim of his saucer and almost causing
a flood. "Such a colourful manner of disposition. The modern
murder is so lacking in aesthetic appeal. As a man of the cloth,
I naturally cannot approve of breaking any of the Lord's com-
mandments but . . ."

He did keep harping on about being a man of the cloth, didn't he?

"Ve take your point, sir." Herr Wortter was not looking at the Reverend Snapper but at Primrose. "Either leave your enemies to make their own destruction or do them in vell and good."

I watched in surprise the faint smile that flitted across Primrose's face before she wiped it away with her hand, and so heard rather than saw Reverend Snapper rise from his chair. When I did look he was gripping his belt buckle convulsively. His nose had deepened to a Rudolph glow but the rest of his face was ashen.

"Excuse me, most embarrassing . . ." And legs wedged tightly together he shuffled in short rapid steps through the archway, leaving us in varying stages of astonishment.

"I say," guffawed Mr. Whitby-Brown. "Seen plenty of men who can't hold their liquor but haven't met one yet who can't hold his murder!"

A flare of lightning cut through the candlelit room, sharpening the faces around the table. They all betrayed varying degrees of astonishment at the sudden exit. But apparently it was not considered the "done thing" to question where Snapper was headed.

"No disrespect to Ethelreda or Godfrey, it was really a rather unexceptional murder." Hyacinth's voice broke the silence. "Apart, of course, from that frilly touch—the drain. Eldest son threatens to marry someone unthinkable, and the family, sitting over their glasses of hock, decide to uplift the family motto: Strike While the Sword Is Hot. Yes, Godfrey"—she inclined her head—"ours doesn't translate well from the Latin either, but my point is that your little murder is not nearly as pleasantly macabre as . . . as some in other families."

Godfrey pouted and opened his mouth to reply when the butler edged to his side and informed him that the cleric had remembered that this was the Feast of St. Vitas and hoped his excuses would be accepted. I wished Dad had been around to hear that one. My eyes met Angus's and I longed to ask him what he was thinking. If the Reverend Snapper had been suddenly taken ill, why had he been embarrassed to say so?

"No great loss." Godfrey heaved, prissing up his mouth.

"Really didn't want to invite him but he practically went on his knees to come."

"On his knees, eh? Force of habit," chortled Mr. Whitby-Brown. "Ah well, I would have felt a qualm or two if the fellow had lost the collection money. Don't know about the rest of you, but I am feeling lucky tonight."

A change came over the group, a thickening of excitement. Only Mrs. Grundy and I seemed to be outside it. Rising from her seat she said, "Yes, Goddy dear, I know when Mumsie isn't wanted. Unnecessary of you to ask Maude Krumpet to come and spend the rest of the evening with me, but I will go up to her now." Chairs creaked as everyone stood up, echoing her goodnight. Angus was rubbing his hands together the way he often did when waiting at the back door of The Heritage for some precious shipment. That "one vice" he had mentioned, could it be cards? Mrs. Grundy bent to whisper a special farewell to me. "Now remember, don't be a stranger. Some nasty-minded people have called me an overzealous mother, but all I have ever wanted is for Goddy to be happy . . . and you really are so pretty!"

Away she trudged, Angus moving ahead of her to open the drawing-room door. Fingers elevated like birds on the wing, Godfrey ordered the trailing butler to fetch in the brandy. "My, this is such fun!" An ecstatic squeeze of those soft white hands, then a flourish indicating a table prepared for cards at the south end of the room. "Shall the play begin? And, remember—no whiny thumb-suckers!"

"Excuse me, I should explain . . ." My confession that I did not play whist, bridge, or fish trickled in tepid pursuit of retreating backs. Hyacinth was rummaging in her tartan bag, unwinding from its depths a flaglike object in shades of purple and brown, its pattern so varied that no four-inch span was alike.

"I absolutely cannot play without my knitting," she said. "But don't worry, it's not the least hindrance. I have become highly adept at working with both pins under my arms."

"Do as you please, madam," came the voice of Fritz Wortter, "but please bear in mind that some of us take the cards very seriously."

"My good man," huffed Primrose, now delving into her

black bag and to my horror bringing out a green eyeshade, "so indeed do we."

Oh, what could I do with them! They were incorrigible. How could I endure sitting idly by, watching my very own pigeons get plucked?

9

A vicar's daughter need never sit idle. She can always pray. But Dad's influence was sometimes tempered by Fergy's belief that God was a very busy man with little patience for trivia. And, alas, it had to be admitted that the sisters were behaving in a deplorably trivial fashion. Bleating at each other in fretful accents, one was moaning that she had forgotten to wear her talisman purple garter, while the other was lamenting that this was the fourth day of the fourth week and that she never, never did well with a pair of fours.

The book I had lifted from a table, piquantly titled *One Thousand and One Practical Jokes,* lay unopened on my lap as I sat in my priceless velvet chair a few yards away from the table. Herr Wortter kept muttering "Ach, mein Gott." And Godfrey was making further disparaging remarks about the green eyeshade. "Vastly vulgar, Primmy dear."

Primrose bristled. "I see nothing vulgar or ludicrous about it. Do you never watch American cinema? Those documentaries on Old West culture classify these as the emblem of the dedicated card player."

Mr. Whitby-Brown looked pointedly at his watch, but the fray continued. "Honestly, Prim," fumed Hyacinth, "I wish you hadn't mentioned that. Now I'm remembering Dr. Holiday and the dead man's hand. Should I get aces and deuces tonight I won't sleep a wink when I get home."

"If ve may begin," snarled Herr Wortter. At last! A basic seven-card stud was decided upon. (Meaning poker, I supposed.) Primrose beckoned me to come closer to the table, but I shook my head. Really, it was a bit much my being stuck with no better means of entertaining myself than listening to

113

"four over, two down, dealer picks, first ace bets," or reading this silly book. Better means of entertaining myself! Of course there was—and work to be done! Maude Krumpet was in the house.

Like a thieving parlour maid I stole across the room, but at the door I risked a glance back and noticed a thoughtful look on Angus's St. Bernard face as he fanned out his cards. Beside him Hyacinth clicked away at her needles making another snide remark to Primrose sitting opposite.

The staircase at Cheynwind, unlike Cloisters, was carpeted. I padded up it soundlessly. I would have to come up with some reason for speaking to Maude away from the presence of Mrs. Grundy. But first I had to find her. I had just reached the last stair and was wondering how much time I could take before the butler was despatched to find me, when a voice called out, "looking for the loo?" And there was Maude Krumpet coming along with a blanket over her arm.

I couldn't waste time on blatant lies. Shaking my head, I slipped on a wistful smile and said confidingly, "They're playing cards downstairs and I got restless. Is Mrs. Grundy asleep already?"

"Not a bit. She had something she wanted to do, and didn't want me hovering. How are you feeling, dear?"

"Better. I remember things in—patches. But the patches are getting bigger."

Could what I had said be medically unlikely? Maude's broad face certainly held what appeared to be a look of disbelief.

"I'm sorry." She took a few steps forward, hoisting up the blanket, which had slipped a little. "I must have been staring. Funny tricks light plays sometimes. Caught as you were in the shadow of the bannister rail, for a moment you reminded me of someone. Not often I show signs of Bertie's fertile imagination."

Here was an excellent wedge into her good graces, and I would weave the conversation back to the someone Maude remembered when she looked at me. "Did Bertie tell you we met again? That he was my rescuer from another close call?"

"He and the invincible Fred? I expect the Misses Tramwell have told you about him." Maude still had an odd expression on her face. She must be listening for Mrs. Grundy, so I had better get a move on.

"They may have mentioned Fred," I moved my two index fingers forward and twirled escaping curls around them. "Such wonderfully kind people, the Tramwells, taking me in as they have. Fascinating and unusual, too. All the sisters being named after flowers." Here I gave a surprised little gasp. "How strange your saying what you did about my looking like . . . because earlier Mrs. Grundy said, in passing, that I reminded her of Violet—the one who went to America."

"Perhaps that is it," Maude said, and I thought to myself what a comfy sort of face she had when she smiled, "although it would have to be some mannerism in common—the determined set of the mouth maybe, because you are nothing like her in build or features. She writes to me occasionally, you know, we were—rather good friends. Violet was never the sort to be bothered by such things as social position. She did her own thing, as they say nowadays."

Excitement surged through me. Friends! Friends helped one another in times of trouble. Admittedly I wished Violet could have been a more glamourous figure, living in England and without quite so many children, but Lily was dead. As out of reach as Mum. And Hyacinth and Primrose . . . no, I still could not visualize either of them taking the steps necessary to become a mother.

"I can't help wondering"—the quiver in my voice was perfect—"if my being in that avenue . . . could mean that I was actually on my way to visit the Tramwells. It does seem odd that in two hours two people have linked me with Violet."

"You mean that, unbeknown to the Tramwells, you may be related to the family?"

"It does sound far-fetched," I sighed, "but if it's true, and if I could find out how, I would be closer to discovering my own identity." Fergy had said once when I was little that I never told the truth when a lie would do. But now the truth served very well.

"There's the heir, a cousin of sorts." Maude took the blanket off her arm and folded it. "He didn't visit for years; something to do with his father having married a divorcee or a widow. Old Mr. Tramwell had some very odd ideas, considering he wasn't in much of a position to throw stones. But I understand contact has been resumed, so the Tramwells would know if there were any girls around your age in that branch of the family, wouldn't they, dear?"

"I'll have to ask them. . . ." The person I wanted to ask Maude about was Lily, but I felt a hesitancy, almost a fear, whenever the face of that enchanting little girl came into my mind. What had she looked like when she grew up? If she grew up. Strange that there were no portraits of any of the Tramwell sisters as adults in the gallery.

I had hesitated too long. Maude was saying that she really must get this extra blanket on Mrs. Grundy's bed. "Have to do something to earn my pay. Most of the time she's no trouble at all, and I sit sewing or writing letters. You know, I think I will drop Violet a note, tonight. Goodnight, dear. And take care of yourself."

The way she said those last words gave me a funny feeling. Why? Why take care? I felt sort of lost, almost abandoned as she disappeared down the corridor. Stupid! My situation was tricky, especially now with the complication of Angus—but not dangerous. Peering over the bannisters I saw no sign of life and decided while up here I might as well make a trip to the loo. If I could find an old lipstick lying around I could write a note to Angus and try to sneak it to him. Several doors opened into ruffled and quilted splendour, and I was enticed into entering some of the rooms. Tomorrow I must attempt a similar tour of Cloisters. Could the portrait missing from the gallery be one of an older Lily? Or Violet? Banished out of . . . guilt or grief? My hand turned another knob.

If this wasn't a loo, I was going back downstairs. I stepped into a laboratory, not a lavatory. Test tubes, fizzing and frothing like mini-geysers all over the place. Something vaguely resembling a red-hot TV aerial sat on a table near a sink shooting off lightning sparks. A figure in a grubby white coat appeared from a side door. Thick safety glasses hid the eyes, but I would have recognized that beautiful crop of white hair anywhere. Mrs. Grundy!

"Hello," I said feebly, leaning up against the door, the popping and hissing throbbing in my ears. What kind of experiments were conducted here? A poor thing he might be, but I could understand Godfrey's concern if this was the form

116

his mother's turns took. Cripes! Was there anything in the
Bible to suggest that the end of the world would come through
the intervention of a stout old lady who took out her teeth at
the table? Some detective I was not to have recognized the
sinister aspect of such behavior.

"Tessa, how dear of you to come up and see me!" She
picked up the rod thing and was coming towards me like Florence Nightingale with the lamp. As I backed up, the doorknob
stabbed me in the back, and I almost pitched forward. A savage
gust of wind blasted the windows and something gurgled nastily
inside the room.

"You will be careful not to touch anything, won't you,
child?" It was amazing; we might have been in a china shop.
"Godfrey worries so about accidents, but really I take every
precaution. My late husband taught me everything he knew.
Such wonderful times we had puttering about up here before
he went and poisoned himself."

"Poisoned himself?"

"On cigarettes." Mrs. Grundy set down her "lamp." "Such
a dreadful, costly way to go. The price per packet! Did everything I could, but Hector's one fault was extravagance. As I
always say to Goddy, look after the pence and the pounds will
look after themselves. And I can tell you, Tessa, I do look after
the dear boy's money." Several of the tubes burped coarsely,
letting off ghastly fumes. "Don't be intimidated by the explosive aura, dear. Nurse Krumpet has complete faith in me. I
only let her come here because it pleases Godfrey. Provides
her with a little extra money—which I don't begrudge."

"This is all wonderfully well equipped," I said inanely.
Was it right of Maude to leave her unattended like this? I felt
a pang of guilt at having kept the nurse talking.

"How kind of you to say so." Hands deep in her pockets,
spectacles glinting, Mrs. Grundy looked every inch the dedicated scientist. "Still playing those silly card games downstairs,
are they? Oh, it is naughty of Goddy, neglecting you like this.
He could be showing you the gardens."

In this weather? Rain bouncing off the roof made the room
vibrate. A draught caused my long skirt to flutter dangerously
near the rods. Snatching it back, I explained about the loo and
she kindly gave me directions. We said a second goodnight.

On reaching the safety of the downstairs hall—Mrs. Grundy's experiments were surely not sophisticated enough to blow up the whole house—I felt vaguely depressed. I had found a lipstick and written my note to Angus and somehow I would get it to him. But my talk with Maude had not provided anything concrete. Just more snippets of seemingly trivial information. Mr. Tramwell hadn't liked widows or divorcees, and he was a man who shouldn't have thrown stones. Why? And did it matter? Was I any closer now than three days ago to uncovering my mother's identity? I had this prickling feeling that I was—*if* only I could sort out the wheat from the chaff. As I opened the drawing room door I thought, Tomorrow I will look for the missing portrait, find out when and whom Violet married. And Lily . . . I would have to know what happened to Lily.

Within the drawing room something was very wrong. The atmosphere, like the lab, positively fizzed. Herr Wortter's guttural rumblings reminded me of Minerva. Mr. Whitby-Brown was gnashing on his cigar, Angus Hunt was staring at his wallet, and Godfrey was pouting like a thwarted child. Now for the bad part. Hyacinth was stabbing viciously at her knitting while Primrose dabbed a lace handkerchief under the green eyeshade, her voice a plaintive kitten meow.

"Always the same—from when we were small children. If I ever won anything—like that wax doll at the summer fête, remember how you put her near the fire so her face went all cross?—you had to spoil things. I detest playing with you Hyacinth. Is it my fault I got four kings?"

"What I resent," flared Hyacinth, knocking Mr. Whitby-Brown's cigar out of his hand with her knitting needle, "is your continually demanding . . ."

"I do not demand."

"Excuse me! Your petulant requests to have every raise repeated sixteen times because you will not wear your hearing aid."

"Ladies, may ve please play." Veins bulged in Herr Wortter's neck and the distended eye behind the monocle flashed red. "Unless you vould prefer to retire after your surprising run of luck?"

"Surprising?" Primrose's silvery curls bounced up and down. "I do hope you are not suggesting . . . that a lady's luck may not be the equal of any gentleman's. You have been winning quite handily yourself, sir."

"And I have been losing quite handily." Angus Hunt tapped down a thickish wad of notes on the table. "My apologies, ma'am, but it would seem I am a wee bit short o' the ready. Will ye no take what I have here, on account, and trust me as a man o' honour to bring the rest round to your home in the morning?"

Canny Angus. He was forging a reason to see me.

"The lady does take cheques—even from her sister on occasion," came Godfrey's plaintive voice.

"Mr. Hunt must handle the transaction as he so wishes." With a delicate blush Primrose swept up the notes into her open black bag. I stood up and shook hands with Angus when he left. His expression of impersonal benevolence did not change as I slipped my note into his capacious palm. And the feeling of guilt swamped me again. All I wanted was for this evening to end. If we got home early enough I would try to see Harry in the Ruins. I had nothing much to tell him . . . but I wanted to know if he had collected any letters for me from Dad or Fergy. I was falling asleep in my chair and might have nodded right off if Hyacinth hadn't asked me to pour some brandy for the remaining gentlemen. My lovely ivory dress floated out around me as I drifted around the table nearly getting caught alight by Mr. Whitby-Brown's cigar. I didn't like the way Herr Wortter looked at me or the way he flicked his finger when his snifter was empty again.

"Do let us try something new," Hyacinth was saying. "What was that game we used to play as children, Primrose?" Hostilities seemed to have ceased temporarily. "Ah, I've got it—a high-low hand, divide the pot, last raiser declares first —two down—four up, last down."

Primrose squinted through her green eyeshade. "Must we play that one! It's so conservative. Can't we go with something a little more . . . peppy? That's it—a most refreshing game—Dr. Pepper!"

"Do ve drink it or deal it?" sneered Herr Wortter.

"I do adore the German sense of humour," said Primrose.

Hyacinth laid down her knitting. "Our young nephews in America taught it to us by post. Probably made it up themselves; such ingenious children! Really rather a fun game. Twos, fours, and tens wild, the one-eyed jack and the king with the axe wild—but only in a pat hand, full house, flush, straight, and five of a kind. How does that sound?"

I could not help myself. I dozed off in my chair, dreaming of being chased by an alligator into Mrs. Grundy's lab, where she stood stirring a bubbling pot in which sat the Reverend Snapper. I woke to see Mr. Whitby-Brown leaving. Disgruntled voices and Primrose's delighted laughter followed me back down into sleep until I snapped fully awake, as if someone had switched me on, to hear Hyacinth cry, "Herr Wortter, I am appalled by your suggestion."

"Shocking," twittered Primrose. "No Englishman would suggest playing for such stakes. You insult my sister's and my integrity."

What was going on?

The eyeshade was now pushed up atop Primrose's silvery curls, and her whole body was shaking. "Hyacinth, I think we should bid Godfrey goodnight and be making tracks for home. I really don't think Dr. Mallard would approve . . ."

"Ven you have settled your debts, then you may leave." Herr Wortter's voice stabbed like a bayonet; poor Primrose shrank back into her chair looking every minute her age. How dare he do this to her, and how dare Godfrey sit there smirking! How much could she have lost in an evening, above what she had collected from Angus Hunt—ten pounds?

I was in the act of standing up when Herr Wortter pressed the monocle closer to his eye and flicked out at a sheet of paper. "Two thousand pounds is vot you owe me. Does anyone vish to check my figures?" For twenty seconds I remained half up, half down, before sagging back into my chair. As I stared, frozen, at the foursome the tableau seemed to be lit from within by an ice-cold fire. The tips of Hyacinth's needles shone silver. Godfrey was panting gently. But it was the faces of the two antagonists that dilated slowly as if viewed through binoculars. I could count the bristly hairs on Herr Wortter's head and the grains of powdered blush standing out on Primrose's cheeks.

Thank God the Tramwells were rich. Godfrey should be ashamed of himself, enticing them to play with hardened gamblers; but perhaps after this they would stick to whist. Best for me to pretend to be asleep while Primrose dealt with the embarrassment of settling up. Two thousand pounds!

"You leave me no choice, Herr Wortter." Primrose drew the green shade back down on her forehead. "I vill—will play."

"My dear, you can't!" expostulated Hyacinth.

"I must."

"Naughty of me, but I can't help but enjoy myself." Godfrey squirmed in his seat. "Better than a ringside chair at the Colosseum."

Those shocking stakes discussed while I slept . . . surely Primrose would not be so reckless as to risk Cloisters on the turn of a card? Mesmerized, I watched through half-closed lids as Godfrey unwrapped a new deck of cards and removed the jokers. If Primrose would not listen to her sister, could I hope to achieve anything by begging her to halt this folly?

"So, my dear fräulein, I am to understand zat you in no vay misunderstand ze payoff? Should I lose zis hand you vin back all the moneys you have lost to me zis effening. . . ." Herr Wortter's face cracked into a mirthless smile and I bit the edge of a nail. Even if Primrose were incensed at my interference, I had to speak. "But if I vin"—now came a ghoulish wheezing—"I get to spend vot is left of zis night, in any manner I choose, vith the young and so lovely Miss Tramwell."

No! Only the onset of total paralysis prevented my leaping screaming from my chair. This sort of horror only happened in those hateful Regencies, the only difference being that usually it was the sozzled Papa tossing the heroine into the gaming pot. And in the way of happy endings, she was always rescued before the actual despoiling. Primrose understood the Barbara Cartland rules on chastity; she would never permit my being dragged screaming from the room. Breathing like a dying kitten, I gripped the sides of my chair, feigning sleep with all my might. Primrose must have an ace up her sleeve.

"I trust I have your word as a gentleman of sorts that you will not resort to violence or anything of a particularly sordid nature," she tweeted, head nodding emphasis. "My sister and I are so opposed to that kind of thing."

She was mad! How could I have not seen it before? Some feeling was creeping back up through my limbs. As soon as they became absorbed in the cards I would slip away.

Dorothy Cannell

"Madam"—an even deadlier sputter of laughter—"force vill not be necessary. You underrate my powers of persuasion. And don't tell me a vager of zis nature has not occurred before. Vat other reason vould there be for a presence so enchantingly frivolous?"

No response to this. For a full minute the only sound was Godfrey's hands squelching together, and then the mode of play was discussed. I was not listening. With my eyes narrowed to slits, I saw the cards whizz across the table like plastic missiles. All four heads were bent now. Hyacinth still knitting. On my mark, get set—go. I eased from my chair and made for the door. A channel crossing for a novice swimmer could not have seemed more agonizingly long, and the hall, when reached, was grimly hostile country. How could I get across its length before footsteps pounded after me? Silly, cowardly me! Footsteps were not coming after me, they were coming towards me, and the butler was asking with freezing deference, "Does Miss require anything?"

Fergy said bribing God was not something to be attempted lightly, but there *is* a severe shortage of Protestant nuns, and celibacy isn't much of a penance. If Dad's Boss would only turn the butler into a pillar of salt . . . He didn't. My past life didn't merit such favours. I would have to go it alone, and trust my smile to reach the man beneath the servant. "Thank you, but all I require is a little fresh air."

"Excuse me, but I really must warn against that—so very unhealthy at this time of the night. Mr. Godfrey would never forgive me if I let you leave the house."

"What nonsense. Why, I shall do exactly as . . . you advise." My voice ended not so much in a whisper as a whimper. He had not moved except to flick a speck of invisible dust off his sleeve, but the slow intentness of the gesture was translated by my paranoid brain into a warning.

"Good evening, miss." He escorted me back to the drawing room door, opened it, and saw me safely imprisoned once more. Shuddering, I moved blindly back to my velvet chair, sank down, and picked *A Thousand and One Practical Jokes* off the floor. Not much of a weapon, but I'd chuck it *and* the chair at Herr Wortter's first step towards me. My gaze was fixed miserably on Primrose. How could she do this to me? No wonder I had made no progress in finding my mother when

I was such a gullible fool. And did I want to be associated with such a family? Harry had warned me I might not like what I was looking for when I was good and stuck with it. But all was not lost yet. Primrose had a fifty percent chance of winning.

A terrible broken sigh, cards fluttering like dead leaves upon the table. And the dread paralysis of my legs set in once more as Primrose's frail body slumped across the table. But hold on! Fergy always chided me for jumping to conclusions. Primrose may not have lost. She could as easily be fainting from the excitement of winning.

"My regrets, madam." Herr Wortter ground out the words. "But you never had a chance against zis friendly pair of aces."

Godfrey's moist rosebud mouth opened to a gleeful O; Primrose remained in a limp huddle; Hyacinth had stopped knitting; and I thought, in dazed outrage, that the vilest part of all this was that no one—including Herr Wortter—even glanced in my direction.

Hyacinth squared her wilting shoulders and lifted her chin. "Surely, we can appeal to your honour as a man who poses as a gentleman. This jest has gone far enough."

"Only children think card playing a game. As for my being a gentleman . . . I thought you English had a monopoly on zat breed. Time for me to claim my prize, ja?" Sweeping his hands across the table in a dismissing gesture, Herr Wortter rose, and without looking at me, bent a finger in my general direction.

I wasn't frightened anymore. I was livid with anger. Herr Wortter was evil personified. Godfrey was the ultimate weed—and the sisters! To say I was exceedingly disappointed in them was an understatement. As I stood up, my book at the ready, Primrose raised her head from the table, removed the eyeshade, and slowly smoothed out her silver curls. "It would seem, Hyacinth, my love, that the sacrifice must be made."

How dare she, a sixty-year-old spinster, speak with such placid regret? Where was the broken woman of seconds gone?

"As our dear father always said"—her voice held only the merest suggestion of a tremor—"one must face our losses as impassively as our wins. Herr Wortter—I am ready."

"You—for vot?"

"Why, for you, sir." She was fussing with her cuffs now. "Pray don't be shocked, Hyacinth, but as resistance would obviously be futile, I must confess I am prepared to make the best of a bad business. Needless to say, I do wish Herr Wortter were a trifle younger, and a great deal better-looking, but I shall just close my eyes and think of Maurice Chevalier."

"Vot in Gott's name are you talking about?" My words— but uttered by a man who looked as though he had stumbled accidentally into the trenches during an evening stroll with his Dachshund.

"My dear barbarian." Dimpling coyly, Primrose walked around the table, holding out both hands. "You did say, didn't you, that there must be no misapprehension? Forgive me, at my age one does tend to be a little hard of hearing. One gets muddled and forgets things, but I was so certain that I understood the terms of play. 'The young Miss Tramwell.' Were those not your words? And no offence to dear Hyacinth, but I would have thought it quite apparent that she is years my senior. As for Tessa"—she smiled sweetly, if vaguely in my direction—"I said she was a family connection, not a word about her last name being Tramwell. You may take my word that it isn't, so—shall we go, Fritz?"

10

During the drive back to Cloisters I pretended to doze. I wasn't the least tired but that climax to an incredible evening had left me speechless. Besides, I felt safer with my eyes closed. A decided worsening of the weather had not forced Hyacinth to resort to the wipers.

"A splendid evening." Her voice was a bare whisper. "My dear, you were marvellous. I thought the spluttering beefburger would get apoplexy. Ranting on that it had all been a 'leetle joke' and begging to play one more hand."

"His winnings against my little seed pearl necklace," tush-tushed Primrose. "But he was all to pieces, poor man. My dear, I would appreciate your carrying my bag into the house; my arthritis is bothering me in all this damp, and carrying anything that heavy would just be too much."

"No trouble, General. Brilliant, the way you unsettled Herr Wortter early in the evening!" chortled her sister.

Whatever had happened to the sibling rivalry and petty squabbles? A flash of light penetrated my lids. Wild honking as another vehicle sloshed past us.

"Fool," snorted Hyacinth, forgetting to whisper. "Some people shouldn't be allowed on the road. Would you believe it—more lights heading straight for us!"

"Could you be on the wrong side of the road, dear?" enquired Primrose placidly.

I clutched the door handle of the hearse. Oh, God, save me! I am sorry for all my wickedness. We were going to be killed and I would go straight to hell in the company of the Tramwells, for surely there were no heavenly harps for those who gambled away the family fortune.

"Dear me," chirped Primrose as we entered the house.

125

"Butler has properly let us down, Tessa; usually he is in the hall to greet us and announce the imminent arrival of a cup of tea. The lazy scamp must be in bed." He was not. When I entered the nursery after bidding the sisters a groggy goodnight, and went to take a hanger from the wardrobe, Butler stepped out.

"Pardon me, miss." He bowed. "Just checking for moths," and he sailed loftily from the room.

Nothing surprised me anymore in this house, but what had been Butler's *real* reason for sneaking up here? As a former crook, did he suspect me of invading the premises with villainous intent? Had he hoped to find some hint of what I was up to? The clocks went into action in all parts of the house. Three A.M. Harry would undoubtedly be in the Ruins, waiting again. I had to get to him. He had a right to know what was going on and I . . . needed to know if Dad and Fergy had written. Like many unpunctual people I had known, Harry did not like being kept waiting, but I could not risk descending the apple tree until I had given the sisters time to drink their cups of tea and go to bed. Stepping out of my fancy attire I dressed in my day clothes. The clocks chimed the half-hour and the house buried itself in silence. Tiptoeing to the window I found it fogged with damp although the rain had ceased. The wind blew my hair around my face as I inched out the casement and crawled over the sill. Careful, those branches looked slick. But luck was with me, and apart from grazing one shin I reached the ground not only safe but cheerful. A two-minute dash, and I would be across the lawn and narrow lane to the Ruins. A pity the moon chose that moment to sail out from behind the sheepskin clouds, but unless one of the sisters was in the act of drawing her curtains I should be all right. I was at the lane, heart thudding more in pleasurable excitement than fear, the humped stones awash with silver light, when a form separated wraithlike from the shadows. "Harry," I whispered, flinging myself forward.

"Heavens above! If it isn't the second Tessa," came a voice I knew and loved to hate. Chantal. My feet skidded on the mushy ground and I swerved to a standstill.

"Minerva got out, and I thought I had better fetch her in before retiring." As she spoke, a hollow barking came from deep within the Ruins. "Hush, you terrible dog. Come here and I'll give you a bone." Moonlight highlighted the curve of her cheek as she turned away from me. "I think the faithful hound may be chasing some tramp away; I was sure I saw someone lurking about." She shrugged, and as Minnie came spiralling up to her, I tried to get my breathing under control. She couldn't possibly know that the man was Harry. Could she?

"You exited by way of the apple tree, miss?" she continued.

"It seemed quickest, and I didn't want to wake the Misses Tramwell by going down the stairs."

"How thoughtful. And you were also bent on rescuing this ungrateful cur, weren't you miss?" Minnie's paws were on her shoulders and she stroked the flattened ears.

"What else?" My shrug was as good an imitation of hers as I could make it.

"Listen to that, Minerva, isn't it fine to be loved by so many so well?" This received a snuffle of approval. Was it true that gypsies could charm animals?

"Why bother with the apple tree for the return trip?" Chantal said as Minnie and I crossed the lawn with her. "We can all go in by the back door, for I'm sure, miss, you overestimate the noise you would make on the stairs."

She was remembering how I had surprised her in Harry's bedroom! The light of the kitchen almost blinded me as we entered and I was afraid of what she would see in my face. Giving Minnie a dinosaur-sized bone and wiping her hands on a tea towel from the draining board, she said, "Did you pause a minute outside to look up in the sky and see if your fate was written there?" She had dropped the "miss."

Was she serious? Was her reason for being in the attic the other afternoon exactly what she had claimed—stargazing?

"If it's all up there in the heavens, why do you people tote around your crystal balls?" Picking up an apple from a bowl on the table, I polished it on my sleeve and studied her as she filled the kettle from the gurgling brass tap. Every movement was graceful. How could Harry fail to be bewitched by her, even without her dark powers? Unless caring for—make that loving—me made him immune. And he *did* love me. I had proof. Why else would he have involved himself in what he insisted was a mad scheme?

Dorothy Cannell

"The crystal is only one of several forms of focus." Impossible not to notice what beautiful hands she had: long tapering fingers and unbitten nails. "And you people like the drama, the slow removal of the red velvet cloth, our evil black eyes peering into tomorrow."

I stared at her. "You despise us, don't you?"

"Despise everyone different from myself? Why, that would be dreadfully bigotted—and ungrateful. Reading the crystal paid my way while . . . ." She set the kettle on the cooker and turned on the flame.

"While what?" Sitting on the edge of the table I bit into the apple.

"While I was experiencing some financial difficulties. I sat in tents at church bazaars wearing a red bandanna and gold loop earrings." She was coming towards me and I felt a pang I couldn't explain. "Mostly I dredged up the usual old stuff; nothing to send my customers fleeing home to stick their heads in the gas oven about. . . . But sometimes I do see things. Will you have some tea with me and let me read your cup?"

"You don't have to don the red bandanna for me. Besides, tea will keep me awake."

"A pity, seeing that I have this feeling you and I are destined to drink out of the same cup—of life. But don't rush off yet. Remember, 'tis terrible misfortune to cross in front of a gypsy. Let me take a peek, missie at what lies down the road." Her head was bent, but I could see the curve of her lips as she picked up my limp hand. "I see soft green fields and movement. Some animals grazing. It is close, very close —and I see a man. A handsome man, as they always are—but this one is not dark. His hair gleams in the sun. I hear laughter, and I see great friendship, but something . . . intrudes."

I tried to wrench my hand away; the other holding the apple was stickily wet. "Not the other woman!"

She lifted her face and I was startled to discover that the laughter, the mockery, was gone. "You are the other woman," she whispered. "You are the silken thread that leads him into the maze. I see deceit, whispers in the night, and . . ."

"What are you saying?" I could tell myself that she was toying with me, testing to see if I would crack—but why had her face whitened? Why was Chantal staring at my hand as

128

though it were lit with flames? My elbow jabbed painfully against the table as I cringed backwards. "What do you see?"

"Death," she said in an infinitely sad voice; and it must be true that animals are plugged into the supernatural, for at that moment Minerva let out a howl that jarred through my skin to the bone. "Death. Someone comes in the early morning. The ground is soaked with blood. I see a man lying . . ."

"I don't believe you." The apple fell with a lurching thud onto the floor. *"I don't believe you!"* And to prove it I covered my ears with my sticky hands. "Why don't you read Minerva's paw—she's practically begging—and let me get to bed."

"Go to bed." She backed away from me, her eyes darkened and made brilliant by tears. "Go to bed and try to sleep, Tessa. You have a letter branded on your palm, and that letter is 'H.' "

11

She was vengeful and vicious and I refused to believe she really cared about Harry. Besides, she was wrong about those "whispers in the night." I had been foiled in each attempt to meet Harry. Angus's untimely reappearance in my life was forgotten. The consequences, while awkward, could not be very dreadful. Not like . . . Don't think about the ground soaked in blood. Oh, Harry. You and your beloved horses— what if one of the beasts kicks you and you are left bleeding, with no one to help you? Tossing in my dwarf bed I thumped my pillow. Stop this. The "H" didn't have to stand for Harry. I knew several people whose name began with "H." Lots of people. Fergy's cousin Hubert, for example, and . . . Hyacinth! I sat up in bed gripping my knees. The way she drove that hearse! And . . . could her sallow skin and razor-thin figure imply something medically wrong? A woman her age should see a doctor regularly.

But at breakfast, she and Primrose both looked a lot fresher than I felt after my forty-five-minute sleep. After greeting me and passing the toast rack, Primrose asked after the amnesia. Blearily I informed her that large "swatches of memory" kept slipping into place but one or two important facts, such as my name and address were still missing. The sisters nodded sympathetically as I slathered marmalade on my toast. Both assured me that they were delighted to have my company, but I knew time was running out. I could not prolong my visit beyond tomorrow. Dad and Fergy were expecting me in Devon, and I wanted time to say goodbye to Harry. Not that we would be parting forever. He would come down to see his Aunt Ruth and me . . . he wouldn't wave me off on a train and

130

out of his life. Chantal's face drifted before me, but I blinked the apparition savagely away. Nothing would happen to Harry; I wouldn't let it, even if I had to scour the earth for a white witch to put a safety spell on him.

"I am afraid our social life is not very exciting," said Primrose, "but I know the Grundys would be delighted to see you again."

Before I could think of an appropriate reply, Butler entered carrying a small salver heaped with the morning post. As he passed it to Hyacinth I noticed that the envelope uppermost was stamped airmail.

"At last, word from Violet." She set it down in front of her plate and I was able to read with ease the name in the left-hand corner. Mrs. Arthur Wilkinson. A tiny bell rang inside my head; one of Fergy's cronies was a Mrs. Wilkinson, but that did not explain why I got this slightly morbid feeling. As Butler left the room, Hyacinth handed Primrose two letters. "The gas bill and the estimate for the roof."

Primrose took the letters, then turned towards the French windows. "Dear me! I wonder who this can be coming up the verandah steps? Oh yes, I remember—it must be that Mr. Hunt."

Angus! I hadn't even thought of what I would say to him. Now I was afraid. Afraid that I wouldn't get to speak with him, afraid that I would . . .

"Somewhat informal, his coming around the back." Primrose smoothed the lace cuffs of her black wool dress. But as Hyacinth whisked toast crumbs from the tablecloth, Clyde Deasley, not Angus, knocked and peered through the window, winking saucily as he caught my eye.

"Nuisance," hissed Hyacinth. "Any other time I would be delighted to see the man but, Tessa dear, when our tartan friend *does* arrive, would you kindly take Mr. Deasley into the kitchen and have Butler show him the Georgian silver tea service? Not the one we use every day, but the best one. Mr. Deasley did say he might know of someone who could"—she dabbed at a stray crumb—"straighten the spout."

Outside the window Clyde Deasley's face contorted into a ruddy balloon and he entered on a gigantic sneeze. "Hay fever gedding wor-worse." His mouth extended into a huge oval and his nostrils dilated. Pulling out an enormous navy blue handkerchief, his face disappeared until he finally recovered from the paroxysms that claimed his whole body.

"It would seem, Clyde my dear," declared Primrose, displaying her pretty dimples, "that Hyacinth and I are the only flowers that do not disturb you."

"Ah, but there you are wrong, my lady!" Mr. Deasley replaced the handkerchief in his breast pocket and fussed the tip back to its former jaunty appearance. "Your presence also reduces me to a state of quiver."

I stood shaking out my serviette, grateful to Mr. Deasley for providing me with some amusement. Hyacinth hurrumphed, "You should have shaken the dust out of that dress, Prim. If getting too close to you starts Clyde sneezing again, we will have all the ornaments flying off the mantel. Ah, the doorbell! Who can that be?"

She knew only too well. How would the sisters introduce their card playing cohort to Mr. Deasley? Puzzling about that kept other thoughts at bay, and it was Angus who handled the minor social dilemma. Shaking hands all round (his smile for me was no more than casual), he spoke of his two aunts in Dundee. Without actually saying so he conveyed the impression that they were old acquaintances of the Tramwells.

"So considerate of you to take the time to visit two doddering old women," gushed Primrose. "Such a treat! You positively must have coffee, and bring us up to date on Gertrude's lumbago. My dear Tessa, I do hope that you and Clyde won't be thoroughly bored, but . . ."

This was my cue. With my eyes on Angus's watch chain, straddling the hummock of his yellow-and-black-plaid waistcoat, I mentioned the wonky teapot spout. While the sisters took my former employer away from the breakfast dishes into the sitting room, I ushered Mr. Deasley to the kitchen, where we found Butler at the sink, up to his elbows in suds.

"Ah, Butler, hard at it, I see." Mr. Deasley seemed to me to be making light conversation (due to embarrassment at my having pushed his hand away when it accidentally brushed my thigh), but Butler calcified.

"I begrudge my ladies no effort, Mr. Knees—Deasley."

"Good to hear." The gentleman named stuck his thumbs

under his lapels and oozed unction. "Value a full-time job, I suppose; your former occupation was seasonal, I gather?"

I had better things to do with my time than listen to these two gibe at each other. Certainly it did not require three people to remove one teapot from a dresser so, excusing myself, I went into the hall. As I passed Tessa's portrait, she smiled down encouragingly and I whispered up at her, "Any ideas how I can collar Angus and tell him the whole story without the sisters' knowledge?"

As I drew near the sitting room door voices rose from within.

Glancing quickly around to make sure that Chantal was nowhere around, I bent low. A row of sorts was in progress. Hadn't I always thought from those Regencies that debts of honour were settled in a gentlemanly fashion? Alas, Hyacinth and Primrose were not gentlemen. One was snorting outrage and the other twittering outrage. Only Angus spoke in calm level tones.

"Be still, ladies. I didna mention the Aunties just to pass the time o' day. Sisters under the skin they are to the pair o' ye. A more cheaty set of bessoms than Jessie and Ida could no' be found between here and Aberdeen, or so I thought until I came up against the Misses Tramwell. Ye make the Aunties appear the rankest amateurs. The wee scamps, they only use the distraction approach—pretending no' to hear, fretting back and forth, dropping things. Aye, they should see you at work! The knitting is downright canny. An extra loop for an ace, a dropped stitch for a king!"

"What arrant nonsense!" flared Hyacinth as I sagged against the door. They were *card sharps!* Hardened gamblers and, what was worse, they had raked me into their seedy business. How could I have been so blind?

"If dear Papa could hear us being humiliated in this fashion," whimpered Primrose. I could picture her sobbing into her embroidered handkerchief.

"Tell me," said Angus musingly, "why? Jessie and Ida do it for the kicks and only in a wee way. They don't have a Godfrey Panty-Legs setting up weekly games, or have a fair young lassie to catch the lecherous eye of bristle-headed nasties."

My hand gripped the doorknob. It gave a quarter-turn,

and if the door had opened I would have pitched into the room. What must Angus think of me? A lure. Could he be wrong about that part? No. The Tramwells had been so anxious for me to look pretty for Cheynwind and . . . that conversation I had overheard the first night when I came downstairs; they had spoken about my being useful. It was all falling into place. And to think, in my charming naïveté, I had believed them to be speaking of a pair of non-arthritic hands for winding wool or washing Minerva! Such deceit. My own sin paled in comparison. Was none of their pleasure in having me stay based on altruistic motives? I shivered. Their reluctance to fetch in the police or a doctor, so glibly attributed by simple-minded me to old-maidish eccentricity and sensitive scruples on Butler's behalf, now revealed itself as decidedly sinister. I was biting my nails again. How dare they use me?

"Tell me," Angus repeated, "why? You have a fine home—this room itself is a rare gem. So many bonny pieces! If ye were straggling along on your old-age pensions, going without light or heat, I would ken fair enough, but . . ."

Angus dear, I thought, why ponder further? Like Jessie and Ida, they are in it for the kicks. A pleasant change of pace from potting petunias and dwelling in the past.

"I have already advised you, Mr. Hunt," came Hyacinth's frigid voice, "that you are talking absolute piffle. Now, if my sister may have the money you owe, we will be pleased to offer you that cup of coffee before you catch the London train."

"I could stop ye both, be well aware o' that. A word in the right places that the play at Cheynwind Hall is rigged, and Godfrey Grundy would be blackballed from his club. That's where I met him, and I imagine he does a fair bit o' his business there. 'Want to play a real feisty game o' poker? I know these two wee old maids who claim they can beat the trews off any man alive.' Aye! What red-blooded, cigar-smoking, card-shuffling male could resist that challenge?"

"Such a shockingly poor loser you are, Mr. Hunt." Primrose tweeted like a ruffled sparrow. "I cannot conceive that dear Godfrey may not invite what friends and acquaintances he wishes to his home for a quiet evening of . . ."

Quiet. Last evening she had come close to being deflowered.

"Tush." Angus's voice rose. "Either you gels cease of your

own accord, or I'll see ye stopped. It's no' just the principle. Aye, and I do believe in playing by the rules, but what I fear is that one o' these fine days ye will land yourselves—and the pretty lassie—in very hoot water. All it will take is tangling with the right tough customer."

Herr Wortter. An exceedingly unpleasant vision came of his stalking the sisters on their way to church. . . .

"Enough said. I'll take that wee cup of coffee." Someone crossed the room and as I backed away from the door I heard the jangle of the bell rope. Butler or Chantal would be coming, but I couldn't get myself moving. Angus's voice now sounded mumbled. He may have been bending down to pat Minerva, because I caught, "How long have ye had the dog?" before propelling myself towards the front door end of the hall.

Godfrey Grundy! The taste of the name was enough to make me want to rinse out my mouth with salt water. I should have been tipped off—when the sisters referred to him as the present Squire—that he didn't do a lick of honest work. Being as rich as Midas, he might not have the incentive; but to feast off two elderly women and their ill-gotten wins was wicked. Yes, what they were doing was reprehensible. I wished Dad had been there to give them a good talking to. But Godfrey was the real maggot in the apple.

What now? I didn't want to go upstairs because doing so would make it difficult to waylay Angus, yet neither did I want to be found loitering. Best to slip into one of the rooms and remain with my eye at the ready. Turning the nearest knob, I entered, to find myself in the library—and not alone. Chantal was at one of the shelves, a duster in one hand, but not in action. She was bent over an open book. I was about to turn around and find a more auspicious place to hide, when all those leather-bound volumes reminded me that I must not let what I had overheard entirely deflect me from my purpose for being at Cloisters. Chantal did not turn as I came up to her, and over her shoulder I read the words *Monasticism in the Middle Ages* along the top of the right-hand page.

"Not the latest best seller," I said.

She turned, the book closing with a thud. Making no excuse for reading on the job, she dusted off the binding and returned the tome to the shelf. Fleetingly a deflating thought intruded. In addition to her other attributes, might Chantal be a secret intellectual? More than I could bear. But, not being a total twit myself, I remembered that mediaeval times were fraught with witchcraft and devil's curses. Was Chantal doing a bit of brushing up on the good old days?

"May I help you, miss?" She smoothed out the white half-apron covering her dark blue skirt. The nerve! Acting as though she had never hissed horror in my face last night? I told her distantly that I wanted to read up on local history. As I scanned the shelves she reached up and pulled down a thin olive book titled *The Tramwell Family*. I was impressed. She did get around with that duster.

"You'll not find it highly entertaining," she offered. "Having been written by a local nineteenth-century curate, it's been well-laundered. All the tasty bits—such as how the Tramwells connived to get this land at the Reformation—have been either adjusted or totally deleted. Old Sinclair the pirate comes off like a missionary, and, need it be said, the Tessa story is the trumped-up version."

"Trumped-up?" The book stabbed into my rib cage, but I felt no pain.

"How foolish of me to keep forgetting you know nothing about all that. In brief, the lavender-scented version is that her father, Tessail the monk, committed suicide. But between these walls"—she lowered her voice to a husky purr—"what really happened was that the God-fearing villagers murdered him. And who could blame them, miss! Only doing their yeomanly duty, same as they burnt my people's caravans when they camped on the common."

Murdered. Tessail murdered.

"And the amusing thing is, miss, that for all the righteousness of hanging the fornicating celibate, the present-day villagers would rise with their pitchforks against anyone who let that old truth leak out. Doesn't flatter the Sunday school image Flaxby Meade chooses to present to the tourist bureau."

I could hear voices in the hall. Clutching the book, I left Chantal without another word. Poor Tessail and that unknown girl who had been Tessa's mother. Angus was saying goodbye to the sisters in the hall and I went up to them. It was now or never. I had to find some acceptable reason for speaking to Angus alone, but for the life of me I couldn't get my lips to move. He was looking at his watch, saying he had ample time for the walk to the station, and then, miraculously, Primrose helped me.

"In about ten minutes Butler will be finished washing the car, but if you wish to take Shank's pony, Mr. Hunt, I am sure Hyacinth would be pleased to show you the short-cut through Abbots Walk. I want a word with our friend Clyde Deasley who is"—she fussed with her seed pearl necklace—"yes, I am sure he is somewhere about. Ah, here he is coming downstairs, he must have popped up to use the—cloakroom. Otherwise, Mr. Hunt, I would be pleased to show you the quickest possible route to the station."

Setting my book down on a chair, I said, "If Hyacinth isn't absolutely pining for fresh air, I would enjoy getting outside, and I think I remember the way to Abbots Walk." It was agreed.

Minutes later I found myself outside the house, with Angus hefting along beside me. We passed Butler, lathering up the hearse, and I felt his eyes upon our backs as we crossed the narrow road. Could I be catching Chantal's ESP? The vibes I was getting struck me as decidedly hostile. Didn't Butler like his ladies to have gentlemen callers?

Neither Angus nor I spoke a word until we were well out of earshot and eyeshot of the house. Then he planted a heavy hand on my shoulder and said, "Your noot said 'all will be explained.' Oot with it, Miss Fields, if that is still your name. All the gory details for old Uncle Angus, if you please."

Taking a deep breath I spilled the beans. We had reached Abbots Walk before I had finished.

"Your friend Harry needs his head examined on a butcher's block," he growled.

"No, you mustn't blame him. I made him help me."

"Such an honest cheat you are, Tessa." And then he roared with laughter. "My dreary bachelor existence has been fair illuminated by knowing you. But that's not to say that if I were your father I wouldn't flay you alive. What would he say if he knew you were holed up with as canny a pair of card sharps as ever dwelt among the Cotswolds?"

Ridiculously I felt an urge to defend the Tramwells. "Don't be too hard on them, Angus." I tucked an arm cosily through his. "Being old must be desperately boring. All they have is their library books, afternoon tea, and knitting." My eyes swerved up to his and I winced. "Forget the knitting."

"Shame, lassie, you were at the keyhole."

"The house echoes." I shook back my hair. "The butler was giving us jim-jam looks back there. I wonder if he had his ear glued to the wall and overheard what you said to the old ladies."

"Oot and away! What difference if he did? He must know what they're aboot."

He was right. Butler must have known a fair bit about the Tramwells before he dropped by that night to burgle the house. Why, they may have been out playing cards on that very occasion. We were in the walk, under the rustling archway of the trees, and stealthily, chillingly, terror soaked through my pores.

"What is it, lassie?"

"Nothing. Only that this place gives me the spooks." We stopped and he tilted my chin up with one of his enormous fingers. "Go home, Tessa; forget all this hashing and be a daughter to a man who loves you. Aye, I know he does, because if a wee bairn could have been dropped on my doorstep I'd have liked it to be you."

I picked at his silver watch chain so he wouldn't see my tears. "If you had had me to raise, you wouldn't have been able to indulge yourself at every pokey clockmaker's in every village you amble through."

"On the subject of extravagance"—his voice was pensive—"do·you think, Tessa, that despite appearances, the ladies of the manor may be noon too flush in the pocket?"

A fierce tooting of a car horn burst into the stillness of the walk and, turning, we saw Mr. Deasley's car across the lane. "Want a lift into the village? Going that way and more than happy to oblige any friend of the Tramwells."

"Aye, I'll no refuse. I'm noo much of a walker," said Angus.

How could he rush off like that? I thought of all the things I wanted to talk with him about—the missing picture in the gallery, Chantal's shattering words last night. . . . He winked, then said in a rumble, "A rare pleasure meeting you, young lady—and one I hope will be repeated soon." The last I saw of him was his trying to unravel the seat belt to accommodate his vast bulk before the gleaming Vauxhall chugged away, Mr. Deasley's mouth opening and closing faster than the wheels turned.

Time for a stern self-to-self lecture. Saving the sisters from their nefarious practices was not my job—yet. If and when I discovered we were related I would take them in hand. Now I would return to Cloisters, write a letter to Dad and Fergy, and make notes of all I had learned about Lily and Violet. Busy work, but I would have to wait until everyone was in bed tonight before scouring the house in a last-ditch effort. Quickening my step, I passed the Ruins. Crumbs! Was that the Reverend Snapper standing behind a crumbling pillar? It was. And how peculiar, he pretending not to see me. Unless he was remembering his undignified exit of the night before.

As I crossed the back lawn I saw Chantal exit from the side of the house. A series of gurgling yelps, and Minerva came romping up to me. By the time I disentangled her paws from my neck, Chantal was gone. So was Minerva half a second later, diving off towards the Ruins.

Thoughts of her chasing the Reverend Snapper up a pillar cheered me as I went into the empty sitting room. Good—as long as the Tramwells weren't in the hall I should be able to get upstairs without being hailed for a chat or a cup of coffee. Despite my defence of the sisters I still wasn't ready to face them without feeling angry with them. I didn't feel I would be very adept at hiding my emotions at this time. And was proved right. A faint, distant, tinny clatter caused my hands to clench in the pockets of my borrowed skirt. My nerves must be in a bad way if a saucepan dropped in the kitchen . . . Walking slowly to the wall on the left of the French windows, I said softly, "If I could hear that *and* Chantal's singing, part of one of the kitchen walls must back onto this room." Even so, with the notorious thickness of old walls it was surprising that sound travelled so well. Perhaps not. Two feet from the edge of the curtain was an unobtrusive hatchway. How delightfully convenient for passing through a plate of sandwiches when the family was alone and informal, and the servants all down with the plague. The shutter was closed, but I lifted it an inch, without making a sound, and spied the top of a dresser. Not all that convenient, after all, to pass anything through, one would have to stand on a step-ladder.

Out in the hall I picked up *The Tramwell Family* and, thumbing through the pages, mounted the stairs. In the nursery I placed it on my bedside table to read that night while I waited for sleep to overtake the other inhabitants, and automatically fingered my wrist. I hadn't put on my charm bracelet that morning and it was gone from the table. Neither had I worn my watch—doing so would have made me feel even more unworthy when meeting Angus—but it still lay coiled up like a sleeping dormouse on the scarred wooden surface. Think! I hadn't worn the bracelet last night. Very fishy: first the watch is missing, then returned, and now this. Either I was going demented in true Gothic fashion, or someone was playing Gothic games. The same someone who had locked me in the priest hole? Looking for moths in the wardrobe—fie on you, Butler! What a pity Detective Fields is here on personal business, or she could have a lot of fun pondering your checkered past.

Back to business. Seating myself at the ink-stained desk, I tore a sheet of paper out of a dog-eared exercise book, picked up a pencil, and scribbled a quick letter to Dad. Quick because I did not wish to dwell on the reassuring fibs I was telling. Ah! Here was an envelope and Harry would provide the stamp.

Now to seine the subconscious. I wrote "Violet" in square stubby strokes. Move, pencil! And it took off as if bewitched by Chantal. *Mrs. Grundy said I resembled Violet but Maude said not physically, Maude writing letters to her. Airmail letter this morning—Wilkinson* (and now the pencil went wild) *She once gave Godfrey a dead frog . . . "morbid girl," he said, turned Catholic, the hearse, Wilkinson . . .* the pencil lead snapped off and I sat staring down at the paper. Spooky—not that I seriously believed some unseen force had guided my hand any more (a shiver) than I had believed in evil atmospheres before entering Abbots Walk on Monday. My mind was just spilling out fragments of information it had filed away and which . . . Why did the hearse and the name Wilkinson go together? Then I had it! On the way to Cheynwind Hyacinth had said the vehicle had been sold to them by Wilkinson's, the undertakers, who had gone heavily into cremation.

Violet married into a family of undertakers? Rather gruesome. But perhaps she had been driven into it, on the rebound from the ill-fated union that had produced me. Absently touching the exercise book as I reached for the paper, I read in the top right-hand corner the words "Violet Tramwell." Hands shaking, I flipped it open, calling myself all sorts of names for not searching this gold mine of a room sooner, and found that all the writing on the filled pages was in French. Never mind, there were plenty more exercise books on the shelves next to the desk. Piling them onto my lap, I went through them for fifteen minutes. I found two belonging to Lily. I touched the pages lightly, trying to get the feel of this child who had been terrible at arithmetic but a good speller—or so her tutor father had thought. Remembering when I had done similar work, I decided that Lily must have been about eight at the time of both books. I thumbed past *Latin* by Hyacinth and *Literary Analysis* by Primrose and came to *Composition* by Violet. In the front pages was a loose piece of paper. On it was a drawing of a coffin with two beaming stick figures seated inside holding hands, with a fancy scripted legend below—*Violet Tramwell loves Arthur Wilkinson*. Okay, she'd had a crush on him as a child, and the woman she had become had left home and country, and changed her religion for a man her family considered beneath her. None of that made Violet an unlikely candidate for the role of my mother. She could have fallen prey to some passing philanderer while Arthur was getting established in America; or perhaps Arthur was my father, and . . . I chewed the end of the pencil. Part of me found it difficult to imagine Violet depositing darling Arthur's baby on a doorstep, but she was obviously a very determined character—and if an untimely pregnancy had threatened her relationship with the man she loved, wasn't it perfectly understandable that she would have chosen the lover over the baby? No, it wasn't— not when the baby was me. But then, my mother wasn't some fanciful extension of me. Harry had tried to instill that realization in me often enough. The distant orchestra of clocks punctured the silence of the nursery, and I realized I would have to go down soon for lunch and face the sisters without revealing any knowledge of their guilty secret. "Guilty secret! Who are you to judge others?" Dad's voice was so close, so clear, that I almost expected to turn around and find him behind me.

A lovely, peaceful feeling came over me as I remembered what else Dad was wont to say. "You don't love people despite their faults but because of them." In coming here I had committed myself to finding my mother, and I would just have to take her as I found her. Should, incredible as it seemed, her name be Mrs. Arthur Wilkinson, undertaker's, wife, or even Hyacinth or Primrose Tramwell. Writing the word "Lily," I underlined it and added *Her father never recovered from her death*.

After staring at those few words for several minutes, I found I could write nothing else about Lily. Had the gallery contained portraits of the other sisters as adults I could have assumed that she had died in childhood—but until I knew the how and when of her demise I was stumped. Fear that the Tramwells would think it odd that someone in the throes of amnesia would show extreme curiosity about their past family history had prevented me from asking too many probing questions. But I would now have to take the plunge.

The nursery had grown stuffy. I opened the window, leaning out to look at the garden. How peacefully innocent it appeared, washed sparkling clean from yesterday's rain. A blackbird zoomed down from one of the elms, settled on the edge of the sundial, then fluttered off. Was the cat out? My eyes searched the flower beds for a skulking black form and then I saw what had disturbed the bird. Bertie was crouched behind a wooden seat. That boy! Was he playing Robin Hood? On impulse I leaned out the window and called down, "The Sheriff has Big John and Friar Tuck!"

Bertie's face inched over the top of the seat and he gaped. "Cripes, how did you know, miss?"

"I know everything. Why didn't you ask your friend to play?"

"Fred?"

"Don't you have another one?"

"You mean Ricky? Fred doesn't like him anymore."

"And if the Tramwell ladies catch you skulking around they may not like *you* anymore. Better scram."

Leaving the window open so the nursery would catch a little sun, I went into the hallway, and on impulse decided to look in some of the rooms in the hopes of finding portraits of the four sisters as adults. Down the whole length of the hallway I tiptoed, opening one door after another into—nakedness. Not one was furnished. Yesterday, when I had opened the wrong doors looking for the bathroom, I had thought how sensible the sisters were to have cleared a few rooms to save on work for the servants. Now, a deep sense of foreboding moved within me.

At last; here was a room furnished and obviously occupied. It was crowded with black lacquered furniture decorated with Oriental panels which did not complement the hyacinth-patterned wallpaper. Next, a large linen cupboard. And then, a room with primroses on the paper, a dainty frilly room with a canopied four-poster bed and an ornate French armoire cutting one corner. Mm . . . None of the previous, barren rooms had possessed floral wallpaper that I could remember. A creaking below the bannister rail brought me up short. I paused, listened, and went on past the bathroom. But yesterday, when I had opened those doors by mistake, surely I had seen a room with flowered paper.

Here it was. Empty of all furnishings, except for the faded mauve-blue curtains at the window; a blue that picked up the colour of the violets garlanding the walls. Not even a footstool. I bit down on a nail. Even if Violet had never come home for a holiday, I would have thought her old room would have been kept in readiness, just in case. The room next door did possess a footstool, pushed up against the far wall. Above it was a small plain brass cross. I was standing near the door, tracing the shape of one of the lilies on the paper, when a hand came down on my shoulder. A scream rose in my throat which I barely managed to swallow.

"After Lily's death Father used to come here and pray." Hyacinth spoke as though we had been in the middle of a conversation. Her black hooded eyes were on the cross.

Now I could ask the big question. So easy, but my voice crawled out in a whisper. "How did your sister die?"

I thought at first she would never answer. Then, leaving me standing in the doorway, she went and stood with her back to me in the middle of the room. "I suppose one could say Lily was a victim of the Tramwell family curse."

12

"What?"

"Lily fell down the stairs, like our ancestress, Tessa."

Instinctively I said, "Your poor mother. I can't think of anything worse than—"

"She never gave way. Never cried. She had Father to tend, you see. His hair went white in a week. Outsiders thought they knew him, that he was mainly interested in his wines and in sporting his fancy waistcoats. But his children were everything to him. He was the perennial child himself. Father was the one who put the swing in the nursery. The house would ring with laughter. Lily had the most infectious laugh. Rather like yours. Sometimes even now, I can hear . . . such a merry sound, and then the screams. . . . But enough of that." Hyacinth turned and came back to me. "It was all a long time ago."

Laughter, minutes before she fell? Then Lily had not been driven from the house by irate parents who had discovered that she was pregnant. Unless . . . unless she was defiant, spirited, determined to brazen matters out—I shivered—and an infuriated someone had come up behind her and given her an angry shake or a shove.

"A terrible accident," I said.

"Yes." Was Hyacinth agreeing that it was terrible or that it was an accident?

Fergy says prying into people's grief is like going through someone's handbag, but I persisted. "Was Lily very young when it happened?"

"Naturally." Wasn't Hyacinth paying attention? Old people fell downstairs.

"How old was she?" I asked.

144

Hyacinth took my elbow and guided me from the room. "Come away. No point in focussing on the morbid. Chantal has lunch ready, and I thought that afterwards you might like to help me with some weeding in the garden. Nothing like fresh air for curing all manner of ills."

Not only was she unwilling to discuss Lily further, but those last words were perhaps a hint that I was beginning to outstay my welcome. I was being hurried towards the stairs, Hyacinth explaining that since Butler and Chantal were both having this evening off we would have a substantial meal now and a cold one at dinnertime.

After lunch, which was a rather silent meal—Primrose appearing rather abstracted—I did go out and help Hyacinth weed the rose beds. The sun was warm on our backs as we knelt companionably, prodding our trowels into the damp earth. I thought of Mum. So long ago, those afternoons when I had sat beside her dropping stones in my small bucket as she worked. Often when I thought of her my sense of loss was a dull ache, but now it was raw and fresh as though dragged to the surface like the weeds in my hands.

The rest of the day passed and I found I was counting the minutes until I could get to Harry in the Ruins. *If* I could get to him. At six o'clock precisely Butler served us a ham salad and cheese and biscuits in the parlour, and announced that he and Chantal would be leaving in half an hour.

"Have a pleasant evening," said the sisters.

"Thank you. I h'always find my therapy sessions most rewarding, mesdames." He swept a cracker crumb into his open palm and padded noiselessly from the room.

"So pleased he is getting this release." Primrose poked at a lettuce leaf.

"But I thought . . ." I could not help myself. "I thought you didn't believe in psychotherapy."

"The home-brewed kind we do," replied Hyacinth. "Pass the mustard pickle, please, Tessa."

Who could Butler be seeing? A sympathetic woman? The curtains had not been drawn, and in looking towards the windows I was overcome again by the feeling that someone was lurking in or near the grounds watching. Bertie? But I hadn't experienced this prickly chill when I had caught him playing Robin Hood earlier in the morning. Chantal crossed the lawn, a scarf fluttering around her head. Off to some pub, I was sure: Perhaps the Traitor's Head?

The meal over, we removed to the sitting room, and I had to fight to keep my jumping limbs still. The sisters picked up books to read, and suggested that I might find *The Dutiful Daughter* soothing. Burying my scorching face in it, I turned a page every now and then without reading a word. Hyacinth was sitting on the same couch as I, and Primrose on the one opposite. When I did lift my head briefly I noticed that although the silvery head was intently bent, one hand was lying across the open pages. Five minutes later I looked again, and the hand was in the same place.

This time Primrose caught my eyes on her and closed the book. "Dear me, I can't settle," she said. "I haven't heard Minnie, and wonder if she got out when Butler and Chantal left. I'll go and have a quick peek round for her."

About ten minutes later she came back to inform us that she could not find Minnie anywhere in the house, and that Clyde had warned her that morning to keep a watch on the dog because several animals had been kidnapped in the village in the last week or so.

"Crime rampant in Flaxby Meade," sniffed Hyacinth, but she looked rather anxious.

"My dear, if you and Tessa will look in the Ruins and around Abbots Walk, I will go down the other way and call for her." Primrose ducked back out the door.

Half an hour of searching and cajoling brought no sign or sound of Minnie, and I began to fear that a ransom note might soon be winging its way to Cloisters. Leaving Hyacinth still circling the grounds I went back into the house. With all those rooms it would be easy for the dog to have burrowed away behind a piece of furniture and gone unobserved by a nervous Primrose. I searched the kitchen first, then the parlour and sitting room in hopes that Minnie had wandered into one of these friendly haunts the minute we all left the premises. Not a sign, so I started opening other doors into rooms that were almost as empty as the ones upstairs . . .

I stood in the centre of the hall, the wind knocked out of me as though I had been hit with a mallet. Angus had been right when he had suggested that the sisters might be in financial trouble. *They must have been forced to sell their fur-*

niture in order to retrieve the funds they had gambled away!
Now I began to wonder if their choice of servants was as liberal
as I had supposed. An ex-burglar and a gypsy would never be
sponsored for membership in such groups as the Joyful Sounds.
Everything began suddenly to fall into place. Godfrey Grundy
would know the Tramwells' financial state, but his lips would
be sealed for his own purposes; and I would bet his mother,
when she came to Cloisters, would never be allowed to set
foot beyond the sitting room. Maude Krumpet seemed to be
only an occasional visitor, and Clyde Deasley . . . how much
did he know? Clyde Deasley, antique dealer! Wasn't it likely
he was the one who was buying up the furniture and other
items of value? Or at least offering valuation estimates. That
book Primrose had handed him yesterday, *Evelina*, volume I:
Was that really a loan to a friend of Mr. Deasley's, or was he
taking it to show a client? This morning when I had been told
to ask him to look at the silver teapot, had the spout needed
repairing or was the pot off to the auction block? What sort of
detective was I? A detective wearing rose-coloured glasses. I
had liked the idea of the ancestral home having its ghosts, yes,
but that one of them should be poverty . . .

I was so rooted to the ground that when Primrose leaned
over the bannister rail and let out a small cry of surprise, I
couldn't move. All I could do was stare blankly up at her.

"How you startled me, Tessa dear. I imagined you were
still outside. When I couldn't find Minnie down the lane I
decided to look up on the third floor."

Footsteps. Hyacinth entered the hall saying she hadn't
had any luck, and Primrose came down the last few stairs,
hands twisting, eyes directed at the floor.

How could they bear it if Minnie was really gone? Hadn't
they lost enough already? They had been foolish and impru-
dent, but everyone needs a little fun in her life. I went to
where they stood close together and put my arms around them.
"Minnie will be back. She's romped off with her boyfriend the
way she's done the last couple of nights."

I made tea and, coming down the hall with the tray, I
heard the phone. It was Maude, ringing to ask how I was doing.
Kind of her, but I was glad when she rang off quickly, saying
she was on her way out to spend the evening with Mrs.
Grundy, who seemed to be on the brink of another of her

turns. The slight tension in her voice was thus explained, but Maude wouldn't buy my delayed recovery much longer.

At ten o'clock Hyacinth suggested an early night. I heaved a silent sigh of gratitude. By three, when Harry would be waiting in the Ruins, the sisters would surely be asleep. And, if I did bump into either Butler or Chantal returning from wherever they had been, I could say I was searching for Minnie. Chantal might find the excuse repetitious, but she had been out after the dog herself the night before.

In the nursery I lay down on my bed fully dressed, the letter to Dad in my pocket, and picked up *The Tramwell Family*.

When I opened my eyes I felt as though I had slept for hours, but my watch said only 10:45. I wound it, retrieved the book, and opened it to the chapter on Tessa Tramwellyan. Eyes striving to blink awake, I skimmed lines. The author related numerous incidents of Tessa's nobility—her love of her family, her generous nursing of the sick during an epidemic of scarlet fever, her sewing of altar cloths, her generosity to the poor. But as I turned each page I felt, as Chantal had said, that the curate would have laid on the same fulsome commentary if Tessa had been a mass murderess. As to murder—nothing was said about Tessail other than that Tessa's father had died before she was born. I came to Tessa's death, and was pleased to learn that it had occurred when she was past eighty. The gypsy curse had been getting a little rusty.

Reaching under my head to draw down my pillow something crackled under my hand. I drew out a square of folded paper, and wonderingly unfolded it. On it were printed the words "If ever you need me hang something orange out the window." And then a scrawled signature. Was it "Your Harry" or "Yours Harry?" Hard to tell, but a lovely warm glow suffused me. He was worried that I had not made it to the Ruins the last two nights.

What a chance he had taken breaking into this room—up the apple tree, I supposed. How fortunate I had left the window open. Carefully I refolded the paper and, leaning over the edge of the bed, tucked it under my mattress. The hands on my watch showed half-past one. I was surprised I had been reading so long. If only I had found something about Tessa that would have given me a clue to my origins. As last night, when I had been talking to Maude, I had the feeling that I had walked past something important without seeing it. Maybe it wouldn't come to me until I had left Cloisters—which I had to do the next day. I couldn't feign amnesia any longer. And yet I hated to leave with so many questions unanswered. Funny . . . several of those questions had nothing to do with my origins. But in the time left I had better concentrate on those that did.

I had hoped that the missing gallery portrait might mean something—that, if I could find it, it might prove to be a face that resembled mine—but now I thought it as likely it had been sold as removed in disgrace. *The Tramwell Family* was sliding off the bed and I reached for it. Still, if that portrait was in the house, my guess was it might be in the attic.

My candle singed a small pale hole in the velvet darkness of the hallway as I stole towards the attic staircase. When I came close to Hyacinth's and Primrose's bedrooms my feet stopped on their own accord; stupid, when what I wanted was to get past those potential trouble spots as quickly as possible. As I stood cupping the flame I heard a faint buzz of voices and almost retreated back to the nursery, until common sense insisted that one of the sisters must have fallen asleep with the wireless on. I took a step closer to the door in question but could not judge whether this room belonged to Hyacinth or Primrose. Didn't matter. The voice speaking now was deeper than either of theirs. It could have been a man's or that of a woman of low pitch.

Move, Tessa. I got up the attic stairs as fast as I could, glad that I had put matches in my skirt pocket in case the candle went out. It did so halfway up and time was wasted when I pulled out three dead matches from the box. Finally, a live one; guarding the candle so close my hand grew hot, I made it up the last few steps and pushed open the door. Two o'clock. Not much time. I placed the candle on a trunk near the window. Chantal had been standing right here. . . . Suddenly I realized that the shock of finding the girl in Harry's bed had imprinted the smallest gesture she had made during our attic meeting on my mind. That picture, lying face down on the trunk under the window—she had picked it up and placed it there! Putting the candle down on a trunk I bent and lifted the frame. In the misted yellow glow a face looked up at me. A face that I felt I would have recognized if some amateur had not topped the owner's puffed and cascading white wig with a wide-brimmed black hat—along with other concealing flourishes. Why? Hands shaking I scraped around the mouth, paint clogging under my nails. In order to see better I hoisted the picture closer to the candle, and my foot came down on something that felt like a folded rug. Jerking my leg sideways I tried to shove it away. But it wouldn't be shoved.

And then I looked down and saw that the rug was Minnie.

The picture, whatever its secret, would have to wait; I leaned it against the wall and sat on the floor, lifting Minnie's head into my lap. The yellow eyes were glazed, and kept drooping closed.

"Wake up, old girl," I whispered, stroking her ears. An awful thought came: Primrose had been afraid of kidnapping, but what if someone was *poisoning* dogs? I shook Minnie hard, and her head came up, eyes open. What an idiot I was. If she had been poisoned she would have been dreadfully sick. But perhaps she had been, somewhere else, before crawling up here . . . to die.

13

Die! She wouldn't die if I could help it. The rough part would be getting her downstairs in the dark, for I could not carry both her and the candle. It was a long slow descent but it gave me time to decide against waking the Tramwells. Old people shouldn't be startled out of sleep in the dead of night. Not unless absolutely necessary. If I could not bring Minnie round they had the right to be informed, but I would do what I could first. After getting Minnie to the kitchen and in a big chair by the fireplace, I made strong instant coffee, using luke-warm water and, prying those massive jaws apart, poured it down her ungrateful throat. The rumble rising deep from within her belly was not going to deter me; the more horrible the medicine the better it works. So I told Minnie and, miraculously, by the time I had emptied a third jugful into her she was up on all fours and frisking at the garden door, begging to be let out.

Fickle creature that I am, my enthusiasm for her waned fast. She would follow me to the Ruins and raise enough racket to wake the dead monks *and* the Tramwells. But I was wrong. Minnie showed her appreciation for my endeavours by abandoning me before I was halfway across the lawn. If I found Harry still waiting, I would forgive her. If it was past three and he was gone, that would be something else. I couldn't see my watch in the dark and I hadn't thought to look at it while trying to resuscitate Minerva. I had hardly heard the random chiming of the clocks. A shadow disconnected itself from the other shadows in the Ruins and stepped towards me.

"Damn you to hell and back," Harry greeted me, and I was so pleased to see him, so reassured by his nurturing, protective attitude, that I ran the short distance towards him,

151

twined my arms around his neck, and pressed my lips breathlessly against his. For five seconds he responded, his arms crushing me to him, his breath every bit as ragged as mine, and then—frigid creature—he pushed me away.

"Only two nights, two and a half hours late," he informed me icily, studying his watch. Unlike mine, his was a modern one with a luminous dial.

"But I never promised I would be here on any specific night," I began.

"Nearer three hours late than two," he said. "It's almost six o'clock."

"But it can't be," I cried. "Your watch must be wrong, or . . ." Oh no! I remembered that feeling of having dozed longer than my watch had indicated. It must have stopped at 10:45.

Brushing past him I sat down on a broken piece of wall. Its being damp and cold did not mellow my mood any. Through two of the crumbling pillars I could see a reddening of sky. Harry came and sat beside me. His hand hovered over my hair for a moment, and then came down to touch it gently.

"I'm sorry, Tess. I was worried about you, not angry. This obsession of yours—won't you give it up? You haven't come up with anything, have you?"

"Why so sure? As it happens I have discovered a host of interesting facts since coming to Cloisters, including one that seems to be of particular interest to you." I hunched my shoulders and scowled.

"Why that tone of voice?" He moved his hand away from my hair and brought it down to catch hold of my hand. "Tessa, you know how much I care about you." With his free hand he was turning my face to his, his voice warm and caressing. "If I have done anything that has made you think otherwise, please understand that it was only because . . ."

What was he saying? "You knew," I cried, breaking away from him to stand, arms folded, eyes flashing. "You wretch, you *knew* when I came here that your gypsy love was the maid in this house. . . ." The words slowed to a trickle, then ceased. The surprise on his face was so blatantly genuine that I sat down again. My hand stroked the sleeve of his jacket. "Harry, I'm sorry. That was beastly of me. I know that if you had realized Chantal worked at Cloisters you would have warned me." He said nothing, and I stared around the Ruins. "Last night when you came here you saw her, didn't you? Didn't the sight of her almost bowl you over? It hit me hard, I can tell you. Did she see you? Did you speak to her?" My hand was clutching at his sleeve now, and I despised the note of desperation in my voice. Her face illuminated by moonlight had been so lovely. "A real comedy of errors this."

"No," he said. "She didn't see or speak to me. Her being here is certainly a complication, but if she hasn't revealed your identity to the ladies of the house, I think you can safely assume she isn't going to."

Men are so gullible, but I didn't pursue the matter of Chantal. I remembered my letter to Dad and gave it to Harry. He tucked into his jeans pocket and then began stroking my hair again, and I felt safe. Really safe for the first time in days, which was odd because nothing terrible threatened me. Even if Chantal did her worst I faced nothing more than acute embarrassment. Hyacinth and Primrose were the ones in trouble. I touched his sleeve again.

"Harry, I'm worried about the Tramwells. Wednesday night we went to a card party at Cheynwind Hall—that's the home of Godfrey Grundy, the local Squire—and although they won, I'm afraid they aren't always as lucky, because they've sold off nearly all the furniture and are now starting on the silver and books. And the most unfortunate thing . . . you won't believe who was among the guests, along with . . ."

Harry laughed, sliding a hand over my mouth. "Oh, Tessa! Your imagination is a witch's cauldron."

I pushed his hand away. "I tell you, those two women are hardened gamblers, and what is more, they cheat. Rather creatively, to give them their due, but someone recognized what they were up to—and that someone was Angus Hunt."

"The man you worked for at The Heritage?"

"Exactly."

"I gather he didn't give the game away where you were concerned." Harry stood up and paced slowly up and down in front of me. It was now light enough for me to see the olive green of his thick-knit sweater and the faded blue of his frayed jeans. "You say that Hunt caught on to what the women were doing. Did he start some sort of row?" His voice was so grim that I was afraid he now viewed Cloisters as a gaming hell and that he'd carry me off to prevent my being totally corrupted by two sweet old ladies. (Sweet! Whatever else they were, they certainly weren't *that*.) A straggle of hair tickled my nose, and I blew it away.

"Angus is too much a gentleman to verbally attack anyone publicly if it can be avoided. And there was someone else present—one Fritz Wortter, who was thirsting to do Primrose bodily harm. Angus came over yesterday morning to admonish and warn the Tramwells. . . ." My words were interrupted by a soul-wrenching howling in the distance.

"Some animal is in deep trouble. Either hurt or trapped somewhere." Harry slid off the wall and grabbed backwards for my hand. "We'd better look."

"It must be Minnie, the Tramwells' dog. I found her semi-conscious in the attic just now. I thought she was all right or I would never have let her go off." I watched Harry's face as he listened. The sound came again, still anguished.

Harry was yanking me forward. "I was wrong. That sound isn't pain. It's more like . . ."

"What?" We scrambled over a broken ridge of wall. If anything happened to Minnie the sisters would be devastated.

". . . Terror. That dog is deathly afraid. Listen! The sound is coming from the walk. Let's go." He dragged me to the lane, and as my feet sent pebbles and twigs scattering, I thought, Who would want to harm Minnie? But someone apparently did. I had been too preoccupied after finding her to consider the significance of the attic door being closed when I went to enter. Minnie couldn't have shut it behind her and it could not have swung to on its own. And as for an accident, who would go up to the attic at night? Primrose had said it was rarely used, and Chantal . . . Chantal was out.

The leaves on the elms were olive, almost black. No light penetrated beneath the canopied branches of the walk. The secret patter of the trees deepened as we walked beneath them. The air was cold. Why did I hate this place? Was it only that it was steeped in my guilt? I would go back to Cloisters; I would confess all to the Tramwells and beg their forgiveness. What was a little cheating at cards compared with my deception?

"Look!" rasped Harry. He pointed forward, the other hand digging into my arm. About halfway down Abbots Walk a giant shadow lay sprawled on the ground. A mansized shadow. A dark brown robe stretched wide across the splayed legs. Even when Harry dragged me down with him to kneel on the ground we could not see the face for the attached hood that covered it. A thin rope was knotted around the waist. A monk's habit. Someone wandering away from a fancy-dress party in a drunken stupor? But who would blunder into this lonely spot at this lonely hour? Harry was reaching forward to draw back that hood, and I wanted to stop him. Stop time, or push it back behind the day when I had first come to Flaxby Meade.

My hand moved to clutch Harry's wrist, but came down instead on brown cloth. When I raised my palm it was dark and wet with blood.

"Poor devil," said Harry. And now I had to look at the face because anything was better than staring stupidly at blood upon my palm. No . . . not better. Not better. I tried to scream but my throat locked. Somewhere close by a dog howled.

"Angus," I moaned, reaching out with both hands to touch his face. "Don't be dead. Please, please, don't be dead." Tears were dripping on to my hands. "It's Tessa, and I love you."

"Angus Hunt," said Harry very low. "Give him room, Tessa. He is alive, barely. He needs every breath of air he can get. Be a good girl and run for help. Phone for an ambulance and then notify the police. I'll stay with him."

The police. They would find who had done this, who had dressed Angus up in this grizzly costume and lured him here. But I didn't care about who or why, if only . . . "I can't leave him."

"For God's sake, Tessa, I can't let you stay. The maniac who did this may still be lurking nearby."

I had found one of Angus's hands and was rubbing it. How cold it was. But if I could only keep him going—will him to live. It seemed to be working. Through my drenched eyes I saw the white lips struggle to form a shape. A sighing breath, and then, as I bent my ear above his mouth, I caught the word "Dog . . ."

"Yes, she told us you were in trouble. But now you are going to be all right."

A bubble of pinkish foam appeared at the side of his mouth. Again that agonizing striving to mould words.

"The dogs . . . Min . . ."

"The dog's what?" asked Harry gently.

Angus's eyes opened and he looked at me. His lips didn't move, but somehow he was smiling. And after that I couldn't see him anymore. "Tessa, lassie, glad you're here." His voice was laboured but clear. "False friend . . . phoned . . . told me she was going to kill herself . . . hang herself here . . . tell them I am sorry . . . never could keep my mouth shut . . . tell them I am very fond of my two old aunties in . . ."

He was dead. I had never seen anyone die before, but I knew that Angus had just died. My fault. All my fault, for Angus must have come back to see me. Yes, he had told the Tramwells he wanted the card games stopped, but he wouldn't have hounded them.

"Tessa, I'm so sorry, but I don't think even if we had got to him sooner that anything could have been done to save him. Poor devil . . . did he have any family other than those two aunts in Dundee?"

The hand I had raised to wipe my face stopped an inch or two from my cheek. "How did you know they live in Dundee? Oh, never mind. What does it matter?" I rubbed a knuckle under my right lid. "Whoever did this is going to pay."

"We should have asked him if he recognized his assailant. But at least we know that it was a woman, and that she got him into the walk by threatening to hang herself from one of the trees."

A woman.

"From the looks of this"—Harry's fingers hovered, without touching, over the sodden chest area—"he was stabbed. I suppose it's too much to hope that the murderer dropped the knife when the dog gave chase."

"Don't," I said. "I don't want to see any of it in my mind." A scuffling sound brought us both to our feet. The killer was returning. To retrieve the murder weapon or to silence Harry and me in case Angus had told us too much? I was remembering the last time Harry and I were in Abbots Walk and Primrose came pouncing through the trees with . . . Someone dropped with a skidding thump behind me and I whirled, bracing myself.

"It weren't me," whined Bertie. "Honest it weren't. An' I didn't see nuffink. Don't let the rozzers pin it on me!"

"Don't talk rot. No one could think this the work of a child." Relief blending with misery made my voice curt as

Harry drew me to stand with him in front of Angus to shield him from Bertie's view. But with leaves and dust still clinging to his jersey and trousers, he inched around us.

" 'As 'e croaked?"

Harry nodded. Kicking aside a fallen branch, he took hold of Bertie's arm, walked him over to the edge of the walk, and eased him down on the ground. "You're doing fine, old man, but murder—especially on an empty stomach—is rough. Easy. Put your head down between your knees."

"I ain't gonna faint," Bertie quavered. True enough. He looked closer to being very sick. His face was the colour of Spirogyra. Crouching down, I hugged him. The silence all around us grew so dense that when it was broken by a twig snapping I clutched Bertie convulsively. His head came up.

"Sorry," I said. "A mouse or a bird, that's all. You're going to be all right, Bertie. Honest."

"Better than all right." Harry's voice was soothing. "The police aren't going to give you a bad time. They'll be as pleased as ninepence with you. Their star witness. The newspapers will refer to you as assisting Scotland Yard in its enquiries, and you'll be able to watch your mates at school turn green with envy."

"I told you. I didn't see nuffink."

"Tess, get him to the house."

"In a minute." Reaching out I touched Bertie's hair. "What about Fred? He's not as sensitive as you, is he? I bet he looked out through the leaves when he heard . . ." I couldn't go on.

"Fred? Another child was with you?" Harry dropped the hands he had been impatiently holding out to assist us up. "Where is he now?"

Bertie scraped at his scuffed red knees. "Scarpered, 'e did. But 'e told me 'e didn't see much. The leaves was in the way an' 'e were afraid to lean out. . . ." Another twig snapped.

"But he did see something?" I pressed. And suddenly I was afraid of his answer. I wanted to know, needed to know who had done this loathsome thing, but I also wanted the murderer to be someone I could hate without reservation. Someone with a motive unconnected with Flaxby Meade and Cloisters.

157

Harry pressed a finger against his lips, and I stared at him numbly for seconds before grasping what I would have realized sooner if shock hadn't sent me out of my head. It was folly, dangerous folly, to sit here—screened only by the trees—discussing what had been witnessed. The killer might be miles away; but he could also be cowering within hearing distance.

"Come on, Bertie." I dragged at his hand. "We'll talk about Fred later." He didn't move and I got up.

Contrary child—words suddenly began to gush out of Bertie's mouth, and I was afraid to tell him what I feared in case he went into a screeching panic, which in turn might panic the killer if he heard. (We were dealing with a madman, weren't we? The monk's robe indicated as much.) "It were 'alf dark—an' it all 'appened so quick. All Fred knowed was that they was coming through the walk, two of them. Then one of them bends down and picks up a branch an' coshes the other. An' then 'e what done it starts looking around on the ground, like for something. After that Fred didn't look no more. Everything went real gruesome quiet until the dog come and starts up a ruckus."

"Get going, you two." Harry sliced out the words.

"I don't want to leave you here."

"Don't be silly." He pressed a hand into my back as I stood hesitating. It was Bertie who pulled me forward, and we were halfway down the walk when Harry called out "Tessa." I spun Bertie round with me. "Tessa, there's something . . . but this isn't the time. Just please always remember . . . that I do love you."

The words went drifting up into the elms and the birds came back to life chippering and chirping disdainfully. But Angus would have understood my half-strangled surge of joy.

Bertie squeezed my hand tighter. "You'll think me bonkers, miss, but that gent's voice sounds like the man what attacked you; you wouldn't remember, but . . ."

I yanked him around and started running. If I told Bertie he must be mistaken, and later, during the murder investigation . . . As we neared the end of the avenue the trees crowded closer and the effect was claustrophobic, ensnaring. So much was bound to come out during the investigation. Harry's and my deception. Oh, God. Hadn't Maude said that first evening that such an attack could lead to murder, next

time? When I explained to the police that I knew Harry, that
it had all been a masquerade, he would be safe from suspicion.
Or would he? Might they not categorize him as an unstable
type, along with me—the bad seed? They would leap to the
conclusion that Angus had discovered my hoax. They would
imagine him threatening me—but wasn't that better than their
finding out that he had threatened the Tramwells about their
card playing practices?

A woman. Harry had taken Angus's dying words as definitely indicting a woman as the murderer. Into the brackish
light ahead a woman came pedalling a bicycle at a smooth fast
clip.

"Bertie," Maude cried, braking to a standstill with her
foot, her navy blue cloak flapping up and down at her sides.
"What are you doing here? You should be at home having
breakfast. So sorry, I was delayed at Cheynwind; there's been
a real set-to up there."

Arms outstretched, Bertie scrambled towards her, half
bawling, half whining. "Don't be cross, Aunt Maude. Somefink
awful's 'appened. Some gent's bin done in."

"My word, no!" Maude side-stepped off the bike and
propped it against a tree, looking at me. "This isn't another of
Bertie's yarns, is it?" Her big comfortable arms went around
him and I wanted to run and throw myself against her cushiony
body, too. Lucky Bertie.

"It's true. A man is dead." I came slowly up to them. "His
name is Angus Hunt and he was one of the guests the other
night at Cheynwind. We're on our way to Cloisters to notify
the police."

"But not *murdered?* Surely not?" She removed a hand
from Bertie and held it out to me. "I do remember the man,
if he was the one with the Scottish accent. About fiftyish and
very overweight—a prime candidate for a heart attack. I must
get to him at once, it may not be quite as bad as you fear."
She let go of my hand and eased Bertie towards me.

"There's a man named Harry Harkness with him. I am
sure he will appreciate your waiting with him until the police
arrive, but Mr. Hunt is definitely dead." I rubbed a hand down
the side of my face, feeling my jaw muscles swell out like a
boil. "He was stabbed, and poor Bertie was in one of the trees
when it happened. You can be proud of him, he's doing very

well, aren't you, pal?" I tweaked one of his ears, my eyes focussing on a damp spike of hair where a tear of mine had landed.

"Bertie, my poor little Noddy." She enveloped both of us in her cape. "Will you be all right while Aunt goes back and has a look at the poor man?" Bestowing on Bertie one final hug, Maude asked me to see he got something hot and sweet to drink as soon as he reached the house, and started off at a fast pace down the walk.

Shoulders squared, chin raised, Bertie ran beside me into the lane. As we came up to the Ruins, I suddenly felt I didn't want to reach the house. I didn't want to face the sisters. What if . . . ? But no; the belief that they might be my relations had nothing to do with my conviction that they could have had nothing to do with Angus's murder. Whatever their faults, they weren't bad people. How could they be when they had put faith in a social outcast like Butler, and had taken pride in Chantal's heritage rather than throwing salt over their shoulders every time she came near? They were amusing and hospitable and loved that exceptionally plain dog. You see! After only a few days at Cloisters I balked at the idea of terming Minnie ugly.

Minnie. As Bertie and I came into the garden I saw her. She was leaping in circles around the Squire, who was trying to stroke her. As he saw our approach he jerked his hand away from her sharply displayed teeth, rubbing his clenched fist before shoving it to safety in his pocket.

"The exquisite Tessa." He minced a smile. "Rather pitiful, really; my trying to make nice with this revolting flea-bag. Doggies have never liked me and rejection does terrible things to my sensitive soul. How cruel life is—and this morning I am so particularly vulnerable. Tell me, have either of you dear people seen my mumsie? The old darling has run away from home in the most frightful tizz. That overpaid nurse promised to check Abbots Walk while I came up here."

"I'm sorry, but we haven't seen Mrs. Grundy."

"Thank God for that!" Godfrey clutched his cashmere bosom, and I walked round him, not caring that he wasn't making any sense.

"Between you, me, and the gatepost"—Godfrey tripped after Bertie and me up the verandah steps—"Mumsie can't stand the Tramwells. But she only enjoys visiting people she doesn't like, so even disregarding her threats, which I didn't take seriously, I half suspect that we will find her seated within."

"Then she is going to be in for a shock, along with Hyacinth and Primrose." I was speaking in a stone-cold voice as the sitting room French windows opened and Hyacinth stepped out.

One look at both my face and Bertie's told her something was dreadfully wrong. "Tessa, what is it? What has happened?" The earrings seemed to glide in slow motion and I had to clutch at the windowframe to keep myself steady. My legs had turned to porridge and, although I opened my mouth, I couldn't speak. It was left to Bertie to chirp out the news.

"The man in the walk, miss. He's bin 'orribly murdered."

"What are you saying, child? The man in the walk? You don't mean—not the man on the motorbike the other day who . . ." She was clenching my arms. "Tessa, it *can't* be! Not Harry! Tell me it's not Harry!"

14

Anger was an iron curtain for the moment blocking out grief. The traitor. And with those words I condemned Harry, not Hyacinth. She and Primrose were victims in his despicable double-cross, but I alone was his dupe. They had acceded to his fiendish request because they were fond of him. He was their distant cousin, the heir of whom they had spoken. No wonder I had experienced that feeling on first being admitted to Cloisters that All Was Going Too Smoothly! Harry had perverted my sensitively choreographed Regency masquerade into a Gothic frolic.

Think back! Remember: He had spoken of knowing Flaxby Meade. Or had he actually said that? I had been so tense the day I had gone to visit him, what with feeling the desperate need to recruit him, and then finding Chantal in his bed. Oh, Chantal! You are much too good for him. Now I understand why you did not denounce me. Harry must have told you everything and in his inimitable way procured your silence. No wonder in the Ruins just now he took the news of my "interesting discovery" so placidly. I bet he thought I had found out everything. Yes, that day at his house was all coming back to me. His knowledge of the Ruins had impressed me because they were not famous and I had never found Harry particularly fascinated with that kind of stuff. And hadn't he said that Flaxby, while lacking the prestige of being the birthplace of Shakespeare, was the birthplace of some of his relatives?

I was seated alone in the sitting room. Hyacinth had despatched a cringing but gleeful-eyed Godfrey to phone the police and had gone herself to fetch a bowl of water so I could wash my blood-stained hands. Now she returned and stood over me while I let my hands float in soapy suds and stared at the wall. She was so relieved, she said, that Harry was not the one dead (as she had first feared) that her exclamations of regret for Angus sounded mere politeness. I must have told her when first entering the house—five or ten minutes ago—about my previous acquaintance with Angus, because she now wondered aloud what in the world could have brought him back to Flaxby and to the walk at such an uncivilized hour? Patting me on the shoulder, she handed me a towel and apologized for distressing me. Then she again made a gallant attempt to turn Harry the Heel into Harry the Hero. When I recovered from this shock I would understand that his deceit had sprung from the purest of motives.

"My dear Tessa, when you and Harry have a quiet moment alone together I am sure he will explain everything to your complete satisfaction."

"He tricked me. I know that my wishing to trick you was wrong, but it wasn't the same. I didn't know you."

"Nor we you, but we have become so fond of you. And you must not imagine for a moment that Primrose and I have not been delighted to have you with us. When Harry first unveiled your scheme to us we were highly intrigued and most impressed. So many young people these days have no sense of adventure."

I looked down the room to where Bertie was sitting. How awful of me. I had forgotten him, but he looked absorbed, stroking Minnie's drooping ears. From her slack jowls and occasional mournful yelps she had not recovered from what she had seen in the walk, and guilt merged with my fury. I should be thinking only of Angus, but I couldn't escape the realization hammering away in my head that the Tramwells had known what I was after, what I wanted to know. So, if they weren't afraid to have me in the house—prowling around in the dead of night, listening at keyholes—they either knew my origins were not rooted in this house (in which case why hadn't they told me so?) or they felt the secret was secure from my snooping.

"You are probably wondering why we didn't just have Harry bring you here to tea one afternoon and tell you whether we knew anything about your parentage," Hyacinth said. "I am afraid I can't answer that; I don't feel I have the right. But both Primrose and I felt you had the right to conduct your search. If we hadn't, well, by now you know that we have our reasons for not entertaining much at Cloisters."

"You're saying"—the towel slipped into the bowl—"that you *do* know the identity of my mother, but that revealing her name would be to break a trust? But please tell me one thing: Does Nurse Krumpet know?"

"A child hasn't been born in Flaxby Meade in the last thirty years with which Maude hasn't had some dealings. But she may not be willing to talk, should you tackle her," Hyacinth said soothingly. "Excuse me, my dear, I must go and find Primrose. So unlike her to be down late for breakfast, but I expect she had trouble sleeping through worrying about Minerva. You understand—I don't want her to come down unprepared to a house full of policemen. By the way, I think we should tell them that you are romantically involved with Harry and are spending the week here so that we can all begin to feel like a family."

"And what if Bertie pipes up with what he saw in the walk the other day?" I lowered my voice so he wouldn't hear.

"He's a highly imaginative child who talks to a friend who doesn't exist. Not that we would accuse him of lying—that would be dastardly. We will say that what he saw was a game. A practical joke pulled by you and Harry which has had Primrose and me in stitches ever since."

Practical joke. Had the dressing up of Angus in that monk's habit been someone's idea of a twisted practical joke? Something prodded at my subconscious; a memory bubbled slowly up towards the surface and then submerged again.

"And as for Maude"—Hyacinth was on the move towards the door—"she won't say a word about the amnesia. You can count on that. Being no fool, she sensed that everything was not as it seemed. The boy playing in the walk that afternoon made it impossible for Primrose not to call her in, but perhaps it was for the best."

"Her loyalty to the family must be extreme if she will keep quiet," I said.

"Loyalty?" Hyacinth's hand turned the doorknob as I took the washbowl from her other hand. "Now I didn't say it was a matter of that, did I? Look, the boy is coming over. Why don't you take him to the kitchen for a hot, sweet drink."

A hot drink! I had promised Maude that I would see that

Bertie had one the moment I reached Cloisters and broke the news. Instead . . . but I wouldn't think about Harry. What had Hyacinth meant by that last remark? How soon would the police be here? Oh, Angus. They will be grouped around you now. They and some doctor, referring to you as the body.

"You all right, miss?" Bertie reached out to touch my arm, eyes under the spiky ginger hair wide with concern.

"Fine." I squeezed his hand. We were at the kitchen door, and I didn't remember coming down the hall. The room was empty, and I blindly filled the kettle while Bertie climbed on to a stool. My hands lit the gas, reached for the tea caddy, pulled down cups from hooks. Keep going—that was the secret. The kettle sang out shrilly, and when I picked it up water sloshed out, but I didn't feel any pain. So quick. Had Angus's death been quick? Who was the false friend who had telephoned? Who was the woman who had threatened suicide? Were they one and the same? Harry had thought so, but . . . *Don't think about Harry.* I couldn't help it. I was back on the ground with him kneeling over Angus, listening to those words about Minnie, and trust, and the aunties in . . . I could see Angus, hear him take that last sighing breath—and he hadn't said the word "Dundee." And yet Harry had asked me whether he had any family other than the aunties in Dundee. Ah, but that was all easily explained now . . . wasn't it?

How soon until the police got here? Hyacinth had pointed the way out of my dilemma—or had she? Harry and I were the ones with Angus when he died. Bertie would tell his story; but would the police believe him? He hadn't been able to describe the killer to us. The police might think Harry and I were in the murder together, but there had to be a motive. And neither of us had one for killing Angus, unless . . . I came back to the card games. How much of what he had said to the sisters would come out?

"Tell them I am sorry," Angus had said. But had he been talking about the Tramwells or the aunties in Dundee? If the former, then neither sister was the "false friend." So who . . . ? I had slopped half of Bertie's tea into his saucer and now tilted it back into the cup. "False friend"; what I must not do is assume that everything Angus said was in context. Had he been speaking about himself, believing that somehow he had failed me? Knowing Angus, that almost seemed a probable explanation.

And what would the police make of the monk's habit? Would they decide this was likely to be the work of some religious fanatic? A member of some goat-worshipping sect that every hundred years made a sacrificial offering of a Christian? A vision came of a group in flowing robes, holding black candles, chanting mumbo-jumbo—and led by, of all people, the Reverend Snapper.

"I think you're a real smash! That's what I told Aunt Maude." Bertie was leaning forward on his stool as I poured the tea. His hands still twitched a bit on his knees and his colour wasn't too great, but he seemed to have got himself together very well for a boy who had just witnessed his first murder. His life at the orphanage had bred a unique brand of stamina. Looking at him as he sipped his tea I felt a loving, protective kinship. I wanted to tell him that I was adopted, too, that we were members of the same special club, but this wasn't the time.

"Aunt Maude thinks you're pretty, too. She asked me if I thought as 'ow you reminded me of anyone."

"What did you say?" Yesterday I would have waited desperately for his answer, but now I was no longer clear about my desire to find my birth mother. I'd had so much and been so greedy. Now Angus was dead. If I hadn't been here—if he hadn't come back to Flaxby Meade—I want, I need; that had been my cry. No thought about the hurt I might be dishing out, or whether the woman who had given birth to me wanted or needed me. I lifted a teacup, watching a thick leaf—a stranger—floating on the top.

"I says, did she mean someone famous like on the telly an' Aunt Maude says no, someone local—from the village."

"And did she tell you who that might be?"

"Well, I says back to 'er, was she meaning a gent or a lady, an' . . ."

Before Bertie could finish, the door from the servants' staircase opened and Chantal came in, moving as always with a careless, sultry grace. Her dark dress emphasizing her glowing skin and her hair was drawn back into a coil low on her neck, giving her the appearance of someone from another century.

"I've been talking with Butler," she said, her voice flat. I continued staring at her. She was afraid, and afraid of showing she was afraid. For Butler or for herself? Either way I should have been relieved. Looking down at my hands I said, "Have you also heard that Harry was with me when I found Angus Hunt?"

"Yes."

I forced my eyes to meet hers. "Nice that Harry's name is no longer taboo between us. Knowing about his relationship with the Tramwells finally answers the question of why you did not give me away."

She was standing next to the big deal table, the black cat sidling up against her. "What a perverse creature you are," she said. "You're actually angry with him for asking me to keep quiet because nothing—nothing must be allowed to spoil your little masquerade."

I bit my lip, hoping she would not see the tears that filled my eyes. "Perverse, but not helpless. Maybe I can assist with breakfast."

"Sit down," she said. "You've been through enough. Butler got the news from the hero of the hour."

I winced and turned my face away.

"I'm sorry. That sounded rather brittle didn't it? And I meant Squire Grundy—not Harry."

"Don't apologize. None of us know how to handle this kind of situation. How is Butler doing?"

"As expected. With his past he's not exactly serene. But I assured him he wouldn't be the only one whose life would be turned into a dustbin for the police to rummage through. They're likely to be prejudiced against all kinds of minority groups besides burglars. Gypsies and . . ."

"Impostors?" I squeezed both hands together.

Chantal stood beside me. "Don't get an undue sense of your own importance, Tessa dear. I've been amused by your little masquerade. We are all members of that faction—one way or another."

"Are you telling me that you are not . . . ?"

"Culturally entitled to bang a tambourine? Oh yes—I am certainly a gypsy."

"In that case, what kind of impostor are you?" I asked.

"I prefer to wait to be found out." She was looking at my

167

right palm. "It's gone." Her head turned slowly from side to side. "All finished. The future is now the past. The horror I saw the other night, the sense of advancing evil, misled me. I thought 'H' represented Harry because the brand was so deep on your palm; and I don't understand why, when the murdered man was a stranger to you . . ."

"Hunt," I whispered. And Harry slipped through our hands like a shadow. The idea of the "H" representing a surname had never crossed my mind. "He wasn't a stranger. I worked for him in London and we were friends."

"I'm sorry," she said gently. Moving to the marble counter, she opened up a cupboard, took down a tin of biscuits.

"Don't you think it's mean, frightening people by seeing dead people in their hands?" Bertie had been hovering a foot away from my chair, but his angry growly voice startled me.

Chantal smiled faintly at him and handed him a biscuit. "Most of the time I make stuff up, the kind of gibberish guaranteed to provide pleasant chills. The other night I even frightened myself. There is certainly something about this house . . ."

The servants' door opened again and Butler appeared. My first impression was that the impact of murder had not affected his demeanour. But as he came across the room I saw that the image of the impeccable servant had intensified and the real Butler, whoever he was, had crept further down into the shell of total anonymity. And there was something else about him. Why was I looking at his feet? Then I realized that for the first time I was seeing him wearing shoes. Sensible. The police would have wondered about his padding around in his socks. But wouldn't they also wonder why he was wearing women's shoes? They were lace-up brogues, but even so . . .

When Butler spoke his tone was as lofty as ever, but his "H's" had rather got the better of him. A sign to anyone who knew him that he was nervous, but meaningless to the police. Now why did I feel such relief at that? Was it because of Butler himself, or because I didn't want anything to perk police scrutiny of Cloisters?

" 'orrible h'experience you've been through, miss. And the young boy. H'everything being at sixes and sevens I 'aven't got breakfast started yet, but I think the ladies will require something steadying on this mournful h'occasion, like bacon with their h'eggs."

Noises. Voices raised, feet trampling in the hall. "I should be getting back to them," I said standing up. "If Bertie can stay with you until his aunt arrives, I think it would be best."

A violent pounding on the kitchen door caused us all to move closer together. Had the police already decided on an arrest? Were they here to haul one of us away? A nose nudged around the door and Minnie trundled drearily over to her Chinese bowl. Butler reopened the door for me and Chantal came up to us. "We'll see the child eats some breakfast," she said. "He and I should get along splendidly, having in common that we both see the invisible."

"So you know about Fred."

"Nurse Krumpet talked to me about him. She is a believer in my powers and wanted to know when Fred would leave; I told her I didn't know."

"I think h'under the circumstances I will set a place at the kitchen table for Fred, miss. H'it's not as though he will make any extra washing up." Butler disappeared back into the kitchen, but Chantal went with me into the hall. Other than ourselves it was empty.

"Tessa, I want to say something to you." She touched my arm.

"Yes?"

"Our first meeting was unfortunate, and finding me at Cloisters cannot have spurred any friendly feeling on your part. But despite my background I am fairly civilized. Shall we call a truce in the hostilities until the outcome of this morning's happening is settled?"

I ran fingers through my tangled hair. "I bear you no animosity. Believe me, I'm not the least jealous of whatever you and Harry have going, for the simple reason that he now means absolutely nothing to me at all. Invite me to the wedding and I'll be happy to bang my tambourine in the choir loft." Awful. I sounded pettish and hateful and every bit as jealous as I was insisting I wasn't.

"I don't believe you, much as I would like to. Harry thinks your—"

"I don't give a damn what Harry thinks."

"He thinks your fertile imagination is winsome and madly appealing, but I find your genius for pretence a sign that you haven't grown up yet. You view me as a woman who plays musical beds, don't you? Wrong. If Harry didn't mean a great deal to me, I wouldn't have gone through the hell of listening to him extolling your charms, anguishing at your pitching his ring at him. Both of us always looking over our shoulders watching for you to waltz back into his life."

"Oh, don't you see," I said, "we're both better off without him."

"True; you because you don't love him, and I because I do."

"I have to go into the sitting room," I said, taking a few steps away from her. "As I'm not the total spoiled brat you think me, the truce is on. Permanently if you wish."

Her husky reply reached me as I touched the doorknob. "No. We won't swear undying affection. Let us leave it until the case is solved, whether or not one of us is found to be the guilty party."

I turned to stare at her, but she was gone.

The sitting room was a fairground of people milling about. In addition to the Squire I spotted his mother. (No sign of men in blue.) She was trotting around in circles with a vase of daffodils in her hands.

"Really, Mumsie, they won't bring the body in here," twittered Godfrey. A violent sneeze burst through the room. Three more sneezes, and I understood why Mrs. Grundy was holding the daffs. Mr. Deasley was also present, and she was looking for a place where they could cause him the least irritation. Primrose, her face crumpled like a wad of tissue almost the colour of her dove-grey dress, took the vase—setting it inside a cupboard—and returned to help Hyacinth plump up cushions. Mr. Deasley graciously assisted in tidying by pushing a couple of magazines under one of the sofas.

Mrs. Grundy whispered in my ear, "Do you have a duster, dear?"

"Not on me."

"Where would one be? We must have the place all spruced up for the police. An untidy room is so unwelcoming. Isn't this murder shocking?"

"Dreadful." I had trouble forming the word.

"But one can't help experiencing a slight thrill. You know we haven't had a really good murder in Flaxby Meade for years. One could say hundreds. Naturally, Goddy—do you see him looking at you, dear? Why, I think the boy is blushing . . . but as I was saying, we are rather partial to our own ancestral caper. A natural bias, some might say. But then again, that Reverend Snapper is going to use us as a chapter in the book he is writing. Only one thing worries me, you don't think outsiders might think drains rather non-U?" Mrs. Grundy had picked a lace doily off a walnut what-not and was vigorously dusting the bureau shelf.

"Not at all."

"Thank you, dear. And at least our murderer wasn't a copy-cat like this one. When Goddy broke the news my first reaction was that we had been presented with a blatant take-off of the Tessail murder."

Yes, of course. How could I not have seen that before now? But not everything slipped by me. "So Godfrey told you about Mr. Hunt being dressed in a monk's habit?" Keeping my tone politely curious was hard but I didn't want her to realize what I was thinking.

"Monk's habit? No, he didn't say anything about that. What absolute impudence on the part of the murderer."

"If you didn't know about the habit, what did you mean about a take-off?"

Mrs. Grundy flapped her duster, sending motes flying into the air. "Why, the deed being done in Abbots Walk, dear. That's where that prurient monk Tessail got what was coming to him."

No wonder I had felt no sense of evil in the Ruins, only under the living gallows of the walk. How long did elms live? Could the one from which the villagers had strung up that poor young man still be alive? Had the first Tessa hated the walk, too? Another parallel in our lives—someone close to each of us dying violently in that place. Did I really believe in ghosts, or was the sense of watching menace I had experienced since coming here something human?

Mrs. Grundy patted my arm and moved on to wield the doily over other surfaces while I tried to straighten the objects she had scattered on the bureau. They did not look quite right, but I could not remember how they had been arranged. Fergy always got the shakes if anything was moved from its appointed place.

The others in the room were either fussing about like Mrs. Grundy or talking loudly, binding themselves together. Butler appeared with a tray laden with a teapot and crockery. He set it down on the coffee table, and I went over and started setting out cups.

"Tessa dear." Mrs. Grundy appeared again at my elbow. "I want you to know that the reason I came here this morning was to talk to you."

"How nice," I handed her a cup.

"About Goddy." She rested the saucer in the crevice between her bolster bosom and her bolster stomach. "To be perfectly frank"—Fergy always said that the minute someone said that you could bet they were being less than frank—"we had a little mother-son tiff about you last night. Nurse Krumpet was quite worried about my blood pressure, and the upshot was that eventually I went out to walk off some steam."

"In the middle of the night? What could you have to say about me that could be so upsetting?" I asked.

Mrs. Grundy gave me a saucy wink. "We won't get into that now, dear. Murder comes first. The bitters before the sweets. That poor Mr. Hunt. I am very relieved I did not come round by way of Abbots Walk. My word, I might have stumbled over the body."

"Or collided with the murderer." I poured more tea.

"That would depend on when the act was committed, wouldn't it, dear? And I am afraid I can't even be exact on how long I was out. All I know is that I left Cheynwind at about six. Before that, I hid in the grandfather clock, you see. At times even the best son needs a good shaking up." Mad! The woman was quite mad.

"So you saw no one out and about?"

"Only Goddy and Nurse Krumpet. Well, I didn't actually see her. I saw her bicycle propped against a tree."

"Far from the walk?"

Mrs. Grundy was pondering on that when Mr. Deasley's voice came from right behind me. "Ghastly business, eh? Although, human nature being what it is, my sales will treble during the next few weeks." My hand jerked the teapot, spilling the brown liquid in an ugly pool onto the tray. The room shifted slightly. I felt queasy and giddy. I couldn't hold on to the pot. It went down with a crack on the table.

"Hold on—I've got you, my dear" came Mr. Deasley's concerned voice. I felt his arm encircle me, a little higher than necessary, and he edged me down on the sofa.

"Bend forward, you will be better momentarily." Over his voice I could hear Mrs. Grundy saying she would look in her bag for something to revive me.

"I don't need aspirins or smelling salts." The pressure of Mr. Deasley's hand rubbing my thigh was bringing me round with great speed. "Thank you, I'm recovered now." Seeing that tea dripping made me remember the blood, pooling on the ground. I accepted the cup Mr. Deasley handed me and found my hands were quite steady.

"Ghastly business," he repeated, his glasses glinting as he shook his head. "Positively couldn't believe what I was hearing when Primrose met me at the front door with the news."

Primrose, across the room from me now talking with Hyacinth, glanced up at the sound of her name and began fidgeting with her cuffs.

"Happened to be passing and thought I would invite myself to breakfast," he continued. "Confounded nerve perhaps, but a man gets tired of eating on his own, and you must have gathered that I'm deuced fond of the Tramwells. Consider them family, being rather lacking in that department. No wife, no children, as far as I know." Behind the glasses Mr. Deasley's right eyelid quivered as though about to wink but he resisted the urge.

I stared at him over the rim of my cup. Mr. Deasley was exactly the kind of man who would have progeny that he knew nothing about dotting the countryside. How long had he lived in Flaxby Meade? I didn't dislike him exactly, but neither had I any burning desire to pass his genes along to my children. All those allergists' bills.

Why hadn't I taken a harder look at the men of Flaxby before now? A sideways glance at Godfrey provided one good reason, but surely . . . no, the thought was too grim to contemplate. Mr. Deasley shifted a little closer and patted my knee. My skin retracted. Thank heaven for Mrs. Grundy. Taking advantage of the freed space she sat heavily down beside him, her pointed glance inducing him to move his hand. Then

Primrose crossed the room to hover in front of us and Mr. Deasley rose, offering her his seat.

"Boggles the mind to think that only yesterday I gave the man a ride to the station from here, and now he's snuffed it. Had a great chat we did about eighteenth-century painting, I have a portrait in the shop . . ."

"Did he say he would be returning today? It does seem rather precipitate, doesn't it?" murmured Primrose. "He would have had to drive down in the very early hours."

"He did say he would gladly take a look at that portrait, but we arranged nothing definite." Mr. Deasley looked at Primrose and cleared his throat. "The man was most congenial, flatteringly so; not that I made out the picture was a masterpiece or anything of the sort." He looked again at Primrose, then as Hyacinth came and poured herself a cup of tea he went off to talk to Godfrey by the French windows. Was he expecting the police to come that way? Why were they taking so long?

I was thinking about Angus talking to Mr. Deasley about a portrait. His interest would have been genuine; he loved small antique shops. A man of such enthusiasms. I reached up to finger the watch chain around my neck and as I did so I saw the strain etched in deep lines around Primrose's eyes. Slipping a hand on her shoulder I asked, "How are you holding up?"

Reaching up she patted my hand. "Fine, dear. Mustn't give way, must we? This will take its toll on poor Hyacinth. That little difference in our ages shows up at times like this. She looks quite haggard."

To the contrary. Hyacinth looked crisp—and was the word invigorated?—as she stood with one hand on the curtain, looking into the garden.

Her wait and ours was now over. A rasp of the French windows opening. Everyone braced, but the police had not descended yet. Harry was entering with Maude. My cup rattled in the saucer. I stood up, stumbling over Mr. Deasley's feet. *Don't look at Harry.* But I knew his eyes were on me as he spoke in low tones. How entrancing Hyacinth and Primrose must have found his performance as Dr. Hotfoot. I caught the word, "Aunty." So much cosier and less Victorian than "cousin." Maybe he hadn't believed me when I informed him in the Ruins that the sisters had gambled away most of their substance, but he would have to face the raw truth soon enough.

He was coming towards me, closing in, Primrose tweeting something incoherent as I made for the door. Across the hall in a dozen flying steps . . . my hand was on the bannister knob when his hand yanked me backwards.

"Not so fast, Tess, you and I have some talking to do."

"Surely not. Dr. Hotfoot's place is with his relations in their troubled hour. Forget me, because you and I are through!"

"God, I hope so."

My hand flew back ready to come cracking down against his face, but he was too quick for me. He had both my hands now.

"I meant as conspirators. I'm sorry you had to find out this way, Tessa, and I can understand your need to hate me as an escape from your grief over your friend, but—"

"Don't bring Angus into this. He was the most open, honest man I ever knew apart from my father. You are a loathsome liar. Snickering behind your hand while I made an utter idiot of myself."

"I never . . ."

"Don't speak to me, and take your hands off me." He did. Sinking them into the pockets of his jeans he stood, mouth grim, eyes sparking blue fire. His hair waved against the collar of his white open-necked shirt rising over his olive-green sweater. For a man who had been up all night he looked offensively alive. Utterly arrogant. An infinitesimal hunch of his left shoulder reduced my rage to trivia. The aunties' pride and joy couldn't wait to return to their doting presence.

Damn him. I was biting a nail. "Don't you even have the decency to defend yourself?"

"You told me not to speak."

"That was a minute ago. With your intimate knowledge of the female mind you should know how very changeable we are." Mounting a couple of stairs I leaned over the rail. "Tell me, has it all been great fun, keeping tabs on me on the sly? Have you had a good few cackles over the telephone or in person with the Tramwells while I've been upstairs sewing or sleuthing?"

"I haven't spoken to them since Dr. Hotfoot's visit, and

then we certainly did not subject you to ridicule. Hyacinth and Primrose both said then that you were everything I had ever claimed."

"I can imagine! Well, if the sisters weren't your confidantes, what about your mistress? On the nights I couldn't make it to the Ruins, did you rendezvous with Chantal instead? Aha!" I gripped the bannister rail, my hair tumbling forward and covering one eye. "I'll bet you did see her the other night; she was out—looking for the dog. But which dog?"

"Yes, now you mention it, I did see her."

I tried to speak but I was impotent with rage.

"But only from a distance, and, as I told you earlier, she didn't see me, someone—a tramp, hitch-hiker, I don't know which—was hanging about inside the Ruins, so I stayed behind one of the trees in the lane. Believe me or not as you please, I have not spoken with Chantal since you came to Cloisters."

"Why should I believe you? Besides, I know that you've spoken to someone from Cloisters. Right after Angus died, you asked me if he had any relatives other than his aunts in Dundee, and he *didn't say* they lived in Dundee; they do, of course, but . . ."

Harry's calm was evaporating. His mouth slid into a hard angry line. On the defensive, was he? Good! But I didn't feel good. My anger was seeping away, leaving me feeling empty as an abandoned building.

"What is this? Have you suddenly become possessed by the spirit of Miss Marple? Picking through my words like . . ."

I interrupted him. "You know, despite everything, I'm not sorry I came here. The last few days I have listened harder and watched closer than ever before. I'm not quite as gullible or readily distracted as I used to be. The murderer had better watch out for Tessa Fields." I looked into his eyes. "Harry— you still haven't explained how you knew . . ."

"And I don't intend to explain or defend myself. But if your detection skills are polished to such a high sheen, I suggest you offer your services to the police."

"Sorry, Harry, I don't have your arrogance; I will work unobserved on the sidelines. Because you can bet I intend to know who killed Angus, even if"—I brushed the hair out of my eyes—"the truth isn't one I like. And you know, don't you, who I can thank for that toughening of the spirit. No more fantasy life for me." My eyes stung but I kept going. "Everything is smashed up . . . I'm not sure I really want to know who my mother is anymore. I don't welcome the idea of loving one other person. Too many risks. But I suppose I am stuck with being the kind of person who has to know."

Harry was coming up those few steps to me. "That's because you are your parents' daughter. Tessa, can't you understand why I had to let you go through with your amnesia plot?" He caught my hand and drew me down to sit beside him. I wanted to resist but I felt too tired to do so. "I wanted you to work through this search so that one way or another it would be over."

"You tried to talk me out of it."

"Sure I did—until I realized the women you had seen in the café were Hyacinth and Primrose and there would be no danger to you. Tess, I couldn't have let you play out your masquerade on strangers. God only knows what kind of people you might have got in with."

"How solicitous. Life at Cloisters has been a Sunday school picnic enlivened with gambling and murder." I burrowed my chin into my hands.

"Don't link the two. I didn't see Hyacinth and Primrose until a few years ago—didn't know they existed because old Mr. Tramwell severed contact when my father married a divorcée—but I have grown very fond of them. The gambling and murder can have nothing to do with each other."

"Now who's fantasizing? Of course they do, but that doesn't mean I think the sisters did it, singly or together. There are all kinds of possibilities."

"Including me?"

I stood up and walked down the stairs. "If they had been forced to stop playing cards because of Angus their only source of income, precarious as it was, would have dried up. They might have been forced to sell Cloisters, and the heir might have found himself highly disgruntled."

"But the heir knew nothing about this. Ah-ha, now I understand your concern about the aunts in Dundee." Harry caught hold of my arm and spun me round to face him in the hall. "Can your anger really cause you to suspect that I would murder *anyone*, and for money? And could I also lead you calmly into that avenue to watch your friend die?"

I didn't believe it, but something bitter twisted inside my throat. "Money can buy a lot of horses, a lot of women."

He stepped back from me as though the thought of ever touching me again made him cringe. "Sometimes I have fantasized, too," he said; "told myself that I didn't love you, that I could live my life blissfully without you, but I always thought I was deluding myself until now!"

The numbness I had experienced when Angus died was returning. I couldn't hear how my voice sounded because of the static inside my head. "I'm glad you don't care about me anymore. That way, if ever our paths should unfortunately converge . . ."

"I'm pretty sure they will." Harry smiled in sardonic amusement. "I received a letter from my mother yesterday. It appears there's been a whirlwind romance in Devon. Your father and Aunt Ruth have fallen for each other. Tea together every afternoon, quiet strolls down leafy lovers' lanes. Think of it, Tessa, if they should marry, you and I would be related and my aunt would be your stepmother."

The numbness left me. "Dad would never do that. He'd never replace Mum. Never. Fergy would never let him." With that I flew past him and up the stairs. I'd go to my bedroom and stay there.

A piercing ringing of the doorbell. This had to be the police. Suddenly everything except Angus's death retreated. My life until the investigations were completed would be here at Cloisters, whether I liked it or not. I started to run back down the stairs and Harry called, "Tessa, be careful." And as I slowed, "Remember Lily. Seeing you lying at the base of the stairs might evoke the old suspicions surrounding her death."

I stood on the last stair. "What suspicions?"

"That she might have been murdered by a member of her loving family."

15

The police entered the premises. There were only two—
a short, fat detective-inspector and a tall, fat constable—but
immediately the hall seemed overrun. A buzz of introductions
with the short Inspector Lewjack displaying the embarrassed
air of a guest arriving two days early for a dinner party. He
was an unattractive man with a splayed nose that twitched
slightly above his pencilled black moustache. Did old murder,
like old brandy, have its own special bouquet? A gentle apologetic smile hovered beneath the moustache, but Inspector
Lewjack's eyes weren't smiling.

Strictly speaking that should have been "eye," singular.
His left orb was three-quarters concealed by a puckered and
drooping lid, but the one open to the public looked like it was
never off duty. He stepped off the doormat, casually scraping
his shoes on the parquet floor. A black spider of a man. Greasy.
Even his good eye was greasy. Far more like an ex-criminal
than Butler. I fought the urge to bite my nails.

"A terrible sad business this." Constable Watt removed
his helmet. Holding it over the front of his tunic, he tapped
out a few bars of "Rock of Ages" with one finger, mournfully
shaking his bald head. "My Missus is going to be none too
pleased, what with me not about to see home nor a hot dinner
till we've nabbed our bloke."

"Food!" breathed Inspector Lewjack, and his rich, fruity
voice deserved to inhabit a far more attractive body. His nose
twitched more blatantly. "I smell breakfast. An early morning
corpse always makes me ravenous."

Oh, Angus! But he would have enjoyed the inspector's
irreverence immensely. Constable Watt's shocked expression
indicated he was thumbing to page 696 of the police manual.

179

Must not partake of victuals on premises associated with unnatural death. He turned to Harry.

"You're some roundabout cousin of the Tramwells, right?" Bending over the inspector he stage-whispered, "This here young man's related to the Tramwells."

The inspector's manners were more polished than his appearance. He refrained from responding that he wasn't deaf. His good eye was on me.

"Tessa, you said? Tessa Fields. The nurse said you and this young man found the deceased."

"He wasn't dead when we found him," said Harry. "This has been a dreadful shock for Tessa; he was a friend of hers. She worked for him at The Heritage Gallery in London."

"Deepest regrets, Miss Fields. May I ask your connection with this house?"

"I've been a guest here for the past few days." My voice was surprisingly steady. "Harry and I are friends and he wanted me to get to know his relatives."

Constable Watt placed a beefy hand between his mouth and the inspector's left ear. "He's in line for all this here property, stands to reason the old girls would want to give her the once-over."

The eye moved from me to Harry. "The nurse said she would go in round the back and wait with the ladies of the house, so if you would please direct us to where they are gathered . . ."

"This way," said Harry, but it was Constable Watt swinging his truncheon who took the lead. The inhabitants of the sitting room—the Tramwells, Mr. Deasley, Mrs. Grundy and Godfrey, Bertie and Maude (her cape still around her shoulders)—were all seated, balancing plates of bacon and eggs on their laps. Constable Watt introduced the inspector over the general flurry of everyone standing up, and Hyacinth announced that Butler and Chantal were fetching more coffee and toast. Bertie's eyes were big as currant buns, and the hand that wasn't holding his plate had his jersey pulled up and was scratching away underneath it. The others had become a semicircle of mouths. The room was dominated by mouths, all of them wary. Nothing moved, save Bertie's finger and the pendulum of the mantel clock. A shaft of sunlight beamed across the room. Flashbulb. Picture taken. Subjects blinking back to life.

Hyacinth and Primrose began talking over each other.

"So kind of you to come, Inspector, I know we all feel so much safer already."

"And we do hope you will not think us heartless to be eating breakfast, before closing all the curtains and wrapping the door knocker in black crepe." Hyacinth stared down at the plate she was holding, removed her sister's eggy platter, and over the inspector's black curly head addressed Constable Watt. "Ah, George, if you would be so kind, set those down on that table beside you. And do please close the door you left open. None of us will benefit from a draught."

Flushing up to his bald dome, Constable Watt shrivelled before our eyes. In a pathetic attempt to re-elevate himself he put his helmet on, took out an official-looking notebook and red pencil, went to make a notation, realized the pencil had no lead and, under cover of Primrose's twitching and stammering, sidled it into his front pocket. Primrose was in the throes of her favourite character part again: tedious elderly female on the loose. But I could not feel she was enjoying herself this time. She might well deem the pose deadly necessary. No one that inane could plot murder. Could she?

"One feels one must keep going. It is what is expected of those in our position, as I was saying to dear Ethelreda, Inspector . . . forgive me, I did not quite catch your name. What was that?" Primrose daintily cupped a hand behind her right ear. "Coatrack? What a very odd name, to be sure, but memorable."

"Lewjack, you ninny," squealed Godfrey. The inspector urged everyone to be seated and immediately the company relaxed, except Mrs. Grundy, who had sat down on her plate. I went to assist her as Harry stood resting his elbows on the top of Hyacinth's high-backed chair.

Godfrey shuffled his feet on a footstool, murmuring to no one in particular, "I do hope the body can be whipped off to London soon so the sanguinity of Flaxby Meade can reign once more."

The door opened, bumping Constable Watt in the rear. Chantal entered with a plate of toast, followed by Butler with the teapot. My eyes couldn't avoid his shoes. He was treading gingerly as if they pinched. The inspector watched him briefly as Hyacinth offered assurance that she and her sister would be gratified to offer their home as a headquarters for questioning.

"Indeed yes," quivered Primrose. "And I am quite certain, sir, that you will not inconvenience us long."

"Not a moment more than necessary." He fought his way out of his raincoat, his eye pursuing Chantal as she laid it on an unoccupied chair. Was he admiring her beauty or wondering what Holloway might do to that complexion? Constable Watt was fumbling furtively inside his pockets, a look of desperation heightening his already ruddy complexion. Hopes of promotion dashed! He couldn't find another pencil.

"Your cooperation is much appreciated." The inspector's moustache crept into a purely routine smile. "We so often find a homey atmosphere sets people more at their ease than if we have to haul them down to the police station."

Silence most profound. Again the door nudged open and in came Minerva, head lolling, tail drooping.

"Your most vital witness, Inspector." Mr. Deasley's tone indicated that he was bent on lightening the mood. Standing with one elbow on the mantelshelf, he fingered a small ivory elephant. "Minnie, the noble beast you see before you, was the one who set up the alarm—bringing Mr. Harkness and the young lady, Tessa"—he bowed gallantly in my direction —"onto the appalling scene of murder."

Butler stood in the middle of the room clasping the teapot in its bright bumble-bee cosy. "H'excuse me, sir, but mustn't say 'murder,' must we? Murder is a very libellous word. Not to be used until all the h'evidence is h'in." The spout had taken a downward tilt and brown liquid dripped on to his shoes. Brought to a realization of his intrusiveness, Butler cleared his throat and sailed off on his rounds with the pot.

Constable Watt gave the inspector a poke in the back, followed by one of his raucous whispers. "Knows a deal about the law, does that one—if you get my meaning." Fishing the red pencil out of his pocket, he portentously licked the tip and remembered it was unloaded.

"H'inspector, may I h'offer you tea?" The mask of impeccable servant had ravelled upwards and I caught a glimpse of crafty terror as Butler removed Mrs. Grundy's cup, even then raised to her lips, arched the teapot over it, and handed it to the inspector. The mask came down as if pulled by an inner string. "If that will be h'all for the present, Chantal and I will retire to the kitchen."

Inspector Lewjack took a sip of tea and nodded. The door closed and he moved into the centre of the room. Under the pretext of feeding Minnie a piece of toast, I handed Constable Watt a pencil from the bureau. Wouldn't hurt to keep in his good books—but the ingrate merely checked the point for sharpness.

Putting his cup on the coffee table the inspector rubbed hairy hands together. "For such a quiet little village you certainly seem to have a bustling social life, and so early in the day, too."

Constable Watt looked affronted. "Only among a certain set. My wife will have been at the washtub for three hours."

"Don't be such a snob, George. Your wife told me that watching her Bendix was better than television. A clearer picture and she got to read at the same time." Hyacinth stared him down.

"Such a particularly spiteful crime, murder!" sighed Primrose, "but I don't think it can permanently tarnish Flaxby Meade's reputation."

"Tarnish! It will do it the world of good" came Mrs. Grundy's comfortable voice. "Excuse us, Inspector. You were about to say?"

The puckered eyelid drooped. "As this is the only house close to the avenue where the murdered man was found, and as all of you appear to have either been here or en route, I will speak with each of you in turn."

"And don't miss the point that we all knew him to some degree or other." Mrs. Grundy's hands were folded complacently over her stomach.

"I suppose there can be no doubt that the man is Hunt," enquired Mr. Deasley. "His being here at such an hour has us all rather puzzled. He took the train back to London yesterday, or I assume he did. . . ." His voice petered out.

"We are basing our belief that he is one Angus Hunt from the contents of a wallet found on the body and from the identification of Miss Tessa Fields." Inspector Lewjack nodded at

me. "Now, young man"—he levelled a finger at Bertie—
"would you like to come with me first?"

"I didn't see nuffink. I didn't hear nuffink. Fred was the
only one what saw . . ." Bertie's eyes threatened to pop out
and roll across the floor.

"If we could use a room on this floor? The library, last
door on the left towards the front door? That will be ideal."
The inspector was speaking to Hyacinth. Maude had her arm
round Bertie's shoulders.

"If you want your mother along, that's fine. This has been
a shock for her, too, and if I know beans about mums she'll
be carrying you around in a backpack until you're twenty-one."
The inspector ruffled the ginger head.

"No, I won't." Maude's voice came at a clip, but I noticed
her blue eyes were extra bright as she prodded Bertie forward.
"Don't need an echo, do you, dear?"

It could have been Mum speaking. Bertie's eyes ceased
popping and his stance grew soldierly.

"Thank you, ma'am," the inspector said. "They do talk
more easily when the parents aren't around."

The sitting room door closed and Constable Watt was once
more The Law in Flaxby Meade. He swelled importantly, the
helmet strap threatening to lacerate his chin.

"Ladies and gents, there will be no discussing of the
murder."

"Oh, stop huffing and puffing!" whined Godfrey. "If you
are so highly dedicated to caution, why aren't the servants in
here with us? We wouldn't have to talk to *them*." He gestured
vaguely from his chair with a limp hand. "They could be kept
busy dusting some of these fussy little ornaments, or by lighting
the fire. I tell you, I've come over all shivery."

"He's absolutely right." Mr. Deasley tugged at his handkerchief. "Please don't think I am implying that they are in
the kitchen cribbing up on their stories, but . . ."

"My darling Goddy! Shivering! You must be coming down
with one of your colds. Let me give you something to make
you feel better." Mrs. Grundy was digging into her bag. "And,
Tessa, you are trembling, too."

She was right. I was besieged by a dense chill, but it had
nothing to do with the temperature in the room or anything
physically wrong with me. I looked from face to face, thought

about Butler and Chantal somewhere outside this room, and struggled with the truth. Whatever I tried to tell myself about vengeful artists pursuing Angus to Flaxby Meade, I still grappled with the strong possibility of the murderer being someone in this house. (Is it quite as much fun playing detective now, Tessa?)

"Forget it, Mumsie. Should I drink one of your poisonous potions when we already have one body too many?" Godfrey shifted irritably on the sofa, snatching his hand away from his parent.

Planting enormous feet apart, the constable blew out his chest. "Let's have some hush, if you please. I will decide whether the other suspects will be brought in for surveillance." His face grew a little less assertive as he spoke. If he went to fetch Butler and Chantal he would have to leave us untended.

Mrs. Grundy inclined her beautiful white head. "Murder, like parenting, is something certain people find they should never have attempted until it is too late. Now, my dear husband and I took the matter very seriously. We viewed raising Goddy as our ultimate work of science."

I was close enough to Mr. Deasley to hear him mutter, "And botched the experiment, by God." I could feel the tension mounting in him and the others. Harry was pacing up and down, Primrose was fussing with oddments on the bureau, Mr. Deasley was fiddling again with the ivory elephant, Hyacinth and Maude were sitting on one sofa and the Grundys on the other. No one was making eye contact.

I got up from my chair and brushed against Harry. His fingers touched mine, and weakly I wanted to hold on to him, keep us both safe. If the murderer were here he or she perhaps knew that Harry and I had been with Angus at the end. And perhaps crouched behind the trees, listening. . . . I stepped away from Harry. We should have been together in this, united as I had believed us to be in the search for my origins. Anger was a powerful shield; it would guard me against fear as well as grief. I didn't need Harry. Detective Tessa would go it alone.

I'd had such dreams when I entered this house; of romantic lineage and of seeing, for the first time, a reflection of my face in someone else's. Now what did I have? The possibility that my mother was linked to a house of old secrets and present-day murder. Fergy always said that wishes are gilded carriages that turn into overripe pumpkins. I had told Harry that the fantasies were dead, and they were. Even if I found my mother she would not be the magical figure I had searched for all these years. That woman was as much a ghost as Mum. But I had wished this family upon myself and now I was stuck with it. The detection business wasn't fun anymore, but I had to discover the identity of the murderer. I had to discover the identity of my mother because, bad seed or not, I had to know who I was. Horribly egocentric, and yet I felt Angus would understand.

I looked from Hyacinth to Primrose. How terrible for one if the other . . . but how much worse to live with suspicion. The sisters couldn't live out their lives, each wondering, fearing, perhaps growing to hate the other. Unless . . . unless they had collaborated. I sat down and found myself praying, "If it *is* them, remember they are old and have been kind to me."

I studied Mr. Deasley. On the drive to the station, might Angus have confided in him? Asked for support in persuading the sisters to give up the card games? Discretion was never Angus's middle name. But I couldn't see Mr. Deasley committing murder purely on chivalrous grounds, not unless he was truly in love with Hyacinth or Primrose. As for the card games—their being halted would surely be beneficial financially to Mr. Deasley. With the sisters' nefarious source of income removed, they would have to sell off the silver teapots even faster.

What was Bertie saying to the inspector? Hyacinth had almost convinced me that the word of a highly strung, imaginative child would be taken with a large pinch of salt, but now I wasn't so sure.

I focussed on Maude. If this were a thriller, it would be discovered that she harboured an insane hatred for all men—because the ones of her acquaintance sat in the pub quaffing Guinness while the wife was in labour. But what did I know that might place her on the suspect list? She had telephoned last night. Suppose Primrose, distracted by the loss of Minnie, had phoned her back at Cheynwind and confided in her about Angus's morning visit? Had Maude plotted to incriminate the sisters as vengeance for an old family feud? My heart beat quicker . . . old family feud. I leaned forward watching her. I wasn't sure I wanted to believe, or suspect that . . . but something about the way she sat, so solid, so steady, in her rumpled uniform with the white frilled collar, made me realize that I had never really seen Maude before—not as a woman. Until now I only thought of her as a nurse, Bertie's parent, and a source of information. A woman alone, taking into her life a troubled child, she must be an extremely strong and indomitable woman.

My heart slowed and I made myself look at Mrs. Grundy. Now here was a woman capable of murder, especially if anyone threatened her darling Goddy. The notion that she might have done away with Angus because she hated porridge would never occur to the police, but I . . . Godfrey was speaking, and in my mind the words "false friend" fitted him better than anyone else in this room. Far better than Angus thinking himself a false friend to me, or the sisters. Godfrey was the corrupting force behind the Tramwells' folly. He said, "Nurse Krumpet, knowing my weak stomach as you do, you should be able to persuade the police that I could never commit murder. Thinking about that knife sliding into flesh is enough to make me turn the colour of those putrid dragons." He pressed a soft white hand against his angora jumper and grimaced at those beasts on the hearth. "Really, Hyacinth and Prim, why don't you let Deasley cart those off to his junk shop? And I'll have my decorator scurry around here with something tasteful in brass. My treat. No? Then at least get them plated."

"Enough, Goddy," admonished his mother. "We don't want to upset the Tramwells."

"Plated!" huffed Hyacinth, eyes on the beloved son. "I'll have you know those two—Marco and Polo as our father named them—are solid bronze. Admittedly not particularly fashionable, with chrome being in, but if they were composed of cow manure they would still stay. Primrose and I are excessively fond of them."

"Would we get rid of our beloved Min because she is"—Primrose, rigid in her chair, spelled out the word—"p-l-a-i-n?"

Up leapt the object of this praise, woofing enthusiastically, and reaping an automatic chorus of "Enough of that" from Constable Watt.

"You know"—Harry bent and patted Minnie as she

whirled in a tailspin—"your abbreviating her name like that makes me think of Mr. Hunt. Those last words of his—I hadn't thought before, but it is interesting . . ."

"What is?" asked Maude.

"Enough of that . . ." But the door grated open, admitting Butler and Chantal, claiming Constable Watt's complete attention.

"That Hunt remembered her name," said Harry. "The dog, Min. He had trouble getting the words out, but whether he was rambling or trying to tell us that the dog had given chase, or . . ."

"Oh, this is dreadful!" Primrose heaved Minnie onto her lap, where she lay dangling like a lumpy travelling rug. "If the murderer should be afraid that somehow a certain dog could give him away—Hyacinth, we must not let her out of our sight for a moment!"

Godfrey, still staring in an ecstasy of revulsion at Marco, froze. His hands stroked his turquoise wool trousers. His breath when it came, formed a slow hiss. "What else did Hunt say?" Uncanny to hear the Squire speak without his babiefied flummery.

"Nothing that made any sense." Harry avoided my menacing glare, and stroked the tip of one of Minnie's ears as he sat down next to Primrose.

"A little more hush, if you please." Constable Watt was finally ready to operate his pencil. "It seems the inspector had those two show our reinforcements from Warwick the Ruins and the gardens." He directed an official stare towards Chantal and Butler sitting in chairs against the wall facing the fireplace; she exotically lovely, he innocuous apart from the female shoes. "Very important those areas in relation to the scene of the crime. I now require all names and addresses for the record. Starting, if we please, with you, young lady." He bounced importantly on the sides of his feet as I rose. "Tessa Fields. The Vicarage, Kings Ransome. Oh no, that's wrong. I *did* live there, but my father is now at Doxbury in Devon." I tugged at a straggle of hair. "Goodness, I can't remember the exact address. You see, what should have been my father's new vicarage was recently purchased by the local historical society, and . . ."

"Tessa Fields, of no fixed abode." Heavily underscored. "Next, if you please."

"Harry Harkness, of . . ." He was giving me a half-amused, half-sympathetic, thumbs-down sign, which I ignored.

"Such nonsense," burst out Hyacinth. "Here, George"—striding towards him, she flicked a flat leather volume into his hands. The pencil went into a flying spin, caught deftly by Harry. "Take that into a corner and scribble to your heart's content." Hyacinth pursued her brow-beating tactics. "Tessa's address as of now is Cloisters. And if you can't spell it, not C-l-o-y, George—at least you know where to find her. Unlike my car, the time you confiscated it for illegal parking on the zebra crossing."

"Just doing my job, ma'am."

"Lent it to his wife for her Christmas shopping in London was the story I heard," said Mrs. Grundy.

"Now, now. One does appreciate your dedication, my good man." Mr. Deasley's voice was soothing. "But wouldn't you be better occupied fetching in this other child—the one the boy indicated was with him in the walk?"

"Other child?" exclaimed Mrs. Grundy. "Would that be young Ricky?"

Maude bent forward and said something I could not catch, causing Mrs. Grundy to shake her white head in dissatisfaction. "Fred! I might have known. Maude, you really should put a stop to this unfortunate association. Couldn't you tell your boy that Fred has been murdered, too? Goddy's father always said . . ."

But I was never to learn what the late great Mr. Grundy had to say for himself. With a lollipop stick extending from his lips, Bertie burst back into the room to announce indistinctly that the inspector was now ready to see me in the library. Following me to the door, Harry tried to catch hold of my hand, but I evaded him. All the remorse of which he was capable could not make things right between us.

Out in the hall, sunlight beaming through the windows on both sides of the door gilded the particles of dust floating in the warm air. The chair which the inspector pulled out for me had its back to the ceiling-high library window overlooking the side lawn. To prevent my hands shaking, I gripped the edge of the table and looked the man straight in his bad eye. Remember Fergy's advice on applying for a job. Always mentally strip your interviewer naked. Nothing in the world is more ridiculous than a naked man peering down his nose at you from the seat of power. But I had not got past removal of Inspector Lewjack's tie when my right leg began to jerk violently. I had to move my hands off the table and hold it down. That eye was considering whether to press obscenity charges. My other leg took up the rhythm.

I was thankful for the wide expanse of table between us. He was flopped in his chair, hairy hands outstretched, absently smoothing out a crumpled grease-stained paper bag. I conjured up a wife who packed sandwiches for him. Anything to make him marginally human.

"Smoke?" He pulled out a packet of Players, also spattered with grease spots.

I shook my head.

"Smart girl. Don't start, won't have to stop." He lit up, inhaling with closed-eyed pleasure. "Pleasant room, this. Makes me wish I hadn't wallpapered my flat. Books are a lot classier. But I suppose they have to be old and out of print to have the right ambience." He burrowed his nose into the air. "The smell of old money. Pack that into an aerosol can and I reckon Sainsbury's wouldn't be able to keep it in stock."

"The Tramwells aren't rich people." The words were out before I could stop them.

"Proper let-down, then, for any burglar who might stray this way. Although his ideas of what constitutes wealth might not coincide with yours, or the Misses Tramwell, for that matter."

I felt a pang of pity for Butler. He wasn't nearly as unpleasant as, say, the Grundys, but he had the criminal record. The inspector was back to smoothing out creases in the paper bag. His next words shot across the table catching me in the midriff. "Do you know why Angus Hunt was in Flaxby Meade this morning?"

"No. Well, perhaps he wanted to see me."

"You were very close friends?"

Surely he wasn't thinking something vile—that Angus and I were having an affair? "He was like an uncle to me. He had no close family, only a couple of elderly aunts in Scotland."

"And when was the last time you saw him, prior to this morning?"

"Wednesday night at Cheynwind—the home of the Grundys. His being there was a great surprise to me, a complete coincidence, and the following morning he stopped by here for a chat."

"With you, particularly?"

"Naturally he wanted to talk with me, but he also liked the Misses Tramwell. They reminded him of his aunts, I believe."

"And he said nothing about returning so soon?"

"No."

"Do you know anything about his friendship with the Grundys?"

"Nothing, only that he liked to play cards, that was the form of entertainment that evening."

"Can you name the other guests for me?"

"There was a Mr. Whitby-Brown. He smoked cigars and dropped ash everywhere."

The inspector looked at the wobbly end of his cigarette and tapped it on an ashtray. "Who else?"

"A clergyman named Egrinon Snapper, he . . ."

"Oh?" The inspector turned the paper bag over. "What have you remembered about the clergyman?"

"Well, the really unusual thing about him was that he was interested in murder. I think he is even writing a book about ones of historical interest and . . ."

"And here we have a body dressed up in a monk's robe. It's common knowledge hereabouts that a monk was murdered in that avenue in days of yore. The constable informed me with some reluctance on that point."

"I believe the villagers are ashamed of that old tragedy. Incredibly silly after hundreds of years; but the story offered to outsiders is that the monk, Tessail, committed suicide . . ."

"Any other guests on Wednesday night?"

"A Fritz Wortter; he was German."

"Do I sense, Miss Fields, that you didn't like him?"

I twisted my hands together under the table. "He and Primrose—that is, the younger Miss Tramwell . . ." The card game scene replayed itself for me. I was back in that exquisite chair at Cheynwind, holding that book on practical jokes in my hand and watching Primrose appear the victim and arise the victor. If ever a man had displayed hatred for a woman, that man was Fritz Wortter. But (and here my spirits, which had lifted a little, dipped) for Herr Wortter to have revenged himself upon Primrose in such a way—murdering a man who might be viewed as her enemy in the hope that she would be found guilty of the crime—he would have had to have known about Angus's visit to Cloisters, and been mad as well. I thought of Angus sprawled across the walk, reduced to a macabre joke in that monk costume, and could not believe that anyone sane would commit such an act. The police would check on Herr Wortter and his movements, wouldn't they? Again I breathed a little easier.

"What about Miss Primrose Tramwell and this Fritz Wortter?"

"They didn't hit it off."

"I see. You left the house this morning at what time, and for what reason?" The thug look intensified as he fired the question.

"Somewhere around six. Yes, I remember—Harry mentioned the time because my watch had stopped. We met in the Ruins. It's quiet there, and . . ."

"A chance to be out from under the eyes of the old ladies. Don't blame you. Do you know how long your boyfriend had been waiting for you?"

I hedged. "Harry always complains that I am late, but we didn't have time to talk about anything much, because almost at once we heard Minnie howling and we dashed off in the direction of the sound. Harry knows a lot about animals. He's wonderful with them." Whatever his other vices, that much was true.

"Give me the time, if you can, when you and Mr. Harkness found Mr. Hunt."

"I'm not sure." Having fudged about how long Harry had been in the Ruins I was in a tight corner here, but my evidence wasn't vital. Maude and Bertie and Harry, too, could pinpoint the time for the inspector. I kept looking straight into his bad eye, hoping my leg wouldn't set the table vibrating.

"And Mr. Hunt's condition, please. According to the doctor who examined the body, death had occurred within the hour. Is it possible he was alive when you found him?"

"Yes. He was, barely."

"Did he speak?"

The heavy mustiness of the room was closing in on me. I had to brace myself against the table. My determination to know the name of the murderer hadn't faltered, but I didn't want to say anything that might lead the inspector to a wrong conclusion. So much depended on how Angus's dying words had been phrased. And I couldn't remember. Harry had believed that the person telephoning Angus and the woman threatening suicide were one and the same, and thus the false friend. And maybe I was wishing myself into believing that the false friend was the one on the phone, and that the woman supposedly threatening to kill herself was someone else. Someone with no idea of what was being said about her. But if that were the case the false friend, alias the murderer, could have been male or female. Awful—but this sounded like one of those long-winded brain teasers: If Tom was Bert's best friend's wife's uncle, who was the man on the train . . . ?

Trains. *Angus didn't drive*. And trains didn't run from London to places like Flaxby in the early morning hours.

"Yes?" prompted Inspector Lewjack.

"Angus said someone had phoned, luring him to Abbots Walk on the pretext that a woman was threatening to hang herself from one of the elms. He said something like 'Tell them I'm sorry,' and then he mentioned his aunts in Scotland." There, I had fudged again, but really I would do much better ferreting out the identity of the murderer myself than trusting in policemen who knew nothing about the personalities involved.

"Anything else?"

"Only a reference to the Tramwells' dog, Minnie."

"Such as?"

"He didn't say anything more than her name. Have you . . . have you found the weapon?"

He shook his head. And a picture came of Minnie running off with a knife between her teeth. But surely she would later have dropped it in the garden or the house? How simple for anyone to have scrubbed it off and replaced it in the cutlery drawer, to be handed out later with a fork and a plateful of bacon and eggs. Now I was being stupid. Murders weren't committed with pieces of cutlery!

"Don't look so worried, Miss Fields. Our men are outside. There goes one now, searching the grounds."

Jerking around to the window, I was in time to see a hunched, man-shaped shadow creep past. I wasn't comforted. That shadow personified more than anything else the menace that besieged the house.

"The possibility of the dog making off with the weapon will not be ignored. Once the search of the grounds is completed we will request permission from the Misses Tramwell to go through the house."

And if they refused? He must have seen me shiver, for he said, "Relax, Miss Fields. In addition to Constable Watt, and myself, we now have two other policemen stationed indoors. Now, one or two more questions." He jabbed another battered cigarette into his mouth. "Have you seen that monk's robe or one similar anywhere in Flaxby Meade?"

"No. And I was up in the attics the other day, going through some trunks of old clothes, which is where costumes left over from pageants or fêtes would be kept."

"Why assume, Miss Fields, that I meant Cloisters, not Flaxby Meade in general?"

"I didn't. Well, you might . . . with this house, but it doesn't mean—" I took a deep breath and something weird happened: I got angry. Thrusting my hair back behind my ears I leaned my elbows on the table and stuck out my chin. "Inspector, will you stop trying to intimidate me by blowing smoke in my face? If I am going to say something stupid I can do so without any assistance. One thing I am certain of"—and I almost believed it myself—"is that the Tramwells are too proud of Cloisters' heritage to capitalize on it in such a way. What I think is that someone used the monk's robe to focus attention here."

"Ah, so now we have a murderer who not only had a vendetta against Angus Hunt, but the Tramwells, too. Anyone else in his little black book, do you think? What about you?"

"Me? Why, that's ridiculous." But was it? What if someone didn't want me at Flaxby Meade because they had guessed at my origins? I had read many books where one murder was committed purely as camouflage for another. Kill Angus and then do away with me; it would be thought that I had guessed too much.

"I am not trying to frighten you, Miss Fields, but I feel you should exercise a certain amount of caution. The boy Bertie will need to be safeguarded, but I will speak to his mother about that."

Maude. I could see her with her arms around Bertie in the walk. She would do everything she could to protect him.

"Do you think Bertie is in special danger, because even though hidden he was present during the murder?" Fear was back in full force. I felt a special closeness towards the boy; if anything happened . . .

"Until the murderer is brought in, the witnesses are inevitably in a precarious position. Nothing we can do about that, I'm afraid, except to advise discretion. No lonely walks, no more rendezvous at dead of night—with anyone."

"But, Harry . . ."

"Can you remember what Bertie said to you in Abbots Walk?"

"He said that the killer hit Mr. Hunt over the head with a tree limb and then hunted around on the ground for something."

"And what did you make of that?"

"That someone must have planned this, hidden the monk's robe in readiness, knocked out Angus, and then dressed him up." My eyes smarted, and I wished I had a handkerchief until Inspector Lewjack handed me one. It looked used, and I shook my head.

"I know this is difficult for you, but if you will bear with me—did you know anyone from Flaxby Meade before coming here this week?"

"I had briefly met Chantal, the maid, before my visit. Harry had taken her out a few times while I was in London, and I ran into her once at his farm." Full marks, Tessa, for nonchalance.

"You were not previously acquainted with the Tramwells?"

"No. Harry had mentioned them, of course." My leg started twitching again. What had Bertie told Inspector Lewjack about my arrival? And had he mentioned recognizing Harry's voice this morning and connecting it with the man who had "attacked" me? If he had, then the inspector's silence on the matter meant that I was a mouse being pawed around by the big tomcat until I squealed.

Inspector Lewjack stroked his moustache. "And as far as you know, you had formerly met none of the other locals?"

I grabbed the chance to side-track. "The first time I met Mrs. Grundy at Cheynwind, I had one of those vague feelings you get about having seen a person somewhere before, yet not being able to place when or where. Probably she reminded me of someone else, not anyone I knew well, but a person I had seen in a shop—a café—the library, that sort of place."

He made a notation, out of mere politeness I supposed, on the paper bag. "What was Mr. Hunt's occupation?"

"He was an authenticator at The Heritage Gallery. Highly renowned for uncovering art frauds."

"Ah," said Inspector Lewjack. "A detective of sorts, eh? Thank you for your time, Miss Fields. Send Mr. Harkness along next, please."

I deliberately slowed my steps in making for the door, and he let me get within inches of it before stopping me. "Miss Fields, I almost forgot." Here it came. He was going to pounce with a demand to know what kind of charade Harry and I had been playing in Abbots Walk on Monday afternoon.

"Did Mr. Hunt wear a watch?"

For a full ten seconds I gaped at him. "A watch? What do you mean, wasn't one found on him? I'm sorry; if one had been you wouldn't be asking. . . . Yes, he wore a watch, a pocket watch; they were sort of an enthusiasm of his. He must have had dozens." I fingered the one around my neck. "He gave me this one." I was remembering how it had disappeared and then returned.

"Any rings?"

"No. But I see what you mean. It is interesting that the watch was taken and his wallet left, and besides . . . the entire staging of the murder seems too elaborate for simple theft, doesn't it?"

Was the watch a bonus? The icing on the cake? Or a deliberate ploy to implicate someone who was known to be light-fingered?

The policeman standing at the foot of the stairs strongly resembled the wax one I had seen at Madame Tussaud's. Not a flicker of an eyelash as I passed. The sitting room was as I had left it—Constable Watt still planted in the middle of the room—but otherwise highly reminiscent of a doctor's surgery. The only homey touch was provided by Minnie, lying on her patchwork blanket. If her grunts and groans were any indication, she was in the throes of a nightmare. But at least she had the benefit of being asleep. I wished I could wake and find I had brought all this terror and grief upon myself by eating cheese late at night. When I passed Maude she smiled at me but I couldn't meet her eyes. Sometime I had to talk to her alone about her relationship with the Tramwells, and especially her friendship with Violet, but now I was cloaked with fear—even of her. That missing watch bothered me terribly.

Tonelessly, I told Harry he was next, and went over to sit by Primrose on the sofa facing the windows. She looked so frail and old that I picked up one of her hands and held it.

"You're not cross with us, are you dear—about Harry?" she whispered. "I've had a talk with Maude, and you have nothing to fear from her or Bertie when it comes to blabbing. It seems the boy had said several times that the incident was like a play, and he has made quite a heroine of you. Before he went in to see the inspector, Maude warned him not to mention anything about the amnesia or its cause. A very intuitive woman, Maude, she had guessed that some charade was afoot."

"How very nice and convenient for Harry and me."

"Now, you mustn't blame him," begged Primrose. "Men tend to bungle things—that's their way. But think how sweet it was of the dear boy to want to help in your search. I remember how concerned he was on first broaching the subject to us, and how intrigued Hyacinth and I were! We thought you such a sport but, perhaps . . . attacking the matter from the wrong end."

"How?"

"Instead of focussing on which Flaxby Meade female might have been pregnant twenty-odd years ago, we felt it might have been more advantageous to look where the trouble always begins—with a man. The type of man who fathers a child and does not or *cannot* marry the mother. Ah! There a host of possibilities spring to mind."

"I have never felt any interest in my biological father. He may not even have known that my mother was pregnant, so why should I care about him?"

"But as an avenue to your mother . . ."

"Yes—you're right." I looked over to where Godfrey was nattering away to Maude. Surely he wasn't capable of a normal man-woman relationship! And yet the way he had looked at me sometimes . . . I began to feel rather queasy.

"Two of my favourite ladies engaged in a tête-à-tête, I see." Mr. Deasley loomed over us. The tone was as hearty as ever. But did I detect an undercurrent? Reaching into his breast pocket for his handkerchief, he patted his reddened nose. It's colour was reflected in Primrose's cheeks. Everyone, in fact, was fidgeting, pacing, or fussing, except Chantal. She sat as still as the Mona Lisa in her straight-backed chair.

Mr. Deasley pushed the hanky back into his breast pocket, but its dispirited droop indicated a lessening of his usual persnickety attention to detail. And when he spoke, he had lost some of his Lothario suavity. He sat down in the space I had vacated, fumbling for Primrose's hand.

"You will be seeing the inspector any moment, my dear," he said, "and I cannot let . . ."

"Please, Clyde, I must . . ."

Constable Watt, whose glum face had borne tell-tale signs of a man wanting his midday meal, came smartly to attention. The pencil assumed ominous proportions.

"Knew one of you would crack. When the wife hears—"

"George! Tell your wife anything and we will have her drummed out of the Mothers' Union." Hyacinth's voice was hailstones dropping on a tin roof.

"Miss Primrose Tramwell and I are not discussing the murder." Mr. Deasley sounded as though he would much prefer that they had been. "Miss Tramwell is completely in the clear, because at the time of the murder she and I were together. We were, in fact, together all night. Oh, my dear lady"—he flushed out the handkerchief again, his voice disintegrating—"if I could spare you the conjectures, the corrupting of something noble and beautiful into the sordid—but I care for you too deeply to let the foul suspicion of murder cling to you."

The pin that dropped was Constable Watt's pencil.

"Hyacinth," came Primrose's broken voice, "don't look at me like that."

So! Those voices coming from her room late last night had

not been the wireless. I pictured myself passing the door on my way to the attics, and a dreadful thought came. Had Primrose drugged and hidden Minnie? A ploy that had two plusses: no wild barks to announce Mr. Deasley's arrival and she had been able to get him secretly into the house while Hyacinth and I were out searching the grounds.

Dreadful silence, wrenched open by Godfrey's giggling voice. "My, oh my! I feel another murder coming on."

Chantal rose as smoothly as a sea wave from her chair. Fingers pressed against her temples. Eyes closed.

"Evil. It is in the room with us. Shall I look into the crystal and tell what I see?"

16

Constable Watt made a token protest. But he had long since lost all control of the group. His cohort on the stairs was summoned to escort Chantal to fetch the crystal. Butler stole across the room, drawing the curtains across the harsh morning sunlight. Harry was still absent. Maude came up to me, Bertie clinging to her hand, his round eyes aglow with excitement.

"Poor Miss Tramwell," she said, and I wondered which one she meant. "An awful thing. I'm glad the girl spoke up when she did. Anything to take our minds off all this waiting."

"Do you believe Chantal may see something?"

"I'm not sure." Maude was looking over to where Hyacinth and Primrose stood like two statues in a park and I wondered if her mind was on our conversation—any more than mine was, really. "A while back Chantal told me something that gave me rather a jolt at the time, and—"

"An' did it come true?" cawed Bertie.

"I think it may have done," said Maude.

Chantal returned, and as Maude, Bertie, and I moved to join the group surging around the card table, which Butler had set up, the boy tugged at my arm, whispering, "Miss, I 'ave somefink to tell you about. Somefink bad."

"Could we make it later, Bertie?" The sisters gravitated to opposite ends of the table, Constable Watt directing traffic.

"No shoving. No crowding. Give way, if you please." But it was Chantal's lifting of the red velvet cloth that made the crowd fall back.

Mrs. Grundy whispered in my ear, "We really must have her put on a little show like this at the summer fête." Mr. Deasley, self-consciousness apparent in his gait, pushed forward a chair for Chantal. The rest of us remained standing. I wondered if she would ever speak. And then I was thinking of nothing but her graceful hands moving in a swirling motion over the glass. Those hands were birds—seagulls—fluttering in ever narrowing circles.

"Cards," she murmured throatily. "Cards falling upon the table, and the dealer is death." The words were trite, yet they frightened me. Chantal was too clever to use such patter without good reason. Or was it the truth she saw in the crystal? Constable Watt was breathing hard in excitement. Chantal drew the palms of her hands outward over the globe as though brushing away cobwebs. "The game isn't poker or whist. It is patience."

"The stakes?" When Primrose spoke I jumped and had to steady myself by clutching at Maude's arm. She put it round me.

"Very high. I keep seeing two aces." Chantal's voice picked up breathless speed. "I see the boy, Bertie; he must be placed in safety, watched, but he is not the danger—it is the other one, the one who saw . . . the one who knows . . ."

Shuddering, but with thinly veiled pleasure, Mrs. Grundy cried, "But that is awful. I was near the walk close to the time of the murder. She or he may think . . . and Goddy! My darling boy, you must promise never to leave my side. I will not rest for an *instant*."

Chantal was replacing the velvet cloth over the globe. "Once anyone speaks, the core of flame which sparks the light is extinguished." Again terribly trite; but Chantal's voice was so empty, so lacking in drama. She had frightened herself, I was sure of it.

Edging towards her, Constable Watt said, "While you're at it, girl, how about a quick peek to see if a horse, name of Skallawag, is going to place this Saturday at Foxhill?"

Chantal shook her head. She was moving away from the table as Harry came in. Hyacinth left us. Then, half an hour later, she returned and Primrose went out.

The morning wore away into afternoon. A drab silence settled upon the room like a bad cold, broken only by the occasional opening and closing of the door and the musical tralahs of the clocks throughout the house. Angus's missing watch, somehow it was the key. My eyes roved across the room, lighting on one face and then another. But it was really Angus I was seeing and hearing.

Godfrey got up and left the room. Harry was reading a book. From where I sat the title appeared to be in Russian. Then I smiled sourly. He was holding it upside down.

Another literary enthusiast. Godfrey returned from the library with a tombstone-sized volume on *Art Through the Ages*.

"Always so artistic." His mother patted my knees. "Such an exemplary trait in a man, I have always thought. A sure sign of sensitivity. And sensitivity is what makes a man a good husband, don't you agree, dear?" I nodded, watching the hostile contours of Hyacinth's face. Minnie's head rested in her lap and she stroked it protectively, eyes on Primrose, who was bent over a strip of lacy lavender knitting. That knave of hearts, Mr. Deasley, sat in a chair next to Harry, pondering his feet. Bertie was lying on Minnie's rug. What bad thing had he wanted to tell me? The mantel clock stopped, and the absence of ticking was as explosive as a bomb detonating in Piccadilly Circus. Primrose wound it and we all sank back, the pendulum moving once more. Chantal was summoned and I fell asleep. Someone tucked a rug around me. A someone smelling of aftershave and outdoors. Dreaming. I was outdoors and Angus was coming towards me through the mottled shadows of Abbots Walk. He wasn't quite close enough for me to see his face, but I could see his hands. They were filled with torn pieces of paper. A wind crept between us and all those fragments, each containing one letter of a name, fluttered up into the elms, but I didn't want to look up into the elms because in one of them someone was hanging.

When I woke I was clutching the rug, and the person absent was Butler. The last to go, and the longest kept. Hyacinth and Primrose made no move to speak or even look at each other, but the expression in their eyes was the same: concern bordering on alarm. Another half-hour. When I looked, the clock said two-fifteen. At last the door opened, but no Butler. The Madame Tussaud policeman entered. Would we all do the inspector a small favour and agree to be searched? A policewoman who had arrived from Warwick would see to the ladies. No one protested. Who could do so without looking guilty? Mrs. Grundy sounded rather pleased when she said, "I shall write to *The Times*."

I had not forgiven Harry. I would never forgive him, but I had difficulty restraining an anguished glance in his direction. Those grisly women with the bobbed hair and arms like tree trunks—I had seen them do the strip-and-search routine on the telly. Yet the reality was bearable. I trooped into the room next to the sitting room, a blond girl constable patted me over, had me empty my pockets, and said, "Ta, love."

Search over, we were now all set at liberty. Orders of the inspector. At first we displayed a tendency to continue huddling together, but when Hyacinth offered everyone a late lunch the atmosphere returned almost to normal. Chantal walked towards the kitchen and I followed her—I wasn't sure why.

"Have you come to help fix lunch?" she asked. "Or to see I don't make a break for it? Sorry." She laughed without merriment. "I was the one who called for a truce, and now I'm starting up the hostilities." She opened the bread bin and reached for a knife.

"You frightened yourself, didn't you, looking into the crystal?" I unwrapped a packet of butter.

"I'm not sure if I really saw anything, or if I was reacting to feelings of guilt."

"What do you mean? You can't be saying that . . ."

She sliced away at the bread. "That I murdered your friend Angus Hunt as a revival of an ancient rite?"

"I didn't mean anything of the sort. But when you mentioned guilt, I wondered if you somehow blamed yourself for what happened. I know I do. If I hadn't come here, maybe Angus wouldn't have got involved, although knowing him . . ." My lips were trembling and I had to bite down hard on them.

"Yes, I do wonder about my part in this." Chantal put down the knife and looked at me. "If I hadn't come here, would he be alive?"

"Are you suggesting that the murderer may have decided that you would make a great scapegoat because of Tessail and the old curse?"

"I've thought of that, but, no . . . the reason I feel guilty is that the Tramwells have been marvellous to me, and I haven't repaid them well."

"That's nonsense. You work extremely hard."

"I get a lot of fringe benefits. I think I told you I am interested in monasticism, but what I didn't tell you is that I am doing a thesis on the subject for my degree. What better place to do research than at Cloisters—being as suggestible to atmosphere as I am? And also, I suppose I have grown soft." Her eyelashes cast a shadow across her cheekbones. "I began to find that studying at a bonfire bothered my eyes, and I had lost the taste for poached rabbit. This job was a godsend. The Tramwells have offered to eat spaghetti on toast every night, so I could study, but I could never quite shake the feeling that they were on the enemy team."

"So now what do you do? What do we both do? Stand wringing our hands?" I wasn't sure that I liked her any better, but I felt a closeness to her, a trust. I scraped a knife over the butter and started spreading. "My dad says guilt is nothing but an excuse for doing nothing to change things. If you and I want to make some return to the Tramwells for imposing on them, then we must find the murderer so their lives can return to normal. Unless you think one of them did it?"

"I don't. Do you?"

"No." And I meant it.

She pushed the butter dish closer and her lips curved slightly upwards. "And perhaps I am wrong in what I fear."

I was afraid to ask her what she meant in case she said Harry's name. She continued: "I have always thought the police labour under a decided disadvantage, coming in as they do at the last scene while we have been here for the entire performance."

"Only if we believe that the source of the murder is here—in Flaxby Meade," I said.

"You knew Angus Hunt; is there any other possibility?"

"I don't think so." Placing sliced corned beef on top of bread, I told her about the reason behind Angus's visit to Cloisters. Perhaps that was foolish of me, and I faltered when I saw a glimmer of relief in her eyes. "I told you," I said, "that I don't believe the Tramwells are guilty. But I am convinced that the card games are in some way the reason for Angus's death."

"Godfrey, that squelchy creep." She was slicing cucumber. "He would be capable of almost anything if someone threatened to take away his toys."

"And his mother would kill without a qualm to keep him happy."

"Who else was at that game?"

"A Mr. Whitby-Brown, a man named Fritz Wortter, and a clergyman."

The knife had slipped and blood beaded up from the tip of one of her fingers. As she ran her hand under cold water, I asked, "When you spoke about seeing a game of patience in the crystal, was that just gibberish to turn everyone's mind from what Primrose and Mr. Deasley had just revealed?"

"No." She turned off the tap. "I felt it—an overpowering sense of watchful waiting."

I had felt it in the garden. Someone hidden behind the bushes, biding his time. And that was before Angus had come to Cloisters.

"Patience is also the gypsy's stock in trade. We get a lot of doors slammed in our faces."

"When did you ever peddle wax flowers door to door?" My voice was irritated.

"I didn't mean that kind of door. I wonder if that shrewd Inspector Lewjack will recognize the type of mind he is up against? Or if Mr. Hunt's having only recently appeared on the scene will lead him to suppose this is a crime of mad impulse?"

Our hands touched as we placed sandwiches on a plate. "Gamblers," I said, "are creatures of impulse."

Chantal looked up at the clock on the wall. "At this moment, I am more worried about Butler than the Tramwells. If his interview with the inspector had concluded he would be out here. I warned him that he should be straightforward about his activities last night and about his shoes, but he was so unsettled by his feeling that anything he might say about his life at Cloisters would shed unpleasant light upon—"

"His past?"

"Upon the Tramwells, revealing them as a pair of eccentric old ninnies. He is absolutely devoted to them. You know he came here to burgle, and their only complaint was that he smoked on the job and didn't wash up after making himself a cuppa. I truly believe Butler would die for them."

"At least Primrose has an alibi." I arranged sliced cucumber and tomato on a glass dish. My voice petered out; I was recalling the murderous look in Hyacinth's eyes when she looked at Mr. Deasley. Under normal circumstances I would have been horribly shocked myself. I picked up the dish, Chantal reached for it, and between us we nearly dropped it.

"We should get these sandwiches in, I can come back for the tea," Chantal said as she loaded up a tray. "But I do want to say something to you about Harry." Her face was turned slightly away from me—and that perfect profile could still rile me. "I can understand your shock at discovering the truth about him, but misguided or not, he—"

"I don't want to listen to anything about Harry." Her making excuses for him put me on the outside of their closeness. How long had I had this headache? It was a pressure on the top of my skull, so powerful that I was sure my forehead must look like corrugated paper.

"Did you ever listen to him, or were you too busy sobbing out your tales of woe? I listen"—her lips moved into a slow self-mocking curve—"when he talks about you. I love him. I've loved him for a long time; didn't I say that gypsies are good at patience? So be warned—when you have driven him away, I will be waiting for him."

"In his bed, I suppose. Oh, I'm sorry; I was forgetting our little truce." The furrows in my brow were now deep enough for the planting of seeds, as Fergy would have said. If only I could see her, see Dad; but most of all I wished I could see Mum—hold on to her and tell her all about Harry.

"*I* wasn't forgetting our truce," said Chantal. "A week ago I wouldn't have believed it possible, but I almost like you, and I want to be fair with you." Brushing stray bread crumbs into the sink she handed me a tray, picked up another, and without further talk we went out into the hall.

Harry was coming towards us past the portrait gallery, and I seethed as he took Chantal's tray. "Don't speak." I glared as he elbowed the sitting room door open for me. Chantal returned to the kitchen to make tea. "You might break a blood vessel in your tongue."

"Know something, Tessa?" He looked tired. "I've spent a long time loving you, and I guess I'm finally bored with the whole stupid business."

My lips pried apart. "Suits me."

"Splendid. But should you ever chance to change your mind, you will have to be the one who comes running with the ring in the velvet box. All right, sweetheart?"

Never. I would never grovel. Especially to a man I didn't want anyway. And he needn't stand there like one of those damned Regency heroes glowering down his arrogant nose at me. Those dark blue eyes of his couldn't throw me into a fit of the transports or convince me that my life would be total emptiness without him. I had Dad, I had Fergy, and I *would* have my mother. She would fill any void. I was sure I was right in what I suspected. I would talk to Maude; she would tell me the truth. But what if . . . what if my mother's life had no voids? Would she want a stranger bursting in upon her world? In giving me a new life, hadn't she earned one for herself?

"A shallow pair, aren't we? Intruding our personal disputes into the midst of murder and mayhem?" Harry edged my tray to one side and set his down.

"Considering you are the walking definition of the word shallow—" I began, but mayhem was re-emerging with the opening of the sitting-room door. Hyacinth, Primrose, and the other witnesses had been congregating in the parlour, assuming that was where luncheon was to be served. But when I explained that Chantal and I had automatically returned here, Primrose absently patted me on the arm, saying that informality was much cosier.

The mood wasn't cosy. Butler was still incarcerated in the library, or so we believed. Barely had Chantal appeared with an assortment of teapots and we had begun filling our plates than Inspector Lewjack ambled into the room with Constable Watt in tow.

My mind focussed on incidentals. The wrinkles in Maude's blue dress, Mr. Deasley's red nose, Hyacinth's earrings hanging motionless against her neck, Godfrey still holding the volume on art, Mrs. Grundy opening up her sandwich to peer inside, Bertie . . . What had he wanted to tell me?

"Mr. Jones has agreed to accompany us down to the station to clear up a few remaining points," announced the inspector.

Jones! My surprise was not that Butler was being taken away, but that his name was Jones.

"Oh, but surely we haven't made you feel so unwelcome that you have to rush away," protested Primrose. "The library is at your disposal for as long as you wish, and as for Butler, I cannot see that he could possibly be of the least use to you in your enquiries."

"Miss Tramwell is right, you know," decreed Mrs. Grundy. "I'm sure you won't get a word out of him at the police station. He'll get lockjaw, remembering what it's like behind bars." That woman!

"Just doing our job," said Constable Watt.

Ten minutes after the official departure, the luncheon party broke up. We all gravitated to the hall, informal departures by way of the French windows being socially inappropriate in a house of death. Hyacinth and Primrose were both grey with fatigue. Neither looked at the other as, echoing general farewells, they went up to their rooms. Harry was standing talking to that other gay blade, Mr. Deasley. Godfrey disappeared to use the phone, and his mother fished in her bag for change to pay for the call. Maude, buttoning her cape at the neck, came up to me.

"I am glad the Misses Tramwell are going to get some rest. Too much for them, all this, at their age. Terrible. The memories it must bring back of Lily's death. Police in the house then, too—and that dreadful inquest! They never talk about it, but . . ." Bertie had sidled up and was clinging to her hand, whispering something. "Shush," she admonished gently. "I know you want to talk to Miss Fields, dear, so do I—when there are less people around. Remember the man who died was her friend."

Would Maude's talk deal with the immorality of feigning illness? What had the Tramwells told her? A hammer started beating inside my head. Bertie had said she had asked him if I reminded him of anyone. Did she mean a man or a woman? But I couldn't wonder about my father now—I wasn't up to it.

"What is said about Lily's death?"

"Nothing much now. Gossip fades." She touched back that strand of hair that kept falling over my forehead. "You should get some rest yourself, dear, or you won't be of use to anyone, and I do think you are the best therapy for those two ladies.

208

Nothing like someone young about the house." She smiled down at Bertie.

"You take care of yourself and Bertie. Do you have someone he can stay with while you are working?" I was tired. I felt like crying.

"I'm going to take him on my rounds for the rest of the day, and the Tramwells did say we could spend the night here if I think there is any likelihood of my being called out. Very kind of them, I thought."

"Very kind," I said.

Bouncing up and down against Maude's arm, Bertie oohed, "Can we really stay here?" Not a boy consumed with fear that the murderer might seek to silence him before he remembered who fitted that murderous shadow in the walk. But if I were Maude, I would not sleep until the case was closed. For that matter I doubted the murderer would get much rest knowing that Bertie's very vital subconscious— Fred—might come alive at any minute. Of course, it was possible that the net was already being drawn over the murderer's head . . . that Butler was the one . . .

Only Mr. Deasley displayed signs of a struggle in making his departure. He was still casting anguished bassett-hound glances up the staircase as he followed the Krumpets and Grundys out the door. A week ago I wouldn't have believed that an elderly man could be passionately in love with anyone, but I myself had aged a lot. I thought of Dad and Vera's sister, hoping that Fergy would put her foot down—and yet I did want him to be happy. Nothing could change the way he felt about Mum.

Harry's farewell to me was brief—a mere pause in his offering to give Chantal a lift into the village in the Tramwell hearse on his way home. The motorbike was temporarily out of commission, and my heart almost softened towards him when I heard him telling Chantal that he had hitchhiked here last night. Then I asked myself why she was leaving the house. Only one good reason sprang to mind, and I hoped the horses rushed to welcome Harry back by biting off huge chunks of his anatomy.

What would Dad think if I became a nun? I pictured myself wan but alluring in my habit and felt faintly cheered.

I would begin my life of penance with the washing up. Totally irresponsible of Chantal to leave me to it, but I would grow inured to the selfishness of others. She probably never did the washing up anyway. I had seen Butler at the sink. . . . What was happening to him now? Could it be that Chantal had gone down to the police station to try to see him? Now she was making me feel ashamed of my prurient thoughts.

Someone had to prepare the evening meal. I discovered a pork roast and shoved it, surrounded by onions, leeks, and potatoes, into a slow oven. Would Butler be home for dinner? The clock on the wall dauntingly informed me that it was after four. Could listing his aliases be what was taking so long? I closed the doors on the Welsh dresser from which I had taken the casserole dish, and looked at the step-ladder leaning beside it. Had Butler stood upon it yesterday morning and listened with his ear to the hatchway to what Angus was saying? The same could be true of Chantal. She would then have had to go through the garden and enter the library via a window. Had I been foolish to begin to trust her where Harry was not concerned?

Minnie scratched at the door and I let her in. "If you weren't such a close-mouthed female, you could tell us a lot." I broke up left-over sandwiches and tossed them into her Chinese bowl. "This is an incongruous house—the Tramwells gambling for a livelihood yet here you sit, you revolting hound, gobbling up your grub from a vessel most people would lock away behind glass doors." The bowl reminded me that I had not yet finished reading that elevating book, *The Tramwell Family*, and that I *did* want to know more about Sinclair.

As I went by the portrait gallery, I thought about the picture I had seen in the attic, looked up, and met Tessa's eyes. Today, they seemed sad, as if she knew all that had happened and wished to comfort me.

I found the volume where I had left it in my room and settled down for a read. Make that *tried* to settle. My head still ached dully. I found the chapter on Sinclair, but he did not fit my image of swashbuckling pirate leaping from a chandelier to steal a giant ruby out of some maharajah's turban. No, indeed! He had replanted twenty elms and sired seven children. (Was that in order of importance? Yawn.) He had given money to the church even though he had not attended

210

regularly, due to his travels. (And an allergy to prayer books, I'll bet!) On those travels Sinclair had attempted to impart the joys of English civilization to the heathens. Another yawn and the book ruffled shut—but I mustn't fall asleep reading it as I had done last time. The roast might shrivel. Reopening it, I retraced to the line where I had stopped. "A deep appreciation of art and ancient dynasties . . ." Wouldn't he and Angus have got on splendidly together, ambling through The Heritage discussing the early Ming dynasty? I must have been half asleep, because I was seeing double. Angus dying in the walk and Minerva at her Chinese bowl. The book fell from my hands as I sat up slowly. *That was it!* Hadn't Harry said it was odd, Angus referring to Minnie by name? And to think I had stood minutes ago gabbing to that spoiled dog about her Chinese bowl! Angus had not agonizingly struggled to say "The dog's got the weapon," or "The dog's chasing my assailant." What he was trying to tell me was: *The dog's bowl is Ming!*

Unable to sit still, I climbed off the bed and sat on the swing. The gliding motion helped me think. Angus's expertise was his destruction. His impulsive, impassioned enthusiasm. He had confided in someone about his discovery—no, suspicion—for if Angus had been certain, he would have told the Tramwells at once. He must have said he would go back to London and confer with other specialists in the field; then, if the news was good, return to Flaxby Meade. And the person in whom he had confided must have nodded, smiled, said how nice for the Tramwells, whilst secretly thinking, *How nice for me if I can prevent you opening your mouth*.

The most promising candidate for the role of confidant was Mr. Deasley. He dealt in antiques and to have such a prize as this fall into his lap . . . but in his favour was the fact that he was highly trusted by the sisters. They were apparently in the habit of selling to him, so he would have had little difficulty in wheedling that bowl out of them, or, better still, could have swapped it for something similar. Or, easier yet, walked off with it under his arm along with the silver teapot. I thought again about Angus's missing watch. . . . A pity about Mr. Deasley. He had his alibi of sorts . . . but Primrose could have fallen asleep. No—the risk of her waking and finding him gone would have been more dangerous than no alibi at all.

Who else might Angus have spoken to before catching the

London train? Chantal had been leaving the house as I went in, but I would have heard the sound of the Tramwell hearse if she had taken off after Mr. Deasley and Angus—meaning the only way she could have caught up with them would have been by thumbing a lift from a passing motorist and doing the same on the return trip. Could she have made it back in time to serve lunch? I supposed it was possible. I had spent a good deal of time poking around upstairs. But Angus wasn't a fool. He would have thought it extremely strange, her appearing beside him on the platform. How could she have explained that? Let me tell your fortune, sir?

The watch. It would have been silver. All Angus's watches were silver. Whoever had taken it had either craved it or been afraid of it. Butler . . . If Chantal could have followed Mr. Deasley's car, he could have done the same. But again, how could he have explained his reason for pursuing Angus? That left Maude and the Grundys. I forced myself to imagine Maude pedalling up to the station as Angus entered, and . . . no. My imagination simply wasn't good enough to make me believe she would care two hoots whether that bowl was Ming, or one of Woolworth's seconds. Unless . . . revenge for past wrongs? Her father had not got on with old Mr. Tramwell. The swing travelled upwards and my mind went with it to the Grundys. Mother and son. Godfrey . . . Angus would despise him—feel greater anger towards him than the Tramwells. What if Angus had telephoned or met him, and said, "You can wave goodbye to your card-sharp operation? Those two elderly ladies have been sitting, or rather tripping, over a gold mine." Admittedly, Cheynwind oozed all the trappings of wealth, but for all I knew it was up to its roof in second mortgages.

Forget Ethelreda Grundy. She might be as loopy as a wire spring but Godfrey was a far better candidate. He had displayed the same kind of cunning in luring card players to Cloisters that had been used to lure Angus to Abbots Walk. Patience, Chantal had said, and anyone living with Ethelreda Grundy would have learned a great deal about patience.

My headache was quite gone. If I were right about the Chinese bowl, Hyacinth and Primrose would have had every reason to bless the day Angus entered their lives rather than viewing him with anger or fear. Relief surged as I scraped my feet along the floor, then . . . down to earth in a grinding halt.

They were only in the clear if he had dropped some hint of his suspicion. And I felt strongly that he had not, because, although Hyacinth had seemed very much as usual after Angus's visit, Primrose had grown increasingly distracted. More than distracted . . . troubled.

How horribly ironic if one of them . . . No, I wouldn't think along those lines. I was still prepared to face up to the truth—whatever it might be. I would ferret it out. But the sisters had taken me into their home. I had grown fond of them, I had adopted them. Impulsive? Not especially. Mum and Dad had made up their minds about taking me on in under five seconds. The Tramwells weren't the only gamblers. Mum and Dad were gamblers, too, of a different kind—and I was their daughter.

I slid off the swing. It was time to look at the Chinese bowl and confirm my belief that it was the focus of someone's greed. The house, dimly shadowed, was very still as I went down to the kitchen, to be confronted by Chantal coming in through the back door.

"Had a pleasant afternoon?" I asked with genuine goodwill. But for her having gone out and my starting dinner . . . blast! Minnie was sitting guard over the bowl. My hand inched forward in a fake pat and shot backwards. Glib thoughts of risking all for the cause were all very fine, but I wasn't prepared to risk three of my favourite fingers. I was saved—not by the bell but the cat. It appeared from under the table, hissed, and Minnie was off after it.

As I staggered up from my knees clutching my prize, Chantal slipped off her black cardigan and laid it over the back of a chair. Idly I tossed undevoured scraps in the rubbish bin and tilted the bowl over.

"Thank you for getting dinner started," she said.

"What have you been doing?" I asked automatically. The bottom of the bowl was stamped "Hong Kong." My brilliant theory blown to dust. Up close, this bowl wasn't as fine a sample of Oriental ware as the one in our china cabinet at home. The Tramwells were not as unobservant or Minnie as privileged as I had dreamt. And, if I had been thinking straight, I would have realized it was highly unlikely Angus had ever entered the kitchen or any room other than the sitting room. Oh, it was such a shame! If the bowl had been Ming, it would not only have helped solve Angus's murder but would have solved all the Tramwells' monetary problems.

Chantal was checking on the roast. "I stopped at the village school to talk to the headmaster, so he could warn the children to be careful walking to and from school. And I asked him if any of the boys was named Fred. I didn't think it was likely, as it is so old-fashioned, but I wanted to be sure."

"But I thought you understood that Bertie's friend is imaginary," I said. She must have spent her time doing something other than visit the school if she had only just returned.

A funny, persistent buzzing sound came from the hall. I had left the kitchen door open, but if the house had not been so silent I doubt that we would have realized the phone was ringing. Chantal dropped her oven cloth and brushed past me. "Butler, that has to be Butler." They're friends, I thought. Not just fellow employees.

Better perform some useful work, like basting the roast. I had just closed the oven door when Chantal returned.

"Was that Butler on the phone?"

She shook her head. "Godfrey Grundy for you. He wants you to go over to Cheynwind, to discuss something of the utmost importance. Probably nothing more than whether he should wear a black or purple bunny-wool jumper as a sign of mourning, but you would still be crackers to go."

"You're the one being silly. Come off it! If our boy Goldilocks wanted to murder me, wouldn't he have devised a way of meeting me secretly? The fly in the ointment is that, as Harry has the car, I will have to walk."

"Tessa, I wish you wouldn't go." She followed me to the back door. "I'm not only worried about Godfrey harming you; it's growing dark, and if you should meet anyone along the way—"

"Cross my heart, Grandma." I touched her arm briefly. "I won't talk to anyone I . . . know."

"At least take the bicycle from the garden shed. It's a modified penny-farthing but not difficult to ride."

"Sorry. I've vowed never to ride a bike again as long as I live."

As it happened I met no one on my half-hour walk to Cheynwind, and I wasn't nervous. I found that I felt better away from Cloisters. I must have needed fresh air. The evening was softly purple and the scent of approaching autumn in the air was rich and tangy—like fresh gingerbread. I was ready for crisp golden days, snuggling with a book by the fire. Whose fire? I knew the house in Devon could be my home for as long as I wished—but what if Dad and Vera's sister were romantically interested in each other? Weren't they entitled to some time alone together? How foolish I had been to think that life would go on in the old pattern forever.

If Dad married this Ruth, Harry and I would be bound to meet at family get-togethers, he with his dark and lovely wife, me . . . but it was all right. I had forgotten that I was going to become a nun.

I found myself turning in to the driveway at Cheynwind, and now the nerve endings throughout my body suddenly began to prickle. An all over case of pins and needles. I was mounting the massive front steps. What did Godfrey want with—from—me? I should have listened to Chantal. I dabbed a finger at the bell and retreated back down a step. If no one came immediately . . . but then I might never know what Godfrey wanted to say to me. I marched back up the steps and punched the bell again. The sound of miniature church bells floated back to me, and at the same time I heard a window being raised above me and a dash of water landed on my hair.

"Tessa, I am so sorry," exclaimed Mrs. Grundy. What was she doing? Watering the ivy? "Do excuse me. I was afraid that if I called out to catch your attention, Godfrey would hear. I'm his prisoner, you see."

"Prisoner?" I would run for help—stop a passing car.

She chortled. "In a manner of speaking. The dear boy asked me to stay up in my room during your visit so he could get you quite alone. The best of luck, dear, and I do hope I haven't dampened your spirits." The window glided down.

The church bells kept tolling and Godfrey opened the door. It was now or never if I wanted to make a break for it but, chin raised, I stepped into the hall. The marble chill deadened the air as, responding to Godfrey's chirrupping greeting, I followed him into the drawing room.

"I can't stay long," I informed his back. My fingers had got themself tangled into such knots I doubted I would ever get them apart. "With all that has happened at Cloisters things are rather at sixes and sevens."

Dorothy Cannell

"I'll say!" Godfrey giggled nastily. "Murder and intrigue. The blushing Primrose baring her petals and letting that busy bee Deasley nuzzle her stamen. But do not fret, my sweet, I will not detain you long. Yours very truly has an appointment to keep e're long."

Frigidly I accepted a seat on the edge of one of the daffodil chairs and refused a glass of sherry.

"A girl who likes to keep her wits about her. Delicious." Another giggle. Godfrey seated himself directly opposite, holding his rose-coloured glass delicately by its stem with thumb and index finger, the other fingers elevated—like fat white grubs. "Isn't it exquisite to be alone? Mumsie desperately wanted to share this intimate moment—interfering bitch that she is."

"Your mother appears utterly devoted to you." Why hadn't I taken a glass of sherry so I would have something to clutch?

"Passionately devoted. Especially," he snickered, "in regard to my trust fund. Your kittenish naïveté enchants, but do you seriously suppose I would spend one hour under the same roof as that obese woman with her frumpy clothes if she weren't the administrator of my money? That rat—my father—tied it all up until I reach his definition of the age of reason: fifty, or—and here is the only loophole—when I enter the blissful state of matrimony. But for my delightfully lucrative arrangement with the Tramwells, I would be a complete pauper."

"A slight exaggeration, surely?" My eyes strayed around that treasury of a room.

"Girls are so dense." Godfrey set his glass down in something perilously close to a slam. "I'm speaking of cash. Money in my pocket." His voice siphoned out in a hissing gush. "Get this through your adorable little head. My mother—loathsome word—has not increased my 'pocket money' since I was ten years old. I still get a pound a week for sweets at the corner shop, like some snotty-nosed tradesman's kid. Oh!" His fat hands caressed each other. "I could have killed her many times, but this is better!"

"My visit has been delightful," I said, "but I do have to be going." An absolute truth. I would head for the police station and inform Inspector Lewjack that Godfrey was a dangerous maniac. They would have to release Butler.

216

Down the Garden Path

"Go? You cannot go. I won't let you. Don't you understand, my dim but exquisite Tessa, that you are the answer to all my problems? The only way for me to be free of Mumsie and savour the bliss of bunging her into a home is for me to marry." He picked up a Dresden shepherdess and fondled her with his obscene white fingers. "And you, you, who outclass even this, are to be the lucky girl."

"Thank you so much, but I am completely ineligible for the honour you are bestowing upon me." If he touched me I would hit him with the poker . . . if I could reach it in time.

"How exciting; the girl is toying with me! Life with you will be constant titillation." His frizzy hair glowed like a devilish halo in the lamp light. "Oh, and think how dreamy, Mumsie has not the teensiest suspicion that I plan to be rid of her at last. Ecstasy! She has been trying to marry me off for years. Proof to one and all that her Goddy is a real man! And a daughter-in-law to dominate! Actually, Mumsie was the one who fell for you first. Absolutely terrified she was when Angus Hunt visited Cloisters. She thought he had gone to propose."

"How did she know about that visit?" I managed.

He flapped a hand at me. "We will have to do something about these tell-tale signs of your middle-class upbringing, won't we? The servants—they tell Mumsie every morsel of Flaxby Meade sublife. And, my flower, pray don't interrupt me again. Where was I? Ah, yes, Mumsie's passion for you. It should have been enough to make me loathe you, if you hadn't been so decorative. People think I'm gay, you know— as if anyone living with Mumsie could subscribe to such a merry-sounding group. Have no worries, my diamond, I have long yearned for the delights as well as the freedoms of marriage. The row I had with Mumsie last night was over you, you know. The bitch actually insisted on grovelling over to Cloisters and proposing to you on my behalf. Marriage, saith Mumsie, is a subject more comfortably broached woman to woman. You cannot conceive my ghastly humiliation when I realized she had escaped from the clutches of that Krumpet woman and was going to declare herself before breakfast. She's had these turns before—picking on women I wouldn't have brushed against in the street—but she has never got away from me or Nurse before. She thinks it's her heart I worry about, as if I wouldn't stop her wretched ticker like a watch if I could."

217

Curiosity won over revulsion. "So what makes you now think that I would—"

"Accept my hand, when I bend the knee?" Godfrey suited action to words. He knelt before me, his red-rimmed, almost lashless eyes on a level with mine. If I were to poke at those eyes with the toasting fork . . . "Oh, you will, my beloved; I now have no fear of being spurned. I am, you see, making you an offer you cannot refuse."

He rose, pounced across the room to a cabinet, and came back carrying a small fold of tissue paper.

A gentle but terrible rustling. I did not have to look to know what would be revealed. The murder weapon. But when I forced my gaze downwards I wasn't prepared for the rusty stains still coating the blade, or for its being a fish knife. A fish knife I recognized as the one that had lain on the open bureau shelf at Cloisters.

Now I understood the full horror of blackmail. No need for Godfrey to verbalize how incriminating this missing item of cutlery would be to the Tramwells.

17

How I yearned to throw Godfrey's proposal back in his teeth with the authentic Regency cry, *I would die rather than marry you!* But the ones who would die languishing deaths in prison were the Tramwells. Play for time. I told Godfrey his possession of the murder weapon, if it *was* the murder weapon, placed suspicion squarely where it belonged—on him. He bounced off the balls of his feet in glee. His fingerprints weren't on the knife. He had used his handkerchief when removing it from Minnie that morning in the garden. And Cheynwind had hiding places that made the priest hole at Cloisters resemble a toy cupboard.

"And, my beloved intended, supposing for the fun of it the Tramwells were innocent, but the murderer had wiped off his prints? You do see what a pickle the sisters are in? Pilchards and pickles, oh! it is all too delicious for words."

I wished Minnie had bitten him.

He gloated down at the knife surrounded by its frill of tissue. "See how sharp it is? What fun the murderer must have had, honing the blade! And what fun the press will have linking this crime to that long-ago duel. Mother England, bored with the coarseness of women's lib, frozen quiche, bossy computers, and punks, will positively thrill to the upper-crust drama of ancestral home, a body in fancy dress, and two elderly spinsters tottering into the Old Bailey in appalling hats."

Alas, alack. Godfrey made an excellent case—not against the Tramwells; I believed in their innocence more vigorously than ever—but for himself as my prospective bridegroom. I wanted to charge at him and yank out his hair. One strand would be enough, along with some fuzz from his angora jumper—Chantal could make me up a voodoo replica of him, and I would stick pins in his lemonade-coloured eyes.

"What did you do with the knife while the police were looking for it?"

Wrinkling his nose, Godfrey made a grotesque attempt at looking lofty. "Haven't you realized by now that I have a genius for psychology? Policemen are usually tall. And tall people suffer from lumbago—they don't like low places. My dimpled darling, I hid the knife inside the fuse box in the cupboard under the stairs. How convenient that Hy and Prim are such sentimentalists. Their father objected to a telephone disrupting the mood of outmodedness at Cloisters, and they won't move it from the cupboard. Another little eccentricity sure to delight the press. How about that sherry to celebrate?" Godfrey was reswaddling the knife. "So sorry I can't offer you any nibbles, but the servants are all out."

Mum's voice was as close as when I would call out for her in the night. "All that matters right now is getting away from this house, then talk to someone you can trust."

"I need time to think over your . . . flattering proposal."

"My flower, you can take all the time you desire—until tomorrow morning. And by the bye, don't worry that ours will be a marriage in name only. I am not impotent any more than I am gay. Neither am I marrying you entirely to get rid of Mumsie and my paws on my money. It's an ill wind . . . and, quite unexpectedly, some other financial irons have dropped into the fire."

Somehow I would save myself from this ghastly misalliance. On the road back to Cloisters I came to a telephone kiosk, hesitated, and entered it. Purely for the sake of the Tramwells I would phone Harry. If he should suffer anguished remorse at the thought of my being laid upon the sacrificial altar, I couldn't help that. One ring, two, three . . . No reply. He had failed me again. I dialed the operator and got Maude's number. If she were home I would go to her cottage and tell her everything. Someone rapped on the glass. I hung up and went outside. A man stepped around me, lifting his hat. Reverend Snapper. The light thrown by the street lamp was poor and he did not recognize me. Or he pretended he didn't.

Bleak hopelessness was my escort the rest of the way back

to Cloisters. As I entered the grounds Hyacinth appeared out of the shadows. She apparently thought I had only been out for a walk. All she asked me was whether I had seen Primrose. She had told Chantal she was going for a stroll, but Primrose never walked at night, being deathly afraid of stepping on and injuring any mice that might be nocturnally traversing the lawn. Butler was still not back, and now Primrose was missing.

"This is all my doing." Hyacinth was working her hands together. "My reaction to Primrose's spending the night with Clyde was not as much outrage as sibling rivalry. I couldn't stand the idea of her knowing something I didn't. And now Prim has done something foolish, before I can beg her forgiveness for my immature churlishness."

"Primrose won't have done anything foolish." Putting my arm around Hyacinth I guided her back to the house. That remark of hers had certainly implied that, up until now, both sisters had been virginal.

"Nonsense. The ability to make incredible fools of ourselves is what sets humanity apart from the animals." We stepped into the sitting room through the French windows. "Tessa, one thing I do want you to believe is that, although Primrose and I are not without our faults, we are not . . ."

"Murderers? I know you are not."

"Naturally. That goes without saying. What I am saying is that we are not cheats. Neither of us would dream of fixing the deck or taking a peek at someone else's hand. Our form of—collaboration—takes acute observation, quick thinking, and an aptitude for making others less . . . aware." Hyacinth remained at the window. "We know, don't we, that the murderer must be skilled in those traits himself?"

"If he is to succeed."

She moved the curtain back an inch, staring into the dark garden. "I have talked to Chantal and agree with her that the police do not have the best qualifications for solving this crime. Inspector Lewjack strikes me as an able man, but the old saying, it takes a thief to catch a thief, is very sound."

I lifted the crystal decanter from the top of the lacquered cabinet and poured us both a glass of port. The thought of sherry made me shudder. "Don't you think it biased, expecting Butler to . . ."

"I wasn't thinking only of Butler. The word 'thief' is used

loosely. Within this house we have a wide range of unorthodox talents. Butler's snooping expertise, Primrose's and my gifts, already stated, Chantal's mystic vision, and your . . ."

"My credentials as a confidence trickster?" I handed her a glass and replaced the stopper in the decanter. "They don't seem too impressive to me."

"My child, you must not be so harsh. Your performance since coming to Cloisters has been first-rate. Harry's intervention does not diminish your talents as an actress. That wistful charm of yours will certainly have its uses. The villain has to be brought centre stage for the unmasking."

This conversation was taking my mind off Godfrey. I joined Hyacinth at the window. "Maybe I am being thick, but doesn't your premise create its own problems? If we can enter the mind of the murderer—because it takes a wily bird to know one—the same is true in reverse. And much as I hate saying this, we can't be positive that we don't have a Judas among us, nodding agreement, putting in his tuppeny-worth, waiting to stab us in the back." I almost said with a fish knife, and the dark horror of Godfrey squeezed again.

"Ah, my dear! That is where faith comes in."

As Fergy would say: "Vicar's salve for hopeless cases." Night was swooping down upon the house like a vast black crow. No sign of Primrose, no sound of her feet mounting the verandah steps. Hyacinth, saying she would go out and look for her again, asked me to delay the roast. By now it would be shrivelled to nothing. This whole day had been one of waiting. Waiting for the police. Waiting to be interrogated. Waiting to find out what Godfrey had to say. Waiting for Butler's return. And now, waiting for Primrose.

As I entered the hall, Chantal emerged from the cupboard under the stairs, holding out the phone.

"Godfrey Grundy."

Ignoring the questioning of her dark eyes, I doubled over and, fighting nausea, followed the cord into darkness. This was what prison would be like—a cramped black hole. The sisters would never survive. I raised the receiver to my ear.

That terrifying, simpering whisper. "Have you decided to make me the happiest man alive? My sweet, impatience is utter anguish. When I envision marriage with you I get delicious tingles up and down my spine, and—would it be naughty

o say—in other parts of my anatomy, too. You are so exqui-
itely right for the drawing room. Or you will be, when I redo
'ou in softer, more muted shades—tone down your hair and
'ersuade you to glide rather than pounce. Knickers! There
;oes the doorbell. Where are those wretched servants? Both-
'ration, I'd forgotten. Well, nighty-night, my treasure. I will
ing you again in the morning. Must trip along now." Clunk.

In relief at escaping his voice I stood up and cracked my
\ead. But pain in this instance was therapeutic. I returned to
ny senses. I wasn't a mesmerized rabbit. At the moment I
:ould not see an escape from Godfrey's trap, but I would not
un whimpering in circles.

Voices out in the hall. Butler! And Harry—the childish
irge to run to him had to be fought back, although telling him
about Godfrey would perhaps be the responsible, mature thing
o do. As I crawled out into the bright light of the hall, he was
alking to Chantal, and I heard Godfrey's name mentioned.

"How are you, Tess? Anything much been happening?"
Harry dug the fingers of his right hand through his chestnut
\air and looked at me intently. How long until I could fully
appreciate the peaceful emptiness of not loving him?

"No more murders, if that is what you mean."

"I had just got back into the car after posting the letter
o your father when I spotted Butler walking from the village
ind brought him up. The poor bloke's had a muck-raking time
of it, but the police couldn't hold him. When he left, they had
ust brought a chap named Whitby-Brown in for questioning.
3ut he doesn't sound too promising. Claimed he was in a minor
notor accident and at the time of the murder was sitting in
utpatients'. Butler's gone in to the sitting room to announce
\is return. Was that the police on the phone?"

Chantal stood watching us.

"No, it was—" I hesitated and saw Hyacinth coming towards us with Minnie bounding at her heels.

"My dears, Primrose has returned. Dinner will be served
mmediately, and then we will get down to business."

Harry was graciously offered a share in the now anorexic
oast, but he just as graciously refused, saying he had already
'aten. The meal was self-serve owing to protocol having been
abolished. Chantal and Butler joined us. Conversation, mainly
a matter of "pass the gravy," "more peas, please," and between

Dorothy Cannell

Harry and me, silence was absolute. But Hyacinth and Primrose were reconciled. They were once more a team. Butler, despite his extended visit at the police station, was his old self—almost. Behind the immobile, featureless face I sensed excitement. The ticking of his wits.

"Time's a-wasting," said Primrose with the slightest quiver in her voice. We all looked at the clock on the mantel. Nine-thirty. Rolling up her serviette, she replaced it in the silver ring by her plate. "And I have already wasted enough precious time today by behaving very childishly. Disappearing like that, causing Hyacinth so much anxiety. I am horribly ashamed. But if you can all understand, I felt I had to be alone to think. About repentance, primarily. My mind kept flitting back to poor dear Father and what he . . . might say to me now. And suddenly I felt extremely vexed. Was the murderer suffering even one shred of guilt while I agonized over my sins? Not a scrap, I'm sure. Dressing up poor Mr. Hunt like a joke indicates to me a smugness incapable of remorse. But I am wasting more time. Shall we have coffee in the sitting room? If instant will suit, I'm willing to make it myself as part of my penance."

"But I am not doing penance, and you never boil the water, Prim," retorted Hyacinth. Chairs scraped and we all rose. Butler moved soundlessly out to make the coffee.

A memory nudged the back of my mind when Primrose spoke of Mr. Hunt being dressed up like a joke . . . but it was gone before I could snag hold of it. Another intrusion was the wind. Heard as a faint hum while we dined, it now gathered momentum until its force shook the house, rattling windows and shuddering down the sitting-room chimney. Entering that room, Hyacinth drew the curtains more tightly closed. But a draught kept them billowing out. The lights flickered and dimmed. As Primrose reached into a drawer for candles, I thought of those old black-and-white films: Dracula's latest victim lying in her coffin, a spray of lilies covering her breast. The only living inhabitant of the House of Menace an ancient housekeeper with a pet rat tucked in her apron pocket. Outside, the Visitor approaching, his black cloak battling the wind, rain streaming off his low-brimmed hat.

The lights went out completely and I let out a silly screech, drowned by the harsh rattle of rain against the windows. What was that? Someone at the door? The living or the dead? Angus

224

coming back to warn us . . . ? Harry's hand found mine, sending a warm comfort up my arm and through my body until the blaze of Primrose's candles brought the room back to wavering light.

"A pole must be down," she said. "Who would believe such weather after so mild and balmy a day?"

"You okay, Tessa?" Harry's voice was pleasant, concerned; he might have been addressing Minerva after treading on her tail. He released my hand and I felt completely alone. Trust Minnie to rise from her blanket and release a curdling yowl.

"I am sure I heard someone at the front door a moment ago," I said.

"Really?" Primrose looked at Minnie. "Usually our friend here would be halfway down the hall at the first sound of footsteps on the garden path. Oh, I do hope she is not going to suffer serious psychological damage as a result of witnessing the *m-u-r-d-e-r*."

Butler arrived with the coffee, followed by Maude and Bertie, each carrying a small overnight bag.

"What a way to greet guests." Primrose pattered forward. "All the lights out! Inexcusable of us, Butler, not to have sent a candle out to you."

"Not at h'all, madame. My father would have disowned any of his children that could not see in the dark."

"Ooh, an' it were fun coming down the 'all, like playing blind man's bluff." Bertie was grinning at Primrose.

Maude looked apologetic, strained, and plain tired out. "Please excuse us taking up your kind offer at such a belated hour, but Florence Smith may go into labour any time now and I was afraid that should I ask anyone in the village to have Bertie, they might get to worrying about their own children."

Where would Maude and Bertie sleep? Had Hyacinth and Primrose been too preoccupied to think that one out?

"I think," said Maude, "I will take Bertie up at once if you don't mind. Get him settled and turn in myself. If you will tell me which room . . ."

"Could they share the nursery with me? I would like company tonight, and the extra beds are all made up." I waited rather breathlessly for the answer. This was my chance to talk to Maude.

The sisters beamed approval. Maude said "Splendid," refused the offer of a hot drink, and thanked Chantal for offering to act as escort upstairs.

When Chantal returned she set her candle down and joined the rest of us huddled around the card table. Butler poured coffee as Hyacinth called the meeting to order. She explained her theory that the crime could best be solved from within, and suggested that we go around the table, each presenting our ideas and disclosing anything that had struck us as odd or inconsistent.

So much had struck me as odd since coming to Cloisters. I had listened and watched, but did I have the ability to recognize what might be important concerning the murder? I let my mind float. And as when I had written down what I knew of Violet it was frightening how fast those flashes of memory came. Angus's missing watch, Primrose's alibi, Minnie drugged in the attic, Godfrey holding that enormous art book, Godfrey—I couldn't, wouldn't think about him now. Hyacinth suggested that Chantal begin the proceedings. She was sitting beside me, and in the candlelight her skin had a wonderful translucence. But I felt if I touched it I would find it ice cold. Did she too sense an unseen presence among us—a visitant from the long dead past who wanted the Tramwell family curse ended at last.

"Looking into the human mind is rather like looking into the crystal," Chantal said. "You face the possibility of seeing what you don't wish to see." Her hands moved in front of her, forming an invisible globe. She turned to me. "When I told you I saw death and an 'H' in your hand, the presentiment may have sprung from some psychic gift I possess. The 'H' would fit Mr. Hunt, but isn't it as likely that I was reading a different kind of sign? The sign of mounting tension and danger, governing the lives of those connected with this house? Those card games worried me; and as the apparently more forceful of the two sisters"—she looked at Hyacinth—"perhaps I did feel subliminally that you might be the one to move into danger. But the one I consciously feared for was Harry. I was afraid of the 'highwayman' story leaking out, and I was concerned about the game he was playing with Tessa."

Yesterday I would have stormed at her, but now . . . now I was caught up in wondering what it was she feared, but had not revealed. How on earth did she know so much?

"I don't have any answers." Chantal's hands moved up her arms as if she were trying to keep warm. "Only questions."

Harry was looking across at her with something deeper than admiration. He was fond of her. More than fond. And hadn't he said liking was the most important aspect of any relationship? "What questions, Chantal?"

She sat with that curious stillness that intensified her dark beauty. "Will there be another victim? And if so, who will it be?"

Her words were the more chilling for being spoken so calmly.

"A dreadful possibility, but are you sure that when you looked into the crystal this morning you saw no glimpse of the murderer's face?" Hyacinth's voice was matter-of-fact but the earrings were going round and round.

"I saw my own face," said Chantal.

Rain hurled against the windows, but silence blanketed the room. "My dear, you don't mean that," exclaimed Primrose.

Harry shifted in his chair. "Of course she doesn't; the idea of Chantal harming anyone is utterly preposterous."

"You have no need to assure me of that," replied Primrose with quiet dignity. "What I wondered was whether Chantal might be afraid for her own safety."

As Harry subsided back in his chair Hyacinth turned to me. "Your turn, Tessa." Her brief smile, pale lips outlined in orange, offered encouragement, but I could not see her eyes. Her head was slightly bent, her lids more hooded than ever in the shifting pale light.

"Okay." I clenched my fists between my knees. "My questions may all sound rather trivial, but here goes. Why was Mr. Hunt not found wearing a hat? Who locked me in the priest hole? Why is Butler wearing Chantal's shoes? Why—" Stupid as it might be I could not bring myself to ask who had taken my watch and returned it, then taken my charm bracelet and kept it. Fergy would have considered such a question wickedly rude, whatever the circumstances.

"Why what?" asked Harry. "Do go on, Tess." His tone was so different from the one he had used to Chantal that I couldn't help myself—the words just fell out of my mouth.

"Why did you say that Angus talked about his aunts in

Dundee, when he didn't?" I had asked that question before. So why was I raising it again, bringing it out into the open? Because I needed an answer, or because I needed to hurt him?

"You have decided to place me at the top of your suspects list, have you?" He leaned back in his chair, lips curving in a slight smile. Was the pain in his eyes a reflection of my own?

"If you two are going to be at each other's throat we'll get nowhere." Hyacinth's earrings knocked vigorously against her long sallow neck. "Tessa, when were you incarcerated in the priest hole?"

"Tuesday morning." My mouth quivered childishly and I kept my eyes on the table.

"Then I cannot see any connection to Mr. Hunt. Most unpleasant for you, but that wretched door does stick, and we have been afraid of such accidents, haven't we, Prim?" said Hyacinth.

"Indeed we have!" responded Primrose.

I waited. Wasn't anyone going to ask why I had been snooping inside the priest hole? The omission should have been comforting, but wasn't. I felt more guilty than ever. Not up to asking how that door could have been closed on me accidentally when I had left it open.

"As for Butler's shoes, I am sure he can explain them— when we get to him." Hyacinth sounded as though she were chairing a board meeting where the rules of protocol had to be rigidly followed. "What else did you mention, Tessa? Oh yes . . . the absence of a watch on Mr. Hunt's person. Does anyone have any ideas on that?"

A flicker of something—fear, interest—passed behind Butler's eyes and was gone. The other faces were blank. I was about to tell them about Angus's passion for pocket watches when Hyacinth turned to Harry.

"I think you should go next as I am acting as a sort of monitor, unless you feel you are not in a position to contribute."

Harry leaned forward, elbow on the table, chin resting on his thumb. "I'm hung up on motive," he said. "If we disallow the contingency that Chantal is mad as all Bedlam, wreaking vengence upon a house which long ago oppressed her people." His smile reached out to her like a comforting hand. My pain mingled with surprise when she flinched. "Or," he continued, "or that Hunt was a threatening figure rising up out of Butler's past—a long-ago robbery at The Heritage perhaps, a scenario into which, at a pinch, Clyde Deasley or Godfrey Grundy might also fit. One sells antiques and the other . . ."

"We know. Cheynwind looks more like a museum than The Heritage, but if you are going that route you also have to include me. I worked there. Angus could have discovered me here and accused me of ripping off master—pieces." I lifted my chin and waited for him to disclaim.

"Disallowing all those contingencies," Harry continued, "we are left looking at the obvious motive—Mr. Hunt's desire to see the card games stopped. But that doesn't make sense."

Butler sat so still he might have been dead. The rest of us leaned closer to the warmth of the candlelight.

Harry's eyes narrowed into slits. "Anyone murdering Mr. Hunt to ensure the continuation of those lucrative card games would hardly have performed the deed on his own doorstep. As matters now stand, the police are bound to check into the set-up at Cheynwind. Word will leak out, and"—he turned from one sister to the other—"dear relatives, your fiendish poker days will be as effectively axed as if Mr. Hunt had lived to blab to prospective victims about your methods. And, as for anyone wishing the games stopped, they had no need to murder Hunt; so I have to conclude that the games are only incidental."

"Dear boy, you are absolutely right." An excited pink flush warmed her cheeks and Primrose clenched her hands. "So much more sensible for Hyacinth or myself, if we could be so wicked, to have followed Mr. Hunt to London and arranged a tidy little accident." The flush faded. "But will the police credit us with such good sense, or will they think that one or both of us went berserk and wanted to get the job done willynilly?"

"H'excuse me, madame." Butler coughed with acute deference. "But what the police think and what they can prove are two different kind of vege—or I wouldn't be here right now. What they don't have—yet—is the murder weapon."

But they would if I didn't play my cards according to Godfrey's rules. Feeling Harry's eyes on me I stopped biting a nail and forced my hands down into my lap.

Pursing her crayoned lips, Hyacinth said, "If that Inspector Lewjack is as bright as he looks, he will realize there is nothing willy-nilly about this crime. Impetuous, but certainly not staged in a bustle. Too many frills."

That word staged. If the murderer knew of Harry's and my performance, could he—or she—be trying to throw suspicion on one of us? Inspector Lewjack had warned me to be careful that I not end up another victim, but I had never thought I might have to tread carefully lest I find myself a scapegoat. And Harry, his position as the heir was even more volatile. . . .

Hyacinth's eyes travelled around the table. "Don't all look so glum. The murderer emerges as a creature of somewhat vulgar imagination who wanted Mr. Hunt's life terminated as well as the termination of the Tramwell family. The only good thing we know is that he is an early riser, which leads to another question. How did X lure Mr. Hunt into the walk at the crack of dawn?"

I opened my mouth but Primrose rushed in with, "Excuse my interrupting, dear." Her eyes sparkled like jewelled raindrops in the candlelight. "But isn't that question an offshoot of another? Where and with whom did Mr. Hunt spend last night?" A brief flare of lightning pierced the room, and in the harsh brilliance I saw Butler's face. A face that was real for the first time, blazing with malevolent joy. I thought he would speak, but Primrose still had the floor; the light in the room receded to its pale golden haze, and Butler's face was expressionless once more.

"To know where Mr. Hunt spent last night would, I think, be to know all." Primrose fussed with her cuffs. "Because we do know that he must have spent last night in Flaxby Meade or somewhere close by. This morning I discreetly asked that Inspector Coatrack if he knew what form of transportation Mr. Hunt had used; and he told me that a return railway ticket had been found on the body. Now we are all aware, aren't we, that the first morning train from London does not arrive until 10:42? Yes, Hyacinth dear, I see you are bursting to suggest he may have stayed at the pub. But only last week Mrs. Burrows informed me they were in the midst of redecorating and positively would *not* be taking any overnight guests until the middle of October. Yes, dear, there is no gainsaying she may have made an exception, but . . ."

"Why don't I go and telephone the pub?" Harry suggested.

"H'excuse me, sir." Butler rose to his feet. "Before you leave, H' I think H' I must state that I believe myself apprised of Mr. Hunt's whereabouts last night. But for my being somewhat distressed by my concern for the Misses Tramwell, I would have realized sooner who it was I saw." His voice and various excited exclamations were temporarily drowned by a shuddering boom of thunder which set the overhead light rocking crazily back and forth. The French windows rattled wildly, and an icy gust set the candle flames flickering like devils' tongues. Instinctively I gripped hold of Chantal's hand. The earthquake noises and vibrations receded to a dull throb, but I still shivered violently. Butler knew, or believed he knew, the identity of the murderer. Was I ready to hear the name? Butler was about to speak when he was interrupted again, this time by the doorbell. It was Chantal's turn to reach for my hand. Something more ominous than thunder sounded in that urgent pealing.

"What a time for anyone to come calling; why, it's gone eleven." Hyacinth was looking at the mantel clock illuminated by two candles. Harry brushed past me on his way to the door.

"Dear heaven, I hope he looks out the hall window before letting anyone in," Primrose cried, as though Harry were a child who might be snatched out into the night never to be seen again. But the phantom of the doorbell proved to be only Constable Watt. Only? Something about his measured stride told me that there had been a new development in the case. Even more alarming, he was holding his helmet like a flag at half-mast over his stomach, one finger again tapping out his rendition of "Rock of Ages."

"Forgive the uncivil hour, but I come here in the painful pursuit of my duty." Rising, we faced him in a tight-knit group.

He had come to take one of us away. But far from experiencing any desire to succumb to the vapours, fury flowed through me at the sight of his pleased face made redder by candlelight. Stepping outside the protection of the group, I glared up at him. "I won't let you take anyone away and lock them up. We had the crime almost solved when you came barging in."

"Be quiet, Tessa." Harry moved to my side and gripped my arm.

"That's all right, sir. I won't book the little lady for contempt, seeing as how this here murder business is hard on women. Don't seem able to stomach it like us men—in the general way of things, that is. There's one what's took to it like a duck to water." He cleared his throat. "It is me solemn and unpleasant duty to inform all here present that Mr. Godfrey Grundy has been foully murdered. And his poor old mum tooken in to custody for doing him in and Mr. Angus Hunt afore."

Godfrey killed! And by his mother! No! But if a lowly constable felt free to refer to the lady of the manor as a "poor old mum," her case was desperate indeed. I was clinging to Harry, afraid if I let go I would fall. Constable Watt grew puffy with importance as the others milled around him.

"Surely there is some mistake," cried Primrose.

"The making of mistakes is not a police hobby, madam. We've had our suspicions regarding the lady for some time—from late afternoon, to be exact. Enquiries in the village brung out certain suggestions that the old girl has, on occasion, put poisonous substances in people's bevs at the local café. The proprietor had been hesitant to kick up a dust, but he has now stated for the record that whenever Mrs. Grundy come in, someone was took bad."

Now I would have gone down if Harry had not twined an arm more tightly around me. The coachman—the one who was taken ill on my first trip to Flaxby Meade! He had been sitting opposite a white-haired old lady. Hadn't Harry joked when I told him that story, suggesting that the woman might have slipped arsenic in the coachman's tea? And hadn't I felt on meeting Mrs. Grundy that I had seen her somewhere before? Why had she pulled such stunts? And how often? Reverend Snapper . . . she had put some of her "glucose" in his coffee minutes before he staggered from the room. But he had lived, as had, I presumed, the coachman.

"Why did she kill Mr. Hunt?" asked Chantal. Her voice conveyed shock, disbelief, and could it be . . . hope?

"Motive? The likes of that one don't bother with motives. Completely barmy she is. Said so for years has my missus. Went all to pieces, did Mrs. G., when Inspector Lewjack and

I went up to the Hall to inform her that her son's body had been found stabbed and stuffed into one of the drains. The butler was the one what summoned us. Very distraught he was. Devoted to his master; meaning he must be a pretty 'queer' customer, if you get me, sir." Constable Watt winked man to man at Harry. "Wept, he did and all, to think he had bin away from the house, along with the other servants, to-night. I ask you! If he had any sense he'd be laughing, wouldn't he, at having an alibi?"

I drew away from Harry, staring into Constable Watt's fat red face.

"It was the butler," he continued, "what took us up to that wicked laboratory where Mrs. G. concocted the stuff she put in the bevs." Probing into his pocket, Constable Watt drew out his notebook, flexing his lips before opening it up and reading out one word: "Phenolphthalein." He flipped the book shut. "Admitted to making the stuff, she did; said lots of kids hear about it in chemistry class. The old girl said the phe-nowhatsit wouldn't kill no one—just send 'em running to the toilet—pardon me, ladies—in a horrible hurry. Nothing more'n a joke, said she. Told us she'd always been partial to practical jokes. 'Struth, I says to the inspector, this joke's on her. She'll get life and rightly so. Doing in of her own son to keep him from blowing the whistle on her! Almost makes me ashamed of being Flaxby Meade born and bred, it do!"

That book, *A Thousand and One Practical Jokes*, the one I had picked up and tried to read at Cheynwind! Now I understood why the idea that the murderer had made a macabre joke of Angus in dressing him up in the monk's robe had not only repulsed but niggled at me.

Everything neatly solved. It would have been hypocritical to pretend any regret that Godfrey was gone. He had been a reptilian creature and would have made a shocking husband. Conversation flowed around me but I could not escape to the security it offered. My thoughts kept circling around Godfrey's proposal. The certainty grew that the charges against Mrs. Grundy were nonsense. Yes, she was mad. I could even believe that she might have murdered Angus, poor dear Angus, be-cause she imagined that he was keen on me and therefore a blight on Godfrey's hopes, but didn't each brand of madness follow a certain pattern? One of the most crucial aspects of

Mrs. Grundy's wackiness was her obsession with getting Godfrey married and, with my arrival at Cheynwind that evening, she must have felt that her goal was within reach. If he had attempted blackmail, wouldn't she have smacked his bottom and sent him to his room rather than killing him and stuffing him down a drain in a re-enactment of a murder way back in the annals of the Grundy family? She had spoken with immense pride of that murder but even so . . .

I must protest Mrs. Grundy's innocence even though, in doing so, I would have to own up to the nature of my conversation with Godfrey this evening. Where would that place me as a suspect? Nowhere . . . because I had an alibi. Chantal—*she* had answered the phone when he called. *Both times!* My heartbeat slowed. If Godfrey had never previously performed a decent deed in his warped life, he had performed one tonight when he made that second call. My mind played over the chills it had inspired and the relief when he had hung up to go to answer the door and admit the unknown visitor with whom he had an appointment. Rain lashed the windows and the wind blurred Primrose's rambling enquiries concerning poor Ethelreda's present mental state.

Constable Watt was folding up his notebook with official deliberation. Into his pocket it went and on went his helmet. I would have to speak, explain how certain I was that Mrs. Grundy . . .

"Well, we won't keep you, George," said Hyacinth. Butler raised a candle for the journey down the hall and in its hazy glare I saw Chantal's face. The black eyes looked blind. She lifted a hand with infinite slowness to one cheek.

"Yes, best be pushing off." Constable Watt's chest expanded. "Have to notify Nurse Krumpet that her boy's safe now, and then it's back to the station for more paperwork."

"Nurse Krumpet and Bertie are staying here tonight, and we will certainly tell her the good news. Well for her it is good . . ." Primrose faltered.

"I suppose I should speak to her myself, but I really must be off. One of the young nippers in the village—name of Ricky—was knocked off his bicycle this evening by a hit and run. Lucky to be alive, fractured skull and a broken leg, but . . ."

"These maniac drivers should be locked up." That was

Hyacinth. I was picturing that child lying broken in the road. Chantal must have seen the same image. Her hand dropped from her face, and I had never seen such glistening pallor.

"My fault," she cried. "My fault, all my fault. I was so afraid that he would try something like this, but at the school they said that there was no child named Fred."

18

Constable Watt naturally enough thought he had broken the hit-and-run case. Out flew the notebook, despite Primrose's protestations that it was apparent Chantal was rambling and that everyone knew gypsies tended to be vastly dramatic.

Harry put an end to Constable Watt's hopes by informing him that he had taken the Tramwell car that afternoon and not returned with it until evening, since which time Chantal had never left the house.

Upon the constable's departure we instinctively regrouped around the table. Several of the candles had burned low and new ones had to be fetched by Butler. Outside, the wind assumed an almost human wailing. And during the brief interludes when it did quiet down, the hush became menacing, as if the night, too, held its breath—waiting for what Chantal would say. Fred. What had she meant about being afraid for him? The child did not exist, except as part of Bertie; and Bertie was safe upstairs. It was that other child who had been hurt.

"You can wait no longer, Chantal." Primrose spoke in a sadly pensive voice. "Whatever my many failings, I am not a coward. I was raised to face what needs must." So she did not believe any more than I did that wacky Mrs. Grundy was the murderer. Her suddenly fragile face turned towards Hyacinth and they clasped hands.

Chantal sat motionless. "I have betrayed you, but that wasn't my intent on coming to Cloisters. I had no thoughts of revenging old wrongs then, but he—he—came with his thirst for murder, and . . ."

Swaying forward, Primrose gripped the table edge. "Don't—don't say you were in this with him?"

Harry uttered an exclamation of protest, rising out of his chair, and Butler peered over steepled fingers as I cried, "Chantal—who is this man?" She couldn't mean Harry. If she did, I would want to die.

"His name is Egrinon Snapper."

"The Reverend Snapper!" Hyacinth had been chafing Primrose's hands, but she now sat rigid; stunned like the rest of us.

"He claims to be a clergyman, but I suspect that is a fiction." Chantal looked around the table. "He was at Cheynwind the other night, prepared to fake an interest in cards because he wanted to learn more about their antique murder for the book he is writing. But it is Tessail's murder which most intrigued him, and no one from the village would provide him with any details. He talked to me one morning in the Ruins, and I . . . I agreed to try to uncover information for him. He particularly wanted the names of Tessail's murderers."

"But obviously you did not give him all the information he wanted or he wouldn't have continued lurking around Cloisters." I drew a deep breath. "And several times I have sensed someone in the garden." I looked at Harry. "Didn't you tell me that the night before last you glimpsed someone you took for a tramp in the Ruins?"

Chantal broke in. "I had arranged to meet Snapper there, to tell him that I had changed my mind. But first you, Harry, and then Tessa came, making a meeting impossible."

"My dear Chantal," Hyacinth interrupted, "I must tell you I am relieved that you did not meet such a man in the middle of the night and that you did think better of assisting him in dredging up past sins. Our Mrs. Mudd would undoubtedly feel compelled to resign as chairwoman of the Women's Institute if it were revealed that one of her ancestors was not only a murderer but a fishmonger; but why do you think Snapper responsible for the murders?"

"Because"—Chantal lifted a hand to her brow and swept back her hair; shadows lay in dark pools under her eyes—"he is obsessed with old murders, and Mr. Hunt's death was a costumed reproduction of Tessail's death, and . . ."

"And Godfrey went down the drain like his ancestor," I said. The urge to giggle was pure nerves.

Harry pushed up the sleeves of his sweater. "Chantal,

aren't you building a case against this man out of misplaced guilt? Your thinking about spilling the beans is not the same as spilling them, and a penchant for writing about murder is not the same as a penchant for committing murder."

"What if he is mad? What if he wanted to be revenged upon me and close-mouthed Flaxby Meade? But the most telling piece of evidence against him is that he didn't know that Fred was imaginary, and that boy Ricky has been struck down. I had such a fear when I looked into the crystal. This afternoon I tried to find Snapper and couldn't, then I went to the school and asked the headmaster if he had any pupils named Fred. He said no, not realizing (as I didn't) that Ricky is an abbreviation for Frederick. I think his grandparents now live in Florida, and he may have adopted that nickname when he went out to visit them. I don't know. All I do know is that the murderer must have thought 'Fred' needed removing, which leaves out everyone in this room since we all knew about—"

"I didn't know Fred was an imaginary friend," said Harry, "and I was out in the car this evening."

"Oh, don't be so silly," I snapped. "Someone else thought he was not imaginary, too—Clyde Deasley. Remember, he asked why the police weren't out looking for the other child." I had spoken in a burst of bravado, not daring to think of Harry driving that hearse through the night, but now I looked at Primrose's face. She couldn't think Mr. Deasley the murderer, could she? What about the alibi? It was the alibi that had made me think I must be wrong about Angus's watch . . . that Mr. Deasley could not be the one. But now I was seeing things differently. That alibi should have strengthened my suspicion of him. What gentleman would have exposed his lady love in public, without compelling reason? And what more compelling reason could there be than deflecting suspicion from himself?

"Oh, Primrose, I'm so sorry. It would be a lot easier on everyone except Chantal if the murderer could be Reverend Snapper. But you don't believe it, do you?"

She shook her head. "Dear me, I have been such a fool. Completely taken in; and now I suppose it will be thought that I was his conspirator in Mr. Hunt's death. I cannot expect the police to believe that had I concocted an alibi for myself, I would have provided equally for Hyacinth. That smoothongued traitor. My dears, when I lay on my bed this afternoon began to remember how drowsy I had felt this morning." She blushed. "And not for the reason you may suppose. I believe now that Clyde drugged me. I had a packet of herbal sleeping draught in my room, because I had given some to Minerva earlier so I could let Clyde in unnoticed. He must have put it in my sherry after we had . . . sat talking for a long time." Primrose was now fidgeting in her seat, hands fussing with her curls. "Dearest Hyacinth, the reason Clyde . . . Mr. Deasley was in my bedroom last night was not for immoral purposes, although perhaps you will consider the breach to which I must now confess even more onerous. I have broken my solemn promise to you. The promise that whatever else we might be forced to sell, I would never part with my share of Mother's jewellery. When the estimate for the repairs to the roof came yesterday (along with Violet's letter saying she was regrettably in no position to help financially), I was in despair. We cannot get through the winter without the roof being fixed, so I felt compelled to part with one or two brooches and rings without your knowledge. I spoke to Mr. Deasley when he was here and he later telephoned to tell me that he had a client who might be interested, but that he must have the pieces immediately. Never, never will I forgive myself for having unwittingly aided that duplicitous creature. I remember wishing that he would go so I could get to bed—and then his shaking me, telling me I had begun to nod off. Wicked, wicked man; I must have slept, under the influence, for as long as he needed. Dearest Hyacinth, how can I ever hope you will forgive me for what I have done to you and dear Minnie?"

As usual at the mention of her name Minnie lurched up off her blanket, barking hysterically.

Hyacinth coughed and her voice emerged unsteadily. "I am not angry with you, dear. On the contrary, I am extremely proud." She turned to me. "I feel you have something else to tell us, Tessa."

"It's about details," I said. "I think that Mr. Deasley got carried away with details. He shouldn't have taken the watch. He should have left it and admitted that Angus came to his shop and bought it, but I suppose he was afraid the police would make something out of that visit."

"How do you know Hunt bought his watch from Deasley?" asked Harry.

"Well, I don't for certain, but I remember Hyacinth or Primrose saying that Mr. Deasley specialized in timepieces, and as his is an antique shop, and Mr. Hunt never passed a small village antique shop without indulging in adding to his collection, I think I'm right."

"I think you h'are, miss." Butler's expression was almost jolly. "Ever since I met him, I have thought the gentleman in question a very nasty customer, fawning over my ladies like they was a couple of fancy pieces propping up a wall at the Palais."

"Now, Butler," said Hyacinth, "please get on with what you have to say."

He murmured an apology and looked at Harry. "You, sir, and the young lady, I dare say, do not know how I spend my h'evenings out, but I occupy myself in the perusement of h'architecture. Meaning I keep my hand in, professionally speaking."

His words sank in slowly. "You don't mean burglary?" I asked.

"In a manner of speaking." Butler adjusted his cuffs. "You see, miss, it's in my blood, and for all I've tried to put the past behind me since coming to Cloisters, there has been the occasional lapse. It's the thought of all those years of h'apprenticeship going to waste, my father always said he would rise from his grave if any of his h'offspring went straight. Fortunately, when I discussed the matter with them, the Misses Tramwell were most understanding."

"How nice," I said weakly.

"It were Miss Hyacinth what devised the plan. One night a week I go out and case a particular premises, setting up a job, so to speak. Often I return to the same premises a dozen times, checking on the comings and goings of the h'inhabitants, doing the rounds of the doors and winders. All merely practice, you understand, quite harmless . . ."

"Harmless? When someone pops up in bed and catches you leering at them through the window?" I said.

Harry cupped his chin in his hand, elbow on the table. "Last night were you casing Deasley's place?"

"Precisely, sir. In the general way he is home of an evening, so I hadn't previously had the pleasure of shinning up his ivy—very partial I am to ivy—but last night I passed him on the road to Cloisters and decided to indulge myself. Imagining myself stripping that place down to the last teacloth was an h'enormous pleasure, but when I shone my torch through one of the bedroom winders I saw a man seated in a chair, his back to me. As I looked he started to get up, and I slithered down that ivy at such a pace I lost one of my shoes."

"Didn't you think it odd at the time that Deasley would have gone out when he had a guest?" Harry asked.

"I imagined the man in the chair might have been a customer, interested in purchasing something from Cloisters, as that's where Deasley had looked to be going sir. I never thought of him again until the question was raised as to where Mr. Hunt, rest his soul, spent last night."

"You say you only saw the man from behind?" said Hyacinth.

"Yes, madame; but when he stood up, I saw that he was very large."

"I'm becoming convinced." Harry relit one of the candles that had blown out. "But we need a motive."

"Oh, I've got that all figured out." I shook back my hair and arched my neck to ease its growing stiffness. "It has to be something to do with antiques. The Heritage deals in more than pictures, and Mr. Hunt was highly knowledgeable about all kinds of valuable artifacts. My guess is that Angus suspected something at Cloisters was immensely valuable, and sensing in Mr. Deasley a kindred spirit—that shared interest in pocket watches, remember—confided in him."

"I wonder if that is why Hunt said 'tell them I'm sorry,'" said Harry. "He and Deasley chat in the shop; Deasley is all enthused at the Tramwells' possible good fortune; Hunt agrees to check out his suspicions; and, if the news is good, return to Flaxby Meade that evening. He accepts an invitation to spend the night with Deasley, arrives, and is somehow put off from calling at Cloisters at once."

"Deasley could easily have said they would be out," Chantal said, speaking for the first time since she had broken the news about her relationship with Egrinon Snapper.

"He must have invented some excuse for going out himself." I nibbled at a fingernail. "And then telephoned his house

241

in the early hours saying he was at Cloisters and would Angus please come immediately to Abbots Walk, because one of the sisters was threatening to hang herself from one of the elms."

Drawing herself up in outraged hauteur, Hyacinth snorted, "I am rather disappointed in Mr. Hunt, if such is the case, for believing such twaddle. Neither Prim nor I would make so rude a spectacle of ourselves in a public place."

Harry turned to Chantal. "You talked about a game of patience. I wonder . . . I wonder if Deasley already knew that there was this valuable 'whatever' in the house. That would account for the frequency of his visits. A man biding his time until he could get his claws on the grand prize."

"He certainly paid us very fairly—even handsomely—for all the furniture, silver, and books he bought from us." Hyacinth's eyes gleamed like jet under the hooded lids. "When it comes to money, Primrose and I do have our heads screwed on right. We did a deal of checking as to market values before letting Mr. Deasley handle our sales."

"As he must have guessed you would—at first. But have you been as cautious lately? Patience would seem a pretty sound investment. Would you have disbelieved him at this time if he had told you a certain item was worth very little?" asked Chantal.

"Probably not," sighed Primrose, eyes misting as she dabbed at them with her handkerchief. "Particularly if it were something that we would prefer to let go over something else. Having always lived among old things, we don't have the *nouveau-riche* appreciation of antiques, whereas Clyde craves history in his hands. To think! Even when it came to murder he could not resist putting on a pageant."

"Especially when doing so focussed attention on Cloisters until Mrs. Grundy became a handy scapegoat," I said.

"Godfrey murdered presumably because he guessed the culprit." Harry looked at me. "What did Godfrey have to say for himself when you went over to Cheynwind?"

"Oh, my dear . . . when did you go?" asked Primrose.

I told them everything, wondering as I did so if the police had found the fish knife and whether it still represented a danger to the Tramwells. From their faces I knew they were wondering the same, but Harry concentrated on something else.

"You say he mentioned the possibility of coming into un-expected wealth. That, coupled with his expecting a guest at a time when all the servants were off the premises, sounds like he was about to indulge in a spot of blackmail. Grundy guessed that Deasley was the murderer—but did he also know why Hunt was killed?"

The electric lights flared on, causing us all to blink rapidly. For about ten minutes we sat pondering what we could do to bring Mr. Deasley to justice. The small difficulty we faced in accomplishing this end was that we had absolutely no evidence and the police had batty Mrs. Grundy. Butler went out and made cocoa, and when this had been drunk it was agreed that we would all think better after a few hours of sleep. Harry offered to spend the night at Cloisters but the sisters grew quite flustered at the idea. They had no bed to offer him and would not hear of his sleeping on the sofa. Plausible. But I think the real reason they were so opposed to the idea was that they thought it unseemly for a single gentleman to sleep under the same roof as two young females. They need not have worried on my account, and I'm sure the only reason I was irritated by their antiquated attitude was that it was so utterly snobbish. (Butler no threat to virtue because he was a servant. Huh!)

Bidding Harry a cold goodnight in the hall I watched him walk out the front door without a pang. He was not the least necessary to my security. Maude was in the nursery, and if any danger threatened during the night we would manage very well. As I started up the stairs, Primrose handed me a brass poker. I saw that she was equipped with its twin, whilst Hyacinth wielded a toasting fork. Surely they didn't think that Deasley would . . . ? The baby alligator grinned down at me from his shelf on the landing. I no longer thought him adorable. His smile was very much like Mr. Deasley's. The urge to run back down those stairs, throw open the front door, and pelt after Harry receding in the hearse reared up inside me. But I had promised never to run after him, never beg him to shield me from the wicked world, never beg him to love me. But surprisingly the sisters kissed me goodnight, and I felt some-what comforted as I went down to the nursery. Maude was asleep when I went in—would it be selfish to wake her? I tiptoed up to her bed, reached out a hand and then drew it back. Tomorrow. Bertie was breathing in short gruff little snores in the bed nearest the window. The bright orange of his pyjamas clashed with his hair. Did he know anything about his origins? Did he care?

As I sat on my bed, kicking off my shoes and unbuttoning my blouse, Maude turned over, opened her eyes, and sat up. She had brushed out her hair, and I was embarrassed as if I had caught her naked. Long flowing locks did not fit the every-day woman. I stared at her, not knowing what to say, and yet not wanting this opportunity to pass without asking her about my origins.

Moving over slightly, she patted the edge of her bed. She was wearing a pink flannel nightgown of the kind that Fergy favoured. "Come and sit here and tell me what has been hap-pening. Something must have occurred if you are only now coming to bed."

I told her about Godfrey's death and Mrs. Grundy's arrest, debated whether I should reveal our suspicions of Mr. Deasley, and decided that in fairness to her and Bertie someone must. She agreed with me that Mrs. Grundy would never have killed Godfrey under any circumstances but seemed dubious about Mr. Deasley's culpability.

"Aren't you all making rather a lot out of his interest in antiques and in Mr. Hunt's being in a similar field? And his having an overnight guest who may or may not have been Mr. Hunt? Should a man be condemned because he is a flatterer and a bore?"

Was she right? Were we rushing to convict Mr. Deasley because we were afraid to look too closely at other candidates? I explained to her about Fred and her response was that, to her mind, the attempt to eliminate him pointed to an outsider.

"Isn't it possible that one of the other card players the other night had a grudge against Mr. Hunt?"

Of course it was possible—anything was possible. Herr Wortter also had a grudge against Primrose. Had I been wickedly, dangerously arrogant in pointing the finger at Mr. Deasley? Where was Herr Wortter now? Did he, like Whitby-Brown, have an alibi for the time of Angus's murder? Frown-ing, I twined a curl around one finger and looked into Maude's blue eyes.

"You're wrong," I said. "I do have a reason for hoping the murderer isn't a local man, but . . ."

"What reason?"

Bertie stirred and we both watched until he burrowed back down into his pillow and the snores started again.

"I am afraid that one of the local men may be my father." I was clenching and unclenching my hands. "The Tramwells may not have told you about my history or why I came to Cloisters, and I know this is not a good time . . ."

"Tessa dear, they didn't have to tell me anything, I realized who you were almost immediately." She sat up straighter. "The likeness to your father is quite strong. A local man, yes but not Deasley; forget that fear." She studied my face. "And surely you didn't suspect Godfrey Grundy . . . no, no, my dear. Never in a thousand years."

"You must have delivered hundreds of babies"—my voice was barely a whisper—"but did you . . . do you see anything of the baby I was in me now?" Why couldn't I ask her the most important question of all?

She reached out and picked up my hands, gripping them tightly. "Tessa, before Violet took you that morning to leave at the vicarage, she stood in the doorway holding you up. 'The best and prettiest baby in the world,' she said. Dear Violet. I am glad she is happy; she deserved to be . . ."

I was numb, unable to think or feel. All the years of wondering, waiting . . .

A violent scratching at the door caused me to jerk away, and by the time I made it across the room Minnie was barking, small, puppyish, yelping barks. Exploding through the door she surged in a flying leap onto Maude's bed and then dived for my ankles. I tried to hush her but she became more excited, tugging at my skirt, urging me back towards the door.

"Maybe she didn't get fed," I said. And it was strangely comforting to know that in the midst of profound revelations life went on as usual. I was being given time to draw myself back together before asking Maude those many important questions. Any minute Bertie and the rest of the household would be awake. "I'll run down to the kitchen and drop a few biscuits in her bowl, won't take a jiff."

"I would come with you, but I don't want Bertie to wake

and find me gone." She was standing, the pink flannel night-gown clinging to her stocky form, the long hair making her look oddly pathetic.

"Count to a hundred and I will be back." Smiling over my shoulder I followed Minnie out into the hallway. Flipping a light switch I hurried towards the stairs. Minnie was already halfway down, still whining and yipping. What if hunger wasn't her problem? Suddenly I was frightened, terribly frightened. This house was so large. So many nooks and crannies where anyone could hide. How stupid of me to have forgotten the poker. I hesitated, ready to run back to the safety of the nursery. Then I heard a creak; a creak that was definitely a footstep behind me. Another and another, closing the gap. Run, Tessa. My hand left the bannister rail and I whirled down those curving slippery, wooden stairs. A voice called out from above, and I sped faster. Too fast—I was falling, my arms flailing out, searching for the rail.

It wasn't there, but I was no longer falling. Someone held me prisoner. A voice, low and shuddering, said, "Tessa, you could have broken your neck."

"Harry!" I clung to him. "He's coming . . . after me." I tried to pry loose, to point upwards in the direction of my pursuer, but I was too late. A blurred blackness descended on Harry's head . . . and then with a grunt he toppled over, to lie in a sprawled heap before sliding slowly down the remaining stairs.

"Cripes," came Bertie's gasp and I looked up to see Maude still holding the poker aloft.

Harry came round in under ten minutes, accepted Maude's apologies in gallant spirit, and explained that on leaving the house he had set the front door catch so he could return when everyone was in bed. If Minnie had not come charging up to announce his arrival, all would have been well. And if Maude had not decided to waken Bertie and follow me I would not have pelted down the stairs. But everyone had meant every-thing for the best, and the lesson learned was that excessive caution was more likely to be our undoing than anything else. I could see that Harry had a headache, but he insisted that the blow had been a glancing one and that he would feel fine in the morning. Part of me yearned to plump up the pillows on the sofa where he lay and adjust the cold compress on his forehead, but most of me was afraid to get too close to him.

Maude, Bertie, and I returned to the nursery and climbed into our little beds. Hunching the eiderdown up to my neck I hoped that the boy would fall asleep quickly so Maude and I could continue where we had left off. I wanted to know Violet . . . but I found that I was the one sinking into sleep. My last rational thought was that I still hadn't found out what Bertie had wanted to tell me. Monks came flying at me on gigantic bat wings, and I was running past a drainpipe that gushed water onto a sodden pile of clothes that grew into Godfrey. He was reading an illuminated manuscript marked: *Rare Priceless First Edition.* "That's my pretty boy." Mrs. Grundy came riding into view, dressed as a witch on a gigantic test tube. "All dressed up for his wedding, and doesn't Tessa look lovely?" Untrue. The Miss Haversham-type bride posing as me looked more ready for the coffin than the altar. Strike that thought! But it was too late. Mr. Deasley had his hands around my throat and a man wearing a name card saying Arthur Wilkinson—Violet's husband—was informing me that if I wanted cremation I would have to find myself another undertaker, but he would be delighted to tell Vi that he had met me.

At that I awoke, and for a moment I hoped that Angus's death was a nightmare, too. The view from the window did nothing to lift my spirits. The rain had slackened but it still trickled sullenly down the panes and the sky was a dirty grey. Looking across at the other two beds I saw that they were neatly made and that Bertie's pyjamas lay folded on top of the pillow. Reaching for my watch, I discovered that it was past eight o'clock. I was about to slither out of bed when a knock came at the door and the sisters entered. They were both fully dressed, Hyacinth in a purple-and-yellow paisley dress and Primrose in a navy skirt and faded blue twin set.

"We have to talk to you." They spoke in unison, voices lowered for fear, I guessed, that the walls might have ears, or that Mr. Deasley might be listening in the apple tree. Swiftly crossing the room, Primrose drew the curtains tight, and then sat down beside Hyacinth on the bed closest to me.

"Maude has left on a case and Harry—willful lad sneaking back here—has taken Bertie back home with him. The boy wanted to see the horses, and . . ." Hyacinth paused.

"I'm surprised that Maude would let Bertie go with him," I said. "After all, she doesn't know Harry." I drew the eider-down around my shoulders to try to get warm.

"True, dear; but she knew his grandfather. He used to come and visit at Cloisters quite often. A wonderful, rakish old gentleman, and Harry takes after him. Not a bit like his father, thank heavens—no one in Flaxby Meade could stand him. A nasty combination of conceit and simpering bashfulness. The only good thing I can say about him is that he was gen-uinely fond of Cloisters."

"Really!" I hugged the eiderdown closer.

"But never mind him. Maude knows Bertie will be all right with Harry. Primrose and I have not slept all night." From the black rings under all four eyes, I believed Hyacinth. The earrings moved slowly this morning.

"We have come up with an idea, but have said nothing to Harry or Maude." Primrose smoothed down the neatly darned sleeves of her cardigan. "The dear boy would think what we propose is dangerous, and perhaps it is, but Hyacinth and I feel a moral obligation to get Mr. Deasley."

Hyacinth looked at me. "The rogue wanted me to believe the worst concerning his night with my sister. He wanted to set us at each other's throat. But what he did *not* bargain for was the depth of our affection and what he *will* not bargain for is that we are capable of a ruthlessness equal to his own."

A finger strayed nervously to my mouth.

"I suppose it is un-Christian, but I rather think I will enjoy myself." Primrose's face flushed and the shadows under her eyes became less apparent. "We have been playing the same parts for so many years now—dithery old ladies—that a stretch in range will be a real challenge. And in such a good cause, too."

What was she talking about? I nibbled a fingernail while she explained. "We are going to take a leaf out of Godfrey's book. Blackmail. We—or rather you, dear Tessa—are going to lure Mr. Deasley to Cloisters. But don't worry, once he is in Hyacinth's and my clutches you will not even appear on the scene. We will take him down to the priest hole, where he cannot leave until we permit. He has always been eager to see our little hideaway. Dear me, yes, we will get him inside easily enough. Then! We tell him we have the evidence. We won't have to say what evidence, because a guilty man . . ."

I shook my head, causing the eiderdown to slip. "You're wrong. He will ask to see the evidence, and I think you should tell him that Godfrey gave me a sealed letter last night when I went to Cheynwind. It was to be opened in the event of his sudden death and . . . but never mind about that. Why do you want *me* to be the one to lure Mr. Deasley here?"

"Oh, my dear! Isn't that quite apparent?" Primrose shook her head in faint disappointment at my obtuseness. "What we need is to throw him off balance. Playing upon his vanity and his lust for a pretty face and figure may give us the advantage. And then, too, you worked for Mr. Hunt at that art gallery. He may suspect your educated eye of spotting what he's after. Ah yes—I see you understand. What we ask is that you write Mr. Deasley a flowery epistle on pretty writing paper, heavily laced with all the gushing ecstasies of a young girl in the throes of her first passion for an older man of the world. You will beg him to come over this afternoon while Hyacinth and I are shopping for wreaths, because you want to show him something of interest you have discovered at Cloisters. Dear Tessa, it will be quite easy; all you have to do is sound extremely silly and eager to show off for him."

"That's it in a nutshell," said Hyacinth. "With your charming talent for romancing you will do splendidly—and when the old dog comes trotting over, you can remain in this room and safely leave everything to Primrose and me."

"While you two tackle a man we believe has killed twice?" I protested. "I may be a bit thick first thing in the morning, but I am beginning to grasp why you didn't mention your brainstorm to Harry."

"My dear." Hyacinth squared her thin shoulders. "We are old; if something should go wrong, Primrose and I have led full lives."

Beaming bravely, Primrose patted my hand. "If you could—supposing the very worst—see that Harry gives us a good send-off. . . . Neither of us having experienced the thrill of a wedding, we have always promised ourselves rather splashy funerals." She sighed sentimentally. "Now, if you are willing, we will go downstairs and eat a nourishing breakfast.

We'll need all the energy we can muster. You can write that note and we will have Butler deliver it. No pouting, dear, please! Butler is also to be excluded from the final confrontation. We will tell him to go up to London, immediately after seeing Mr. Deasley, and see if he can discover with whom Mr. Hunt spoke after leaving Flaxby Meade, and if he discussed his mysterious find at Cloisters."

"And what of Chantal?" I felt the old jealousy rising.

"When Primrose, Mr. Deasley, and I enter the priest hole," said Hyacinth, "Chantal will station herself by the fireplace. If all goes well and he disintegrates in response to our threats to keep silent regarding the evidence only for the price of a cosy little life annuity, I will rap on the chimney wall. These old houses echo splendidly. When Chantal hears those raps, she will immediately telephone the police."

Typical. Chantal gets the plum role. "But two watchdogs are much better than one," I insisted.

Hyacinth compressed her orange lips. "Harry would be extremely angry if we involved you in any danger. When Prim and I first talked about taking you to the card games we were concerned that he would not be pleased."

Huh! Flinging one end of the eiderdown over my shoulder I flounced across the room. If they were afraid of Harry, I was not. And why did they think he would have no qualms about Chantal? They weren't worried about Mr. Deasley escaping from the priest hole and rampaging through the house—they were worried about my botching the grand plan. I'd show all of them! The sisters couldn't force me to stay in my room like a difficult child.

I was mightily tempted to telephone Harry; not because I needed to hear his voice, you must understand, but because I felt this might be one of those rare times requiring masculine intervention. Should I have done so; much terror might have been spared us. But all I could see were the sisters' trusting faces. And I could not deceive them as Harry had deceived me. I knew too well the bitterness of betrayal after having conceived the perfect plan.

In the parlour I sipped coffee and penned my literary gem to Mr. Deasley on pale pink paper garlanded with embossed flowers.

"My dear Mr. Deasley, or may I please call you Clyde?

I have discovered something of great interest here at Cloisters and, having worked for Mr. Hunt . . ." The pen nib bit into the paper and I had to force myself to continue. . . . "I wonder if—but perhaps it would be best if I explain when I see you. Could you please come here at noon today? The Tramwells will be out, also the servants, so we will be quite alone."

Primrose peered over my shoulder as I wrote the last line. "A pity—it has a nice ring—but upon reflection I think 'Yours devotedly' might be a shade too much. Best keep it simple—your signature followed by an agitated scrawl."

Duly summoned to perform his errand, Butler looked mildly pleased at the prospect of a bit of spying in London. "Anything I can do to be of service, mesdames, to h'insure a certain gentleman being detained at Her Majesty's pleasure is most gratifying." He bowed his way out of the room.

"I'm afraid Butler would never care for any gentleman who called upon us." Primrose preened a little. "I don't think he believes there's a man alive who is good enough for either of us."

"And he's right," said Hyacinth. "Tessa, perhaps you would enjoy arranging some flowers for the sitting room. I have some cut on the hall table."

The rain had stopped and the day was developing a gentle golden haze. It was hard to believe, looking out onto that glorious vista of smooth lawns, variegated pastel flower beds, and the cool darkness of the woods, that anything unpleasant could touch this place. The scent of roses drifted through the room and a bird fluttered singing up from the sundial.

"Nature, how lovely it is and yet so cruel." Primrose came in and sat opposite me, a darning bag placed carefully on her lap.

"My dear, you look tired," Hyacinth cooed. "You know, Prim, I think we could all benefit from some of your splendid herbal tea—the one you concocted from last summer's wild flowers. You remember—such a delicious brew it made."

Her sister nodded. "You must mean the one Minnie enjoys so much."

"Where is Minnie? I haven't seen her this morning." I asked.

"Out of harm's way." Primrose stood up. "Harry took her with him and, although I was a little hurt that she went so readily . . . well, never mind that. Always rambling, that's me. I do believe I have a packet down in the priest hole. Tessa, kindly ring for Chantal and ask her to heat some water. We won't need a teapot as the petals should be steeped directly in the cup. Hyacinth, do you remember exactly where I left those packets?"

"Next to the bottled plums; they're on that old tea tray along with the dried figs."

Primrose was back in minutes with a brown paper packet. Chantal had answered the bell and she returned carrying a loaded tray. Sunlight highlighted the beautiful planes of her face as she bent over the coffee table. Had she also been tempted to telephone Harry—to warn him of the Tramwells' plan? She was moving Primrose's chair forward so the elderly lady could more comfortably reach the water jug.

My reaction to the tea Hyacinth handed me was not entirely favourable. Dabbed on the wrists it might have been all right, but who wants to drink perfume? I took another pursed-lips swallow and another. A man would have to be a fool not to want Chantal. Beautiful, clever, complex . . . Why hadn't Harry telephoned us? The flowery brew began to grow on me. Hyacinth and Primrose should stop tinkling with their spoons and drink up. It was rather nice, really, once it went down. Warming and sort of floaty. Another swallow and I set down my cup and watched it topple sideways onto the saucer. My hand moved languorously to my mouth to suppress a yawn. Very relaxing, that tea. If I didn't stand up I would fall asleep.

"You look tired, Tessa," murmured someone, Chantal, I think, but the figure was rather blurred. As I struggled up I saw with surprise that Hyacinth and Primrose had merged into a two-headed monster, swaying in place. Blinking, I pried them apart, the effort exhausting me. My limbs suddenly felt so heavy. What was wrong with me? A nasty struggling suspicion. Something . . . knock-out powder in the tea. But it couldn't be, they wouldn't. Why, they were even opposed to aspirin! Now I was fully upright I did feel better, hardly acrobatic but at least marginally alert.

I reached the nursery, having spurned the offer of Chantal's arm upstairs. I thought, *Won't lie down yet, must tidy up a bit first*. Spotting a duster draped over the waste-paper basket I lunged for it, nearly losing my balance, and began sliding it conscientiously across the furniture, including my bed-tumbled blankets. But my arms began swerving away from me, going off on travels of their own. Wassat? Wassat I heard? Footsteps creeping up the stairs. In order to hear better I moved to the door, or tried to move to the door; somehow I got entangled in the swing, the ropes spinning around faster and faster, crushing me. It was evil, that swing —it was trying to murder me. I stood still, the swing relaxed its hold, and I made a break for the door but found myself at the window. The open window. I was lucky not to have gone flying through it. The apple tree was staring at me. Was it my friend? Did it want to help me against the forces of evil? My head swam, but this time with a memory—an idea. Orange. I only had to hang something orange in the apple tree and I would be rescued from the swing and those footsteps on the stairs. My knees buckled as I turned from the window, but at once I saw what I wanted. Bertie's pyjamas. Like a tortoise with ingrown toenails I headed for those pyjamas. At last I had them; now the painful return to the window. Could I make it? Yes. My arm jerked outward and the orange pyjamas fluttered onto the branches of the apple tree.

I was slithering down in a heap. I couldn't move a limb. What if I had been wrong about Mr. Deasley? My eyes slowly closed onto nothingness.

19

I had been buried for eternity in a deep dark tomb. Rather cosy and peaceful, but now someone was persistently rattling my coffin lid.

"Tessa, wake up. You have to wake up." The voice was Chantal's, and I resented her ordering me about. The vibrations got stronger. The noise louder. I was awake and I knew the sound of the chisel was real.

"Tessa, do you hear me? They took the key and I can't get the door off. Get out of that bed. The Tramwells are still down with Deasley. It's been more than half an hour, and I haven't heard a sound. I can't leave to fetch help unless—"

"Stop! I'm coming." Throwing my legs over the edge of the bed I struggled up. A creaking started inside my head when I opened my eyes, but surprisingly I felt fairly peppy. I had not—thank you, Dad's Boss—drunk all of my tea. And I did not suspect the sisters of polluting my system with some poison off a chemist's shelf. The tea must have been a natural opiate, nothing artificial added. How healthful!

"Forget the door, Chantal." I pressed my face up against its cool surface, feeling stronger by the minute. "I can climb out the window."

"No you can't. When the Tramwells came up to check that you were out cold, they didn't only lock the door and remove the key—they stuck the window down with Eterna-Hold."

"You mean the glue that sticks airplane wings back on? Blast! But Chantal, you can't worry about me now. The Tramwells could be rapping on the wall this minute. But even if they haven't signalled you can't wait any longer. You have to ring the police."

"The phone's out because of the storm. They should have checked the line this morning—but these are two elderly women, not professional sleuths. We have to help them, but if I go down into the priest hole and Deasley gets me while you are holed up here, we are worse off than ever."

True to the distraught heroine syndrome, I rattled the doorknob in absolute futility. What did I expect? The door shimmied but did not give. Scarred, scratched, and slightly warped, it must be immensely old. Old enough to be eaten up with woodworm?

"Nothing else for it, we will have to knock it down." Despite my concern for the Tramwells, I spoke those words with a spurt of elation. Chantal and I would manage. What was needed was a heavy object with which to . . . My eyes travelled around the room, past my bedside table to the beds themselves. Wouldn't work. Those beds weren't on casters—they were from the days when good quality meant unbudgeability. I couldn't ram one with sufficient force to break down that door. What I needed was momentum—speed, and one sharp thrust after another. The swing! I would swing up high, arch myself back until I was prone, and kick out at the door.

Ignoring Chantal's instructions that I search for an old cricket bat, I sat down on the wooden seat and clutched the ropes. Back and forth, one swooping arc following another until my head grazed the ceiling. Toes up. Heels out. Explosion. A horrific crash and splintering of wood. Only as I came spinning off into full solo flight did I think to squawk out a warning to Chantal to scram.

How that door failed to knock her unconscious I do not know. Even more miraculous was that my only injury was a grazed knee. As I scrambled to my feet and gazed down over the balcony rail to the debris of wood a mile and a half down, I shuddered.

"Foolhardy and noisy, but brilliant," came Chantal's throaty, stunned voice from behind me. When I turned she was leaning against the wall.

"We postpone our nervous breakdowns for a time when we can enjoy them, right?" She said. I nodded and we went down the stairs, shoulder to shoulder. "You go for the police," she said. "Flag down the first car you see, and . . ."

"No—better for you to go. I'm a rotten runner and you

know the way to the village. I will go down into the priest hole and see what is happening."

"All right." She ran out the front door, leaving it hanging open. I was glad she did. The outside world seemed a little closer. The unearthly silence of an empty house in midafternoon surged around me as I fumbled with the secret catch on the fireplace wall. The brick door inched open. I would have to go down without a candle, surprise being my only ally. I began the grim descent. A murmur of voices came up to meet me. I could hear Hyacinth, not frightened—more outraged. I was halfway down the stairs when I heard a laugh. A man's laugh. Dreadful in its joviality. Speak, Primrose! I had to hear her voice, to know she was unharmed. The chill damp seeped through my clothes. I was almost at the bottom; I could see the glow of candles and pressed myself against the wall. Hyacinth was tying up Primrose while Mr. Deasley directed the jagged end of a broken bottle at them.

"How fortunate that I never leave home without my manicure scissors," he purred as I tiptoed down the last step and slithered towards the fireplace wall. "And how fortunate that you ladies wear such serviceable petticoats. Are you sure you have left sufficient strips for your own bondage, Hyacinth, my dear?"

No response.

"Have Primrose lie down before you tie her ankles. I'm a gentle person by preference and don't wish to have to knock her to the ground. Perfect! I am now ready for you, old friend."

The bottle fell from Mr. Deasley's hand—the sound of its shattering hard-edged and spiteful. Binding Hyacinth's arms behind her back he ordered her to join her sister on the floor.

"Really, Clyde, this is too tedious for words." How brave, how clever she was! Not a hint of being anything more than slightly miffed. I was the one having difficulty exercising restraint. Only by focussing on the imminent arrival of the police was I able to keep from bursting across the room and leaping on Mr. Deasley's back. If he only knew that in trussing up the Tramwells like Christmas geese he was knotting the rope around his own neck. . . .

"Down. That's right—face down. Dear, dear! I regret the nasty chill of that stone floor, but I will have you warm in a tick." Mr. Deasley moved away from the sisters, but he did not head towards the stairs as I expected. He was now standing in front of the kegs in the opposite corner. He was heaving one up, wheezing in the attempt. Nothing that I had heard him say was as evil, as menacing as that laboured breathing. He was staggering forward, he was going to drop that keg. Deliberately drop it! Not on the Tramwells' heads, please! Now when I wanted to move I could not.

He dropped it a few feet away from them. A violent thud and the sickly sweet odour of rum soaked into the air.

"Yes, I will have you warmed up in no time." He was walking towards the candles.

"Thank you so much, but I would prefer you take no extraordinary measures to ensure our comfort," trilled Primrose.

"Think nothing of it, my dear. What are friends for?" Mr. Deasley went over to the candles, plucked them from their bottles, walked back to where the broken keg lay, kicked it aside, and set them in a circle around the Tramwells. Five small orange flames licked the dark. "Please accept my apologies for having lied to you when I said I would not harm you if you cooperated in permitting yourselves to be tied up."

"You will achieve nothing by killing us." Hyacinth's voice did not quaver.

"True, dear lady. The life of a fugitive lies before me whatever course I take now, but this time I am not killing from necessity but for pleasure. If you had been the gullible old fools you feigned to be, I could have achieved my heart's ease and lived the life of king instead of a vagabond. An eye for an eye! Ah, I see your eyes are on the candles. Little more than stubs all of them. Soon they will burn down, the rum will ignite, and you two will blaze away like a pair of Christmas puddings."

Silence.

"Dear ladies, you may feel I am an irreligious man, but I do count my blessings this day. What a blessing that your forebear Sinclair brought back those kegs of rum from his travels and that he did not live long enough to consume the contents. What a blessing that his descendants, including your light-weight father, considered rum the drink of able-seamen and peasants. What a blessing this floor is full of shallows so the rum can puddle!"

"Surely you have matters to attend, more important than gloating over our demise," spluttered Primrose. "Pray don't let us detain you."

"Yes, it is time to be away. I have a business acquaintance who will be delighted to conceal me under or in her bed until the coast is clear. By the bye—should I chance to see the luscious Tessa as I pause to pick up my last souvenirs from Cloisters, I will bring her down to join you. A pity if, as you say, she has left the premises in the company of the servants. I would like to thank her for her charming note." Mr. Deasley retreated some distance from the candles, and now made a courtly bow. "And so adieu, My Lady Chickenthroats, squirm —and you may shorten your lives by—minutes."

He was heading for the stairs, footsteps growing softer.

"Don't wriggle dear. You might catch your dress alight and"—Primrose paused—"it is so pretty."

"I wonder how he will react when he finds the priest hole door closed?" Hyacinth wondered with hollow amusement.

"He will certainly not risk being trapped here as we go up in smoke," replied Primrose. "Even should he escape death himself, he . . ."

The priest hole door was not closed. I had left it ajar . . . there, the sound of the door being pushed open! Exclamations of consternation, bewilderment from the sisters. I flung myself away from the wall. My left foot came down on something cylindrical, something that rolled under me, causing me to fall forward with a yelp.

"Who is it? What is it?" came the sisters' voices.

"Don't move," I cried. Bending, I picked up the object so it would not trip me again and stuffed it into the pocket of my skirt. One of the candles was almost down to the wick. Would I be in time? I was afraid to run in case I caused its flame to waver, fanning out across that sea of alcohol. Dropping to my knees, I crawled forward and scooped up the small glowing blob, crushed it in my hand and tossed it away over my shoulder. Then, skirt trailing in the wet, almost drowning in fumes, I inched around the rest of the circle snuffing and tossing as I went. I knew that, for the moment, we were all safe. Untying Hyacinth in the dark took five minutes; Deasley must have been a Boy Scout.

"I dare say it would not have worked." Hyacinth rubbed

her wrists. "A man could not be expected to know that one must always heat rum or brandy before flambéing."

"Not"—Primrose lay perfectly still as I worked to release her—"not that we aren't extremely grateful to you, Tessa."

I apologized for not closing the priest hole door behind me and offered the small consolation that Chantal would be returning any moment with the police.

But would they come in time to catch Mr. Deasley?

"How foolish of us not to have made sure the telephone was working," Hyacinth said. "But no time for recriminations. We have all meant everything for the best. You in coming down here, we in attempting to keep you out of harm's way by giving you that tea. It is what we give Minnie before taking her to the vet's, and what Primrose gave her the other night."

As I stood up, my hand brushed my skirt pocket and I pulled out the cylindrical object. I had imagined it to be a bottle, but now I realized it was too short and squat, with a rough little nub about halfway down. A jab with my thumb and it turned into torch, beaming a frail but beautiful light.

"Tessa, sweet girl," exclaimed Primrose. "How splendid of you to have displayed such foresight." I opened my mouth to say I had dropped the torch when I was last down here but she rattled on. "Foresight and ingenuity. You must tell us later how you escaped from the nursery, but now, if you will give me the torch, we will follow Mr. Kneesley Deasley."

Purely to humour her, I handed over the torch. She was suffering from shock, or paralysis of the brain, as Fergy would say.

"Dear Primrose, nothing is to be done right now but wait patiently until Chantal arrives with the police."

"Wait placidly here, like geese ready for carving! Indeed we will not," stormed Primrose.

"I know it is frustrating, but we have no choice," I said pacifyingly.

"Rubbish, my dear," sniffed Primrose. With the torch held out at arm's length she headed for the chimney wall, Hyacinth and I following in her wake. "We were unable to reach this area to rap for Chantal because of Deasley menacing us with that broken bottle. The villain! Wantonly smashing one of my best parsnip wines. The wasted rum doesn't bother me—we never use the stuff except for a dribble at Christmas in the egg flip—but if he had dared touch one of dear Father's last bottles of French brandy, that would have been a different story! Only a couple left. . . . Poor Father, he always was a hearty drinker. A blessing really he never knew he had brought his family to the brink of ruin by his gambling on the stock exchange. He never noticed all the things we had to do without, like having our portraits painted as adults."

Nothing seemed odd anymore. Not even discussing Mr. Tramwell's financial status while beating our hands against a brick wall. I had relieved Primrose of the torch but my free hand had taken up the drum-rap. What were we looking for?

"Our lives have been spent attempting to retrieve enough of what Father lost to save Cloisters. But I am afraid it has been a losing battle," supplied Hyacinth. "Ah-ha!" She paused, grabbing the torch and beaming it on a nail—the nail I had taken for a picture hook on my last visit. Chuckling in gratification, she pressed down upon it.

"A secret exit, up the chimney!" I exclaimed as a portion of the wall groaned open. Stepping into the brick-lined cavity my voice developed the sort of echo that comes with a bad head cold. "Why—why, this is how Butler got so grimy the day I arrived! He must have been trying to come up this way because the other door was jammed." We stood now at the foot of a narrow staircase running up one side; an acrid smell of soot almost choked me, and I saw a large number of cracks in the wall dividing this hideaway from the chimney itself.

"Dearie me, no. Butler was not using this as a means of exit. This is his Ali Baba cave. Alas, we have not yet completely broken him of his jackdaw tendencies—spiriting pretty trinkets away. Mind you"—Primrose mounted the first step—"he is making remarkable progress. He returns everything in time and what we find highly encouraging is that valuables—watches and good jewellery—always get put back pretty speedily. The cheapies he hangs onto a little longer."

I would be getting my charm bracelet back any day. Starting up the stairs behind Hyacinth and Primrose I looked sideways and spotted a battered suitcase in the corner. Butler's trinket box.

"A priest hole within a priest hole, you see." Primrose was barely panting as she went up. "If the king's men did manage to locate the main area, they would find it empty.

Trust Lily to be the one of us children to find this place. She always was such a spirited, curious child. Careful, Tessa." I had stumbled and had to catch Primrose around the waist.

"Don't fall," called back Hyacinth, our leader. We were almost at the top. "Such a long way down to the cold floor. I remember Lily—that laughter turning into screams. She was playing blind man's bluff with Father on the second-floor landing and he was coming after her with the little stuffed alligator, saying it would eat her up if it caught her. Oh, it was agonizing. I can see him now clutching that alligator to him, the look of a bewildered child on his face as he looked down the staircase to where she lay on the bottom step. No wonder people whispered "murder." He thought of himself as Lily's murderer."

"This place makes for gloomy thoughts, I fear," sighed Primrose.

But I didn't think of them as gloomy—just terribly sad.

Hyacinth's voice brightened. "Here we are. Now, can we all squeeze on to this platform? Good." She had found another catch and again a door grated open. It hit the edge of the bookcase and we each took deep breaths, emerging sideways. Would Mr. Deasley still be in the house? How much time had elapsed since he had left the sisters to burn to a crisp—ten, fifteen minutes?

He was still in the house. He was coming through the sitting room door now, a framed picture under his right arm and a couple of books in his left hand. He saw us and reluctantly I had to give him credit for holding up well under pressure. His eyes flashed behind his spectacles but his lips, under the sliver of moustache, struggled to form a smile.

"Ah, dear ladies! So you could not resist coming to see me off." A trace of a swagger appeared in his gait as he crossed the room. He was coming towards us. What could one unarmed man do against three women? He dropped the portrait and the books on one of the sofas and kept coming. He was at the fireplace, his free hand moving, reaching towards the mantel clock. He was going to pitch that clock at us. I lunged, an inch ahead of Hyacinth and Primrose, and he ducked, dragging up one of the bronze dragons—sending a splay of pokers and shovels scattering. His change in direction was so fast I blinked, and in that instant he grabbed me, while holding the dragon out towards the sisters.

"Come any closer," he wheezed, "and I will crack her head to scrambled eggs. This," he panted in my ear, "is your reward for that sweet, come-hither note of yours. I would not still be here if I had not ransacked the house hoping to find you. Wayward Tessa! You and *Daddy* are going to have some wonderfully jolly times together. I know all about you, Tessa —overhead you talking to Primrose. . . . I am your daddy, you know."

"That's a lie. But even if you were I don't give a damn. I don't believe in bad seeds." I kicked him hard in the shin. He wouldn't crack my skull; he needed me alive.

"I have absolutely no desire to get anywhere near you," quivered Primrose. "Oh, I do feel faint—if only I had my smelling salts." Blindly her hands fluttered outward. She was lifting a vase of yellow roses from the bookcase. "Perhaps a whiff of these will bring me round." She sagged sideways against Hyacinth, head drooping over the blooms.

"My dear, take three deep breaths," murmured Hyacinth. I could not help feeling peeved. What of my plight? Mr. Deasley was dragging me towards the French windows. My heart was beating so fast I could hear it pounding inside my head like rumblings of thunder or . . . hoofbeats? The sound was mounting, drumming to a formidable torrent. Those pounding hooves were not inside my head. The curtain brushed my face. Did no one else hear? Twisting my face sideways, I saw a magnificent black horse emerge from the woods. Mr. Deasley was clutching at the curtain, desperation on his face. Oh, Harry, whatever else you have done, at this moment you are my knight in shining armour!

To give our villain his due, he had not had all the starch washed out of him yet. "He can't stop me," he cried. "No one can stop me. I meant it—I'll crack her head open!"

It was then that Primrose struck. She took aim and flung the vase of yellow roses into Mr. Deasley's open-mouthed face. What a weapon. The man dropped the dragon—thankfully missing my feet—and, clutching himself dementedly, gasping, sneezing, wheezing, sank to a despicable huddle clawing at the floor.

A shadow dark as a thundercloud blocked out all light from the window. The wall shook with violent sound. Hyacinth and I had barely time to yank a screaming Primrose out of the way before horse and rider ploughed into the room. Devastation. Furniture crashed in all directions, but the mighty hooves of the gallant black steed, ridden by a man and a ginger-haired boy, skimmed over Mr. Deasley's body as though it were a pebble on the beach. The room tilted and slowly righted itself.

A new commotion—wild barking—and Minnie hurtled through the window. In a rush of narrowing circles she came at last to rest beside Mr. Deasley, her yellow fangs only an inch away from his throat and a look of bliss on her furry, beautiful face.

"Harry, dear boy." Hyacinth stood holding the chair she had caught one-handed as it flew through the air. "These impromptu visits of yours are charming, but if you had let us know that you were bringing Bertie to tea we would have prepared something *special*."

20

The sitting room looked much more presentable after Harry led Highflyer down the verandah steps to a nearby tree. Bertie, eyes glowing, eagerly agreed to watch him eat grass. A good idea, because he would be better off outside when the police arrived. They did so a moment after Harry rejoined us. Chantal walked in and announced in wry amusement as she took in the scene before her, "Inspector Lewjack and Constable Watt."

Mr. Deasley had recovered from his sneezes and listened to the reading of his rights with only a slender lessening of his usual aplomb. Indeed he had the effrontery to ask if he might take the books he had been planning to borrow so he could have a little read in his cell. I was surprised he did not ask to take the picture, too.

Constable Watt picked one leather-bound volume off the floor and tossed it in his hands. "*Evelina!*" he scoffed. "Sort of romantic bosh the wife would read." A regretful shake of the head. The constable expected his murderers to be of the he-man variety; even had he discovered the 1778 date indicating a first edition I doubt he would have been any more respectful of Mr. Deasley's literary interests.

Handcuffs were snapped on and the prisoner taken away. "Well, that's that. I think we can all do with some tea, don't you, Prim dear?" said Hyacinth.

"Was it *Evelina* he wanted all along?" I asked. "But I thought you gave him a copy the other day to show to a customer."

"We gave him volume one; these are two and three. I can see why he took them—easy to transport and easy to flog for

264

a nice little sum. But they aren't of great value because when she was little Violet scribbled in all three and tore out some of the pages."

"Then it must have been the picture that he especially . . ." I bent and lifted it up, looking down at the canvas. It was a portrait, the portrait I had seen in the attic, but now, without the false black moustache and eye patch, I recognized the face. I hadn't looked at Harry since that first moment he had galloped into the room, eyes searching until he found me, shouting my name, and I had to force myself to look at him now. The painful feelings of restraint were still there. "This man is your double. Dress you up in silk and lace, add a fancy wig, and you would be he, or he you."

'Exactly, my dear." Primrose was fluttering about the room setting chairs upright and resettling doilies. "That is why we had Chantal take it up to the attic before you arrived. And then we became afraid that you might find it, so we had her dab on a few concealing touches. Where is Chantal? Gone to get the tea, I suppose. I must thank her for having washed off the portrait and brought it down again. So industrious—considering everything else she had to do this morning."

"I should have realized that what Deasley wanted and what Angus spotted was likely to be a picture," I said but Hyacinth shook her head.

"Not this picture. I suspect Deasley grabbed it off the wall at random. There will always be buyers for ancestors to hang on their walls, but this one I know was painted by a very mediocre artist." Hyacinth adjusted the curtains which had been wrenched from some of their hooks. "Harry, it was all very noble, your flying in here on that horse, but why did you not drive to Cloisters?"

"The hearse died." Harry picked up the dragon, and looked from it to me and back again, his face grim.

"Amazing," Hyacinth responded. "That vehicle has never given us a day's trouble. Must be your driving, young man."

Harry smiled, a finger tracing the dragon's wings. "Well, Marco . . . or is it Polo? Back to the fireplace with you. Fortunately with no blood on your scales. A bit of a comedown for you and your brother; such grandiose beasts, ending up on a hearth as fire dogs . . . *Dogs!* Dogs—*plural*. No apostrophe, as in 'The dog's got the weapon,' or 'The dog's chasing my killer.' "

Hyacinth and Primrose were staring at him as though he had lost his wits, but I understood. I had been wrong about Minnie's Chinese bowl, but on the right track.

Harry put the dragon down on the coffee table. "Angus Hunt tried to tell us the dogs were *Ming*. If you two hadn't named your dog Minerva, light might have dawned sooner. What do you think, Tessa?"

"I'm sure you've got it. And this explains why Godfrey came a cropper. Remember his ranting on yesterday about how ugly they were? Then, when Hyacinth or Primrose said they were bronze, he shut up double quick. I bet that book he brought back from the library after his session with the police had a page or two of info on Ming. One of our history teachers was rather keen on ancient artsy stuff, and I remember her saying once that most people associate Ming with china—vases and such—but it can be bronze, or . . ."

"Poor Godfrey," sighed Primrose. "One can't help wishing he had used that sharp mind of his in worthier endeavours. Blackmail is so . . . so . . . pedestrian. Still, Ethelreda will enjoy putting up an enormous monument, and she will have nice little visits with her boy. All the nicer now that he can't answer back."

Chantal had come in with Bertie and the tea things, and she and the boy stood listening. Harry took the tray from her as she said, "I wonder if anyone else was ever murdered on account of Marco and Polo."

"One prefers not to delve into how old Sinclair acquired them," sighed Primrose. "I suppose they may originally have come from one of those depressing, overly ornate temples. Silly of me, but I don't think I will ever again experience the same comfy affection for them. Hyacinth, my dear, despite the memories they evoke, I believe I am ready to part with them."

The earrings rocked in vigorous assent. "Yes, I am afraid there is a certain gaucherie in having pet names for objects that must be worth . . ."

". . . Enough to set Cloisters up for the next century or so." Chantal smiled as she poured tea. Harry was studying her face and I wondered if, in the warm glow from the rose wall lights, he thought her beyond price.

The object of our united interest being returned to the hearth and the companionship of his brother, we all sat around the coffee table sipping tea.

"This has all been so very exciting—in a dreadfully sad kind of way, of course." Primrose's cheeks were flushed and she looked almost girlish. "And I have been contemplating how flat life will seem when returned to normal, particularly as the card parties have come to an end. What do you think, Hyacinth, of our going into the private detection business? We could send out little cards to all our friends and acquaintances—the kind of people who when they are in a spot of bother would prefer confiding in someone from their own walk of life. Not some well-meaning rustic with a pencil tucked over his ear."

"What a marvellous idea." Hyacinth's lips cracked into a delighted smile. "Butler will be of immense use to us. As dear Father always said, although he knew nothing of the matter; the sudden acquisition of vast wealth is disastrous unless one keeps busy."

"Ooh, in't it just like the films!" cried Bertie. Bunched down on a hassock, fat freckled knees squeezed tightly together, his eyes grew big and round.

Yes, it was, wonderfully exciting. Happy endings and new beginnings for the Tramwell sisters. Harry, whilst looking pleased for them, did not wear the expression of an heir whose expectations had magically moved into the realms of fantasy. But during all those cosy conversations at his mother's cottage, I had never sensed that boundless wealth was one of Harry's goals. Well, he need not worry unduly, a good measure of the new-found spoils would, I was sure, cross the Atlantic one day to be enjoyed by Violet Wilkinson and her family.

Maude and Butler arrived at the house within minutes of each other, she apologizing for the length of her absence—a difficult and prolonged delivery—he to inform the Tramwells that Angus on his return to London had consulted with a Mr. Henry Falcon. I had heard of Mr. Falcon, and was certain he was the man Angus would have chosen to consult over anything Ming. Dear Angus. The pain was a bruise deep inside me. I would have to find out the day and time of his funeral.

Through the French windows I could see Highflyer tied to a cherry tree. The light was only now beginning to fade, casting soft pearly, shadows over the garden. Beautiful and utterly peaceful. Still, Devon—if not entirely peaceful with Fergy—would be a warm and loving place. My handbag and suitcases were at Harry's house, but he would bring them over in the morning and we would say our polite goodbyes.

Perched on a straight-backed chair, legs negligently crossed, Butler, other than holding his cup with both hands, pinkies quirked, looked very much the gentleman at his posh London club as he listened to the sisters discuss their plans for a detective agency. "I think it might be rather interesting to check into the life of Herr Wortter," said Primrose. "Constable Watt told me just now that the good Fritz was interviewed yesterday by the police in his honeymoon suite at a London hotel. He's over from Cologne celebrating his fourth marriage. It seems the three previous brides all committed suicide."

Hyacinth looked disappointed. "I wouldn't think there's much mystery about that."

Maude and Chantal were talking over the top of Bertie's head, and Minnie's snores rose in a series of highs and lows from the patchwork blanket. The room, despite the French windows being open, felt hot and stuffy. Stepping out into the hall, I closed the door on the cheerful flow of voices. No one would miss me if I disappeared upstairs for a few minutes. Wrong. A click and a quick tread pursuing me. No need to turn around to know it was Harry.

"Tess, are you all right?"

His hand touched my arm and I was glad that my hair fell forward, obscuring my face. "I'm marvellous. And I do appreciate the gallant charge to the rescue."

"I was a bit late, wasn't I?" He had turned me round and lifted a hand to brush back my hair. My skin burnt where he touched me and I still could not look into his eyes. I had such strong feelings for him—anger, bitterness, regret, tenderness, love—and yet everything between us was ruined, smashed to pieces like a broken cup. Fergy would say you can glue the pieces back together but the cracks will always show.

"You came when we needed you," I said.

would have insisted that I had the right to know everything about my origins, but now . . .

"I hope you can accept that, Tessa, that I don't owe you his name. You have a father."

"I know. And I never have been much interested in who sired me. Perhaps if Mum hadn't died . . . I wish you could have met her again."

"I was dreadfully sorry to hear of her death; I wrote and told Violet when I heard. But you are very like your mother, Tessa, in lots of important ways. That first time I saw you I couldn't take my eyes off you—I had such a feeling of recognition. I'm a practical, down-to-earth woman, but a few weeks back Chantal had asked to look at my hand, and she told me that the child out of my past was coming closer. Bunk is what I have always termed clairvoyance. But Chantal is unusual, isn't she?"

I nodded. "One thing still puzzles me. You don't seem the type to use Devon violet writing paper. At first I took that as another sign that Violet was the one, but . . ."

"Didn't I tell you I am a practical woman? Every Christmas I receive all sorts of presents from my patients. Handkerchiefs and bath salts, and boxes and boxes of fancy writing paper. Devon violet was the best of the bunch that year, I remember."

We smiled at each other, our hands coming together again. At least I thought she was smiling. I couldn't see too well because my eyes blurred. This meeting wasn't anything like the old dreams. Maude wasn't glamorous, charming, witty, or beautiful—any more than the Tramwells were the sweet, simple-minded old ladies I had fancied them to be before coming to Cloisters. I was the one who had been simple-minded. Maude had told me about my origins, but that was not the same as telling me who I was. She couldn't give me that information. No one could. I would have to find out who the real Tessa Fields was, a day at a time, like everyone else.

"You look sad," said Maude.

"I am—and for the strangest reason. I feel sorry for Mr. Deasley. Fergy—she's our housekeeper—would say he tried to take a short-cut through life and tripped over his own shoe laces. Perhaps you will meet Fergy and Dad one day. I think

273

you and Bertie would like them. That reminds me, what was it Bertie wanted to tell me?"

"I'm afraid this is going to shock you." She managed a shaky laugh. "Bertie was the one who locked you in the priest hole the other day. He saw you go in from the garden, and shut you in just so he could win points in your estimation by rescuing you. I know it sounds odd, but Bertie is so desperately in need of approval."

"He loves you and knows you love him; don't worry—he will do just great. Would you tell me something? Why doesn't he call you Mother or Mum?"

"Haven't really thought . . . but I suppose I felt I didn't deserve the name."

"And I thought you so sensible. No one deserves the name more than the woman who adopts a child."

Maude stood up and came around the table. "Thank you, Tessa. And now may I ask you a personal question? When are you going to marry that young man who was so busy watching to see if you had recovered from your close call with Mr. Deasley that he gave me a cup of tea with ten lumps of sugar?"

"Harry? But he deceived me, and Fergy says . . ." I told her what Fergy said about broken cups.

"Tessa, I hate to disagree with such a worthy woman, but I think this time Fergy is wrong. Picking up the pieces and sticking them back together is what any worthwhile relationship is all about. It's what life is all about. Men are only human, and when it comes to reality rather than fiction, perfection can be very boring."

"I will not go crawling to . . ."

A firm but gentle shove towards the door. "You won't have to crawl. You are a very creative girl. And, Tessa—"

"Yes?"

"A child can have only one mother and, although I wish I could have been, I am not yours. But a mother can have more than one child. I do love you. I have always loved you. Now do as you are told and get out of here."

When I passed Tessa's portrait she was definitely beaming.

Harry wasn't in the sitting room and when, ignoring the sudden hush in conversation, I looked out the French windows, Highflyer was no longer rambling around on his rope nuzzling grass.

Down the Garden Path

"Tessa, you look horridly peaked," Hyacinth informed my rigid back. "An evening walk would do you a world of good."

"Indeed yes," piped in Primrose. "Harry just left, but you may be able to catch up with him, because he took his horse around the side of the house to give it a drink from the rainbarrel. Do hurry, and apologize for our forgetting to ask him if he will come for afternoon tea tomorrow."

Chantal came up behind me. "I love him enough to let him go. You had better love him enough not to let him go."

I went out, down the verandah steps and across the lawn, but I didn't go round to the rainbarrel. The noble Highflyer was entitled to drink in peace. Instead I went through the Ruins. How serene and empty they were this evening. It was Abbots Walk I feared to enter. Would Angus's ghost have joined Tessail's? At the first step beneath the boughs, however, I realized that the horror of the place was gone. The only ghosts were those of a twentieth-century highwayman and a damsel in distress. Shadows filtered through the leaves, turning the ground to a mosaic of grey and brown. Somewhere in the darkening sky a bird chanted its eternal song. Though the memory of Angus would always be with me, his shade would not haunt this walk, yet surely a monk or even the abbot himself might still pass this way, his tonsured head bent low, fingers tolling the beads with the patient ease of daily ritual. But, hark! Those sounds approaching were not the football of a ghostly monk, but of hoofbeats pounding ever closer.

Horses are not a great love of mine, but I think I prefer them to bicycles. And yes, new-born golden foals are rather sweet. Bending, I picked up a tree branch and began idly flicking off leaves. The amber light at the end of the verdant tunnel clouded and as the great black horse and rider came cantering into the walk I stood in their path, pointing my wooden pistol.

"Stand and deliver!"

A terrible way for a girl of twenty-one to meet her end— to be mown down by a mane-tossing steed. But with scarcely a pause, Harry bent down, lifted me up into the saddle, kissed me with wicked abandon, and galloped off into the sunset.

ABOUT THE AUTHOR

DOROTHY CANNELL is the author of *The Thin Woman*, which won the Best Paperback Novel of the Year from the Romance Writers of America, *Down the Garden Path*, and *The Widows Club*, which was nominated for an Agatha Award as Best Novel of the Year. She was born in England and currently resides in Peoria, Illinois where she is hard at work on her next Ellie Hashell novel.

BANTAM MYSTERY COLLECTION

- 24958 **DEATH OF A GHOST** Allingham $3.95
- 28506 **POLICE AT FUNERAL** Allingham $3.95
- 28073 **JEMIMA SHORE'S FIRST CASE** Fraser $3.95
- 28071 **A SPLASH OF RED** Fraser $3.95
- 28096 **MURDER SAILS AT MIDNIGHT** Babson $3.50
- 28061 **MANHATTAN IS MY BEAT** Deaver $3.95
- 28070 **OXFORD BLOOD** Fraser $3.95
- 27663 **THE RAIN** Peterson $3.95
- 28019 **YOUR ROYAL HOSTAGE** Fraser $3.95
- 28590 **MURDER AT THE CAT SHOW** Babson $3.95
- 28495 **THE DA VINCI DECEPTION** Swan $4.95
- 27860 **THE SCARRED MAN** Peterson $4.50
- 28824 **CUPID** Reid $3.95
- 28044 **SAN FRANCISCO KILLS** Flinn $3.95
- 28816 **FUSE TIME** Byrd $4.95
- 18512 **HOT WIRE** Russell $2.50
- 28926 **BLIND SPOT** Russell $3.95
- 28311 **QUIET AS A NUN** Fraser $4.50

Bantam Books, Dept. MC, 414 East Golf Road, Des Plaines, IL 60016

Please send me the items I have checked above. I am enclosing $_____
(please add $2.50 to cover postage and handling). Send check or money
order, no cash or C.O.D.s please.

Mr/Ms _____

Address _____

City/State _____ Zip _____

MC–4/91

Please allow four to six weeks for delivery.
Prices and availability subject to change without notice.

BANTAM OFFERS THE FINEST IN CLASSIC AND MODERN BRITISH MURDER MYSTERIES

Dorothy Cannell
☐ The Widows Club — 27794-4 — $3.95
☐ Down the Garden Path — 26895-3 — $3.95
☐ Mum's the Word — 28686-2 — $4.99

Michael Dibdin
☐ Ratking — 28237-9 — $4.99

Colin Dexter
☐ The Dead of Jericho — 27237-3 — $3.95
☐ Last Bus to Woodstock — 27777-4 — $3.95
☐ Last Seen Wearing — 28003-1 — $3.95
☐ The Riddle of the Third Mile — 27363-9 — $4.50
☐ The Silent World of Nicholas Quinn — 27238-1 — $3.95
☐ Service of All the Dead — 27239-X — $3.95
☐ The Secret of Annex 3 — 27549-6 — $3.95

Dorothy Simpson
☐ Close Her Eyes — 18518-7 — $2.25
☐ Dead by Morning — 28606-4 — $3.95
☐ Dead on Arrival — 27000-1 — $3.50
☐ Element of Doubt — 28175-5 — $3.50
☐ Last Seen Alive — 27773-1 — $3.95
☐ Night She Died — 27772-3 — $3.50
☐ Puppet for a Corpse — 27774-X — $3.95
☐ Six Feet Under — 25192-9 — $3.95
☐ Suspicious Death — 28459-2 — $3.95

Available at your local bookstore or use this page to order.

Send to: Bantam Books, Dept. MC 6
          414 East Golf Road
          Des Plaines, IL 60016

Please send me the items I have checked above. I am enclosing
$_____ (please add $2.50 to cover postage and handling).
Send check or money order, no cash or C.O.D.'s, please.

Mr/Ms._____

Address_____

City/State_____Zip_____

Please allow four to six weeks for delivery.
Prices and availability subject to change without notice.   MC6 11/91

Kinsey Millhone is...

"The best new private eye." *—The Detroit News*

"A tough-cookie with a soft center." *—Newsweek*

"A stand-out specimen of the new female operatives."
—Philadelphia Inquirer

Sue Grafton is...

The Shamus and Anthony Award winning creator of Kinsey Millhone and quite simply one of the hottest new mystery writers around.

☐ 27991 "A" IS FOR ALIBI $4.95

☐ 28034 "B" IS FOR BURGLAR $4.95

☐ 28036 "C" IS FOR CORPSE $4.95

☐ 27163 "D" IS FOR DEADBEAT $4.95

☐ 27955 "E" IS FOR EVIDENCE $4.95

☐ 28478 "F" IS FOR FUGITIVE $4.95

Bantam Books, Dept. BD26, 414 East Golf Road, Des Plaines, IL 60016

Please send me the items I have checked above. I am enclosing $_____
(please add $2.50 to cover postage and handling). Send check or money order, no cash or C.O.D.s please.

Mr/Ms _____

Address _____

City/State _____ Zip _____

BD26–1/91

Please allow four to six weeks for delivery
Prices and availability subject to change without notice.